THE SUN VALLEY SERIES

bide

EJ Blaise

For Becka
Because maybe if I dedicate this to you, you'll actually read it.

CONTENT NOTE

This story contains explicit sexual content, profanity, loss of a family member, and mentions of a past abusive relationship.

BEFORE

He found the colors to paint her
where the world had left her grey.

PLAYLIST I

S.L.U.T - Bea Miller
Maneater - Nelly Furtado
Rhiannon - Fleetwood Mac
I Will Wait - Mumford and Sons
Cold Coffee - Ed Sheeran
Let Me Down Easy - Daisy Jones & The Six
Happiness - The 1975
Good News - Mac Miller
Dead To Me - Kali Uchis
Wet Dream - Wet Leg

PROLOGUE

LUNA

I'M TIRED, sweaty, and fucking desperate for a beer—something I never in a million years thought I'd crave.

Alas, something about working a solo shift at Greenies while the place is chock-full of students celebrating the end of spring semester drives a girl to yearn for a beverage that tastes like dishwater.

That should be me, I internally screech as I gaze longingly at the throng of people chugging alcohol I'm serving instead of drinking. I deserve to get shit-faced too; I did just survive freshman year. No, I didn't survive—I crushed it. Aced shitty classes, dodged shitty men, found surprisingly un-shitty friends who I plan to cling to for the rest of time, even if they did break my cardinal rule by, *shudder,* falling in love or whatever.

I didn't crumble and fail and move back home to New York like my highschool friends—a questionable term for people I'm beginning to learn I kind of hate. They didn't think I could handle the big cross-country move all by myself, nor did they think I was intellectually inclined enough to actually pass classes. But I did. With flying goddamn colors.

Jokes on you, assholes.

Although, right now, the joke is most definitely on me. A summer job seemed like a great idea, a way to pass time and earn some cash so I wouldn't have to chase Ma for money she doesn't have, until it came down to actually doing the work.

1

I could summon my roommate slash coworker slash newfound best friend; Amelia's holed up in the break room scarfing a pitiful, greasy dinner and hiding from the obnoxiously loud drunken fool she for some reasons calls her boyfriend. I know it would only take minimal begging for her to come running to my assistance but stubborn streak resents the idea of asking for help. It's very insistent I can manage the chaos myself—Ma likes to say I'm chaos personified so this is basically my calling, right? And, come on, wrangling drunk men, whipping them into shape, bending them to my wiles?

Easy fucking work.

Taking a quick moment I don't have, I free my hair from its restricting ponytail, fluffing the blonde waves with one hand while slicking on the lip gloss that lives in my back pocket with the other— only a fool goes to war without their weapons. And, as I catch sight of one particular booth laden with strapping young men, I gather every ounce of charm I possess. God knows with these boys, I'm going to need it.

Baseball players.

There's just something about them. An inherent cockiness. Deeply ingrained, honed showboating skills. The possession of an invisible magnet behind their eyes that connects to the one that must be embedded in my sternum, considering where their gazes are oh-so-often drawn.

Well, most of their gazes.

One, deep brown and always inexplicably warm, remains north of the border as I approach the table, just like it always does every time the Sun Valley Rays' star catcher graces me with his presence.

He's an enigma, Oscar Jackson. An uncrackable juxtaposition of a man. You hear rumors of a guy who throws the wildest parties on campus, you picture one thing. You imagine his roommates. Nicolas Silva, breaker-of-hearts who slings his dick around like it's an Olympic sport. Or Cass Morgan, the second coming of Babe Ruth.

You do not imagine the grimacing man struggling to look me in the eye, tips of his ears painted a blushing pink, fidgeting awkwardly on the edge of his seat as if the woman attempting to hump him has fucking cooties.

He's blushing, for God's sake. The beautiful man with the pretty hooded eyes that crinkle at the corners on the rare occasion he smiles who could convince a woman to drop to her knees with nothing more than the husky rumble of the the quiet 'hello' he sometimes deigns to offer and is renowned for debaucherous gatherings is *blushing*.

I don't get it. I really, really don't get it. If I had bone structure like that—the man consists solely of sharp, defined angles—I sure as hell would put it to good use. Hell, if he ogled me the way his buddies currently are, I wouldn't even mind. To be perfectly honest, I'd welcome it.

But he doesn't.

Ever.

It's a ridiculous thing, pouting over a man not staring at my tits. I blame it on the chaos thing. And on the only child urge to always get what I want. Not that I want Jackson—just a sliver of his attention would be nice.

And I'm going to get it.

One day, I swear to God if it's the last thing I do, I'm going to get it.

1

JACKSON

THERE ARE three things in life I know with absolute certainty.

One; the only good thing my parents ever did was give me my horde of sisters, and drop us on the doorstep of Serenity Ranch.

Two; I am destined to a life of pining after a girl who a.) is way out of my league and b.) probably knows me only as 'that friend of that baseball player.'

And three; Nicolas Silva will never pass up an opportunity to get laid, no matter what consequences he may suffer.

I warned my roommate-turned-best-friend that getting fucked up last night was a terrible idea; hangovers and road trips mix like oil and water. But did he listen? No.

Did he thunder through the front door, drunk off his ass and toting the latest in a long line of giggling women, in the wee hours of the morning? Of course, he did.

Is he now curled up in the back seat of my truck, a grimace twisting his normally handsome face, a sickly green tint to his golden skin, and his brow glistening with a sheen of sweat? Unfortunately, yes—something the man in my passenger seat, Cass Morgan, a trinity of roommate, friend, and teammate, is taking great, mocking pleasure in.

God, this was a terrible idea. I knew it would be the second the eldest of my younger sisters suggested it. But I was blindsided by the shock of Lux, a woman who prefers to be entirely self-sufficient, actually asking for help by subtly implying having a few extra hands around the ranch for the summer would be useful. In my state of surprise, I agreed before I could consider the repercussions of exposing my beloved sisters to my friends.

My equally beloved but lacking in morals and common sense friends.

Twisting in his seat, Cass regards our friend with false pity. "Christ, Nick. What did that girl do to you?"

Brandishing a middle finger, Nick grunts, "Shut the fuck up."

"Who was it this time?"

Despite the dread bubbling in my gut, I can't help but join in. After all, I did have the unfortunate honor of bumping into our half-naked houseguest on the stairs this morning. "The one with the claws." Bright red and fit to gouge an eye out. "Jessie?"

"I thought it was Janice?" Pretending to think, Cass purses his lips, scratching his chin and sliding Nick a look rife with barely hidden amusement. "Care to enlighten us, Nicolas?"

A beat of silence is his only response yet it speaks volumes.

"You don't remember," Cass snickers, "do you?"

Nick's groan echoes around the truck's interior, and I bet beneath the forearm shielding his face from the sunlight pouring in the window, there's a harsh glare lurking. "Fuck off."

A shocked laugh rips from my throat, my head moving in a disapproving shake. God, that's bad, even for him. No one who knows Nick would accuse him of being soft and sentimental and sensitive to the feelings of the many, many women he coaxes into his bed. It's not a secret, his blasé attitude towards sex. In-and-out, one-and-down, hit-and-run, all apply to my dear friend. But it's not like he hides any of that. He doesn't offer anything different.

But, still. Come on. Her *name*?

It's not funny, it really isn't.

Except, *shit*, yes it is.

My humor is short-lived, though. It diminishes as unkempt road turns into a familiar dusty dirt trail, as the place that's been my home for almost a decade appears on the horizon, as we creep closer to the most important people in my life. A nervous feeling of impending doom settles in my gut. Accompanying it; a familiar sense of calm and, most prominently of all, a fuck ton of anger.

The barn catches my eye first. It's impossible to miss, a huge wooden structure in desperate need of a coat of paint that makes me frown and kiss my teeth in annoyance because it's bigger than it was last time I was here. Horses roam free in the nearby paddock, and my suspicions are confirmed when I spot new equine faces grazing.

They fucking renovated again.

If they did up the barn, the guesthouses certainly got some attention too; they're the real money-makers, the mini fucking chalets rich people and fancy companies pay extortionate amounts of money to stay in and get 'the real country experience.'

Of course, my grandparents expanded their cash grab. Why wouldn't they, considering how much money they make from it while doing absolutely nothing other than supplying the funds? The actual work is always shucked onto someone who already has enough to deal with.

Someone who's lingering on the front porch of our home, three figures hovering beside her, their hands a blur as they frantically wave.

"Quick recap." Cass and Nick groan in unison as my truck rolls to a stop. Adopting a stern expression, I shift to face both of them, jutting my head towards the girls already tearing toward us. "These are my sisters. We do not fuck with my sisters. If you do, you sleep in the barn with the hay and the horse manure."

"Sir, yes, sir." It's a playful yet sincere grumble; they know how much my sisters mean to me, and they know—because I told them, intricately and repeatedly—the last thing I want is the girls feeling uncomfortable in their own home.

They've had enough of that to last a lifetime.

Shouldering open the driver's side door, one foot barely hits the grassy ground before a thundering of squealed greetings fills the air. Four girls race toward me, hair every shade of brown and blonde whipping in the wind carrying excited chants of my name.

The youngest of the quartet reaches me first, knocking the air out of my lungs as we collide. "Oscar!" Eliza screeches, further inhibiting my breathing capabilities by snaking her arms around my neck.

Chestnut hair tickles my neck, suspiciously straight compared to the wild, wavy mess I'm accustomed to. Pulling away, my chest pangs at the lack of baby fat rounding her cheeks, but my lamenting is soon chased away by a grimace as I note the black rimming her dark eyes. God, are fourteen-year-olds supposed to wear that much eyeliner?

Wisely, I don't voice that concern aloud; the three sisters that came before her taught me to keep my mouth shut when it comes to things like that.

My arms are only empty for a second—the twins are quick to fill the vacant spot. With equal vigor to our younger sister, Grace and Lottie launch themselves at me. Once more, I have to bite down the urge to comment as I twine a strand of Lottie's unnaturally blonde hair around my finger, a definite change from the usual sandy brown. Swatting my hand away, she meets my narrowed gaze with one of her own.

Again, I choose to exercise wisdom and keep my mouth shut, averting my gaze and finding a small miracle in Grace looking exactly the same. Hair the same brown, eyes the same hazel, no dramatic makeup to be found.

She always has been the easy sister.

Over their shoulders, a face the spitting image of mine lurks, and the goofy smile I'm sporting grows exponentially—I know I'm not supposed to have favorites but, God, Lux is mine.

"Alexandra," I drawl, coaxing a scowl out of the eldest Jackson sister. She hates her full name as much as I hate mine—the only difference is she actually managed to make her nickname stick.

"Oscar," she replies in the same tone, glower relenting when I yank her into a hug. "Nice of you to finally make an appearance."

It's a snippy joke, I know it is, yet combined with the circles marring her under eyes, almost as dark as the irises that match mine, a knot of guilt settles in my gut. "You look tired." An understatement—drained is probably a better word.

The second Lux graduated and decided not to attend college, the responsibility of the ranch fell on her shoulders, whether she wanted it to or not. Further education or family business, that was the ultimatum our grandparents gave all of us. Personally, I suspect she chose wrong but, again, not my place.

Lux shoves me away. "That's how you greet your favorite sister? Seriously?"

"Yeah, Jackson," an accented croon cuts through the round of indignant huffs Lux's comment is greeted with, and I swear, more than one of my sisters sigh. "You're supposed to compliment pretty girls."

"Stop flirting with my sister."

"I'm not *flirting*." Nick rakes a hand through his dark, curly hair before flattening it against his chest. "I can't help if I'm naturally charming."

"Naturally nauseating," Cass corrects mockingly, slinging an arm around our friend's shoulders and tossing Lux a wink. "Leave the poor girl alone. It's bad enough she has Jackson for a brother, she doesn't need you ruining her life."

"I would never," Nick protests dramatically, hitting Lux with puppy dog eyes before pinning Cass with a scowl. "You'd be lucky to have me as a brother-in-law."

"*Lucky*." An exaggerated snort leaves Cass. "Remind me to bulk-buy condolence cards for whatever poor girl's family gets stuck with you."

It should be impossible, after spending my entire life surrounded by them, to forget how loud my sisters are. Yet somehow, the sheer volume they're capable of achieving always shocks me.

Not only loud but hectic, too. Food flying, cutlery clanging, a million conversations happening at once, hard to focus on any one thing kind of hectic. Like four freight trains colliding simultaneously. By the time the guys call it a night and escape to their room, both Cass and Nick look a little shell-shocked. Even I feel a migraine incoming, and I should be used to the nonsense after almost twenty-one years.

The front door screeches as I escape the mayhem-rife kitchen, weathered wood creaking beneath me as I settle on the top step of the porch, tilting my face toward the stars twinkling above me. Besides my sisters, this is one of the things I miss most about ranch life; clear, country skies, nothing but stars for miles.

A moment of peace is all I get before footsteps sound, a body plopping down beside me at the same time a beer, ice-cold and dripping with condensation, nudges my hand. Accepting the drink, I slide Lux a disapproving look as she sips one of her own. She rolls her eyes. "I'm nineteen, not nine."

"Still not twenty-one."

"Neither are you."

Only a couple of months shy, I could argue, but I'm not in the mood to bicker. Instead, I sigh, resting back on one hand and bringing the beer to my lips with the other, an honest admission changing the subject. "This place looks really good."

More understating; 'really good' doesn't begin to cover it. A single walk-through and a glance at the books proved this place is running smoother than it ever did under anyone else's control. Dream career or not, Lux is a natural at this.

"It better," my sister grumbles, her smile weak as pulls her knees up to her chest, resting a cheek atop them. "It's taken enough of my blood, sweat, and tears. The renovation almost killed me." Her attempt at humor falls flat, probably because there's too much truth to be found behind her words.

"They didn't help?" I don't know why I ask when I already know the answer; of course, they didn't. They never do. Our grandparents' idea of 'parenting' involves depositing a hefty cheque in our bank accounts once a month.

Although, that is slightly better than that of our parents, which involves simply disappearing from our lives altogether.

"They paid," Lux drawls, the defeat in her tone hiding behind a layer of sarcasm. "That's enough for them."

I must not hide my annoyance very well because Lux lays a hand on my knee, patting comfortingly. "It's fine. I have help."

I scoff—knowing who her help is, I'm not exactly soothed. "How are Dopey and Sleepy?"

Comforting patting becomes a chastising slap. "*Simon* and *Charlie* are great," she corrects with narrowed eyes, emphasizing the names of the ranch hands our grandparents hired around the time I left for college.

To pick up the slack, they said.

To get in the way, in reality.

Two giant hulking masses of muscles with no brains, good for heavy lifting and not much else, are not the help my sister needs.

"And I have Mark."

A humorless laugh leaves me. Fucking *Mark*. God, I'd rather her have no one.

I've never liked him, Lux's boyfriend, mostly because he's a fucking dipshit. Smarmy, condescending, over-controlling, and Lux is oblivious to all of it. I've heard him talk down to her more than once. Try to diminish the hard work she does. Refer to her as 'nothing more than a housewife' in a derogatory tone, twisting taking care of our home as an insult and dismissing the fact she does so much more than goddamn housework.

She runs a successful business. She keeps three teenage girls, and herself, alive and healthy, as well as a dozen horses. She does a million times more work than that tool, and she's a million times too good for him. But every time I point that out, it ends in a fight, hence the warning look contorting Lux's features.

"You can talk about Mark," she starts, tone too saccharine for my liking, "if I can talk about Caroline."

It's a dirty tactic, bringing up my ex-girlfriend. My sisters' preferred strategy of shutting me up. "You brought him up."

"A temporary lapse in judgment."

"But can I just-"

"So, you really never think about getting back together with her?"

"Nope," I cut her off with an honest, firm answer. Not once in the two years since the break-up have I contemplated getting back together with my high school sweetheart. It was a final decision, the right decision. It never would've worked—she loves the tiny town we grew up in, never wants to leave, and I love this place too but, God, I couldn't wait to get out.

"Fair enough," Lux muses over the rim of her beer bottle, and I silently marvel at how adeptly she shucked the attention off herself. "She was kind of weird."

"She was not."

"I thought she was gonna follow you to Sun Valley."

"Shut up."

"Is there a new girl yet? Just so I know to get slash-proof tires."

Her question is rhetorical, made in jest, yet still, a glimpse of an

EJ BLAISE

image flickers through my mind. Silky blonde hair, enrapturing blue eyes, a sweet yet sultry voice that I could listen to forever, easy.

I shake off that fantasy as quickly as it appears because that's all it is.

A fantasy.

2

LUNA

"You're fucking kidding me."

A single grunt is all Kate offers to confirm that no, she is not fucking kidding.

"He *forgot*?" My enraged screech startles more than one of the families attempting to enjoy the early July sunshine in the park I'm stomping through. I took the long way home with the same intention, wanting to soak up the New York summer I yearn for all year.

Alas, a single call and one infuriating confession has ruined any chance of that.

Offering as apologetic a smile as I can muster in my current fuming state, I hiss at the unimpressed face taking up my phone screen, "He forgot her birthday?"

Kate's sigh is more resigned than surprised. "Hasn't so much as texted her."

"You are fucking kidding me," I repeat my earlier statement, shaking my head and damn near crushing the plastic takeout cup of passionfruit lemonade clutched between my fingers. Not for the first time since I met Dylan Wells, I wish it was his neck straining beneath my fingertips.

Bastard.

I shouldn't be shocked; forgetting his girlfriend's—my best friend's—birthday is the least offensive of a long string of misde-meanors. The guy is a pushy, controlling prick, and I knew as much as the second I met him. He always expects the most while providing the bare fucking minimum—literally the polar opposite of Amelia—and it hurts, seeing my kind, headstrong friend so frequently mistreated, so often reduced to a pretty little ornament draped over an unworthy arm. And it's infuriating that no matter what I do, I can't change Amelia's mind about him because in her eyes, for some unknown reason, the man can do no wrong.

In my eyes, Dylan is a billboard ad for why a commitment-free life of meaningless sex is superior.

For months—honestly, since the moment Dylan strutted into the dorm Amelia, Kate, and I shared and introduced himself to my boobs—I've been searching for an intervention opportunity, and it looks like this might be it.

On cue, a door opens and closes somewhere in Kate's vicinity, and my friend's subtly enraged expression melts into a careful smile. A greeting sounds, followed by a request for Kate's location, and a moment later, another face joins our video call, our trio complete for the first time in a week.

I didn't think time apart from my roommates would be a big deal but after an entire college year practically attached at the hip, I feel like I'm missing a freaking limb.

"Hey, stranger," my favorite little redhead greets.

"Hey, birthday girl," I sing a reply. "You get my present?"

Green eyes shine with humorous gratitude as Amelia nods. "They're bigger than me."

Considering Amelia makes Thumbelina look like a giant—it would probably be harder to find sunflowers smaller than her than it was to find a jungle of potted plants almost a head taller.

Even before the murderous-rage-inducing news of Dylan's forgetfulness reached me, I knew the bastard would fail the girlfriend he doesn't deserve on her special day. And flowers on a birthday are what Dylan Wells is to chemical castration—obligatory.

However, when I voice that thought—that fact—the reactions are far from agreeable.

"It's not a big deal," Amelia defends a man who doesn't deserve it. "He has a lot going on right now."

Yeah, right. An unemployed, unmotivated dipshit who's sole

interest lies in the bottom of a keg has a lot going on in the middle of summer break.

Sure.

"Do something nice today, okay?" I say instead of word-vomiting the many derogatory comments brewing in my brain. Contrary to popular belief, I do know where to draw the line—I just have to squint to see it sometimes. "Go celebrate."

Don't sit at home and wallow over that goddamn dickhead.

"I will," Amelia replies, her poor attempt at a lie evident in the pinkening tips of her ears.

Smile tight, my gaze finds Kate and a rapid, silent conversation occurs between the two of us—something along the lines of *make her go out, I'll try my best, drag her by her hair if you have to*—that Amelia finds incredibly annoying, if her little huff is anything to go by. "Stop it." She elbows Kate, and I feel the ghost of a sharp joint poke me. "I'm fine. I have coffee cake and sunflowers. That's celebratory enough for me."

A sad, slightly pathetic celebration unworthy of such an occasion, in my humble opinion, but I'm not one to kick someone when they're down.

Well, not intentionally.

It takes an impressive display of self-control to keep my mouth shut and my rampant thoughts to myself. By the time the girls bid me goodbye, the poor cup in my hand is as dead as I wish, with zero shame, a certain sorry excuse for a man was.

Tossing the crumpled cup in the trash can at the bottom of my mom's building's stairwell, I climb the three stories to the one-bedroom apartment we shared for almost two decades, feet slapping against the so-old-they-must-be-a-health-hazard-steps with more fervor than necessary. Stomping down the hall, I wrestle my keys out of my bag and unlock the front door painted a faded shade of bubblegum pink— something Little Luna who likened Princess Peach to a god begged for and Preteen Luna who inexplicably thought pink was uncool loathed.

Shouldering the Pepto-Bismol-esque slab of wood open, my nose scrunches as a familiar, overwhelming stench engulfs me. "Ma, I'm home."

No reply.

Unsurprising, considering the volume of the music rattling the walls has not only swallowed my words but has probably severely hindered my mother's hearing capabilities.

Following the telling trail of colorful droplets staining the floor, I find Ma where she usually is; upstairs in the loft area I used to call a bedroom, covered in paint and haphazardly swooshing a paintbrush at a canvas.

"Ma," I repeat louder, simultaneously reaching for the old stereo propped in the corner and quieting the melody threatening to scramble my brain. The blonde woman with her back to me jumps, spinning around and brandishing the brush in her hand like a weapon. It might as well be; paint stains are definitely something to fear.

When blue eyes, the mirror image of mine, land on me, Ma deflates. "Jesus, Lu, you scared the shit out of me."

"Sorry." Thumb swiping at a streak of paint marring her cheek, I'm momentarily distracted by the bright colors as I ponder what Ma's painting now. Last month, she had a thing for oceans, various shades of blue streaking her skin, clothing, canvases, everything. This month, it looks like red is her thing.

Fitting, considering my mood right now.

A mood that I'm apparently not hiding very well.

Brow creased with a frown, Ma scrubs a damp rag over her paint-flecked skin, doing the same to my thumb. "You okay?"

A simple question and her probing stare are enough to have my big mouth opening and word vomit spilling out. Before I know it, I've relayed the entire Dylan dilemma in a perfectly dramatic rant, pacing, erratic arm gestures, spittle flying and all.

Ma regards with a mixture of amusement and concern, gaze flicking from my fidgeting hands to my marching feet as they narrowly avoid colliding with an open paint can. "Lu, did you take your meds this morning?"

With a huff, my eyes roll toward the ceiling. "Yes." I take them every morning like clockwork, habitually, ingrained between brushing my teeth and doing my hair.

"Just checking sweets." Ma surveys me skeptically. "You seem a little off."

"I'm just irritated." And I get a little more so at the assumption that me being in a bad mood automatically means I skipped my meds and I'm displaying signs of hyperactivity rather than just regular fucking emotions.

Expression shifting to one of subtle guilt, Ma swiftly changes the subject. Ushering me downstairs, she deposits me by the small table separating kitchen from living room, commanding me to sit down before snatching up the kettle; it's a strong Isla Evans belief that tea can fix anything. "Any plans for tonight?"

"Going out with Eva and Bea."

Ma grimaces at the mugs—handmade by her—lining our kitchen cabinets. She's never been the biggest fan of my high school friends. *Snooty* and *uptight* is what she's always called them, and honestly, after spending time away from them and returning with fresh eyes, I'm inclined to agree.

When I came home last Christmas, it was a veil lifted and suddenly revealed how rude and self-involved they are. Spending any time with them felt akin to torture. Every conversation felt like a competition, a sneaky battle over who was having the best college experience. And, God, the way they spoke to everyone around them? Bartenders, hostesses, waitresses, old classmates who deigned to say hello? I was in a state of permanent cringe.

Over Spring Break, when I brought Amelia and Kate home, I successfully avoided them for the entire week. Alas, I'm not that lucky twice in a row; my plane had barely landed before Eva was calling, insisting on a catch-up, and I've been bracing myself for scrutiny and pushy questions ever since.

The only silver lining; I'll have alcohol to cushion the experience.

I look fucking hot.

Clad in a little black dress, hair floating around me like a halo, make-up done to fucking perfection. The thumping music guides my body, my fake ID and phone secured in my bra so my hands are free to thread through my hair, gathering it in my hands away from my sticky neck.

Eva and Bea dance beside me, albeit a lot stiffer, more focused on throwing flirty lances and pouty lips at the guys surrounding us, dancing for them while I'm dancing for me. At the risk of sounding like a conceited bitch, I don't need to beg for attention.

They'll come to me.

It's amazing what a head of blonde hair, a decent pair of boobs and a sliver of black material covering next-to-nothing will do. Miraculous, really, especially when they earn me free drinks like the one I receive within minutes of leaving the dance floor in favor of the bar.

If I were a better person, I would reject the gratuitous vodka cranberry gifted from a slightly creepy, greasy-looking man I have zero interest in.

Good is not something I've ever claimed to be.

Snatching the condensation-streaked glass with a coy, grateful smile, my free hand discreetly crumples the accompanying napkin scrawled with his number and drops it into one of the many dirty glasses littering the bar.

"That wasn't very nice, darling."

Another thing I have never claimed to be.

The instinctive grimace that always comes out to play when a man in a nightclub invades my personal space is only slightly tempered by the familiarity of the voice crooning in my ear. "Darling?" I twist to frown at the man behind me. "Really?"

Owen's laughter tickles my brow. "Princess? Lover? Sugarplum?"

"Enough," I groan, shaking my head like that might rid my mind of the offensive pet names. Wretched things. Never seen the appeal.

When you get called 'baby' by some meaningless, random man yelling across the street one too many times, it kind of loses its allure.

Hands settle on my hips, tugging and guiding me back to the dance floor, and I let them. Out of all my hometown friends, Owen is the only one I'm genuinely glad to see. The only one I can tolerate for extended periods of time. The only one with whom absence did, in fact, make the heart grow slightly fonder.

Whether that has anything to do with him being the regular source of my orgasms for the better part of my senior year, who knows.

It's always been a casual thing. Never exclusive. Certainly not something I foresaw continuing during college breaks but hey, it's a comfortable arrangement. A safe one, and sometimes, a girl needs a little safe. Especially on nights like this; not only do I get a guaranteed happy ending but also a handy bodyguard to scare away silly men who can't take a hint.

Owen is perfectly adequate. Not great, but good. He gets the job done. Scratches the itch. Which is more than I can say for every man in Sun Valley; I don't know where the hell the guys who know what they're doing are lurking in that town but I've yet to find one. Sex with Owen is quick and dirty, exactly how we both prefer our hookups. No false promises or fake sentiments or useless expectations.

Just sex.

And that night, when the nightclub suddenly becomes his bedroom, it's just sex.

I barely even take a minute to catch my breath before rolling out of his bed, dark carpet soft beneath my bare feet as I hunt for my scattered clothing. It doesn't take very long—not like I was wearing much.

Owen rises as I'm hooking my bra into place, and I watch him pad naked toward the bathroom, tossing the condom in a trash can. When he leans against the doorway, an amused smile tugs at the corner of his mouth. "You can stay, you know. If you want."

Wrestling my dress up my body, I shoot him a look. He knows damn well I won't. The spare room down the hall has my name on it, as it always does.

A sigh escapes my occasional fuck-buddy, a hand scratching his bare chest. "It's not that deep, Lu. I'm not gonna fall in love with you if we sleep in the same bed."

"Not a chance I'm willing to take, " I tease, bending to scoop up my heels, laughter following me as I dart from the room with an air-kiss and a quip thrown over my shoulder, "Men have fallen for less."

Honestly, I hate sleeping in the same bed as other people. I move around too much. I like my own space too much. I don't like the claustrophobic feeling of an arm locking me in place like a sexed-up seatbelt.

Why share half a bed with a stranger—or, in this case, a friend— when I can have a whole one all to myself?

As I sneak down the hall, squinting against the darkness and wondering when the hell the others arrived at Owen's place—the floor separating us does nothing to dull the sounds of their partying

—when I barrel headfirst into someone. "Jesus, Eva." My yelped groan of surprise morphs into a ragged laugh when I recognize the scowling brunette. "You scared the shit out of me."

One half of the duo I spent most of my high school career attached to doesn't respond. Judging by her tense shoulders and the snarl twisting her lips, her night clearly wasn't as successful as mine. Gaze flickering to the room I just snuck out of, Eva's eyes roll to the back of head when she notices the slightly ajar door. "You're still playing around with Owen?"

If I didn't know any better, I'd say that wild look in her eyes was jealousy.

"If you mean fucking him," she winces at my candor, and yeah, that's definitely jealousy, "then yeah."

Eva does not look impressed. "How many is that this week? You cycle through your little black book yet?"

God, it is too early for slut-shaming. Or too late? I don't know, but either way, I'm too tired for her attitude. "Didn't take you for a prude, Eva."

"I'm just not a whore."

A loud snort escapes me before I can stifle it. "Michael Harvey would beg to differ."

Eva stiffens, snarling something vulgar beneath her breath at the mention of the ex she cheated on.

Repeatedly. Relentlessly. Unashamedly.

Like, the girl didn't even try to hide it.

In her defense, the guy is a misogynistic dick who, more than once, loudly declared he only dated Eva because she was a cheer-leader—I distinctly remember something vomit-inducing about neither her looks nor her personality being the real catch, but her flex-ibility—and definitely deserved to be knocked down a few pegs.

But hey, a girl's gotta defend herself and I'll find my ammo wher-ever it arises.

Like an enraged dog, Eva grits her teeth, metaphorical hackles raised as she readies herself for a brawl. But as much as I adore some verbal sparring, entertaining an unworthy opponent whose peak creativity solely involves digs at who I let in my pants feels like a chore. I'd much rather bask in the lingering remnants of my sleepy, post-orgasm haze whilst sprawled on the cloud-like king-size mattress in the spare room. So, before the bitch can pounce, I yawn, loud and obnoxious.

"I'd love to discuss my sexual habits further," I lie. "But being such a slut is hard work, y'know? I'm beat."

Whatever response Eva conjures up, I don't stick around to hear it.

3

JACKSON

I WAS twelve when Serenity Ranch became mine and my sisters' official home.

Even then, when I was young and naive and still full of childlike hope that my parents would get their shit together, the name felt ironic to me. At the time, it didn't feel very serene. Not when our life was nothing but an endless stream of turmoil, full of adults who didn't love us nor care enough to pretend. Despite the rolling green hills and the postcard-like scenery, the latest set of people tasked with raising us ensured, through thinly-veiled insults and painfully obvious disdain for their new position as guardians, ensured serenity was inconceivable.

It was maybe half a year after our mother dropped us on her parents-in-laws' doorstep that the name started to make sense. When our grandparents left us for the first time of many, the eggshells we'd been treading suddenly disintegrated, and *home* finally formed a meaning for us. We discovered real stability, security we'd never truly had before, a safe haven for us to grow up. Odd things to get used to after so long lacking but we did. We settled. Threw down some roots. Grew comfortable enough to make our own traditions.

One of them; the summer party Lux insists on throwing every year. Midsummer, she says, though I'm not entirely sure she knows what that even is; my sister was a fairytale lover in her childhood, and I suspect she read about it in one of her little books.

Wherever it came from, it's her thing. Her expensive, loud, over-the-top thing that started as a way to piss off our grandparents—or to get them to notice us—and morphed into something more. Something that thrived and blossomed and infiltrated our little community, feeding into Lux's inane need to be useful, to be needed, to help. To hold the entire world on her shoulders and act like she isn't a stiff wind away from crumbling.

She's doing it now, floating around the crowded yard, a smile on her face as she mingles and passes out drinks and refrains from actually enjoying the event she painstakingly planned.

I sigh at the sight of her.

I feel tired at the sight of her.

Even more tired than I already feel because unlike my sister—unlike all of my sisters—a social butterfly is not something I could ever be described as. It's fucking hard, this socializing shit. Harder when you no longer live in the small town you call home because your return is practically headline news, worthy of intense scrutiny and endless questions. And it's hardest when you tote two handsome strangers home with you.

All night, there's been a nonstop train of people pretending they want to catch up when really, they want a quick introduction. Personally, I'm not a fan of feeling like a damn circus attraction but Nick and Cass? To no one's surprise, they fucking love it. Preening and prancing and puffing their goddamn chests, they greedily lap up the attention from their admirers.

It's when the number of girls I went to high school with asking for Nick's number hits double digits that I reach my limit. Luckily, I don't need to fake an excuse to leave; not a soul notices when I slink away, my presence, or lack thereof, shadowed by the shiny light my friends permanently exude.

My breath of relief sounds in unison with soft equine snorts as I seek refuge in my favorite spot on the whole ranch. The musty silence of the barn greets me like an old friend, as do its five permanent occupants.

They're an odd mirror, the Appaloosa horses taking up half of the stalls. A parallel. Unwanted by their original owners because of their maintenance and the odd flaw—a muddled coat here, a limping gait there. Strong, though. Resilient as hell. Powerful if given the chance.

Despite the imperfections, they're the most expensive things on this ranch, and I can never quite tell if it's tragic or hilarious that the beautiful creatures are named after a meddling group of cartoon characters. Lux went through a Scooby Doo phase right around the time our equine counterparts joined the family, and contesting the wishes of Alexandra Jackson is an almost impossible fight to win.

Thus, Scooby, Velma, Shaggy, Daphne, and Fred were christened.

I run my fingers through Scooby's—the stallion I chose as mine—mane as I pass his stall, cooing a hello as I grasp the ladder leading to the loft and hoist myself up. As I lean against the stack of hay bales stored up here, legs dangling over the edge, I find myself feeling grateful that at least, amongst the chaos of renovation, this one place hasn't changed.

It was little Lux and I's hiding spot. Where we fled to when our grandparents were on a rampage or when the house felt too full or when we just needed to breathe. So when I hear soft footsteps and creaking wood, I assume it's her seeking me out, coming to drag me back to the festivities.

When a head of mousy hair comes into view, closely followed by a pair of pale brown eyes, I stifle a groan.

"I've been looking everywhere for you," my ex-girlfriend croons as she crawls toward me, perching gingerly on the ledge with her thigh pressed against mine. "You weren't gonna say hi?"

Honestly, no. I wasn't. I've been actively avoiding her for this very reason; I can't take the unrestrained hope, the blatant want for something that no longer exists.

My smile is as weak as my effort to lie, "It's been a busy night."

Caroline's expression dulls slightly, my answer clearly disappointing her. Throat bobbing with a quiet sigh, the skirt of her yellow sundress rustles as she folds her hands in her lap, the smallest furrow to her brow as she regards me. "You look good." The compliment is soft, hesitant, as though she's unsure whether or not she should make it.

"So do you." And she does. Always has; I could never believe such a pretty girl was remotely interested in me.

It was, *is*, the personality that always left something feeling amiss. *Our* personalities. Not a clash but an eerie likeness; quiet, harboring shy tendencies, agreeable for the sake of not causing problems. We never argued and that was the problem. The absence of passion. The lack of fire.

Lux's previous quip about needing slash-proof tires? Hilariously improbable because I'm convinced anger is not an emotion Caroline is capable of.

She confirms my suspicions as we chat amicably like it's not stiflingly uncomfortable. Like she shouldn't be pissed as hell; I broke up with her a couple of months shy of graduation with very little explanation—I believe the words 'it's not you, it's me' were used—before fleeing town, and in the year that followed, I actively avoided her every time I was in town. If the roles were reversed, I'd be irritated.

But she's not. Not even a little. Hurt, clearly, but accepting of my decision, so much so that she's willing to sit here and exchange pleasantries that make my skin itch.

"So, you're home for the summer?"

I hum in confirmation, restraining a wince because God, the telling expectation in her tone is too much. So is the fraction of distance between us. The fingers drumming against her thigh, occasionally brushing mine. The feeling of her breath brushing my shoulder.

"Do you think," *don't do it, Caroline, please don't do it,* "we could hang out sometime? Bishops still does those wings you like."

There's not an ounce of subtlety, not an inch for misconstruing her question; Bishops was our regular date spot. When I drag my gaze upward to meet hers—I've been staring at my thighs for the past ten minutes, scared what eye contact will bring—the look in her eyes makes me feel like I'm a grouchy old man about to kick a goddamn puppy.

"Caroline," her name is heavy on my tongue, tinged with something bitter that tastes an awful lot like guilt, "that's not why I came home."

"I know." Her tiny recoil is hidden well, her wince covered with a drop of her head. "I just thought we could…" She trails off, chewing on her bottom lip, tendrils of hair escaping her braid and flying around her face as she shakes her head quickly. "Never mind. You're right."

It's quick, the scramble as she gets to her feet, practically throwing herself down the ladder before I can get a word out. She flees my presence, a flurry of rapid blinking and watery eyes and strained noises, and as I watch her disappear out the barn doors and rejoin the crowd, I can already predict the topic of conversation in our tiny, nosy town for the foreseeable future.

Great.

~

"Oscar! Hurry the hell up!"

I cringe, both at my real name and at the volume of my eldest sister's voice as she raps her knuckles on my bedroom door. Once, twice, three, and four times until I'm groaning, grabbing my backpack with one hand and ripping open the door with the other. "Stop yelling. I'm right here."

Fingers yank my hair as I brush past, and I twist to slap Lux's hand away. "Finally," she huffs dramatically, redirecting her attack to my back as she shoves me down the hall. "We were about to leave without you."

Ha. More like her impatient ass was about to herd everyone away without me.

"Sorry, *Mom*," I quip, flicking the godawful floppy hat sitting atop my sister's head.

"Piss me off this morning, Oscar," hisses her dry reply. "I dare you."

"Someone woke up on the wrong side of the bed."

Ratty old Birkenstocks clip the back of my heels as Lux shoves me again, her sarcastic laugh echoing off the walls. "*Someone* woke up to our sister passed out on the bathroom floor reeking of beer and covered in her own vomit."

I don't need clarification on which sister; a certain fake blonde has been inexplicably mad at the world lately and taking it out on us. It turns out the enthusiastic greeting I received at the beginning of summer was a fluke; Lottie is a fucking nightmare.

An alcohol-drinking, curfew-skipping, lip-giving nightmare.

The first time I caught her sneaking in past curfew, I labeled it a youthful indiscretion. The second time, I let her off with a warning. But the third time, when red eyes and wide pupils plagued my little sister, I acknowledged the problem.

What was meant to be a reprimanding but supportive confrontation quickly became a screaming match. The house filled with yelled reminders of how we're not her parents, accusations of ruining her life, claims of hatred. Lux screamed back, calling her every name under the sun, asking if she thought we wanted to be her parents, if she thought she wasn't ruining our lives, if she thought we loved her a whole lot right then.

They've been walking on eggshells around each other since then, both acting like they're not overwhelmed with guilt and regret.

So, I'm not surprised when, upon being unceremoniously prodded into the living room, Lottie is nowhere to be found. Everyone else is here though, looking as disheveled and tired as I feel, as though they too were dragged out of bed at the crack of dawn on their one day off.

A day spent at our favorite creek hidden near the Northern edge of our property—where Serenity bleeds into the dense, beautiful forest immortalized on many a sketchbook page—sounds nice until you're awoken by shouted threats and banging pans when the sun is still kissing the horizon.

My poor, victim-of-circumstance friends greet me with simultaneous yawns, Nick's face like thunder while Cass remains in his permanent state of mild amusement. "Your sister is bossy."

I grunt my agreement. Understatement.

We follow my bossy sister towards the barn, where the already tacked and ready to go horses proof that her work today did not begin at annoying her siblings out of bed. Any reprimand dies on my tongue, replaced by a stifled laugh at the sound of my friends' quiet groans, the instant tensing of their shoulders, the grumbled, undoubtedly explicit Portuguese; it's safe to say my city-bred friends have not enjoyed getting acquainted with life in a saddle. Hell, even I had some trouble the first week, jelly legs and stiff fingers plaguing me as I got used to hours on end atop Shaggy after months not riding.

It was a welcome relief when muscle memory finally kicked in. I'm not sure what was more painful—the aching muscles or the mockery from my sisters.

"Shut the fuck up." Nick cuts me with a glare when I don't quite manage to keep my amusement at bay. In my defense, my oversized, suavely coordinated friend awkwardly clambering atop an equally unhappy recently rescued Percheron named Princess is a sight no one could resist chuckling at. "Go make some more girls cry."

Jesus Christ. I knew telling my friends about the Caroline incident was a bad idea.

A half-hiss, half-laugh of a noise escapes Cass, his shaking head doing nothing to hide his grin. "Because you, Nicolas Silva, have never made a girl cry."

"Happy tears," Nick drawls an amendment. "Very, very happy tears."

Cass blinks, amused expression dying. "I have never wanted to know anything less in my life."

Ignoring our friend, Nick fixes with a look bordering on disappointment. "I don't get why you don't wanna have a little fun this summer."

"Messing around with my ex-girlfriend would not be fun." It would be the absolute antithesis of fun. Long, hot months of stress and tension and the awkward, unavoidable knowledge that come summer's end, I'd be leaving again.

Nick clearly disagrees, his scoff as telling as his words. "Meaningless sex is always fun."

"You would know." Cass slaps him on the thigh, threatening the fragile stability he's achieved atop his steed, before clapping a palm down on my shoulder. "Don't listen to him. Not everyone needs their dick hard to have a good time."

"I'm just curious, asshole." Nick risks face-planting the dirty ground to kick a wobbly leg in Cass' direction. "This is about the blonde, isn't it?"

One question and my face feels hot, my throat oddly dry, a question I already know the answer to leaving me at an embarrassingly high pitch. "Who?"

"The blonde from Greenie's." Nick smirks. "The one you like drooling over."

I cough, shrugging like I'm not dangerously close to bursting into flames. "I don't know what you're talking about."

Nick's resounding laugh is anything but subtle. "Sure you don't."

God, I wish I could truthfully call his claims bullshit. I wish that Nick wasn't there when one of many nights spent at Greenies suddenly offered something different than the usual unwanted drinks and counting down the minutes until I could go home without complaint. I wish that I'd never looked up the exact moment a pretty blonde waitress with eyes the same sparkling, clear blue as the creek we're heading to and a pouty, pink smile that could bring a man to his knees breezed past our table and caught my undivided attention, leading to a infuriating amount of teasing from the friend who witnessed it.

"Come on," Nick pries, smiling mockingly. "You gonna pine from afar forever?"

Right now, that is my plan.

Something about her sucks the tiny shreds of confidence I possess out of me—I can barely smile and order a beer let alone flirt with the girl.

I don't answer aloud but it's like Nick reads my mind, his sigh accompanied with a playful chastising tut. "Let's hope she likes the silent brooding type."

It's my turn to sigh.

I highly fucking doubt it.

4

JACKSON

"WHO IS THAT GUY?"

Metal creaks loudly as Cass leans forward, feet planted on the bleacher bench in front of us as he stares quizzing at the field littered with sweaty, sprinting teenagers.

When Coach mentioned he was running a couple of practices over the summer for incoming freshmen, I thought it was a great idea. When he strongly encouraged—code for threatened—the team to help out, I didn't actually mind. I thought it would be a good way to curry favor with Coach and meet prospective teammates, and that maybe, even if driving back and forth from Serenity sucks, it would be fun.

That, however, was when I had no idea it would involve baking in the hot, July sun for hours, only occasionally pitching in with encouraging words and advice that mostly goes ignored.

Most of the team crapped out after an hour, the threat of sunstroke more daunting than Coach's wrath. But Cass wanted to stay to scope out the newbies, so I stayed too.

One newbie in particular stands out, the one Cass is watching like a hawk. Kid would probably be a better word to describe this guy. Blond, lanky as shit, a face like a *high school* freshman. Even from this distance, I can tell he's got an attitude, cocky as he struts about the field but with one hell of an arm to back it up. Honestly, he rivals

Cass' unnatural talent which is probably why my friend hasn't taken his eyes off him for the last hour.

"I've no idea," I answer his earlier question. "But he's pretty good."

Cass grunts unintelligibly and leans back in his seat, cocking his head thoughtfully.

The moment Coach calls a well-needed water break, Cass is on his feet and working his way toward the stampede of guys desperate for a cold beverage.

Sighing, I follow, nudging my friend in the ribs when I catch up. "Leave the kid alone."

"I just wanna talk," he protests, thwarting any attempt to stop him when he cups his hands around his mouth and the booming sound of his voice echoes around the field. "Hey!"

Multiple heads snap our way but Cass' gaze doesn't waver from his target. The kid frowns at the attention, head shifting from right to left as he checks his surroundings before pointing at himself, tilting his head, and mouthing "me?"

Stifling a laugh, I mimic Cass' nod, hoping my smile is a hell of a lot less intimidating than my friend's downright thunderous expression,

The second he's within earshot, Cass introduces himself but he's abruptly interrupted. "I know," the kid pants, grinning teeth startling white against his flushed skin. "Cass Morgan. You killed it last season."

I groan internally as a slick smile twists Cass' mouth. Chest puffed, he shoots me a smug look, his earlier disdain suddenly nowhere to be found. Rolling my eyes, I shift my attention back to the kid, opening my mouth only for my introduction to be cut off as well. "Oscar Jackson. I know you, too."

I pause a moment before arching a brow. "No compliment for me?"

His smile is nothing short of pure cheek. "You're pretty good."

A glowing review.

"You got a name?"

"Ben. Ben Smith."

"You coming here in the fall?"

"You're a shoo-in for the team," Cass points out when the kid nods, and I pray Ben wipes the starstruck expression off his face before my friend's head blows up. "After today, I doubt Coach will even make you try out."

I hum my agreement; a severe understatement. Like Cass was, he's too good to even entertain the ridiculous idea of not making the team. And like he did Cass, Coach is already looking at Ben with hearts and trophies in his eyes.

The kid doesn't preen under the praise. He doesn't play the modest prodigy. No, he grins lazily, shrugs, and I bet if he had long hair like me, he'd toss it nonchalantly over his shoulder. "I know."

God, him and Cass are seriously cut from the same cloth. Talented and they know it, and they will make sure you know it too.

By the time Coach demands everyone get their asses back on the field, both guys are practically levitating, Ben with the excitement of meeting who's apparently his idol and Cass with the satisfaction and entirely unnecessary ego-boost that comes with being idolized.

"I like him," Cass declares, watching Ben run off with a look I can only describe as fatherly pride.

I snort. "Five seconds ago, you were threatened."

"I was not."

Cass rolls his eyes. "If anything, he reminds me of me."

"Obnoxiously self-confident?"

A fist meets my shoulder. "Incredibly fucking talented, thank you very much."

"I agree," a rough voice chimes in, and I glance aside to find Coach has joined our conversation. The older man's gaze flits between us and Ben, the Yankees cap with a permanent place on his head briefly lifted so he can scrape a hand through salt-and-pepper hair. "I want him on this team."

Just like I thought; the kid's already in.

"You two are gonna keep an eye on him," Coach commands, doesn't ask, and we both nod without hesitation—I don't think anyone has ever argued with Coach Daire Kelly and lived to tell the tale. "Show him the ropes. Make him feel comfortable. If he's not on that field come February, I will hold you both personally responsible."

A hard look follows his words, and neither of us get a chance to reply before he's striding away, hands clapping loudly and a slew of barked orders leaving him.

Hand lifting in a mock salute, Cass huffs an amused yet confused breath. "Did he just give us custody of a seventeen-year-old?"

Raking my hands through shoulder-length hair, I let out a chuckle of my own. "I think he did."

∾

I imagine that when Coach trusted us with taking care of his new favorite player, he didn't anticipate us taking him to a grimy, gritty bar frequented by every student on campus.

Well, almost every student—when I say *us*, I mean *me*, since Cass was banned from the establishment within weeks of starting freshman year.

Ben's got stars in his eyes as we shove our way toward the counter, the sea of people taking advantage of cheap booze and minimal security meaning I have to glance over my shoulder every two seconds to check I haven't lost The Golden Child.

Only my semi-prominent status as Baseball Player and Friend of Nick and Cass gets me through with minimal injury and effort but by the time we make it, a layer of sweat sticks uncomfortably to my skin and I already can't wait to get the hell out of here.

"This place is so cool," Ben yells in my ear as he hops on a rare unoccupied stool.

I stifle a laugh; oh, to be a young, naive freshman again, when warm beer and sticky counters and too many people in your space was *cool*.

And I stifle another when the moment I reach the counter, I spot a familiar face at the other end of the bar, a drink nursed in one large, tattooed hand, an ass cheek in the other.

"Nick!"

Golden eyes laced with irritation flick my way, a dark brown brow quirking as if to say *'yes? Excuse me? Why are you interrupting my very important business of feeling up yet another pretty girl?'*

Rolling my eyes, I crook a couple of fingers to beckon him over, jerking my head toward my new friend.

With a long, tormented sigh that I swear I can hear even over the din of the bar, Nick briefly returns his attention to his new *friend*. Whispering God knows what in the girl's hair, he leaves her with a wink and a slap on the ass before sauntering our way. "Whatever you want, make it quick."

Because in the thirty seconds this introduction is going to take, the girl flashing heart-shaped eyes at Nick's retreating back will get bored and leave. *Sure.*

"Nick," I ignore my friend's comment, clamping a palm on his shoulder and guiding him toward my newest teammate, "this is Ben. Ben, this is Nick."

Behave, I'm tempted to add, unsure who needs the reminder more.

"You're Nicolas Silva." Ben maintains his perfect record, three-for-three at Campus Guess Who. "Heard some people," *girls,* "around campus talking about you. You're popular."

He knows, I think.

"I know," Nick drawls.

I swear to God, I smell the trouble dripping from Ben, sensing the quip a second before he bares shiny, straight teeth in a sorry attempt at an innocent smile. "I didn't think you'd be, like, old, though."

The pride painting Nick's features melts. A scowl contorts that life-ruining face, the mouth so skilled at seduction opening to spit something undoubtedly the opposite but an interruption saves Ben from the wrath of a large, testy Brazilian man.

"What can I get you, boys?"

With a handful of sweetly crooned words, my friends disappear. The crowd disappears. The damn bar disappears. All I see is the blonde waitress planting her palms on the counter and smiling brightly, pinning me with clear blue eyes that render me fucking useless as usual.

She smells like vanilla. Simple, rich vanilla. I want to lean in closer and breathe deep, filling my lungs with the scent until it permeates the organ.

Thankfully, I don't do that.

I don't do anything, actually.

She stands there, so goddamn pretty with full cheeks and fuller lips and cheekbones I could spend hours painstakingly drawing, staring at me expectantly, and I can't get a damn word out.

It's Nick's snickering that drags me out of a blue-eye-addled haze, and his elbow jabbing my ribs. He rattles off our order and the waitress scribbles it down, disappearing into the back before I have a chance to get my shit together.

"You're pathetic," Nick laughs, shaking his head.

I groan, my elbows hitting the counter, my head cradled in my hands as I brace for the incessant teasing I'm sure is on its way.

But it never arrives.

Frowning, I tilt my head toward Nick, brows furrowing when I find his attention no longer on me. Staring off into the distance, his gaze is weirdly intense, unmistakable lust clouding it, along with something else indecipherable.

Curious as to what—or who—has a man the epitome of cool, calm, and collected looking so… *off,* I follow his line of sight. A slow smile spreads across my face when I find one of the only people here as often as we are.

A contrast to her coworker, Greenies' other newest waitress is a tiny redhead with a perpetually worried brow and eerily bright eyes, and all five-foot-nothing of her is currently holding Nick captive.

The guy looks fucking enthralled.

Oh, this is good.

This is so damn good.

"Something caught your attention over there, Nicolas?"

With a cough, Nick rips his gaze away from Red, the curl of his lips flattening as he scowls and shakes his head. Leaning back against the counter, he aims for nonchalance but I don't think a force in the world could keep his eyes from drifting back toward the girl.

And I'm pretty sure he hates it.

Ben, oblivious to how unusually flustered my friend seems to be, breaks his rare display of silence with a crooked lip and pale, raised brow. "Is that your girlfriend? She's cute."

Nick scoffs in unison with my barked laugh. "Nicky doesn't do girlfriends," I explain teasingly, although I wonder if right now, he's regretting that stipulation.

"You don't *do* girlfriends?"

"Nope," is Nick's simple answer to Ben's disbelieving inquiry, his blank tone contrasted by glimmering gold irises.

Ben practically exudes mischief as he cocks his head at Nick. "Boyfriends?"

With a low laugh, Nick copies Ben's stance, tilting his head and crooking a brow. "You hitting on me, kid?"

"You wish, Grandpa."

5

JACKSON

"I can't believe you've done this."

For the third time since we arrived at Sun Valley's only decent pub, Nick huffs loudly, slumping in the booth we claimed with his arms crossed over his chest, muttering something in angry Portuguese before following up in English. "This is a terrible fucking idea."

Across from Nick and I, Cass sighs like one might at a child throwing a tantrum. "He needed somewhere to live."

"Dorms exist."

"Our spare room is nicer."

"He's a *child*."

"You're dramatic."

"Ben is nice," I interject before the eye-poking, hair-pulling segment of their argument begins. I ignore Nick's scoff as I crook a brow at Cass. "But you should've asked us first."

"I didn't think it would be a big deal!"

"*You didn't think it would be a big deal*," Nick repeats, eyes rolling toward the ceiling. "Inviting a fetus to live with us is a big deal."

"He's seventeen!"

Nick blinks. "Exactly."

"Look," Cass starts and God, don't I recognize that troublesome tone. "I know anyone under the age of twenty seems like a child compared to you-"

"I am not *old*."

"You know who says that? Old people."

I'm up and sprinting to the bar before the first Portuguese curse can leave Nick's mouth; I physically cannot listen to another round of arguing without another round of alcohol. They just keep recycling the same conversation.

Cass reveals he asked Ben to move in with us.

Nick is pissed.

Cass tries to explain why.

Nick is pissed.

Cass gets pissed because Nick is pissed.

Nick is more pissed.

Deep down, I don't think Nick actually has a problem with it. Besides the whole calling-him-old-thing, him and Ben got along well. He–and I say this lovingly–just likes to bitch. And Cass–also, with so much love–likes to make him bitch.

It's a dangerous fucking cycle, and being caught up in it?

Actual hell.

It's a hot and sticky tussle to the counter, elbows hitting the wood as a sigh loosens my lips. I want to go home. I never wanted to leave home, actually. I didn't even want to be in Sun Valley this weekend. With a meagre couple of weeks until junior year starts, I wanted to soak up every moment of fresh, country air I could.

Nick and Cass, however, had other ideas.

An obligatory house-warning night out, they claimed, never mind the fact we technically moved into our new place at the beginning of summer, when we transferred all our stuff from what was essentially a shitty, overcrowded frat house without the official title to a slightly less shitty place for the three of us.

Or, I guess, the four of us now.

Learn to say no, Jackson, I tell myself as I contemplate scaling the bar and pouring my own drink since that seems a better plan than waiting for the bartender—whose devout attention belongs to a group of giggling girls—to shift his focus my way. And after a lengthy wait, when my wish for a fresh drink is finally granted, the relief is short-lived.

A full glass barely graces my palm before a shoulder rams into my chest and sticky liquid sloshes over the rim, half the contents staining one of the only t-shirts not splattered in paint I own.

Typical.

"Fucking hell," I swear beneath my breath, brows pulling together in a frown that all but dissipates the moment my gaze raises and lands on the culprit.

The strong scent of vanilla overwhelming the acrid tang of beer should've given it away before the blonde hair does. Or the eyes with the uncanny likeness to the paint that's been frequenting my canvas— Spun Sugar, a pale cyan, a complete coincidence. Or the skin stained a sandy brown from the sun. Or the long legs I really, really try not to gawk at but, in my defense, the gem-adorned strappy heels encircling delicate ankles are hard to ignore.

It's embarrassing, really, that without seeing them, I can recall those features almost perfectly. That I can recall the first time I saw them despite the fact they belong to a girl who's name I don't even know.

It was after the last game of sophomore year, a game we won, of course, because losing is not something Cass Morgan is accustomed to. We were celebrating in the local student haunt, as we often do— minus our star player because getting banned from establishments *is* something Cass is accustomed to but plus the other biggest player on campus because where the women are, so is Nick. I was just sitting there, cringing at my too-loud teammates and trying to politely shuck off an overenthusiastic jersey chaser when suddenly, there she was.

Bright and smiling and so damn pretty it hurt my head.

Robbed me of my speech then too—I barely managed to conjure up a simple request for beer with that smile fixed on me.

Slack-jawed and blurry-eyed, Nick likes to say I was. Tongue hanging out like a dog catching sight of a treat. Wedding bells ringing around me.

The persistent teasing all summer was painful but even worse?

Suddenly, the blonde was everywhere.

It was like I saw her once and I couldn't unsee her.

Every Greenies visit, she was working. The rare times I was in Sun Valley over the summer—I promised my sisters I'd be home and I'm a man of my word—she was always inexplicably in my vicinity too, all swishing hips and flicking hair and melodious laughter.

I'm not sure why I thought tonight would be any different. Greenies' most distracting waitress blinks blankly at the damp spot on my t-shirt, her throat bobbing with a quiet hiccup as she sways on unsteady feet. She's stationary yet she stumbles over nothing, and I loop a steadying hand around her bicep before she falls on her ass.

"Are you okay?"

Shoulders quaking with a shiver, hazy blue eyes slowly climb upward. Pale brows furrow as though she's just realizing I'm here. Full lips painted a glossy pink part, slurred words leaving them in an incoherent gargle.

With my umpteenth sigh of the evening, I turn back to the bar. Wouldn't you know, now that I have a pretty girl by my side, the bartender is quick to appear, ready to take my order with a sleazy smile on his thin lips.

I side-step, blocking her from view. "Can I get some water, please?"

Exchanging a couple of bills for a bottle, I'm checking it's sealed when the warm skin beneath my fingertips suddenly disappears. I glance up just in time to watch Blondie slip my grasp and stumble away, oddly elegant in her inebriated state.

I'm not the only one who notices her graceful yet wobbly strides; it's like a hundred gazes swing her way as she ambles through the club. For once in her presence, my brain stops malfunctioning long enough for me to shove through the crowd after her.

Blonde doesn't notice me looming at her back like a protective shadow as she makes a break for the bathroom—her slightly green sickly pallor gives her away before her wandering feet do.

I don't touch her. I'm just... there. Hovering. A couple of inches between us. Enough to give her space.

Not enough to give any of the leering creeps the impression we're not together.

I wonder, briefly, if they'd still be leering if they too watched her drop to her knees and empty her guts into a toilet.

Honestly, probably.

Awkwardly crouching in the sliver of space between her and the cubicle wall, my fingers skim the nape of her neck as they clumsily twist long, wavy locks into a makeshift ponytail. God, I never thought I'd be grateful for Lux's more rebellious years; they may have been hell on my blood pressure but at least they taught me how to take care of a drunk girl.

"You okay?" My question is drowned out by the sound of retching, followed by a defeated groan as the girl sits back on her heels. When another shiver wracks her lithe body, I wriggle out of the corduroy shirt I'm wearing over my tee and drape it over her shoulders.

Her very bare shoulders.

To go with her very bare body, if I was noticing things like that.

I'm not, though.

A weak smile and quiet thanks draws my attention away from miles of smooth skin. I watch like a damn lovestruck fool as she slips her arms through the sleeves of my shirt, hugs the soft fabric close to her with a small, happy inhale that, God, I don't know what to do with.

Clearing my throat, I crack open the water bottle and hold it out to her, desperate to prove I'm not a creep despite very much feeling like one. Only a moment of cautious eagle-eyeing passes before she sighs and takes it, sucking down the contents so greedily, she sloshes water all over her chin and her chest and *God help me.* "If this is roofied, I'm gonna kick your ass."

My chuckle surprises me, how casually it comes out. "I don't doubt that."

Those diamond encrusted death-trap stilettos could take a man down, easy, if wielded the right way.

A satisfied, agreeing hum leaves her as she suddenly shifts, two palms molding to my shoulders as she hoists herself to her bejeweled feet.

I don't move a muscle. I don't think I breathe for the impossibly long minute it takes her to right herself, nor the following thirty seconds where she simply… stands. Stares. Smiles.

Winks.

And honest to God purrs, "Thanks, handsome."

Death by half-hearted, joking compliment.

That's how I'm gonna go.

Huh.

I don't get the chance to even attempt a response; she pats me on the shoulder and teeters away before my tongue can untie itself. Slender fingers topped with long, bright pink nails clasp the ceramic edge of the sink, narrowed eyes peering into the cloudy mirror above it. Downturned lips part with a displeased puff of air. "Jesus Christ, Luna."

Ordinarily, I would revel in the sudden discovery of her name. I would think, God, how fitting she's named after a goddess.

My brain, however, is caught on the sight of the pearly silk clinging to her upper thighs, riding too high when she stoops to rinse her mouth out with tap water. A hint of curved ass cheek is enough to have my gaze averting. It shoots toward the ceiling for a brief second as I pray the choked noise lodged in the back of my throat isn't as audible as I fear before returning to her reflection.

Clambering awkwardly to my feet, I shove my twitchy hands into my pockets, watching her straighten that goddamn scrap of fabric and fluff her hair and swipe at the errant streaks of mascara beneath her eyes, all the while cursing and chastising herself for being such a mess.

"You look good."

Startlingly bright irises dart my way, as wide and surprised to hear the compliment as I was to say it—I was thinking it one second, blurting it the next. It's hilarious, really, that amidst a sea of instances where my mouth refuses to open around this girl, it couldn't stay shut the one time I wanted it to.

Something between a smirk and a pout flourishes as Luna straightens, one hip cocked as she flicks her hair over a shoulder, intimidating in a way no one as wasted as her should be capable of achieving. "Just good?"

"Uh," I cough, gaze inadvertently raking over her.

Yeah. If I looked like her, I'd be offended by *good* too.

"Beautiful," I correct myself, the tips of my ears on fire as they presumably turn bright red.

A tiny, sharp intake of breath echoes off the tiled bathroom walls. Luna's head drops ever so slightly, waves falling forward to hide what I'm sure are but can't possibly be blush-stained cheeks. It only lasts a split second, the brief lapse in bravado, before she clears her throat and straightens.

"Beautiful, hm?" she croons, twirling a blonde lock around her finger in a way that should absolutely be cringy and obnoxious but somehow isn't. "Lucky you. Trapped in a bathroom with a beautiful girl."

Briefly, I wonder if I'm hallucinating. If I'm the drunk one. If someone slipped something in my drink. Because I swear there's a flirtatious edge to her tone, something sultry and sticky and too damn enticing.

Coy. Curious. Wanting.

God, I might not be Nicolas fucking Silva but I know what a girl looks like when she wants to be kissed. And she, for some unfathomable reason, is looking at me like that right now.

It's so sudden, so off-balancing, so fucking distracting, I almost forget she's drunk. I almost forget she's… *her*. Any thoughts unrelated to the crystal gaze zoned in on my mouth are pretty cloudy. When her tongue darts out to trace her bottom lip, I almost break.

God, do I want to break.

But then Luna takes a single step toward me and trips over her own feet, and reality breaks through the fog.

I catch her before she hits the ground, holding her at arm's length but she doesn't stay there for long. Soft, drunken snickering brushes my neck as she shimmies closer, long lashes casting shadows across her cheeks as she blinks with blatant false innocence. "What, you scared of me or something?"

Terrified, I admit silently.

"You need help finding someone?" I ask aloud.

It's not a dismissal—it's more of a plea—but Luna takes it that way. A full bottom lip comes out to play, disappointment found in straight, white teeth kissing loudly. "No."

It would be a lie, if the universe wasn't evidently on Luna's side. The moment the word leaves her pouting mouth, the bathroom door swings open, wood banging against the wall in unison with an indignant shout. "Hey!"

Survival instincts drive me away from the too-drunk girl with lowered inhibitions; she doesn't get the message. The large step I take, she copies, plastering herself to my side, dead weight leaning against me as one hand loops loosely around my waist in an oddly comfortable way while the other waves lazily at the girl looming in the doorway.

The girl staring at me exactly how you'd expect someone to stare at the random stranger pawing your drunk friend alone in a bathroom.

Dark eyes scrutinize me suspiciously, and when she crooks an accusing brow, I blurt, "I was helping her."

The responding hum is less than convinced.

"Relax, Kate," Luna cuts in confidently, a clammy palm patting my hip. "He did not roofie me."

Kate wears an expression as dry and unamused as her response. "That's nice of him."

A croaky, heaving noise I think is a laugh directs my attention to the lump of pale skin and wild, red hair bundled beneath Kate's arm, and I'm briefly distracted as I wonder how Nick would react if he knew the girl he definitely has absolutely zero interest in was scurrying around the same bar all night.

Very distracting fingers messing with the hem of my t-shirt direct my attention to Luna again. Lashing batting, she does that goddamn purring thing again. "Can you help me into bed?"

"Jesus Christ, Luna." Kate sighs, briefly pinching the bridge of her nose before crooking her fingers in a summoning gesture. "You're done. Let's go."

Luna puts up a hell of a fuss, whining and slurring incoherent complaints, but she obeys her friend. She stumbles over, tucking herself under Kate's free arm, letting her half-lead, half-drag her down the hallway.

Right before she disappears from sight, Luna turns. Droopy eyes land on me, one dipping in a wink as clumsy fingers wiggle a goodbye. "Bye, handsome."

6

JACKSON

I WAKE up with a woman in my bed.

Blonde hair tickles my bare chest, the fresh-from-a-bottle, burns-your-nostrils peroxide kind. Like a mop splayed across my chest, roots tinged rusty.

Oddly, it reminds me of Lux and the time she tried to dye her hair in our bathroom with bleach from the dollar store. Suffice to say, the following day was spent soothing teenage tears and restoring her original dark shade.

I don't remember her name. I only vaguely remember her face. But I definitely remember slamming shots like they were water and bringing home the first girl who showed interest in me. The friend of whoever Nick brought home, I think.

It seemed like a good idea at the time. A release. A distraction from who I wished I was bringing home. Now, though, as I carefully roll out of bed and creep out of the room, the regret hits me pretty hard, and I wonder just how shitty I'd feel if we'd done anything more than kiss and fondle each other before passing out.

Getting plastered and hooking up with randoms isn't me. I don't like it, it doesn't make me feel good. It makes me feel awkward and uncomfortable and out of my depth, emotions I grew up drowning in and now actively avoid. Their occurrence is few and far between, catching me off guard at rare moments, and always, without fail, I wish I could take them back.

Last night especially.

I avoid my friends' gazes as I shuffle into the kitchen. I make a beeline for the coffee pot and fill a mug to the brim, topping the dark liquid off with the hazelnut creamer our fridge has been stocked with since Ben moved in. Gracious man that he is, Nick allows me two whole sips before cooing in my ear, "Have fun last night?"

I hum a yes. Because I did, for a brief, odd moment.

It's just not the moment I gather Nick is referring to.

Hands squeeze my shoulders, giving me a gentle shake. "That's my boy."

From the opposite end of the counter, Ben finishes dishing pancakes onto plates already laden with every breakfast food imaginable. After sliding two mine and Nick's way—I dare not mention Nick's sudden lack of roommate complaining—my younger friend props his elbows on the counter, chin in palm, brows wiggling. "You see Blondie was there?"

Nick's loud groan cuts off my response. "Seriously? I swear to fucking God, I can't get away from that girl."

"No, my Blondie," I correct him, just as quickly correcting myself. "The waitress, I mean."

Luna.

Alas, the damage is already done, Nick's smirk promising trouble. "*Your* Blondie, huh?"

"Shut up." My knuckles connect with his shoulder. "Your waitress was there too."

His smirks drops with his gaze, his breakfast suddenly more enticing than teasing me. "I know."

"The redhead?" Bacon dangling from his fingertips, Cass slings an arm around Nick's shoulders, shaking our friend teasingly. "You know her name yet?"

Curls fly as Nick shakes his head, irritation clear on his face. A hint of confusion, too. Like he's not quite sure why. It's a weird look on Nick, and God, I'd be lying if I said I wasn't kind of enjoying it.

Cass snorts. "That's kind of pathetic, buddy. You're turning into Jackson."

"Hey?"

Cass waves off the middle finger I flip his way, ignoring me in favor of continuing his interrogation. "Just ask her out."

"No."

"Why not?"

"Because I don't want to."

"Liar."

Nick's grip on his mug tightens, face scrunched in exasperation. "Would you drop it already?"

"Is the big bad Nicolas Silva *scared*?"

"Would you shut the fuck up?"

If two years of friendship have taught me anything, it's the skill of tolerating Cass and Nick's bickering. Something Ben has yet to master; his gaze flits between the pair like he's watching a tennis match. When he side-eyes me with a mixture of confusion and amusement, I already anticipate his question. "Are they always like this?"

I take a long, needed sip of sweet, nutty coffee. "Pretty much."

Sometimes, my hands do this thing.

They kind of disconnect from the part of my brain that controls them and imprint my random stream of consciousness onto paper. Draw whatever they want without me realizing. Usually, it's harmless. Usually, it's whatever random shit is on my mind; my sisters or the ranch or, occasionally, the face of a woman, an older version of Lux, who really doesn't deserve to be immortalized in print.

This time, though, the sketch staring up at me, a heart-shaped face framed by wisps of wavy hair, does not feel harmless.

Damn it.

Releasing a frustrated puff of air, I shove my sketchbook away.

The art store I work at is supposed to be my slice of peace. It's rarely busy, which means I spend most shifts with only my thoughts as company, quietly and sporadically interrupted by the scratching of charcoal against paper. My time here isn't usually invaded by thoughts of a pretty girl and what her exact eye shape is or how I'm failing to truly execute the impatient arch of her brows.

I swear, I'm not usually this pathetic.

Elbows hitting the counter, I drag my hands through my hair, head dropping in unison with my eyelids as I will myself to think of something, anything, else. But as the seconds pass, it feels more and more like an impossible task.

I don't know what's wrong with me. I'm not like this, I don't get hooked like this. Not in the way that Cass and Nick don't, where commitment is the issue. It's the opposite, really. Like I said before, casual isn't really my thing, and college breeds casual. It's more like I've never been interested. Not enough, anyway. Never had my eye caught.

Not like this.

It's fucking torment.

My head lifts reluctantly as the bell above the front door chimes, duty calling. But my customer-service-friendly smile dissipates just as quickly as it slips into place when I get an eyeful of who strides through the door and suddenly, I'm hit with the urge to drop to the floor and hide.

Impossibly tight denim shorts.

I'm ashamed to admit that's what I notice first.

Hard not to when they're clinging so tightly to such tanned, toned legs. A flash of something sparkly draws my gaze upward, and a groan builds and dies in my throat at the sight of a diamond belly-button piercing glinting in the light, showcased by the cropped cut of the flouncy, floral v-neck top knotted a few inches above it. I skip quickly over the expanse of freckled chest revealed, landing on a face I suddenly feel embarrassed for having tried to replicate.

I could have all the talent in the world and I'm positive I couldn't do justice to the original.

She's too vivid. Painfully so. Like a beautifully unnerving spot of color in a consistently monotone life. God knows I'd never capture that, and something in me doesn't want to. It doesn't seem right to trap all that within the confines of my sketchbook yet here I am, doing it anyway.

I straighten as she approaches, knuckles white with how tightly I grip the counter, a lump the size of Texas clogging my throat.

On the contrary, Luna is the epitome of relaxed. She breezes over, propping her palms on the counter, arms spread wide, one set of perfectly manicured pink fingernails tapping an offbeat rhythm. A hip cocks in unison with her head.

Not a hint of recognition in baby blue eyes.

She doesn't remember. Of course, she doesn't. Why would she? It's naive to think a ten minute drunken interaction with some random guy would be enough to leave a mark.

"Hi," Luna greets, and I resist the urge to close my eyes and bask in the smooth quality of that single word. "Can you help me?"

My nod is as stiff as my smile. "Sure."

Some of the tension holding me taut melts when she graces me with a beam. I'm so entranced by it, it takes me a full ten seconds to register the Post-It extended my way. Snatching it with a cough, I scan the scribbled list.

Pencils, sketchbooks, a couple of different kinds of paint and brushes. Standard beginner art supplies kit.

Because I need another reason to like this girl.

"This won't take long." With another sorry excuse for a smile, I duck beneath the counter and head for the stocked shelves lining the store walls, expecting my first customer of the day to wait by the register. I'm surprised when, instead, she follows me. Provides me with an endless stream of chatter.

God, did I really ever enjoy the quiet?

"I'm not really much of an artist," Luna muses without prompting, absently brushing her fingertips over a set of fan brushes. "I just had an elective to fill and my mom says it runs in my blood. She's an artist."

I hum quietly, watching her out of my peripheral as she babbles with seemingly no expectations for a response. It's so creepy, I know it is, but she's kind of fascinating to watch. She's got this thing I always notice but can never put a name to. *Energetic* doesn't cover it. It's like she can't stay still. Bouncing on the balls of her feet, touching every-thing we pass, spinning a ring around her finger, all of it absent-minded, like she doesn't realize she's doing it.

Only when I hand her something does she briefly settle, pausing to thoroughly study it. Fishes a pen out of her bag and leans around me to tick it off the list quickly becoming more and more crumpled between my fingers. Breath tickling my skin and her hand brushing mine, I'm reminded of the last time we were in such close proximity, and I wonder if she'd be this close, this oddly comfortable, if she remembered too.

When the scent of vanilla starts clouding my judgment and

convincing me that burying my face in her hair and sniffing wouldn't be that weird, I force myself to step away. I practically sprint to the other end of the aisle, only awarded a few seconds of reprieve because she's hot on my tail.

Whether she blocks my path intentionally or not, I don't know, but she props herself directly in front of the exact pencils I'm looking for, back to the shelf with her hands tucked casually in her back pockets. "You like art?"

I know damn well we're the only people here yet still, I'm tempted to glance over my shoulder to check she's talking to me. Miraculously, I cough out a simple, coherent response. "I do."

Her laugh is soft, quiet, such a juxtaposition to... *her.* "Silly question, right? Since you work here?"

A quirked lip and a shake of my head is all I manage.

"Can you draw?"

"Uh-huh."

"Let me guess," undeterred by my horrific conversational skills, Luna's lazy smile remains intact, eyes narrowed in sparkling scrutiny, "art student?"

Somewhere in the dark recesses of my mind, my grandparents' laughter echoes. As if they would've ever let that happen. "Architecture."

"So you build houses?"

If a smile is what Luna was aiming for, she succeeds. "Something like that."

Her hum is interested, curious, and I find myself standing a little straighter, especially when she squints at me with a half-smile. "I know you from somewhere."

A few places, actually.

Stomach in my goddamn throat, I wait.

"The diner, right?" she proclaims eventually, fingers snapping like she's solved a puzzle. "You and your friends come in a lot."

I'm an odd mixture of disappointed that she still doesn't remember a conversation that's been playing on my mind non-stop and pleased because hey, at least I'm not completely forgettable. "Yeah, we do."

"You guys are on the baseball team," she continues slowly, as if she's piecing something together. When I hum confirmation, a lovely, dangerous smirk forms. "Your friend stares at my friend a lot. The pretty one with the horny eyes."

I swallow a snort. Yeah, Nick would love that description.

In a different universe, maybe I'd have the nerve to offer more than a nod. To ask her to elaborate when she murmurs *'interesting'* beneath her breath. To continue the conversation, keep her here a little longer.

In reality, I hurry back to the cash register, ringing her up and sliding the paper bag full of new supplies toward her. "You need anything else?"

Shaking her head, she props the bag in the crook of her arm, hitting me with a smile nothing short of breathtaking. "Thank you."

Two words, Jackson. You can manage two damn words. "You're welcome."

Luna robs me of those upturned lips when she turns her back and heads for the door, yet another interaction coming to an end too soon for my liking.

But with one hand wrapped around the door handle, she pauses. Indulges me a little more by half-turning. Sighing, big and dramatic, in a way that matches her big, dramatic expression of false exasperation. "You're really gonna make me ask for your name, huh?"

My face fucking hurts with the magnitude of the smile that erupts. "It's Jackson."

"Jackson," she repeats, rolling the word around on her tongue, and shit if my name isn't suddenly the best sound in the world. "It's nice to properly meet you, Jackson. I'm Luna."

"Luna," I repeat the same way she did, reveling in her pleased hum. "It's nice to meet you, Luna."

Again.

7

LUNA

"SHIT, SHIT, *SHIT.*"

A light breeze whips against my bare legs as I rush across campus, teasing the hem of my dress and flashing everyone in my path. If I hadn't woken up late, I would've been able to coordinate my outfit with the blustery weather. Instead, I rolled out of bed with barely twenty minutes to spare before my first class of the semester, and my only choice was to throw on the first thing I saw.

I knew I shouldn't have gone out last night. *Just a couple of drinks,* I'd told myself. *You deserve it.*

Honestly, at this point, I should know better; a couple is never a couple. Every time, a single vodka cranberry turns into *ohh, let's have a cocktail* and before I know it, bottom-shelf liquor shots are scorching my throat and my inhibitions are on the floor and the contact lenses improving my vision might as well have evaporated.

Pro; I wasn't quite drunk enough to try and fail at seducing kind men in a dingy bathroom.

Con; I did, unfortunately, bring yet another unworthy opponent home.

In and out of the apartment in under half an hour, last night's conquest once again made me wonder if this bad sex epidemic is campus-wide or specific to my unlucky self. I can't even remember the guy's name, and I don't feel bad about it; it's an unwritten, steadfast rule in my mental hook-up handbook that if you don't make me come, I don't have to remember your name.

Plus, it's not like I *need* to remember it. A guy who tasted like onion rings and clearly viewed me like a blow-up doll? Yeah, it's safe to say I won't be calling him up again.

I shove lamenting thoughts of mediocre sex to the back of my mind as I rush into class, barely making it on time. With a relieved sigh—I fucking hate being late—I slip into a seat near the back, my thumb already spinning the ring on my pointer finger. It's a two-hour class; my worst enemy. Too still for too long with too little occupying my mind.

It seems I'm not alone in my dread; the chair beside me groans in unison with the girl flopping onto it, her tight expression mirroring mine. I watch her out of the corner of my eye, trying not to chuckle as she curses beneath her breath, dropping her bag on the floor with a loud thump and smoothing back messy dirty blonde hair with a huff.

"Rough morning?"

Head whipping to face me, the grimace playing across her lips deepens. "Is it that obvious?"

"Only to someone who's had an equally rough morning."

The girl huffs a laugh. "You trip up a flight of stairs and fall on your ass in front of a very cute group of boys?"

"No." A corner of my mouth tips upward. "But I did flash a few sprinting across the courtyard."

Another chuckle morphs into a groan as my classmate slumps, voice low like she's half talking to herself. "I don't even wanna take this class."

Preaching to the choir. "Introduction to Political Theory isn't for you?"

Her snort says it all, as does her eye roll. "My dad's the professor and my '*I don't give a shit about politics*' speech hasn't quite gotten through to him yet."

I commiserate, "My mom's an artist so she's making me take an art class."

She side-eyes me, mouth curled in amusement. "You didn't inherit the gene?"

"Stick figures are the extent of my artistic capabilities."

"A woman of real talent."

Snorting in amusement, the girl twists toward me, extending a hand. "I'm Pen. Penelope, actually, but no one calls me that."

"Luna." I accept the oddly formal greeting. "You a sophomore too?"

Pen nods, the only response she has time to give before a door creaking open cuts her off, followed by thudding footsteps as a man strides into the room, coming to a stop behind the desk center stage. Who I'm assuming is our professor—Pen's dad—takes his time setting up his laptop, silent except for the sound of loud, overdramatic typing that every teacher seems to master. When he finally lifts his gaze to scan the room, it snags on Pen, head dipping in the slightest acknowledgement.

Weirdly, I swear it lingers on me too. Just for a second, so quick I definitely could've imagined it, as well as the flicker of something I can't quite name but could be mistaken as recognition. The moment is over before it begins, and I brush it off as my mind playing tricks on me—God knows that's not a rarity.

"Professor Robert Jacobs," the man begins with a brusque introduction, and more than one girl in the room sits up a little straighter at his surprisingly husky voice, interest suddenly peaked.

"Remind me to thank the hiring committee," someone in my vicinity mutters.

"Is it just me," another voice adds, "or do the staff get hotter every year?"

"Jesus Christ." Pen groans beside me , twisting to glare at whoever's eyeing up her dad. I feel her pain—growing up with a young, attractive mom was my own personal hell at times.

Jacobs is objectively good-looking, I guess, if I were into men old enough to be my dad with a very noticeable ring wrapped around his finger. But definitely not my type. Although, these days, I'm not entirely sure what that is.

I never used to be a fan of lean, long-haired men nor the quiet, nice guy yet here I am, mind wandering toward the very epitome.

Jackson.

I like it all on him.

Even the shy thing, I like. I like how nervous I make him. And not in the uncomfortable, harsh way I usually enjoy, the kind that feels like karma for years spent crossing roads or avoiding going out alone after sundown or carrying mace in my purse just in case some entitled asshole got too handsy. That feels like balancing the scales.

This, how Jackson reacts around me, feels different. Nervous in the most lovely way.

He's like karma but the good kind I'm not sure what I did to deserve. He proved it when he rubbed my back and tied up my hair and, after the entire contents of my stomach were flushed down the toilet, proceeded to scoop me up off the dirty bathroom floor and tuck me in his shirt.

A shirt I still have. I woke up in it the morning after, unsure where it came from but obsessed with the scent wrapped around me. Clean and fresh with a faint hint of grass clinging to the fabric, like laundry hung up to dry outside. I can't recall a night since that I haven't spent wrapped in the soft cotton.

I didn't recall everything right away, just flashes of warm touches and a kind smile. But the moment I walked into that art store and saw him, I remembered but I feigned ignorance because I was too mortified to mention it considering the enormous fucking fool I made out of myself.

I was drunk and fumbling and reeking of vomit yet he called me beautiful. *Beautiful.* Not hot or sexy, which I firmly believe is the worst compliment in the world/ It makes me cringe every time it's screamed in my ear over the noise of a club or slurred at me over the counter in Greenies.

No, he called me beautiful in the most endearingly earnest way. Hands fidgeting and cheeks flushed. Unable to look me in the eye. I'm not someone who gets all weak in the knees and weepy at such simple complimentary words but God, I was practically swooning.

I haven't dwelled on that long enough to figure out why. I don't plan on it. I plan on waiting for the odd little crush to pass, for my mind to fixate on something else.

I can only hope it happens soon.

"Assholes," I grumble, mentally sticking my tongue out at the retreating backs of the frat boys vacating Greenies. Two hours flirting my ass off and entertaining their advances and flashing my cleavage on purpose—because, you know, feminism on hold when it comes to earning tips—only for them to massively lowball me.

Two dollars. Six of them clad in fucking Ralph Lauren polo shirts and goddamn boat shoes and requesting top-shelf whiskey—because, obviously, Greenies screams high quality liquor—could only spare two goddamn dollars.

Ass. Holes.

Allowing myself a moment longer of bitterness, I stuff their sad tip in my pocket before getting back to work.

It's busy as hell today, just the way I like it—time goes quicker that way.

Plus, I'm on shift with Amelia, as usual, and I can hardly complain about spending the evening in the company of my best friend. Especially when I have particularly interesting entertainment in the form of the most notorious player on campus simpering at her with puppy-dog eyes.

She's got the guy spellbound without even trying, and I would only be prouder if she wasn't still inexplicably in love with a big dumbass.

It's easier to focus on Nick—Nicolas Silva wasn't a hard name to source—than his company. Not the young blond guy who reminds me of a puppy but the walking pair of cheekbones beside him. Every time I sneak a glance at Jackson, my amusement fades, replaced by sweaty hands and this weird twisting sensation in my stomach that I'd rather not put a name to.

No, instead, I shake it off and blame it on dehydration.

I'm chugging a bottle of water when someone calls my name, and for a split second, bashful hope tickles the back of my neck. That is, until I turn around. A not-so-silent groan builds in my throat when the guy from last night sets his forearms on the counter with a heavy thump, every inch of visible skin slick with drunken sweat. "I had fun last night."

"Well, that makes one of us." My words are a quiet grumble but even if I shouted them in his face, I don't think he would hear. Currently, all his attention is directed south of my face, honing in on the minimal cleavage my uniform tank top allows.

Lacing my fingers together and squeezing, I force a smile. "Can I get you anything?"

Besides a mint.

"Another round." The man who's name I don't feel an ounce of guilt about not remembering smirks, and I wrinkle my nose at the disgustingly obvious innuendo. "Of drinks, obviously."

My only response being a grim nod does nothing to deter the guy; I can practically see the gears in his brain churning as he prepares another dirty comment he, luckily for me, never gets the chance to spill.

The brush of another shoulder against his isn't that hard, only momentarily knocking him off his already precarious balance, but it's enough to direct his attention from me to the guy squeezing in beside him. "What the fuck?"

"My bad," Jackson holds his hands up in surrender, faking a guilty expression and purposefully not looking at me. "Sorry, Billy."

I gape at the pair, not because they seem to know each other or because of Jackson's sudden miraculous appearance, but because of the name Jackson just uttered.

Billy?

I banged a *Billy?*

God, no wonder I didn't remember his name. Blocked it from my memory, obviously. Definitely wouldn't want to associate sex with a name that conjures up an image of an old man with a beer gut and goatee.

Fucking *Billy's* face morphs from angry to calm in the blink of an eye. "Jackson," he greets, pulling him in for one of those bro-hugs. Jackson smiles and indulges him but when he grips the counter, I notice his white knuckles. And I notice how he slaps Billy on the back a little harder than necessary before pointing in Nick's direction, encouraging Billy to amble away and do the whole bro greeting thing again without even a backwards glance at me.

I just watch, a little perplexed by how fucking smooth that was.

Jackson.

Smooth.

Interesting development.

He doesn't linger to accept praise and gratitude like most knights in shining armor would. He tries to leave without a word but I stop him. "Did you need something?"

Jackson turns slowly, just as slow to raise his gaze and finally,

finally, graces me with those beautiful eyes. Dark brown, with hints of gold that glint when the light hits them just right. He must be feeling generous because he indulges me with that voice too—no nodding or head shaking like I've become accustomed. Deep but quiet with a rasping quality that sends a shiver down my spine every day. "Coffee, please."

Unashamedly, I take my time filling a mug with dark liquid. Feeling selfish, wanting his presence longer, even if he's not saying a word. It's... comforting. Warm. Like a little slice of calm. When I eventually slide the drink his way, I wave off the money he offers. "It's on me."

You save me from leering men, you get free coffee.

Jackson's lips purse, unimpressed yet undeterred as he drops what more than covers the cost of a measly black coffee in the tip jar. A dip of his head and he's gone, scurrying back to his friends without a backwards glance.

And what do I do? I watch him go like a fucking creep because I think we've silently established staring is our thing.

8

LUNA

I'M EXHAUSTED.

My legs feel like lead as I scale the stairs to my apartment, my fingers numb as they fish for keys. It's been a long ass day, packed with classes and the longest work shift known to man, and I want nothing more than to curl up on the sofa with a preferably cold and necessarily alcoholic beverage. And food. Lots of food; a day survived on only a couple of sneaked granola bars and a measly apple is not a day worth living.

So, when I shove open the front door and find Kate splayed on the sofa cradling a mug, another one and a bottle of wine set on the coffee beside her propped-up feet, I almost weep. I can't find the energy to shed my coat or shoes, or even greet my roommate. I just kick the door shut and collapse beside her, my head propped on her lap.

Kate doesn't spare me a glance. She just leans forward and fills up the spare mug before transferring it to my greedy hands. "Want some dinner?"

I groan through a mouthful of rosé. *"Please."*

My head hits the sofa cushion with a thump as Kate stands, pausing to yank my shoes off on her way to the kitchen. Shuffling upright, I wriggle out of my coat, replacing it with a fluffy blanket just in time for Kate to return and place a plate piled high with steaming leftover Chinese takeout on my lap. My thanks is muffled by a forkful of mapo tofu, the spicy, salty flavor coaxing another groan out of me.

After a solid ten minutes of stuff, chew, swallow, repeat, my hanger recedes enough for me to notice someone missing. "Where's Mils?" Kate's grimaces answer my question before her mouth does. "She has that thing with Dylan."

Way to ruin my appetite. "The gala?"

Kate nods, and I grunt. I don't know how I forgot about the fucking gala. Amelia's been dreading it all week, therefore I've been dreading it all week. Or, more accurately, loathing it. I'm not a fan of anything that riddles my best friend with anxiety, even less so when it involves that dickhead.

I know Kate shares the same sentiment; she sure as shit isn't obsessively checking the time on her phone for the fun of it. "She should be home soon."

"Alone, hopefully."

"Amen."

Not long passes before it's proven that, for once, something upstairs listened to our prayers. But the relief I feel at the sight of Amelia creeping into our apartment alone, heels in her hand while her small body shivers—I shouldn't be surprised Dylan didn't offer up his jacket—dies as quick as it's born. The moment she fails to acknowledge our joint greeting, shoulders tense and head down with her hair falling like a shield, I know something's wrong, and a loud sniffle proves me right.

"Mils?" I thwart her attempt to rush past us. "You okay?"

It's like the two words break her. Shivering morphs into trembling, sniffling into strangled sobs. In a split second, Kate and I are by her side, simultaneously gasping when I brush red curls aside and reveal what our friend tried to hide.

She's terrifyingly pale, her expression alarmingly blank despite the tears seeping from her eyes, but that's not what worries me. Not what causes red-hot rage to boil my blood.

No, that would be the blood seeping from the cut on her lip. The matching one on her temple, too, and the nasty looking bruises staining her skin.

"Amelia," Kate darts, the question I know she's about to ask needless, "who did this?"

We both know the answer. Without a shadow of a doubt, we know, but we need verbal confirmation. And we get it. One word, one name, one whispered, broken sob that I don't know what to do with. Or, more accurately, I don't *legally* know what to do with.

I know Dylan is an asshole. I know he's a misogynistic, entitled, handsy creep who doesn't deserve to exist in the same space as Amelia. But this...

I'm going to kill him.

I am actually going to kill him.

Like she can hear my train of thought, Amelia grips my wrist, hazy, unfocused eyes scaring the shit out of me. "It was an accident," she whispers quietly, emotionlessly, and I'm not sure who she's trying to convince.

"No," it's hard, so damn hard, to keep my tone gentle and even when I want to fucking scream, "it wasn't."

Amelia blinks, so terrifyingly absent and heartbreakingly confused. She flinches when Kate rests a hand on her shoulder, again when she softly says, "Amelia, you need to go to the hospital."

And, out of everything, the thing that worries me the most?

Amelia doesn't protest.

She doesn't fight us as we hurry her to the car, carefully maneuvering her into the backseat. She's silent the whole drive. She doesn't acknowledge our arrival at the emergency room, nor the nurse who points us toward the waiting room and leads her away. She disappears without a word, and while Kate settles in an uncomfortable plastic chair, my body refuses to do the same.

Instead, I explode.

All the insults and threats I've been bottling up since the moment she stumbled home come out in one long barrage. Shouting and swearing. Threatening things I really shouldn't be saying in public or in a hospital, things involving very vivid methods of emasculation, ignoring all the alarmed looks I receive because if they knew, they'd agree.

When I burn myself out, I throw myself on the seat beside Kate, crossing my arms to stop my fidgeting hands. "Kate-"

Her hands lands on my knee. "I know."

"She said it was an *accident*."

"I know."

Since those words left her mouth, my mind has been racing trying to figure out why she would say that. Why she would make excuses, try to defend someone who left her bruised and bleeding. And I hate the only viable answer I find.

A sense of defeat washes over as I slump in my seat, head falling to Kate's shoulder. "She's gonna take him back."

A beat of silence passes before fingers fold around mine, squeezing as a source and in search of comfort. "I know."

~

It took me days but I've done it.

After hours of coaxing and pleading and promising sweet treats, I got Amelia out of the house.

Claggy, damp sand sinks beneath my feet as I plod towards the sea, Amelia's clammy hand in mine. Salty sea air soothes my lungs as I suck in a deep breath. "See?" I glance at the girl beside me, offering an encouraging smile. "Isn't this better?"

Amelia looks skeptical. "What're we doing here?"

I don't reply as I drop her hand, turning to scan the long expanse of beach behind us. It's empty this close to nightfall with such overcast weather, most people in their right mind avoiding the choppy, gray ocean.

We, on the other hand, are doing the opposite.

One more breath to steel myself and I whip my t-shirt over my head, discarding it on the sand before I can second guess myself. Wariness overcomes Amelia's expression as her gaze darts to my barely-lace-covered chest. "What are you doing?"

Choosing silence again, I grin as I wriggle out of my skirt, a flutter of nerves erupting in my belly. I'm not much of an exhibitionist but neither is Amelia and that is exactly the point.

In nothing but my underwear, I brace my hands on my hands and pin Amelia with a no-bullshit stare. "You know, the most adventurous thing you've done since I've known you is cut your hair."

Amelia flushes, tucking a newly shorn lock behind her ear—no prizes for guessing who insisted she keep it long because he preferred it that way. "What does that have to do with you stripping on the beach?"

"You let other people dictate your life." One person, specifically. "You worry too much and you don't live enough." Unclasping my bra, I let it drop to the ground, quickly crossing my arms to cover my bare boobs before the brisk wind can assault them. "So, let's fucking live a little."

I knew she would hesitate. I can almost see her brain cycling through all the reasons to say no. And even though the one she chooses is exactly what I expected, it still leaves me flushed with anger. "Dylan wouldn't like it."

Because that is still something that matters.

Because, like I knew she would, she took him back. It only took three days for the incessant phone calls and the chocolates she doesn't even like and the shitty bouquets of roses to work. For Amelia to forgive him, welcome him back into a life and a relationship he will never deserve, and no amount of pleading on mine or Kate's behalf could change her mind.

And the most awful part is that even though I don't agree with her decision, I get it.

I understand what it's like to be influenced by the fear of not being believed.

When she prods at her temple where the physical reminder of what could've been so much worse lives, one of Ma's many mantras comes to mind. One that would arise whenever either of us had a particularly bad day and green tea just wasn't cutting it, so we'd brave the nearest beach solely to spend a few hours soaking in the sea air, watching the surfers, occasionally daring the shallows.

"Saltwater cleanses." Sweat, ocean, or tears, and the former or latter simply aren't enough. "Now, hurry the fuck up before my nips freeze off."

It's almost in slow motion, the movement of Amelia's hands towards the hem of her hoodie. They dither there for a long moment, face twisted in contemplation, before, too quick to second guess, she whips it over her head, revealing nothing underneath, her sweats quick to follow.

Before she can change her mind, I lock our hands together and take off running toward the ocean, only having to drag her a little. Our shrieks echo through the air as frigid water smacks against our shins but I keep going, even when my stomach contracts as the breath is knocked out of me. I don't stop until each lulling wave laps at the napes of our neck, sending chills down our spines.

"What now?" Amelia yelps. Bobbing in the water, her skin is pale and her body shivers but her eyes, they're bright. Excited. A far cry from the frail thing that's been cowering in our apartment for the past week.

Finally, she looks alive.

Tilting my head back until it dips beneath the water, I let the cold and the silence take over. Amelia does the same, a ragged breath escaping us in unison. "Just breathe."

~

I jolt awake to the sound of banging.

Blinking groggily, I sit up slowly, careful not to disturb the redhead curled up beside me, buried under a mountain of blankets. We stayed at the beach long after sunset, only leaving the water when Amelia became convinced that every shadow or stray current was a shark trying to snack on her legs. In sandy, soggy clothes, we shivered our way back to the apartment, freezing our asses off but smiling like fools.

Amelia fell asleep smiling, too. Wet-haired and stuffy-nosed and bone-chilled but smiling.

I plan to keep her that way as long as possible, even if it means going to jail for maiming the man attempting to break down our front door.

Even before I haul my ass out of bed and check the peephole to confirm the culprit, I have a warning prepped. "Get the fuck out of here Dylan."

He does no such thing, instead pressing his ugly face closer to the door, insipid eyes glaring. "Let me see her."

"No fucking way."

Fists slam against the door viciously, so loud I'm forced to open it a crack—safety chain firmly in place—just to stop the brutal noise. The last thing I want is Amelia waking up and wandering out here.

"Luna," Dylan warns, shoulders square as he straightens to his full height in an attempt at intimidation, and maybe it would work if he didn't only have three measly inches on me. If I didn't already know he's a coward who slams car doors in girls' faces for fun. If I hadn't long since put a lock and key on the part of my brain that allows fear over unworthy opponents.

"Dylan," I spit back. "Leave or I swear to God I'll rip your fucking balls off."

"You think you're such tough shit." He scoffs, baring his teeth like the dog he is, breath stinking of whiskey and cigarettes. "Let me see my girlfriend or you'll regret it. That's a promise."

"Pretty sure the cops call that a threat." When his mouth opens to retort, I cut him off by holding up my phone, showing 911 already dialed with my thumb hovering over the call button. "You have three seconds before I call them."

I don't wait to see if he makes the wrong decision; I slam the door, triple-check the locks, and pray to whatever high power exists. Jaw aching with how hard I clench my teeth, I glare through the peephole, palms braced as if that could possibly stop it from caving in if he decided he wanted it to. I don't relax, not even a little bit, until the fist hovering mid-air falls achingly slowly. I wait until he's completely disappeared from sight before moving to the window, hands shaking as they nudge the curtains aside so I can watch as he climbs in his car and drives away.

"Who was at the door?"

Swearing under my breath, I spin to find Amelia lurking in her bedroom doorway, heels of her palms rubbing at squinted eyes. "Pitbull," I lie, our drug-dealing lookalike neighbor the first thing that comes to mind. "There's a car boxing him in and he wanted to know if it was us." With one last peek outside, I let the curtains full shut and shuffle toward Amelia, herding her back into her room with an arm around her shoulder. "Let's go back to sleep."

9

JACKSON

WE'RE IN GREENIES.

Again.

A common fucking occurrence lately.

We always start somewhere else yet end up here. Like it's kismet or some shit.

We lost Cass along the way, replacing him with other guys from the team, a swap I'm less than happy about. They're fine. Just a bit... *much* for me. Vinny is loud enough to break eardrums, Jay can't carry a conversation that doesn't involve sex, and Frankie does little more than chug beer and belch.

Plus, I'm not a fan of the girls they brought with them, particularly the one who's ended up perched on my lap through no encouragement of mine. My disinterest is clear—or, at least, I think it is—yet she keeps rubbing my thigh and whispering things I think are supposed to be alluring in my ear but kind of just make me cringe. Only politeness and the lack of room in our cramped booth stops me from shoving her off.

I pretend to listen to her spout incoherent nonsense about baseball but really, unsurprisingly, my focus is elsewhere. Namely, it's flitting around the diner following the path of an uncharacteristically frazzled blonde.

It looks like she's braving the masses alone tonight, the sole provider for the droves of drunk students demanding another one, and as unhappy as the situation makes me—something about seeing Luna so clearly uncomfortable strikes a bum chord within me—I can't compare to the man squished beside me.

I wonder if Nick thinks he's being subtle, with the way he cranes his neck slightly to peer around the diner. Brows drawn together sullenly. Lips pursed in a permanent disappointed pout. The girl perched on his knee has spent the better part of an hour fighting a losing battle for his attention, and with a chime of the bell above the front door, she's defeated. Blatantly rejected as Nick actually shucks her from his lap, the poor thing scrambling for a moment before finding a new purchase on Jay's knee.

The mysterious Red waltzes into the room and everyone else ceases to exist for my friend. His golden eyes glow as she approaches, her pencil poised ready to scribble our order, her smile falsely bright as she asks, "What can I get you?"

Even if he hadn't adopted the unholy trinity of a lazy slouch, a cocked head, and a crooked brow, I would've anticipated Nick's snarky response before it leaves his mouth; the man just can't help himself. The goddamn twinkle in his eyes screams trouble long before he does. "Are you even old enough to be here?"

Red purses her lips, fire flickering in green eyes as they narrow, something saccharine lacing her tone as she retorts, "Are you? I'm afraid I'll need to see some ID."

The burgeoning chuckles die out immediately.

Except for mine; I can't keep from smiling as I rummage for my ID, shaking my head at Nick's expression; nothing short of love-struck. I think he likes the girl even more now. Hell, I like her; anyone who refutes Nick's attitude rather than falling to their knees and kissing his feet is a winner in my book. *And* she, when they fail to cough up IDs, gets rid of the girls with a shrug and a 'hey, what can you do?' kinda smile.

Wins all around.

Ben casts us a forlorn look as he slides from the booth, his fabricated protests futile—no matter how hard he tries to convince Red he's of age, he still ends up trailing towards Greenies' exit, tossing a scowl and a middle finger in Nick's direction on his way out.

It's as I'm watching him leave that, for the umpteenth time, my gaze snags on something else. Tanned forearms propped against the counter and a mouth that makes no attempt at hiding its amusement. When sparkling eyes meet mine, that smile thins to a smirk, lips forming a silent apology that doesn't seem all that sincere.

I last a record-breaking five seconds before all that blue becomes overwhelming, and God, I hope the blush searing my cheeks isn't quite as visible as it feels.

"I like that girl," Frankie muses, watching Red as she retreats with our sheepishly mumbled orders. "Feisty."

An honest to God *growl* rumbles in Nick's chest. Ripping his gaze from his newest—and, I suspect, first—infatuation, he glares at my teammate, the sweet sentiment he doesn't say clear as day; *shut the fuck up.*

I can't help but snort; doesn't like the girl, my ass.

Slumping, Nick hits me with a warning look. "Don't say a fucking word."

"Wasn't gonna." Copying my friend, I lean back and cross my arms before adding in a voice low enough for only him to hear, "you got a ring picked out yet?"

Golden eyes narrow. "Hypocrite."

"Coward."

"Hey, pot?" Sarcasm weighs down Nick's drawl as his beer bottle tilts toward the spot my gaze can't help but stray. "It's kettle, you're black."

The downside of drinking with people you dislike, besides the sudden urge to plug your ears and sing *'la la la la la la'* on repeat?

You always get a lot drunker than you intended.

Self-preservation, I guess; easier to drown out the inanity when you're halfway to a hangover.

I don't realize quite how past my limit I've gone, though, until a full bladder sends me to my feet and I find myself swaying through the diner, bumping into more people than I care to admit. I make quick work of going to the bathroom—leaving Nick alone with my teammates for too long feels like a recipe for a bloody disaster. In my haste, I round a corner too quickly and run smack bang into someone.

Instinct has me reaching out to steady whoever I almost bowled over, an apology on my tongue.

The smell of vanilla hitting me like a slap to the face has a different word escaping me. "Shit."

"You know," a lilting voice cuts through the tipsy haze, "for an athlete, you're pretty clumsy, Jackson."

She remembers my name.

My hands drop with my gaze, finding shelter in my pockets as they fist, palms buzzing with the memory of warm, soft skin beneath them. "Sorry."

Silence follows my mumbled apology, and I'm wondering just how awkward it would be if I turned and ran without another word when an amused question breaks it. "Do you have something against my eyes?"

I frown at the dirty tiled floor. "What?"

"My eyes," Luna repeats slowly, and I glance up just in time to catch her tongue darting out to wet her bottom lip, teeth finding purchase in the plump pink. "Something repulsive about them? Remind you of an ex? Or do you just hate blue?"

Repulsive.

I almost laugh.

Definitely not a word I would use.

Dizzying, maybe. Overwhelming, definitely. Magnetic? Stunning, but not in the beautiful sense, although they are that. In the way that dazes a person and robs them of words and thoughts and the ability to do anything but marvel.

There's a hundred better descriptors yet all I manage is a croaked, "no."

"You think you could manage to look me in them every once in a while?"

The teasing question catches me off-guard, has my wide-eyed gaze meeting one full of roguish mirth. "There you go," Luna croons softly. "Much better."

And there it is, I think as my internal organs begin to malfunction. The reason I avoid looking right at her. The same reason you don't look directly at the sun, I guess; bad for your health. Even as frazzled and disheveled as she appears right now.

One hand smoothes back the wisps escaping her ponytail, the

other swiping a flushed cheek before pushing open the door behind her. She slips into an empty kitchen and, without thinking, I prop myself in the doorway, watching as she yanks open a dishwasher. "Were you looking for something?" she asks, the question punctuated by a grunt, the muscles in her arms straining as she hoists a crate full of freshly washed glasses out of the machine and onto the counter.

"No," is what I plan to say, since Luna's question sounds suspiciously like a dismissal.

I'm not sure where "you need help?" comes from.

It's slow, how she turns to me, a hand on her hip and an incredulously amused expression arching her brows. "You wanna help me polish glasses?" When I shrug, she tuts. "It's a yes or no question, Jackson."

I swallow, I cough, I fucking choke. "Yeah, I do."

A moment of hesitation, a half shake of a head, before an inviting arm waves in the air. "Be my guest."

It feels weird, wrong, and slightly exhilarating, sauntering through a door marked 'staff only.' Even more so because of the pretty blonde watching me like a hawk.

Picking up a rag and a glass, I get to work, trying and failing to ignore the sight in my peripheral vision. It's only when I pass her a rag of her own, slender fingers brushing mine, does Luna let out a quiet, breathy laugh and re-assigns her gaze to the steaming glasses. "Are your friends really that boring?"

"I prefer sober company."

"Sober company," she repeats with a low hum. "And what about mine?"

It's a miracle, really, that I don't drop the glass in my hand. And that it only takes a very long minute to choke out, "Yours is good."

"Help *and* flattery. Your girlfriend is a lucky woman."

I pause polishing. "My what?"

"Your girlfriend," Luna repeats nonchalantly, the glitter in her bright white nail polish catching the light as she holds up a glass for inspection. "The one my friend kicked out. Sorry about that, by the way."

"She's not my girlfriend." I'm really not sure what gave her that impression considering I barely talked to the girl.

Up goes a pale brow. "No?"

"Nope."

"She's busy tonight?"

"Who?"

"Your girlfriend."

"I don't have a girlfriend."

"Oh." Luna hums, a hint of a smile gracing pink lips. "Good to know."

Good to know.

Good to know.

A phrase suddenly so goddamn foreign to me because *what*? What does that mean? What does *she* mean?

I'm too chickenshit to ask. I just cough and nod and stay silent some more until... I don't. Until I find a long-buried, tiny shred of bravery and spit out, "What about yours?"

Luna side-eyes me, head tilted in question.

I swallow hard. "Your boyfriend. He busy tonight?"

Her hesitation lasts forever. Or at least, it feels like it does. I hold my breath as I wait, silently wishing I could pluck my words from the air and shove them back down my throat. When that serious, contemplative look softens and laughter echoes around the room, my breath leaves me in one big whoosh. "No."

An answer but not an answer. An answer that evokes another question. An answer I have a feeling is entirely purposeful.

10

JACKSON

Fire Brick.

It's the name of a paint that lives in my collection, a standard shade of deep red. The exact shade currently staining my younger sister's hair.

It knocked me back a step when I first saw it glowing in the late October sun. I blinked a couple of times, wondering if it was just a trick of the light. I opened my mouth to say something undoubtedly eloquent along the lines of 'what the fuck, Lottie?' But before I could, Lux yanked my arm and shot me a look. A look I know well; shut your mouth or risk the wrath of a hormonal teenage girl.

So, I did. And I have.

But, from where I stand on the front porch, I can't stop staring at Lottie through the kitchen window, hair even more fiery against her prim and proper white dress. She eyeballs me right back, squinting a silent dare as she presumably reads my mind.

Tugging on the uncomfortably itchy collar of my over-starched shirt, I avert my gaze to the girl standing ram-rod straight beside me, glaring at the hem of her knee-length skirt. "Since when does she like red so much?"

"Since she sold her soul to the devil, maybe."

"*Lux.*"

Unbothered by my reprimand, Lux snorts. "See if you're still defending her by the time this weekend is up."

"If we survive this weekend." The slacks suffocating my waist yet billowing too loosely around my calves might kill me first. Or the fancy, previously unworn shoes blistering my feet to hell. Or, more likely, the passengers in the spotless white BMW kicking up dirt on the horizon might be my, *our*, end.

Dragging my gaze from our impending doom, I glance over my shoulder and sigh at all that red. "They're not gonna like it."

"She's their favorite." Lux plays nonchalant but her twisted expression gives away her concern. "She'll be fine."

It's not Lottie I'm worried about; it never comes down on her. The responsibility always lands on the girl fiddling with the tarnished pendant hanging between her collarbones. "Everything looks okay, right?"

I plant a hand on my sister's shoulder and squeeze, the tension rolling off her palpable. "Everything looks great," I assure her, wishing my false optimism was successful in soothing the dread knotted in my stomach.

Our grandparents' visit is a rarity. I was surprised as hell when Lux told me about it while requesting my presence. They rarely leave their Malibu mansion—we called it the Barbie Dreamhouse, back when we still used humor to counter the shit hand we'd been dealt— and we like it that way. We like our freedom, our slice of peace and privacy.

But occasionally, they make an appearance. Usually just our grandmother; the only good thing about our grandfather is his blessed indifference. Mercifully quick visits but still long enough to taint our day. And with every inch closer the ridiculously impractical car travels, the sense of foreboding grows.

The screech of a door opening is as slow and reluctant as the rest of my sisters are to join us on the porch. When a body tucks itself against my side, I wrap an arm around the calm to her twin's chaos. "You think they're coming to congratulate me for making varsity captain?"

It's a joke but still, I wish I could say yes. Instead, all I can do is give Grace's ponytail a tug and say, "I'm proud of you."

"I know." A head hits my shoulder. "Lottie made the track team again."

"She did?" Soft hair brushes my neck as Grace nods. "I didn't know she was trying out."

Grace cracks a smile, I can hear it in her voice. "She didn't. Coach saw her running circles around the boys' team and practically begged her to join."

"Good." Really good. Having something to channel all that anger into can only be a good thing. Maybe she'll run off some of that goddamn attitude. "You know what sparked the makeover?"

Something in Grace's expression falls. She glances toward the far side of the porch where her twin lurks, a sad downward tilt to her mouth as she quietly reveals, "They called her a dumb blonde."

"What?"

"Some boys at school. They called her a dumb blonde so she dyed it."

Fuck.

Well, now I feel like a dick.

No, worse; I feel like my grandmother.

Following Grace's line of sight, my stomach twists as I sigh at my angry little sister. I just don't know what to do with her. I never have, even when there wasn't something so obviously wrong. If she'd just tell me, I could fix it, but unfortunately, it seems Lottie inherited that standard Jackson urge to fix everything all on your own.

Catching me staring, she barges onto the porch, face twisted in all too familiar glare. "Can I help you?"

Deep breath.

Just take a deep fucking breath.

Holding a hand up in innocence, I shrug and avert my gaze. I wait until the glare falls, until that horrid anticipation infects her too, until she starts to twitch and fret as much as the rest of us, before calling out softly. "Hey, Lot?"

"*What?*"

"I like your hair."

Even from a distance, I see my grandmother's pursed lips as she exits the car—mercifully alone—familiar disapproval heavy in the air between us. I'm unsure if she's ever looked at us with anything else.

Especially Lux and Eliza and I; we have the great misfortune of looking like our mother. Dark hair, dark eyes, tan skin. Not a hint of our father's lineage. No, we're all our mother, all Kimura and only Jackson by name.

Sometimes, when she looks at us like that, I get why our mother left. I don't blame her. They must've looked at her a whole lot worse. The twins, though, Lottie and Grace, they look like our dad. Like our grandmother. They inherited their lighter features, the paler skin and the lighter hair and eyes. Usually, that grants them a little extra kindness. Today, though, I hold my breath when my grandmother's gaze lands on Lottie. "Charlotte," she tuts, her heels clacking as she scales the porch steps. Brow raised, she captures a strand of dyed hair between her fingers. "What's this?"

We all wince at our sister's dry reply. "Hair dye."

"The blonde was so lovely." Our grandmother's gaze slides towards Lux, and for a second, I catch a flicker of guilt flashing across Lottie's face. "Honestly, Alexandra. You let her do this?"

There's no chance for a rebuttal; even if Lux wanted to inform our grandmother that no one lets Lottie do anything, she couldn't. With a disappointed sigh and a dismissive wave of her hand, the older woman stalks inside.

"I came to check on the renovations," not to check on her grandchildren, of course, "and to have a little talk," she pauses, eyeing the kitchen with nothing short of a sneer before settling her attention on the youngest Jackson, "about you."

The color drains from Eliza's face. "What?"

"We heard about your suspension," that palpable disapproval—almost as perceptible as my confusion—bounces to Lux, "from Principal Matthews."

Her… "Suspension?" Eliza got *suspended*?

"I was going to tell you." It's unclear whether Lux is talking to me or our grandmother but it's the latter who responds.

"That's not good enough, Alexandra. We allow you a lot of freedom," God, that's a funny way of putting it, "but our generosity has limits. We won't tolerate you disrespecting our trust."

I hate that tone. The condescending dissatisfaction within it has a way of making you feel exceptionally small, and watching my sisters shrink is a special kind of torture.

When I whisper for Eliza to go upstairs, she doesn't need to be told twice. When I nod for the twins to follow, they scarper just as quick. It pains me that I can't sneak Lux out too, shield her from the full force of Ruth Jackson's rage, but I do what I can; I deflect.

"It was my fault," I lie through my teeth, loading my tone with false apology and adopting an expression to match. "I told Lux not to say anything. I didn't want to bother you over something minor."

"Hitting another student is not minor, Oscar."

By some miracle, I swallow my splutter of shock. I resist the urge to gape at Lux—because what the actual fuck—and keep a straight face, an even tone. "It's under control."

An unimpressed hum echoes around the kitchen. Reaching into her purse, my grandmother pulls something out, and my stomach twists when I catch sight of leaflets decorated with kids in uniforms lingering in front of big brick buildings. "Some alternative schooling options to consider."

"They won't be necessary."

My grandmother sighs, readjusting her purse with one hand and patting my shoulder with the other. "If something like this happens again, that won't be your decision to make."

No one wanted to stay in that house tonight.

It was like in one visit, an almighty speech and a hefty dose of thinly veiled threats, all the warmth we've worked so hard to inject into our home was sucked right out. So, after the quickest packing session known to man, I loaded the girls into my car and swept them away to Sun Valley.

Maybe it's the silence that's making the journey drag. It's an odd thing, my sisters being so quiet. I don't mind though; the longer they go without speaking, the more time I have to figure out what the hell I'm supposed to say.

The more time I have to articulate my emotions beyond being pissed off.

Lux should've told me. That's our deal, we both share the girls and any burdens they might induce. I might not be physically there all of the time but I still want to be present. To be involved. There are enough absentee parent figures in our lives, and I have no intention of becoming another.

The girls spark back to life a little when we pull into the Walmart near my house—us Jacksons eat our emotions and my house is pitifully devoid of… well, anything but beer and frozen pizza. When the click of seatbelts being undone fills the truck interior, I shift to face the girl in my passenger seat and the three crammed in the back. "Everyone good?"

Four nodding heads respond, one shakier than the rest.

Sliding Lux a concerned look, we both hone in on the slumped, pale fourteen-year-old. "Eliza?"

The dark eyes looking everywhere but at us shine as Eliza fights a losing battle against a wobbly bottom lip. "Please don't send me away."

God, I'm on a steady path towards heartbreak today.

"You're not going anywhere," I promise. Reaching back, I set a hand on her knee, the fabric of her godawful grandmother-approved dress rustling beneath my fingertips. "Tell me what happened."

Eliza stiffens, glancing quickly at the twin on either side of her before sighing. "Some kids at school make fun of me sometimes."

It's so quick and subtle, I almost miss the slow slide of Lottie's arm as she links it through one of Eliza's, red nails settling against a tan forearm. Grace encroaches on the opposite side, wrapping a protective arm around a pair of defeatedly hunched shoulders.

"Why?"

A hard swallow precedes a quiet, "for not having parents."

Suddenly, my heart is a lump of granite. Lodged in my throat and sitting there uncomfortably, unmovable no matter how many times I swallow.

"I tried to ignore it, I promise I did, but one of them…" Eliza sniffs loudly, and the utterly dejected look on her face causes me actual pain. "He called me an orphan."

Jesus fucking Christ. What the hell is wrong with the kids in this school? "So, you…"

"I punched him."

"Good girl."

I shoot Lottie a hard look, opening my mouth to chastise her but nothing comes out. I don't know what to say. The parental, guardian side of me? He knows there has to be some kind of reprimand for violence, some punishment.

But the big brother?

God, he is trying so hard not to give Eliza a high five.

"I'm sorry." Eliza's voice quivers as a few tears spill. "I'm so, so sorry. I didn't mean to, I swear, it just happened."

Breaths, Jackson. Long, deep breaths. "How long were you suspended for?"

"Three days."

Okay. Three days isn't bad. Three days is redeemable. Most importantly, a three-day suspension is not an expulsion.

Silver linings.

"I'm sorry," Eliza repeats, desperation heavy in her tone.

"I know," I exhale a long breath. "You can't punch people, Eliza, okay? Not on school grounds, anyways. Or with any witnesses present."

Eliza's watery chuckle is echoed by Lux's much more enthusiastic one, but it soon cuts out when I turn my frown on her. "And you," my free hand pokes her on the thigh, "can't keep shit like that from me."

They're my responsibility too, I silently add through raised brows and another, gentler poke.

When her eyes narrow indignantly, I know she got the message. "I had it under control!"

"So you punished her?"

If Lux's sudden silence didn't say it all, the snort and snarky comment from the backseat does. "She took her for ice cream."

A pained half-groan, half-laugh leaves me as my forehead hits the steering wheel.

An early grave. I'm calling it. I have twenty years left, max, before these girls end me.

"Come on." Lux pats my back. "Let's get you a drink."

11

LUNA

You know those shitty high school stereotypes coming-of-age movies love to use? Jocks, geeks, cheerleaders, whatever?

Well, based on looks, I know I'd be labelled The Mean Girl. The Head Bitch. The Regina George of Harlem.

But for a long, long time, I was The Bad Kid. The Class Disturbance. The student jittering and disrupting because my thoughts moved too fast to be constrained in tiny classrooms with insipid lessons for hours on end. I didn't, *don't*, like schedules and deadlines, or rather, my brain isn't wired to obey someone else's, so teachers didn't like me. And they liked me less when I finally got my diagnosis because attention deficit hyperactivity disorder? Codeword for lazy. Unmotivated. Excusatory.

That was when I became 'Too Much.' Too loud, too brash, too impulsive.

Too unwilling to sit on my ass and ignore the shit plaguing my mind, the intrusive thoughts designed to get me in trouble, like other people could.

I lament that quality most of the time. It's hard, living with a brain like that. It's tiring. It leads me to do things like slink out of my apartment dressed all in black with only nefarious intentions because I can't stop picturing my roommate's bleeding face.

They had a fight. Amelia and Dylan. Another loud, dramatic fight that bled through the thin walls between our bedrooms, about that damn Halloween party, of all things. Jackson's Halloween party, I learned when I pressed my ear against the wall because it had gotten a little too quiet for my liking. When Amelia agreed to go like both Dylan and I knew she would, it just got me thinking.

Maybe, if Dylan wants to celebrate Halloween that badly, I should help him.

Hence why I'm skulking around Walmart a few minutes shy of midnight with a basket full of eggs, silly string, and spray paint. And a two pound bag of Sour Patch Kids. Because slightly villainous but definitely deserved deeds require sustenance, obviously.

My fingernails—glossy black because I take my criminal activity very seriously—tap against my basket as I debate whether an addition of something salty is necessary. Flamin' Hot Cheetos are calling my name, and I'm reaching for a party-size pack when I get knocked off course.

"Woah." Gripping the edge of the shopping cart attempting to mow me down, I crack a smile at the young girl driving it. "Relax, kid. There's enough to go around."

Deep brown eyes regard me with panic, and I lose my grip on the junk-food-laden cart as the girl stumbles backward. "Crap, I'm so sorry."

"Hey, I'm a shit driver too. No judgment here," I assure my weirdly familiar assailant. Not *her*, per se, but her face.

Her very sad face.

"You okay?" I can't help but ask, peering around the aisle for whoever she might belong to. "Need help finding someone?"

The girl bristles in that indignant way teenagers striving for independence do. "No."

I hum. "Someone need help finding you?"

She does a terrible job trying to hide her smirk. "Probably."

A voice in my head makes a fond, nostalgic noise; it's like looking in a mirror at my past, troublemaking self.

That's not why she's so damn familiar, though.

I can't put my finger on it. There's just something about her that makes me think we've met before.

And when a yelled, "Eliza!" rings out, I figure out why.

~

It should be a criminal offense for a man to simultaneously look so stressed yet so *fine*. Artfully mussed hair escaping from a loose braid. Furrowed brows I have the urge to call tortured. A white dress shirt with the top few buttons undone to reveal the dip of his throat and a hint of collarbone, the collar rumpled like he spent the day tugging at it.

Drooling in a Walmart. Oh, how far I've fallen.

"Luna," Jackson breathes my name like it's both a strain and a relief. He looks at me the same way, doing a quick yet thorough scan that makes me wish I hadn't scampered out the door in fuzzy slippers and my best attempt at a cartoon robber costume. "Hi."

"Hi, Jackson." God, what is it with him looking surprised every time I say his name? I can't tell if he assumes me to be forgetful or himself to be so unmemorable. When I glance at the girl beside me, I find her wearing just as funny an expression. "Eliza, is it?"

Jackson's little sister—there's no way that's not his sister, they're practically identical—nods as she looks between her brother and I. "You know each other?"

"Luna goes to Sun Valley, too."

And I occasionally need to be scraped off bathroom floors.

Figured that bonding experience would promote a girl to 'friend' but apparently not.

"Really?" Eliza hums, and Jackson cringes. He grips her by the shoulders and starts to steer her away, to say goodbye, but she slips his grasp easily. "Why do you have so many eggs?"

I follow her gaze to the admittedly questionable contents of my basket. "I'm bulking."

Both Jackson siblings arch a brow that so clearly screams 'bullshit.' "And the spray paint?"

"Art project."

"Silly string?"

I wince. "Plausible deniability, kiddo"

"But-"

"Hey, why don't you go find the others?" When Eliza whines at the command weakly disguised as a suggestion, Jackson shoves her gently down the aisle. "I'll be right behind you."

Reluctantly, she slopes off, waving goodbye with a crooked smile so similar to her brother's, it's a little scary. "She's cute," I start to say but the frown on Jackson's face cuts me off. "What?"

"Are you okay?"

My eyes narrow, an instinctive reaction to my least favorite question. "Yes."

"You look a little..." He dithers on a suitable descriptor, and I prepare myself for one bordering on an insult. You know; unhinged, unbalanced, bat-shit. Things every girl loves to be called. "Upset."

Huh.

Okay.

Pleasantly surprising but still, I wave him off dismissively whilst making a second attempt at snatching those Cheetos. "I'm good."

"You're shaking."

A single glance at my outstretched hand proves Jackson's quiet observation correct.

Crap.

Sucking in a deep breath, I drag my palm along a legging-clad thigh. "I'm fine."

My tight smile morphs into the beginnings of a scowl when Jackson laughs softly. "Sorry," he coughs. "I have sisters. I know 'I'm fine' is bullshit."

Annoyance—irrational but tangible all the same—straightens my spine, a huff of frustration leaving me. "To be perfectly honest," I start, voice too sharp, too high, "I'm on my way to vandalize my roommate's dickhead boyfriend's house because he's a giant piece of shit who deserves terrible things and I can't do anything to him, but an anonymous vengeful Halloween spirit definitely can."

Silence follows my outburst. Silence and staring, pretty brown eyes latched on me the way I naively begged for only a few nights ago. Before I knew how much him looking at me could *itch*.

Resisting the shiver tickling my spine, I huff, shopping basket teetering precariously as I shift to cross my arms. "Oh my God, *what?*"

The calmest I've ever seen him, Jackson glances over his shoulder. "Eliza?"

Immediately, a grinning face peeks around the end of the aisle. Not the least bit ashamed to have been caught eavesdropping, Eliza catches the wallet Jackson tosses her easily. "Stay with Lux, okay?"

A sarcastic salute, a cheeky smile in my direction, and Eliza disappears again, leaving the sound of whispering in her wake and making me wonder just how many Jackson women are lurking around the corner.

"What're you doing?" I frown at Jackson when he advances, frowning some more when he gently maneuvers the basket from my grasp and sets it on the floor. "Hey, I'm buying that."

Ignoring me, Jackson nudges me toward the exit. "C'mon."

"Your sisters-"

"-are probably gonna spend the next half hour fighting over ice cream flavors," he finishes for me. "Just come with me for a sec?"

I don't know why but I do. Wearing the frown of all frowns and with a healthy dose of grumbling but with minimal actual fight, I let Jackson lead me outside. Apparently, my survival instincts have taken the night off. Not even when we reach a truck I assume is his do any internal alarm bells start ringing which, admittedly, for me, isn't all that weird but still.

I don't know where this odd inherent trust is coming from and I don't have the time or the brainpower to question it because Jackson is unlatching the tailgate, patting the bed of his truck. I arch a brow. "This is a terrible attempt at seduction."

Even in the shitty street lamp lighting, I see the blush I was angling for. It deepens when I hoist myself up and lie on the cold metal, legs dangling over the edge. "Really?" I sigh and shimmy in a vain attempt to get comfortable. "I'm not worth a couple cushions and a blanket?"

It must be a whole minute, how long Jackson stares at me, mouth open yet nothing coming out. When he does eventually articulate a response, I don't hear it; it's muffled by the truck creaking as he joins me. And then, he's back to silence, lying on his back with his hands folded on his stomach and his eyes on the sky and I'm doing the staring, fingers drumming against my thighs.

I feel the need to whisper as I ask, "What're we doing?"

"One of my sisters, Grace, has pretty bad anxiety," Jackson responds, gaze remaining skyward, voice so calm it could lull a girl to sleep. "When it was at its worst, she had episodes almost daily and the only thing that really helped calm her was being outside. It's called ecotherapy. Stargazing was one of her favorites. Naming constellations gave her something else to focus on."

Heat crawls up my neck, my fingers balling into fists, a defense automatically forming on my tongue. "I wasn't having an episode."

"I know," Jackson murmurs, quiet and calm and honest. "Figured it would help anyway."

Oh.

Well, that's sweet.

I'm not used to sweet.

It's very… different.

Tilting my face towards the sky, I say, "I don't know anything about stars."

"Me neither. Nice to just look, though."

"Hm." Yeah, I suppose they are. But the twinkling lights only manage to hold my attention for a handful of minutes before it flits back to the man beside me. As I scan the unusual combination of slacks, dress shoes, and a button-down shirt, my curiosity gets the better of me. "Were you at a funeral or something?"

Jackson's head flops toward me, an amused frown tilting his lips.

"You look nice," I explain, and immediately amend it, "you're dressed nice, I mean. Fancy."

"I look nice," I might be imagining it, but I swear, Jackson looks a little smug, "so I must've been at a funeral?"

"I would've said wedding but you look kinda stressed. And you were in Walmart bulk-buying junk food at midnight. That's sad-person behavior."

"As opposed to bulk-buying eggs?"

"That's mad-person behavior." In every sense of the word. "So? Funeral? Wedding? Baptism?"

"Grandparents visit."

Huh. I didn't know visits from your grandparents required such formal wear but hey, what do I know? Not like I have any for reference.

I do, however, have many, many references for the uncomfortable tension suddenly holding Jackson taut. And, like so many things tonight, I don't like it.

So, I let my gaze rake over him, slow and purposeful, noting every detail and I hum. "It's not a baseball uniform but you look pretty good."

It's an interesting juxtaposition, the doubtful wrinkles of his forehead combined with the upward tilt of his mouth, the bashful shade of red staining his cheeks and the wisecrack he murmurs. "You got a thing for baseball uniforms?"

"Everyone has a thing for baseball uniforms."

It's not a joke but he laughs, a familiar, quiet chuckle that I'm beginning to think might be the most comforting sound in the world. As comforting as his smile and his eyes, locked on mine with the focus of someone who's actually seeing. He doesn't stare. He... Jesus Christ, fuck me for saying this but he *gazes*.

I'm not sure who exactly moves closer. Both of us, maybe. All I know is one second, there's a decent gap between us and the next, we're practically sharing breath. He's right fucking there. So close I can truly appreciate the depth to those dark brown eyes. The sun-bleached streaks in long, wavy hair. The uneven lips, the bottom fuller than the top.

In any other circumstance, with any other person, I'd be kissing those lips by now. I'd be kissing the hell out of them and hopefully, he'd be kissing the hell back.

But I think it's been established Jackson is not any other person.

He doesn't kiss me. Doesn't even try. He does what could be the very opposite; he sits up, shoulders heaving as he breathes deep, and scoots to the edge of the truck bed, basically as far away from me as he can possibly get.

"Wow," I tease quietly, blatantly ogling the muscles covered by white cotton, letting the sight of them soothe the teeny tiny sting of rejection. "I think that was a record for the whole eye-contact thing."

Broad shoulders rise and fall dramatically once more before Jackson turns, obviously nervous yet oddly determined. "Do you have plans on Halloween?" he blurts, not giving me a chance to respond before continuing, "Because there's a party at my place. My roommates are throwing it. And me, obviously since it's my house too." He laughs awkwardly, a hand rising to rake through his hair. "It should be fun and, uh, you can come."

Propping myself up on my elbow, I cock my head. "I can?"

Jackson swallows hard enough for me to see the bob of his throat. "If you want."

I try so very hard not to grin like a big fool, and I fail so very spectacularly. "If I want."

He nods.

"Do *you* want me to come?"

"If you want," he repeats, and that's just not good enough for me.

My grin becomes a teasing smirk. Joining him at the truck's edge, I elbow him gently. "It's a yes or no question, Jackson."

His lack of hesitation is as surprising as it is needed. "Yes."

"Okay." Humming in satisfaction, I allow myself another indulgent second with the warmth of him bleeding into me before hopping to my feet.

Jackson follows my lead. Leaning against his truck with his hands in his pockets and an indecipherable expression on his face, he watches as I straighten myself out. "So," he coughs. "You're coming?"

Biting down my smile, I shrug.

Jackson shifts, crosses his arms over his chest and coughs again. This time, when he speaks, his voice is a decibel louder, a hint deeper.

"It was a yes or no question, Luna."

I pause my oh-so-casual adjustment of my ponytail.

Interesting.

"I was always coming," I admit, not the least bit embarrassed. "But it's nice to have an invite from the big man himself."

12

JACKSON

"Do you think I got enough?"

I don't acknowledge my friend's skeptical question with anything more than a scoff; his truck is completely packed full of every alcohol under the sun, yet Nick regards it all dubiously. Like drinking the contents of an entire liquor store in a single night is not outside the realm of possibility. I did tell him to go nuts when I gave him my card but Jesus Christ, I didn't realize he was the boozy equivalent of a magpie.

Nick kisses his teeth, both hands braced on his hips. "It doesn't look like enough."

"Are you serious?" I can't even see the bed of his truck nor the leather of the backseat.

"A lot of people are coming," Nick defends himself. Which is true. And entirely his fault. That's the thing about Nick; he likes to pretend he doesn't like people. To be unapproachable and unfriendly and rude. To bitch and moan about his space being invaded by strangers. But at least half of the people celebrating Halloween in our home tonight scored a casual invite from the giant grump with the mushy middle. Not that he would ever admit that; I'd bet my pitching arm he'll blame the whole thing on Ben.

"The entire campus could come," I drawl, hoisting a couple slabs of beer into my arms, "and we would still have enough."

I amend that statement about half an hour later when our loot is spread across the kitchen, covering every inch of counter space. The entire town could turn up, and we'd have drinks to spare. Ben's eyes practically bug out of his head when he catches sight of everything, and I can't tell if it's in horror at the quantity or sheer delight at the many, many options for internal pollution.

"Where's Cass?" Nick asks as we start sifting through the mountain of grocery bags, pulling out booze and cups and mixers while I imagine how wonderfully scandalized my grandparents would be if they knew a substantial portion of the money they deposited in my account this month went towards intoxicating the local students.

Ben and I exchange an amused glance, my friend rolling his eyes as he loads the fridge with soda. "He ditched us for one of the frats."

Nick's lack of surprise is telling, and equal to mine earlier when Cass told me he was bailing; we all know if there's anything Cass loves more than a house party, it's a frat party. Especially on Halloween when near nudity is practically required; my friend will use any excuse not to wear a shirt. Or pants, if last year is anything to go by.

That's not a sentiment I share. I'm not keen on dressing up at all, and I wouldn't if Ben wasn't so damn insistent. I'm only embellishing my jeans and t-shirt with a cowboy hat and boots under his insistent command. And I suspect Nick's costume is a direct result of the same thing; I can't imagine any other circumstance under which Nick would be frowning at a recently bought kid's face paint kit.

It causes me actual, physical pain when my friend rips the thing open and dips a thick finger in the white shade, using his phone as a mirror as he smears it on his cheek. "What the fuck are you doing?"

"Tryna be a skeleton."

Huh. I would've guessed panda.

Bundling up the last of the emptied bags and chucking them in the cabinet beneath the sink, I wet a clean dishtowel and chuck it at Nick, sighing. "I'll do it."

For once, Nick puts up minimal resistance, wiping off his godawful attempt and letting me create something better. It's a soothing process, even if it takes more time than we have. Even if all that work is going to be smudged by some random girl within the hour. Nick lasts almost the entire time with only minimal fidgeting and no gruff, snarky comments.

Almost.

"Your girlfriend coming tonight?"

If I didn't take such pride in my work, I'd smudge the shit out of Nick's perfectly executed skeletal face. "Is yours?"

Nick's scoff is hilariously exaggerated. "She has a boyfriend and it sure as shit isn't me."

Ah, yes. The boyfriend. Neither Nick nor I can tell if the guy was actually familiar or if he just had that recognizably insufferable air all douchebags possess. I would laugh at how quickly Nick's mood changes whenever the guy appears if I wasn't deeply, genuinely concerned about Red and the way she flinches every time the guy touches her. "Since when has another guy ever stopped you?"

"And what, exactly, is stopping you, *seu medroso*?"

Ben snorts from the other side of the counter, head shaking as he stirs a pitcher of too-bright blue liquid. A Cass recipe, if the strong smell wafting from it is anything to go by. "Both of you are pathetic."

Oh, I know. I am painfully aware of my patheticness. And how ridiculous it is, so goddamn ridiculous, to feel sick to my stomach at the thought of Luna turning up tonight. Even sicker at the thought of her not. Which she probably won't. She definitely got a better offer. She probably forgot I offered at all, actually. So, I'm not holding my breath.

Obviously.

~

She's here.

Luna is in my house.

Luna is in my house, dancing in my living room, drinking my alcohol, and I don't know what to do.

I saw her the moment she arrived when my hundredth completely nonchalant sweep of the house finally proved fruitful. When she strutted into my home like she owned the place. When every gaze swung toward her, like moths to the brightest flame. When every eye in the room scanned her from head to toe, noting the fluffy halo hovering above a cloud of wavy hair, the matching wings strapped to her back, the tiny white ensemble showing off enough shimmering skin to short circuit my brain.

When she sauntered into the kitchen, gaze sly and smirk secretive, extended her hand, and pretended we didn't know each other.

"Luna," she introduced herself to me for at least the third time, and I deflated like a fucking balloon. I shook her hand with a limp grip my grandparents would deem unacceptable. I politely smiled at the friend flanking her, ignoring the air of teasing emanating from mine. And then, I mumbled an excuse and fled in search of air that didn't inexplicably smell like vanilla.

I've been hiding in the backyard for half an hour and still haven't managed to achieve that. Slouched in one of the lawn chairs we nabbed from a yard sale over the summer, I stare blankly at the sky, ignoring the beer in my hand and the people around me.

I'm not going to lie, I'm hurt. And confused. I don't get it. I thought... I don't know, I thought we were friends. Acquaintances at the very damn least. Something worth a *'hey, we actually know each other'* when Nick thought he was making first introductions.

Clearly, I thought wrong.

Obviously, I read too much into everything like a big fool with a pathetic crush.

Stifling a groan, I thump my head back against the lounger.

How fucking embarrassing.

I'm so tangled up in my thoughts, it takes me a minute to register the shimmering white floating in my peripheral. When I do, I don't acknowledge it. I just... wait.

A long moment passes before a voice too chirpy for my current mood permeates the night air. "Stargazing, cowboy?"

Fingers tightening around my beer, I force myself to not look. Not to respond with anything other than a shrug. Not to acknowledge how the minute she appears, everything else around me becomes insignificant.

There's a creak of plastic as Luna occupies the empty chair beside me, long legs outstretched, feet crossed at the ankles, and her gaze skyward. Nails tap against the armrest restlessly before she aims a finger at a cluster of stars. "That one's Orion. I googled it."

I stay silent even as something in my chest thumps a little harder.

"That's Leo." She shifts, pointing out a new constellation. "Might only remember that one because it's my star sign."

Again, I say nothing. I can't bring myself to. I don't have the energy to pretend I'm not upset.

Luna sighs quietly, the noise almost inaudible amidst the din of drunk students but distinctly irritated. Another round of creaking sounds as she shifts to sit sideways and scoots closer until her knees brush my thigh. "Hey."

"Hi." I clear my throat, an attempt to erase the kicked-puppy essence to it. "Luna, was it?"

Her laugh is an octave higher than usual. "Funny."

"Wasn't tryna be." I don't mean to sound so snippy but that's how it comes out, and I hear Luna's dissatisfaction in the kiss of her teeth.

"Baby, I'm not in the mood to nurse hurt feelings tonight."

I purse my lips to stifle a bitter laugh. God knows I wasn't expecting her to; I learned a long time ago that it's rarely the cause of the hurt that soothes it.

I've never been one for quick, snippy comebacks, and it turns out, I don't need one. The rest of the world reappears as a drunk guy stumbles over, and my head snaps towards Luna just in time to catch her jolt as a heavy hand jerks the back of her seat.

"Luna fuckin' Evans." Billy leers down at her, and I find myself wishing that when I helped him with his pitch last semester, I'd done something else with the baseball bat instead. "Been looking for you."

Complete apathy paints Luna's face as she drawls, "lucky me," but her sarcasm is lost on Billy.

He smiles, wide and fucking creepy, and agrees. "Lucky you."

Jaw clenched, Luna gestures to me. "I'm busy."

"Ah." Billy's grin redirects, landing on me. "Lucky *you*."

"Fuck off." Luna huffs as she stands. When she makes a break for escape, Billy blocks her path, and before I know it, I'm on my feet and echoing her sentiment.

"Fuck off, Billy."

Billy holds up his hands in innocence, swaying as he claims, "dude, I had her first."

"*Dude*, I'm right fucking here," Luna practically growls, body rigid, scowl deadly. "And the only thing you *had* was the stamina of an eighty-year-old man. Now, get out of my way."

She doesn't wait for him to obey. She simply shoves him aside, her heels sinking into the grass as she stomps toward the back door.

Billy watches her retreat with a whistle—apparently, he's one of those guys who takes a woman's complete disinterest as a challenge. Clamping a hand down on my shoulder, he murmurs in my ear like we're co-conspirators, like I'm not five seconds away from throwing him out of my house. "Watch out, man. She might fuck good but the attitude ain't worth it."

Heat creeps along my skin, and for once in the presence of Luna, it's not from mortification plaguing me. Shrugging so his hand falls away, I turn toward Billy. "What the fuck did you just say?"

"I get it, okay? She's hot. But does hot really outweigh batshit crazy?"

I blink at him. Once, twice, three times, whilst wondering if he really just said that. If he's really smiling while he spouts shit. If he's really waiting for me to laugh and agree.

I don't know who's more surprised, Billy or I, when my palms connect with his chest and shove him backward. "Don't you *ever*—"

"Jesus Christ." Nails dig into my bicep as someone yanks me, hard, away from a stumbling, shocked Billy. "Reign it in, cowboy."

I do no such thing. Unable to shake the surprisingly strong grip, I stab my free hand in Billy's direction. "Get out of my house."

"*Jackson.*" Another hard pull drags me towards the back porch, inside the house where I can't glare at Billy anymore, and doesn't stop until we're upstairs. Luna shoves me into the first bedroom she stumbles upon and storms in after me, slamming the door shut behind her. "What the fuck is wrong with you?"

"He-"

"-has the emotional maturity of a child, yes, I know. I didn't know *you* shared that affliction."

"He said-"

"I heard what he said," she interrupts me again, hands on her hips and fury in her eyes, "and I can handle it. I don't need you flouncing in like some hero."

"That's not what I was doing."

"Well, that armor of yours is looking awfully shiny." Luna huffs, hair flying as she turns away from me, heels clacking as she paces the room. "You gotta pick your battles, cowboy. Drunk dipshits at house parties are not worth the effort."

You are, though, I don't deign to say aloud.

But I don't apologize either.

I just stand and stare and as I do, it starts to sink in that the bedroom we're in?

It's mine.

Luna Evans is in my bedroom.

Standing bang in the center. Arms crossed, back to me. Long hair grazing the curve of her ass as her head tilts toward the ceiling, and when I follow her gaze, I suddenly hate her being in here. With a soft sigh, some of the tension eases from taut shoulders. "These are amazing."

I frown at the rough paintstrokes holding her attention. Almost broke my damn neck, painting up there while trying to balance on an old, rusty ladder. But the view of rolling hills and blue skies reminding me of home is worth it. "They're rough."

Luna glances over her shoulder, pretty eyes rolling. "You're modest."

I drop my gaze before the full effect of that smile hits. Quiet and discouraged, I ask, "Did you bring me up here for a reason or can I go?"

"Alcohol makes you feisty, hm?"

Yeah, the fault falls on the single beer I've had, for sure.

Heels clack against wood as Luna approaches, the tips of her toes just visible as she ventures too close. "I thought we solved this eye contact thing."

Swallowing a sigh, I reluctantly look up.

Luna scans me the same way she perused my artwork, smile as strained as the humor in her tone. "Mad looks good on you."

"I'm not mad."

"No?"

"No, Luna, I'm not."

She doesn't seem convinced. "Billy was just being a drunk dick."

"I don't care about Billy."

"Looked a lot like you cared."

"Not about him."

Pink lips part on a sharp breath, nothing else escaping them. They roll together for a moment, thoughtful and oddly nervous, before she inhales again, slower this time, releasing it with a confession. "I panicked, okay? I saw you and I panicked."

When I frown, Luna rolls her eyes. "Because," she answers the question I only silently asked, "you make me kind of nervous, Jackson."

"*I* make you *nervous*?" I gawk at her, mouth wide open, perfectly aware of how foolish I look and sound yet powerless to stop. "Why?"

Luna doesn't answer. Instead, she cocks her head, eyes narrowing slightly. "Is that really so hard to believe?"

I decide against responding, and the smile that curves Luna's lips in response to my silence?

Downright terrifying.

"It is very nerve-wracking, Jackson," she all but purrs, "to not know when the hell a guy is gonna make a move on you."

Oh.

Oh.

"I thought maybe you were gonna the other night, in your truck," she continues, another purposeful step eliminating the distance between us. "The whole way home, I wondered if you'd thought about it."

I did. There was a long moment where I considered it before common sense kicked in. "Did you want me to?"

I can't tell what answer I'm hoping for. Half of me begs, *please God, say yes.* The other half prays she'll laugh, say no, crush the little hope I have once and for all because Jesus Christ, this is painful.

It's painful feeling so awkward and helpless around her constantly. It's painful trying not to make a complete ass of myself. And, God, it's painful wanting to kiss her.

And I really, really want to kiss her.

As slow as the smile that graces her lips, Luna's hands dance up my chest, toying with the fabric of my t-shirt, until her hands are linked behind my head. "Yes."

I can't speak or move or breathe but it's fine because she does it all for me. Luna leans forward, melding to me perfectly, breath brushing my lips. "I wanted you to, Jackson," she says, and as though compelled by her words, my hands move, landing on the curve of her waist.

Another one of the few inches between us is decimated when her nose brushes mine. "Really, really badly."

It's not the feel of her breath on my lips that does it. Not the feel of her fingers tangling in my hair either. No, it's those goddamn eyes, the soft genuinity in them that matches the upturn of her lips. They provide the encouragement I need.

They convince me to tug her forward, so gently, and press my lips to hers.

DURING

We were together.
I forget the rest.

PLAYLIST II

I'm In Love With You - The 1975
touch tank - quinnie
God Is Fair, Sexy Nasty - Mac Miller (feat Kendrick Lamar)
Electric - Alina Baraz, Khalid
Love on the brain - Rihanna
Throw Me Around - That band Honey.
Stay - Mac Miller
Garden (Say It Like Dat) - SZA
It Will Come Back - Hozier
Tenerife Sea - Ed Sheeran

13

LUNA

Oscar Jackson kisses like he talks. Soft and slow and always leaving me wanting more in the most gloriously frustrating way.

I've never been one to feel... breakable. To be treated as such. *Delicate* is not a word often—or ever—used to describe me and yet, that is exactly how Oscar Jackson treats me. Like I might shatter beneath the gentle thumb sliding along my cheekbone, the fingers cupping my face reverently, with a foreign softness that's as unnerving as it is exhilarating.

God, a girl could get used to this.

Which is exactly why I need him to stop.

I pride myself on my ability to make a man lose his mind, and never have I needed to pull through more than now. Rising on my toes, I eliminate the concept of distance between us, pressing myself as close as humanly possible. When I bury my hands in his hair, nails scraping his scalp, Jackson groans into my mouth, and just like that, a flip switches.

It's like he's suddenly possessed. RIP sweet Jackson, hello... well, not sweet Jackson. Dirty Jackson. Rough Jackson. Kinda Slutty Jackson.

Makes Me Wanna Rip His Clothes Off Jackson.

Teeth spear my bottom lip demandingly, and when I gasp at the contact, Jackson uses the opportunity to slip his tongue into my mouth, tangling with mine, fighting a battle I'm suddenly not sure I want to win. He kisses me desperately, full of want and lust, and I can barely keep up. If it weren't for the hand resting on the small of my back, the other palming the curve of my neck, I fear I'd fall to the floor, shock and desire sending me there.

That hand shifts, settling high on my throat and exuding just enough pressure to tilt my head for better access yet still holding complete control over me. The possessive touch sends a zing down my spine, pooling in the pit of my stomach, awakening a fierce burn that I'm positive only Jackson can douse.

And I'm confused. I'm so fucking confused, my inner monologue a chant of *what the fuck what the fuck what the fuck* because where has this come from? Who the fuck is this? It's been weeks of gentle but obvious flirting and you're telling me all it took was a little bit of straight-talking to get *this* out of him?

A wanton moan leaves me when his touch drifts to my ass, yanking the hem of my skirt up and out of the way so he can palm the bare skin underneath hungrily. Like his kiss, his touch is anything but gentle as he kneads the soft flesh, fingers digging in hard enough to leave evidence. Calloused fingers travel upwards and hook around the band of my panties, a yelp escaping me when he snaps the fabric against my skin.

Unfortunately, the noise snaps him out of his lusty haze.

With a deep groan, he pulls away from me, expression twisted as though it physically pains him to pry his lips from mine. Our heavy breaths mingle in the air, chests rising and falling in unison, the heat of his skin bleeding through me as he rests his forehead against mine. I try to lean in again only to be denied by the hand on my neck tightening, restricting my movement and his strained, husky voice.

"Fuck." Jackson releases me, pushes me away slightly, the back of his head hitting the door behind him with a thud. "Fuck, I'm sorry."

"The only thing you should be sorry about is stopping."

If it weren't so infuriating, Jackson's distressed hesitancy would be adorable. "You were yelling at me ten minutes ago."

"You were mad at me ten seconds ago." I roll my eyes when he starts to object. "Sorry, you were *not* mad. My bad."

My quip earns me no punishment, unfortunately. Just a pained look and, "You've been drinking."

"I had one drink." A single shot of tequila chugged for liquid courage before I skulked after Jackson, scared yet desperate to rectify my royal fuck-up. I never drink heavily at parties like this; too many dark rooms and hammered, handsy guys lurking. And with Dylan in the building, the need for lucidity only increases; beating the shit out of him, if needed, would prove most difficult with vodka coursing through my veins.

Jackson sighs as he brushes my hair away from my face, both of us ignoring my silly costume halo as it clatters to the ground. "I don't wanna fuck this up."

"You are." I deadpan. "Right now. By not kissing me."

He laughs, grinning in a way that makes me feel... weird. Incites a flurry of goosebumps. Twists my stomach. Makes me want to fucking twirl my hair and giggle.

I blame it on being horny. He's got me all worked up and now he won't deliver, that's it. I've been borderline edged and I'm feeling needy. I need release.

And I'm not going to beg him for it. My pride won't let me.

Pasting on a half-hearted smirk, I step away, rolling my shoulders like that might eliminate the odd feeling clinging to my skin. "Fine," I purr in what I hope is an indifferent tone. With a shrug, I gesture for Jackson to get out of my way, and he does, still frowning. "If you won't fuck me, I'll go find someone who will."

I barely manage to open the door an inch before it's slammed shut with a surprising force.

"Luna," Jackson rasps, warning tone sending a shiver down my spine and a rush of heat between my thighs. "Don't."

Instinctively, I lean back into him, relishing in the certain kind of dark wickedness rolling off him in waves, simultaneously warming my blood and sending chills through me. "Don't what?"

"Don't fuck with me." Rough fingers sweep my hair to one side, exposing skin quickly riddled with goosebumps when he lightly caresses the slope of my neck with his lips. "You're under my roof, sweetheart. No one else is touching you."

Well, shit.

If I wasn't turned on before, I sure as fuck am now.

"Well, then." Turning slowly, I quirk a brow. "You better do something to keep me here."

∽

He doesn't.

He wants to, it's so obvious in his tight grip on my waist and that clenched jaw and the rushed breaths brushing my skin, but he's holding himself back. Being so damn careful, so damn honorable.

Admirable, yes.

Necessary, absolutely not.

A slow smirk spreads across my face as I rest my hands on Jackson's chest, the soft material of his t-shirt such a contrast to the tense muscles beneath. Gently but forcefully, I push and, wearing a slightly dazed expression, he indulges me, allows me to walk him backward until his calves hit his bed and he's forced to sit down.

Jackson watches, rapt, as I shuck his hands from my hips. "You want consent, Jackson?"

He nods stiffly, gaze following my fingers where they slide off the costume wings strapped to my back. His expression turns pained when I finger the hem of my top, and I gotta give it to him; it's commendable, how he keeps his eyes on my face instead of letting them dip to the lacy fabric revealed when I tug the thin fabric over my head and toss it aside.

Blood rushing in my ears dulls the sound of me unzipping my skirt, the rustle of satin as I shimmy until it hits the floor, leaving me in just underwear and heels. I wonder if he sees my hands shaking, with equal parts anticipation and apprehension, as I brace them high on his thighs, using him for balance as I bend until we're eye-level.

"I consent." Jackson's breath catches in his throat, both hands moving to cover mine. "Please fuck me."

I think he might choke a little. He definitely groans, a frustrated noise that matches his grip, either prayers or curses muttered beneath his breath. I reckon there's an equal chance of either, but I don't get the chance to ask because suddenly, I'm airborne. Then I'm on my back, a plush quilt soft against my bare skin.

What was a surprised yelp quickly morphs into a moan when Jackson's lips catch mine again without warning, harsher than they were before. Depraved, really. Like he's drowning and I'm his only source of oxygen.

Any earlier hesitation dissipates. Jackson wastes no more time, deft fingers sneaking between me and the bed and making quick work of undoing my bra. I squirm beneath him as he slowly, teasingly, slides the straps down my shoulders before discarding it.

I push him away just long enough to return the favor, desperately tugging his t-shirt over his head to reveal a body I've been dreaming of for fucking *weeks*. God, do clothes not do him justice. Much like his face, his torso is all sharp angles and defined lines, and my greedy eyes drink up the lean definition, the light brown skin covering rippling muscles and ridged abs. Wrapping my hands around taut biceps, I pull him back down to me, and we both groan as our naked chests collide, hard muscles meeting smooth skin.

Jackson works his way down my chest, teeth scraping and tongue worshiping. A tortured gasp leaves me as warm, wet lips envelop a pert nipple, my back arching as if to force more of me into his mouth. I've always had sensitive nipples but God, with the way his tongue is working, it feels like I could get off from this alone. My hands tangle in his hair, an attempt to ground myself as nimble fingers tweak my other nipple before he squeezes the full mound of flesh roughly. It's relentless, his attention, and it only takes a pathetic number of minutes until I'm on the verge of begging for more, back arched completely off the bed, nails surely leaving marks on his shoulders.

And then, he stops.

Ignoring my noise of protest, the bastard *stops*.

He moves until his lips hover over mine again and, looking a little too damn proud of himself, he utters the most infuriating word. "No."

My whine is loud and unashamed. "*Why?*"

"Because when I fuck you, sweetheart, it's not gonna be a one night stand."

"But those are so much *fun*." So meaningless. And meaningless fun is my speciality.

Beautiful brown eyes never leave mine as Jackson shakes his head. "I don't share, Luna," he says so softly, such juxtaposition to the fucking filth that follows, "I'm not fucking this pussy until it's all mine."

Jesus fucking Christ.

Even as an aroused shiver wracks my body, I find myself gaping at Jackson. "Who the fuck are you?"

Dominance shies away for a moment as red stains the apples of Jackson's cheeks. When he retreats, kneeling at the foot of the bed, I follow on bent elbows. "No, seriously, what did you do with Jackson?"

"Luna," he groans my name, and I can't help but grin.

"Are your thoughts this dirty every time we're together? Because if they are I would love to—"

My sentence ends in a shriek when Jackson abruptly gets to his feet and yanks me forward, shutting me up pretty effectively by sinking to his knees between my legs. A hand on my stomach keeps me flush against the bed as he, never breaking eye-contact, starts to trail open-mouthed kisses from my knees to my inner thighs.

Any trace of humor dying, I fist the sheets with a death trip, damn near ripping a hole in the fabric when he traces a knuckle over the white lace of my panties. My breath catches, my blood humming with anticipation. He's so close, so fucking close to where I want him, and when he leans in, hot breath following the path of his finger, I almost lose it.

He pauses.

A boyishly devious grin blooms.

And he asks, no, *demands*, "Go on a date with me."

Somehow, I have enough wits about me to scowl. "That's bribery."

I have to give him props. Clever tactic. And it's sure as fuck working.

Gruff laughter tickles my sensitive skin, the sensation only making me hotter and my panties damper. He nudges them aside and runs a finger along the length of my pussy, his touch featherlight as he circles the borderline painfully throbbing bundle of nerves lightly, teasingly, not enough to get me off but just enough to drive me wild.

"Luna." God, I love the way he says my name. "It's a yes or no question."

I don't respond. I can't respond. My mind is too foggy, my eyes screwed shut as I grind against his hand in an attempt to find some relief before he inevitably deprives me again. When he does, my eyes fly open. A protest forms and dies on my lips when I find him hovering above me. His expression has changed, the softer side of him returning for a moment. He brushes a thumb over my lower lip, along my jaw, tucks a strand of wayward hair behind my ear. "Let me treat you right."

His request makes me gulp. It's so sincere, so simple, yet so hard to wrap my head around. I can't figure out what I've done to deserve him looking at me like I hung the fucking moon. I hate that my hand shakes as I reach up and trace his jawline, hate the vulnerable gaping hole in my chest that makes it hard to get out a single word.

Shoving away the doubts, the nerves, I focus on the warmth of his skin beneath my fingertips, the gentleness in his gaze that I'm not sure how I ever survived a day without, the pit of want in my belly. "Okay."

14

LUNA

FOR ALL HIS TEASING, all his dirty words, all his all-consuming dominance, Jackson somehow still manages to look surprised. "Okay?"

I stifle a laugh, nipping at the thumb still resting on my lip. "What, you want a different answer?"

Jackson smiles as he grants me a long, sweet kiss.

Or at least it starts out sweet. It doesn't take long for the depravity to set in again, all frantic touches and twisted tongues. Jackson kisses his way to my ear, teeth pulling at the lobe, voice low and rife with devious promise as he asks, "You want my fingers or my tongue?"

"Both."

God, does he oblige.

The ripping sound of him tearing my underwear off only pisses me off momentarily, the annoyance drowned out by the sight of him kneeling before me. He looks like some kind of corrupted deity, dangerously handsome. Lips swollen, smudged with my pink lipstick. Skin shiny where my body glitter transferred. Dark eyes frantic like they can't decide where to settle first.

His biceps flex as he rakes his hands through his messy hair before coasting them up my thighs, kneading roughly. As eagerly as he watched me undress, he watches his hand dip between my legs, both of us sucking in a sharp breath when his thumb finds my clit, circling lightly. "Tell me what you like, sweetheart."

My hips rock toward him in a silent request for more, and more I get. "That," I pant on a heavy breath, body clenching when Jackson slips two fingers inside me, the pressure of his thumb changing, intensifying, when it's replaced by a hot tongue. "I like that."

Jackson hums against me and God, is that a sensation.

When he curls his fingers and brushes against that tender spot that has my vision temporarily blurring and a white-hot heat shooting up my spine, I reward him with a loud moan. And when he smirks widely, proudly, I know he was waiting for that reaction. Searching for it. Figuring out what makes me feel good.

Fuck, that's hot.

Clutching at the nape of his neck, I squeeze. "More."

"Don't rush me." Jackson chuckles, keeping the motion of his hand infuriatingly slow and steady, nipping at my inner thigh. "Been thinking about this for a long fucking time, Luna."

Don't ask how long.

Do not ask how long.

The question is on the tip of my tongue when it dies.

When there's suddenly no room for questions, for thoughts, as Jackson tosses my leg over his shoulder, spreading me wide for him. I assist with his mission to get closer, hands in his hair guiding him to a faster pace, and he catches on quick. He groans against me, burying his face in my pussy and fucking *feasting*.

And God, he does not waste any more time.

It's too good. Too much yet not enough. Never have I been the object of so much undivided attention, so much affection, and apparently, it's exactly what I've been missing. What I like, what I *love*.

I come in less than a fucking minute.

Even when I come down, Jackson doesn't stop, and a realization hits me.

Jackson does not do quick and dirty, not the way I do.

I am painfully, terrifyingly aware that with Jackson, sex isn't just sex, but I'm too lost in a lusty, dreamlike haze to care.

Jackson reaches up to palm my breast, rolling my nipple between his finger and thumb and sending me over the edge again, even harder than before. My mouth drops open in a silent scream, my eyes roll to the back of my head, my ears fucking ringing.

In my haze, I hear, or more accurately feel, his chuff of laughter. Teeth graze my clit and my scream is vocal this time.

This.

This is where the good sex on campus has been hiding. In this house where, if the rumors are true, the only men who know anything about a woman's body live. In the body of a guy who I'm beginning to think only pretends to be meek and shy.

A strangled sob rips from my throat when another orgasm builds quickly. It's too much to take, a throbbing kind of pleasurable pain, but my attempts to push him away are as futile as they are half-hearted. His eyes narrow as he relents for the briefest of seconds. "Again."

"I can't."

"I didn't say you could stop." Fingers dig into my thighs, keeping my legs open as he works harder, relentless until I wilt beneath him. "Come on, sweetheart."

I lose count of how many times I come. Of how long he kneels before me, tormenting me. I'm limp and shivering, lost in an endless sea of pleasure. My body isn't my own anymore, it's Jackson's, and I do not give a shit.

When he finally stops what feels like hours later, my whine is a mixture of relief and disappointment.

Mostly the former, honestly, because *Jesus fucking Christ.*

"What," I pant as I prop myself up on trembling elbows, "the *fuck* was that?"

And there it is. A flicker in his bravado. A tiny glimpse of Can I Help You Dry Those Glasses? Jackson. An interesting shade of burnt tan, he rubs the back of his neck. "Too much?"

Oh, I shouldn't laugh.

I really, really shouldn't laugh.

It's such a shame I never grasped the whole concept of 'shouldn't.'

I collapse on my back with a shamefully loud laugh. "*Too much*," I snicker, hair in my face as my head shakes from side to side. "Fucking hell, Jackson."

The poor, confused boy flushes another shade darker. "Did I do something wrong?"

"Absolutely fucking not." I sit up so fast my head spins a little. "Sorry. I'm not laughing at you. I think I'm in shock."

"You, uh," Jackson scratches his nape again, and again, I want to laugh at the whiplash-inducing change in demeanor, "don't normally come?"

"Not like that." Shifting to rise on very unsteady knees, I bat his nervous hand away and replace it with mine, fingers finding themselves at home in his hair again. My free hand skates down his chest towards the hard cock begging for my attention. "And I have every intention of returning the favor."

Jackson catches me by the wrist before I can. "Not tonight. I meant what I said."

"Seriously? That wasn't just a line?" My whine morphs into a shriek when I'm pushed on my back again, then a moan when the warm weight of him presses me against the mattress, every noise swallowed by a kiss that effectively lulls me into submission.

When he pulls away, muttering another "not tonight, Luna" even as his cock digs into my stomach, I don't argue.

I sigh and I huff and I pout like a brat, but I don't argue.

Rubbing my eyes to try to ward off the sudden wave of sleepiness several orgasms causes a girl, I gently shove Jackson off me and rise on unsteady legs, wobbling my way to the bathroom, much to his quiet amusement. I make quick work of cleaning myself up and when I re-emerge, Jackson's settling a pair of sweats low on his trim hips.

Grey, of course, because he enjoys making me suffer.

A very apparent lack of boxers.

Jackson smiles at me where I linger in the ensuite doorway, tossing me a shirt that I promptly toss back. "I should go."

"No, you shouldn't."

I sigh. "Jackson."

Jackson stalks towards me, giving me a real good look at those surprisingly muscly arms as he braces a hand on either side of the door, caging me in. "Stay."

"I don't think I should."

He leans down, nose nudging mine, lips brushing mine in a soft, slow, oh-so-tempting kiss. "Stay," he repeats, "I'm not playing the hot or cold game, Luna. Either you want to be here, or you don't. And I think that you do."

I do. For the first time in my life, I want to stay.

I just don't know if I'm capable of it.

Expression soft, Jackson dips his head. He kisses along my jaw, down my neck, following the curve of my collarbones and back up again to end at the corner of my mouth. "Let's go to sleep."

In hindsight, I didn't put up all that much of a fight. He didn't give me time either. He wrapped my hand in his and with a single tug, I followed him back to bed. He handed me his t-shirt and I took it, slipped it on, tried so fucking hard not to sigh happily at the familiar scent. He pulled back the covers and I climbed in.

I let him tug me close, wrap me in his arms.

I let myself fall asleep in his warm embrace.

I can't help it.

When I wake up the next morning in a bed that's not mine or Amelia's or Kate's, or even some random's, I momentarily panic.

I actually fell asleep. Like deep sleep. Judging by the amount of light flooding the room and illuminating the various sketches and drawings littering the walls, I slept right through the morning until midday.

There's a hard chest warming my back, an arm locked around my waist, a face buried in my neck. A familiar fresh scent washes over me, and I have to force myself not to press my nose to the muscled arm my neck rests on, inhale deeply, and fill my lungs with a big gulp of that smell. God, he's like one of those air fresheners you hang in your car.

But what really makes me panic, wanting to sniff a man I barely know?

For all my lamenting and complaining and avoiding sleepovers over the years, this doesn't feel half bad.

I'm lying here, unsure where I end and he begins, listening to his soft, sleepy breaths and I'm considering letting myself be lulled back to sleep instead of hightailing it out of here.

Shit.

As sneakily as I can, I try to extract myself from the tangle of limbs.

I barely manage to move an inch before the arm around me

tightens and a gravelly voice murmurs in my ear, "Where do you think you're going?"

My escape efforts screech to a halt. I stiffen, and I can't tell if it's because I've been caught trying to flee or because of the hot breath hovering over the sensitive spot on the crook of my neck. A memory from last night of his teeth grazing that same spot, him biting down and sucking hard enough to leave a mark floats to the surface. I mentally slap it away. I'm already naked and crushed in his arms; I don't need to be all hot and bothered too. "Nowhere?"

Jackson hums sleepily as he nuzzles my neck, evoking an involuntary sigh. The hand splayed on my belly coasts upwards, thumbs brushing the underside of my boobs in a tender move. "Go back to sleep, sweetheart."

I wait for the usual feeling of disgust that pet names evoke in me to rear its head. Just like last night when he whipped out that word, it doesn't. Instead, my heart does a weird little pitter-patter thing in my chest, insides nothing short of gooey.

I am a weak woman.

So very weak.

One night of orgasms and my entire ethos shatters.

I attempt a weak protest but my resolve is putty in his hands. Big, strong hands that he uses to flip me over and yank me even closer so my face is smashed against his chest, the content grumbling sound he makes vibrating under my cheek. All thoughts of escape eddy from my head as he strokes the length of my spine lightly, soothingly, until I'm damn near purring like a cat.

Sending up a silent 'fuck it' and going against pretty much every instinct I have, I give in. I fucking snuggle the man that is all lean muscles yet still soft and cuddly. His heart thrumming steadily soothes me, and I don't know if it's that or his husky morning voice or the warmth spreading from him to me or a combination of all three but slowly, my panic ebbs.

Hard to freak when you're this damn comfortable.

Before sleep can claim me again, I reel back slightly, tilting my chin so I can look at the man beneath me. I didn't do nearly enough looking—or touching—last night. I was too caught up in all the looking and touching he was doing. So, I'll get my fill now while he's dozing and docile before whatever alternate ego I met last night comes out to play again.

Closed eyelids hid those intensively rich brown irises. A few wild wisps of messy hair frame his face, and I can't stop myself from reaching up and tucking a silky strand behind his ear. At the contact, his eyes flutter open lazily, lips curling upwards in a soft smile that has my heart doing that silly thing again.

I don't let his gaze deter me. Slowly, I trace the slopes of his cheekbones, the dip in his chin, the crinkles beside his eyes. When my pinky brushes the corner of his mouth, his lips part to nip at me playfully, the corner of his eyes crinkling and his cheeks dimpling.

I can't quite decipher his expression. Content, for sure. A little drowsy. But there's something almost confused about it. Disbelieving, maybe. It twists and becomes something else when I continue my gentle exploration lower.

A low, throaty sound rumbles in Jackson's chest as my hands brush against his lower stomach, nails scraping along the ridges and grooves of his abs lightly. He tenses beneath my touch, a hiss of air escaping clenched teeth. I don't try to hide my smirk—God knows he was plenty smug last night, I think it's my turn—and it widens when my hand trails lower and lower until I find him half-hard and straining against his sweats.

"Luna," he murmurs my name, half a groan, half a warning. "What're you doing?"

"What we didn't do last night."

Instead of, you know, ravishing me or something equally debaucherous, Jackson *laughs*.

He fucking *laughs*.

A big, hearty, booming sound that echoes off the walls and punches me in the gut. Rolling me off him, Jackson gets out of bed. "Nope."

Bitch.

"This is cruel," I whine, slapping my hands against the mattress like a child because I get stroppy when I'm horny.

Jackson bends, a palm smoothing my hair back, lips grazing my forehead. "You'll live."

"You might not," I grumble as I rise and follow him into the bathroom, definitely not eyeing the glorious outline of a perfect, sweat-pants-clad ass.

The stars in my eyes dissipate real fucking quick when my gaze raises to the mirror and I catch sight of my reflection. Fucking hell, what is it with me and looking like a wreck around this man? Remnants of last night's makeup line my eyes, glitter still decorates my skin in haphazard clumps, and my chest and hips? Covered in tiny little bruises that I notice, with no small sense of satisfaction, Jackson seems particularly fixated on, the gleam in his eyes nothing short of predatory.

When he realizes he's been caught, Jackson drops his gaze, clearing his throat and muttering something beneath his breath about spare toothbrushes under the sink.

I don't dwell on why exactly he has a horde of dental care. And I definitely don't dwell on why the most obvious potential reason irritates me. I just take the toothbrush, grateful for its existence, and snag a couple of hair ties too.

"You wanna shower?"

Yes. Desperately. But I've already stayed a hell of a lot longer than I intended, than I should've. It's not in my nature to linger yet here I am. And when Jackson takes the shake of my head for what it is–a bare-faced lie–and leads me towards the shower, I let him, blaming the lure of hot water.

The lure of a gorgeous, naked man is inconsequential, obviously.

So insignificant, actually, that my hands absolutely do not wander freely around that deliciously sculpted torso, tracing collarbones and hipbones and a drool-worthy defined abdomen until Jackson groans.

"I'm trying really fucking hard to be a gentleman."

"What if I don't want you to be a gentleman?"

A momentary dark flare in his eyes is all I get before he composes himself. Big hands smooth along my shoulders, comb through the hair down my back, settle low on my waist. "We've been over this, Luna."

"But I don't get *why*." It's just sex. Hot, sweaty, no doubt toe-curling sex. It doesn't have to be... I don't know, whatever he's trying to make it. Special or whatever.

"Because I like you."

"You barely know me."

Jackson smirks as he twists my hair around his fist and tugs. "I've held your hair back while you vomited. Doesn't that count for something?"

A groan of pure embarrassment leaves. Cringing, I hide my face in my hands. I'm not one to indulge shame but that was a low moment. It's a miracle he stills looks at me the way he does when he's seen me doubled over a toilet, spilling my guts.

Jackson pries my fingers away from my face, pressing his lips to my palm, his laughter sprouting goosebumps across my skin. When I peek at him through narrowed eyes, he's grinning like a Cheshire cat. "So you do remember that."

"I neither confirm nor deny."

My surprised shriek echoes off the tiled walls when a hand comes down hard on my ass in a stinging strike. "Go get dressed."

With a harrumph, I step out of the shower and wrap myself in a towel, playfully scowling at him over my shoulder. "You're kicking me out?" *Oh, how the tables have turned.*

"Not fucking likely." Jackson scoffs like the mere idea is completely ridiculous, biceps flexing and making my mouth water as he runs his hands through his hair. "Just didn't think you'd be keen on a cold shower."

Although probably not his intention, Jackson's joke does nothing but draw my attention to the impressive length between his legs.

Yeah, I can *definitely* work with that.

Jackson groans as my hungry eyes take him in, and I'm half convinced I could make him come from eye contact alone.

An idea springs to my mind.

"I could help." When Jackson pins me with a pleading yet stern look, I roll my eyes. "Not like that."

In one swift movement, the towel covering me drops to the floor, Jackson's gaze dropping too, cock pulsing as he eyes my bare chest.

A boob man, for sure.

As slowly as he touches me, I coast a hand up my stomach towards my tits, letting out a little throaty moan when I palm their heavy weight.

"What are you doing?" Jackson's voice drops a couple levels, his gaze dark and menacing.

"Helping," I say on a gasp. "You were going to think about me, weren't you? While you fucked your hand?"

Another groan rips from his chest.

"Is this not better than your imagination?"

"Fuck, Luna." His eyes stay trained on me as his shaky hand fists his cock and starts stroking slowly. "Sit on the counter." I do what he says without even a moment's hesitation, hopping up on the counter behind me, tensing as the cool surface meets my flushed skin. "Spread your legs."

Again, I do what he says within seconds of him saying it, unable to stop my wriggle of excitement. Shivers of anticipation wrack my body as he zones in on the wet spot between my legs. His throat bobs as he swallows, his eyes ablaze with so much unbridled lust and want, it makes me a little dizzy.

It also evokes a weird feeling of respect towards him because, my God, this guy has restraint.

He steadies himself with one hand braced against the wall, tenses arms ripping with veins, his legs trembling under the effort of keeping himself upright as he pumps himself slowly. *Erotic* is the only word I can think of to describe the sight before me. Hot as fuck, too. The fact that I can do this to him without even touching him... talk about an ego boost.

"Touch yourself, Luna."

He doesn't need to tell me twice. My fingers work greedily, two of them filling my needy pussy while the heel of my hand grinds against my clit, imagining Jackson touching me. Imagining me touching him, bringing him pleasure. It's not long before I'm on the edge, my words strained and whimpered, "I'm close."

"Wait," Jackson commands with a growl, pace quickening. His thumb swipes over the head of his cock, collecting the dripping wetness leaking out and making himself shudder, and I groan at the sight. "Fucking wait for me, Luna."

I cry out as my stomach clenches, the act of holding off my orgasm almost painful when I'm so close. I have no idea how long passes, hanging on the brink, before I hear a groaned, gravelly order. "Come."

The bathroom fills with our combined groans of pleasure as we come together. I watch him through hooded eyes, his movement jerky and frantic as he spills into his hand for what seems like forever, his eyes never leave me.

Chest heaving with panted breaths, I slump against the wall at my back, utterly sated as I let my tired eyes flutter shut.

Jesus.

The shower shuts off and footsteps approach, my eyes barely able to open halfway when hands land on my thighs, crawling upwards up they cup my cheeks.

Lips touch mine, the unhinged way he kisses me a stark contrast to the gentle way he cradles my face. His breath is warm and ragged against my skin as he buries his head in my neck, his groan just as rough. "Fuck me."

A lazy smile contorts my lips as I lace my hands around his neck. "Would if I could."

15

JACKSON

I THINK I might be in shock.

Having an out of body experience, maybe. Like I'm watching myself from a bird's eye view, my surroundings moving in slow motion. All because I can't quite believe I'm sitting in a diner booth with Luna Evans practically on my knee.

I know I'm staring but I can't stop. Everything she does, I follow with an eagle eye because I don't want to miss anything. Not her preferred hangover food order—a grilled cheese with a side of extra crispy bacon and enough hot sauce to kill a small child. Or the way she winces every time she sips the green smoothie her, Kate, and Amelia all reluctantly order. Or how she dithers over which kind of tea to get before muttering a 'fuck it' and ordering three.

Green, peppermint, and passionflower, all of which she made me try, all of which I swallowed with a fake smile because Jesus, herbal tea tastes like shit.

I want to make sure I remember it all because it happened too quickly, the past twelve or so hours. When I woke up this morning, I was half convinced I'd dreamt it. Fuck, when it was actually happening I had to pinch myself more than once.

I just... I can't believe it. Can't believe it happened. Can't believe *how* it happened. Can't believe it's *still* happening. Sure, I practically begged her to stay last night but she didn't have to. Luna doesn't strike me as someone who does something she doesn't want out of pity. And this morning, when a breakfast outing was proposed, it took no encouragement on my part for her to agree.

If she wanted to leave, she would've.

But she stayed.

And I'm choosing to take that at face value.

Doesn't mean I'm any less shocked by it, though.

I don't think my friends can wrap their heads around it either. God, the looks on their faces when I'd followed Luna downstairs this morning, when she'd plopped herself on my lap, casual as anything. I wish I'd had one of Nick's fancy cameras on hand to capture their blatant surprise.

"Blink twice if you're being held hostage," Ben had murmured to Luna in a dramatic whisper, while Cass asked if she'd got lost on the way to his room and Nick wondered aloud how devastated she must have been to be stuck with the runt of the litter.

But there was a moment, in the kitchen before we left when the girls were raiding our closets, where the guys swarmed me like a post-game celebratory huddle and filled ten, maybe fifteen, seconds with silly, boyish back-slapping and quiet cheering.

It's been hours and there's still a general air of disbelief, from my friends and hers. Very quickly, I picked up on the fact this isn't exactly usual behavior for Luna. More than once, I've caught Kate and Amelia looking at her like she's grown a second head, looking at me like they're trying to figure something out, but I don't mind. I'm not going to question it. I'm just going to enjoy it.

Besides, in her defense, I'm pretty sure I keep looking at Amelia the same way. Her being Cass' long lost sister who just so happens to be Nick's little crush—newly single, I should add, much to the delight of Luna—swiftly stole the prize of Most Unexpected Night from me.

It's a comforting distraction, seeing Nick as frazzled as me. He hides it better but if you know him, you can see it. Smiles less easy, quips less frequent, a too-hard set to chronically relaxed shoulders. Amelia's no better, and she hides it a lot worse. Sitting too straight, casting little looks Nick's way and immediately checking to see if Cass caught her looking.

It's because I'm watching them that I see the exact moment Amelia's entire demeanor changes, a second before heavy hands land on the table, dishes shaking with the force, and the girls on either side of me seem to simultaneously stiffen. "We need to talk."

It takes a second to recognize the guy looming over us. When I do, I swallow a groan. Freshman year, there was a mix-up with dorm assignments. Nick and Cass were meant to room together but somehow, they got split up. It worked out for me; I got Cass. Nick, however, got Dylan Wells.

I think Nick slept on the floor of our dorm more than he did in his own bed purely because he couldn't stand being in the same room as the guy.

But the hatred in my friend's gaze right now? A whole lot more than past roommate resentment.

I only met him a couple of times, and Cass never did, which is why he frowns and asks, "Who are you?"

"Her boyfriend."

A flurry of arguments erupt, a hostile air settling. I'm not entirely sure what's happening—he's a dick, they broke up last night, that's all I know—and I don't think it's a great time to ask. To get involved at all, really. I just try to keep the peace, try to stop Nick from leaping across the table and causing a bloody scene.

That is until Dylan turns his wrath on Luna.

"Luna," he seethes when she tells him to fuck off, and his tone alone has my guard up, "for once in your life, shut your mouth."

I'm halfway to standing before I know it. "Watch it."

A hand on my thigh shoves me back to sitting but despite the nails digging into my skin and the stern look burning a hole in my face, I don't relax until Dylan fucks off, Amelia unfortunately in tow.

Arm slung around Luna's shoulder, I squeeze her gently. "Sorry." When she crooks a brow in question, I quote her from last night, "you don't need help."

"I don't," she agrees. A hand slinks up my arm, dancing along my shoulder to cup the back of my neck, fingers toying with my hair. "It's pretty hot when you try, though."

Something in my chest warms. "That right, sweetheart?"

Luna hums, the noise brushing my lips a moment before hers do.

"*Sweetheart*, some of us are tryna eat."

Ben waves a hand in the air, dramatically shushing Kate. "Keep going, this is great breakfast entertainment."

Cass snorts. "This is a great intro for a condom ad."

"Ten bucks says they'll bang in the bathroom."

"Watch your mouth." Luna chucks a fry at Ben, a sharp elbow digging into my side. "He's a gentleman."

LUNA

I'm in a daze as I walk to class.

It's been twenty-four hours and I still feel like I'm floating.

Jackson's face, eyes dark and expression feral, consistently flashes through my mind, and it keeps making me smile. I look like a fucking freak gliding around campus with a big, dopey grin on my face.

I don't recognize myself. I'm not a girl who glides around post hook-up, giddy over a guy. And I'm not a clingy girl either but yesterday? The girls practically had to peel me off Jackson, only the allure of so much gossip—I've never been so proud as I was when I found out Amelia racked up a fucking novel's worth of drama in one itty bitty night—convincing me to part ways. I probably would've been happy curled up in his lap all day and that scares the ever-loving shit out of me.

As much as I want to blame it on being weakened by the multiple orgasms, I can't. I'd be lying.

I like Oscar Jackson and it's fucking terrifying.

Completely unexplored territory.

Everything about him, all the reasons I like him, are completely fucking new to me.

When I'm talking, he looks at me like he's actually listening. Like he's hanging on the edge of every word. Even when I'm silent, which makes zero fucking sense, I know, but it's true.

He doesn't make me feel so… *much*. I spend my entire day, my entire fucking life, searching for tiny snippets of calm just so I can catch my breath and boom, he appears, and it's all goes silent.

It doesn't make sense. I sure as hell don't like it, the concept of a man magically being the solution to my problems.

But that's just how it is.

That's just how I feel.

As I breeze into class, I try not to think about it for just a couple of hours.

Settling in my usual seat, I occupy my mind with firing up my laptop and doodling on my hand but that doesn't work for long. No matter how hard I try, I keep seeing him in my mind, keep feeling his fingers ghosting my skin. It gets to the point where I have to physically shake the thought of him off to clear my head.

I silently rejoice at the arrival of Pen but even that potential distraction doesn't last long. One look at me and she narrows her eyes. "You got laid."

My new friend is a sex psychic. Good to know.

"I did not." It's only half a lie. Technically, there was no laying involved. Just some good old fashioned... groping?

"Liar." Blue-green eyes pointedly flick to the telltale bruises on the base of my neck that apparently, my high-collared shirt does nothing to hide. "It was that guy, wasn't it?"

"What guy?"

My attempt at cluelessness is a monumental failure at which Pen scoffs. "The baseball player with all the hair."

"Jackson," I correct her, and even though I drop my head to hide the involuntary smile his name evokes, Pen catches it. She bats her lashes as she coos his name dramatically. I have to clamp my hand over her mouth to get her to stop.

"So?" She slaps me away, brows wiggling. "I take it he was good."

I take only the briefest of pauses before sighing. "Understatement."

"But you didn't have sex?"

"Nope." I kiss my teeth, still a little disgruntled about that part. "He wants to take me on a *date* first."

"Aw. A gentleman. Rare find," Pen muses, chewing on the back of her pen thoughtfully. Her gaze flits to the front of the room when Professor Jacobs noisily enters the room, and she pouts at the sight of her dad. "Damn it. I wanted details." Turning back to me, she pokes my arm. "I have a class after this but are you free for a late lunch?"

I nod my somewhat reluctant agreement just as the professor

starts talking and for the next hour, I just about manage to keep my mind out of the gutter and on world politics.

Barely.

I practically work up a sweat with the effort it takes. It's uncomfortable as hell, being all hot and bothered as I squirm in my seat, unable to do anything but sit and suffer.

Damn you, Oscar Jackson.

Grateful isn't the word for the emotion I feel when class finally ends and I can finally escape. Pen has to book it to her next class so she rushes out the door, shouting *'details!'* over her shoulder loud enough to draw stares.

I'm slinging my bag over my shoulder and silently cursing Pen's name when I hear my own name being called. When I turn around, I find Professor Jacobs beckoning me over. I frown as I approach him

"Is everything okay?" His question surprises me, even more so the genuine concern on his face.

"Uh," I fidget with the strap of my tote bag, "yeah?"

"You seem distracted today."

I hide my blush with an easy smile. "Everything is fine."

"Good." Jacobs nods, his tone and expression suddenly firm. "Make sure you pay attention in the future. Participation does contribute to part of your grade."

"Understood." And the real message is heard loud and clear too; don't lead my daughter astray.

Luckily, my phone ringing saves me from this godawful conversation.

"Sorry, I need to take this." I flash him an apologetic smile as I hold up my phone, *Ma* flashing across the screen.

He nods jerkily and waves me away, an indecipherable look on his face as he watches me leave.

Weird.

16

LUNA

I DON'T FREQUENT the library often. The quiet doesn't work for me, the people milling around distract me, and I can't blast my music obnoxiously loud like I can at home. But I needed to get out of the apartment and away from the non-stop sibling re-bonding session Cass and Amelia have been on for days. It's starting to get a little nauseating; as much as I love Cass' frequent angry, vivid threats against Dylan's life, there are only so many mushy childhood stories and sappy moments I can take.

So, I'm braving UCSV's draughty library that reeks of old books and mothballs just to escape all that healthy familiar love for a while, tucking myself in a quiet corner in an enormous leather armchair, my laptop propped on my lap and a list of readings to bang out. Or try to, at least. The couple across from me prove a particularly interesting distraction, what with being in the midst of a fantastically dramatic breakup.

I may or may not have purposely lowered the volume of my earphones just so I can eavesdrop. The girl is hurling some exceptionally creative insults at the guy, including colorful language I'm pretty sure is frowned upon being used in a library at a volume I'm definitely sure is frowned upon in a library.

I'm contemplating jotting down a few for future reference when my attention is abruptly torn away. A surprised gasp escapes me as a headphone is yanked from my ear. My head whips to the side, ready to hurl expletives at whoever's so rudely interrupted me but the words evaporate when I find Jackson crouching down beside me. "Hi."

A strange fluttering erupts in my stomach at the sight of him, a feeling that I shut down real fucking fast because I refuse to be a fluttery ditz who melts at surprise visits and single word greetings from pretty men. Though it's not easy with him smiling at me like that, all teeth and dimples and warm brown eyes.

"Uh, hi?" I remove my other earphone, forehead creased in a frown but a smile tugging at my lips. I'm surprised, sure, and slightly confused how he knew where I was, but it'd be a bare-faced lie to say I'm not happy to see him.

It's been three days, three minuscule, inconsequential days, since I last saw him but, fuck me, I felt the loss. Texted him pretty much every damn minute, did my fair share of reliving a certain round of events, yet I missed him.

I hate myself a little for it but I missed him.

And I hate *him* just a little when I lean in, lips puckered and intentions clear only to be bypassed. Instead, he kisses my cheek, and I don't quite manage to hold in my grumbled, indignant complaint. "What am I, your sister?"

"You'd like my sisters." Jackson snickers as he scoops my laptop off my lap, shuts it, and tucks it into the bag at my feet. "They're a little bratty too."

I scoff an offended noise, ripping my hand away when he tries to grab it. "*Rude.*"

Ignoring me, he rises, crooks an expectant brow. "Ready?"

"Ready for what?"

Swinging my tote over his shoulder, Jackson dials his smile up a notch until it's borderline blinding. "I'm collecting on that date you promised me."

It lasts a fraction of a second, my hesitation, but it's enough for Jackson to notice. He crouches again, in front of me this time, megawatt smile becoming nothing short of wicked as he smooths his hands up my thighs. "You need a reminder?"

Need a reminder? Nope—that experience is ingrained in my mind, probably for the rest of time, like a non-stop porny home movie reel.

Wanting a reminder, however, is a different story.

I don't admit that, though.

I do have a shred of self control.

"No," I lie, shucking away his hands so I can think a little clearer, "but I'm not dressed for a date."

Ripped jeans, a white tank, and a fuzzy pink cardigan aren't exactly what I envisioned wearing on my first date. I definitely imagined something with a little easier access. Jeans are cumbersome; too tight, too many buttons, too much material.

"We can swing by your place first."

I hum a non-answer, fidgeting with the ring on my finger as I try to come up with another excuse. It's not that I don't want to go. I'm just... nervous, I guess. Unsure what I'm in for, and I fucking *hate* being unsure. I've never exactly been wined and dined or whatever Jackson has planned before. I'm more of a hit and run kind of girl.

Knuckles graze my cheek before fingers comb through my hair until they reach the curve of my neck, holding firm. "Luna," he says my name low and slow, dragging out the two syllables. "I wasn't asking. Get your pretty little ass up and let's go."

Jackson doesn't wait for a response before hauling me to my feet. A good thing, too, because he probably wasn't going to get one; any and all words I try to speak die in my suddenly parched throat. He places a single chaste kiss on my lips, perfectly appropriate for a library, entirely too appropriate for my liking. I feel his self-satisfied smirk, and I nip at his bottom lip before he pulls away.

Smug bastard.

You know, there was a time I thought Jackson might've been a bit of a pushover. I blame the quiet, nice guy stereotype; they're notoriously easy to bend to your will.

A single real conversation with him changed my mind about that, and when I spend the entire ride to my apartment unsuccessfully grilling him for information, I learn how truly wrong I was.

I don't like it. Both being wrong and not being in-the-know. I like being right almost as much as I like being prepared.

And I can't exactly pick an appropriate outfit when I have no idea where we're going.

"It's dinner, right?" I insist for at least the third time.

For at least the third time, Jackson forgoes answering in favor of continuing to hum along to the music playing from the radio.

"Dinner and a movie," I say more to myself than him. "It's gotta be. I hear that's a classic first date."

"You hear?" Jackson side-eyes me, and suddenly it's my turn not to respond.

Shrugging, I lean forward to turn up the radio, hoping it will drown out the impending conversation.

Jackson turns it back down. "Luna, have you never been on a date before?"

For unfathomable, inconsequential reasons, heat assaults my cheeks. "Define *date*."

The man behind the wheel waits until we're safely parked outside my apartment building before shifting to face me, brows high and mouth agape. "How is that possible?"

I almost lie. I should lie. But that implies shame and my dating history, or lack thereof, is undoubtedly the least shameful thing about me. "No one's ever asked."

"I find that really hard to believe."

It's cute, the look of utter shock on Jackson's face. Good for a girl's ego. But the conversation is a little too serious for my liking, his line of questioning a little too curious.

So, I adopt a sly smirk and try to steer it elsewhere. "Guess it's just not where my skills lie."

My joke doesn't have the intended effect. The opposite, actually. It seems to piss Jackson off, his face falling. "Did someone say that to you?"

Say, no. *Imply*, once or twice.

"Relax." I give his thigh a placating pat. "I don't date because I don't want to. Even if someone did ask me, I'd say no."

"You said yes to me."

"I was under duress." I joke but my smile is soft. "Never wanted to say yes before."

Funny how rejecting a man has never felt quite as terrifying as accepting him did.

A hand palms the back of my head. "That was sweet."

"Sweet enough for you to tell me where we're going?"

Jackson laughs as he unbuckles his seatbelt. "Nope."

I follow him out of his truck with a huff, putting on my best brat act as I storm past him and upstairs, adding an extra sway to my hips and a bounce to my steps because use the tools the Lord gave you and all that.

A sense of deja vu washes over when the moment I unlock the front door and step inside my apartment, I'm pinned between solid wood and an even more solid body. I try to stare defiantly up at Jackson but my bravado falters when he thumbs my bottom lip.

"Sulking?" he croons, dark amusement painting his features. "Really?"

"It's a tried and true method of persuasion."

"Is the ass shaking also a method of persuasion?"

My hands creep up his chest, fisting the collar of his shirt. "It's working, isn't it?"

"Depends what you're trying to get, sweetheart."

The sound of a clearing throat causes us both to freeze.

"As riveting as this is, can you maybe take it behind closed doors? Live-action porn isn't really our thing."

Peering over Jackson's shoulder, I scowl at the two girls sprawled on the sofa. I brandish a middle finger at their grins. "Perverts."

"Exhibitionists," Amelia retorts.

"*Hypocrite.*" Only one of us had a half-naked drunken romp through the boys' house.

Kate rolls her eyes. "Children."

Amidst the bickering, Jackson stays silent. Stays exactly where he is, too. Now he knows we have company, he reverts to his quiet, borderline shy self. Body tense beneath my fingertips, a flush creeping up his neck, face twisted with embarrassment.

I stifle a laugh. Poor boy.

Gently, I push him towards the roommates suddenly deciding to behave and offering him welcoming smiles. Jackson shifts to lace our fingers together, maintaining a tight grip even when I direct him to the empty armchair. "You, wait here."

He flops into the chair obediently, if not a little hesitantly, and reluctantly releases me. Not before kissing my knuckles swiftly, murmuring against them, "yes, ma'am."

Hand tingling with the residual warmth of his lips, I shake it quickly before grabbing Kate and Amelia and yanking them to their feet. "You two, come with me." Before either of them can protest or ask questions, I drag them to my room, casting one last glance at Jackson perched in that ridiculously tiny chair before I slam the door behind me.

Kate flops down in the middle of my bed while Amelia perches on the edge, both shooting me questioning stares. "Where's the fire?"

Raking my sweaty hands over my thighs, I take a deep breath. "I'm going on a date."

"You're *what*?" If I wasn't so nervous, I'd laugh at my friends' comical reactions. Amelia's jaw hits the floor while Kate sits up so fast she almost knocks our tiny redhead right off the bed.

God, you'd think I'd just told them I was going to jail.

"Going on a date," I repeat, enunciating each word sarcastically slowly as though I'm talking to very small children.

"Like a real date?" Kate blinks. "With Jackson?"

"No, a fake one with my imaginary friend." I reach over to smack her upside the head. "*Yes*, a real date with Jackson."

"Are we on Punk'd? Is Ashton Kutcher hiding in your closet?"

"What happened to 'relationships in college are as pointless as a circle?'"

"Yeah!" Kate harrumphs, pointing an accusing finger my way. "Do I get to give you the Great Disappointment Speech now you're shacking up?"

They're kidding, I know they're kidding, yet against my will, my temper sparks. "What, is it really so unbelievable that a guy would want to take me out on a date?"

Immediately, my friends sober.

"Not at all," Amelia replies without hesitation, the shake of her head frantic. "It's more the fact you're *letting* a guy take you on a date."

Kate hums her agreement, a playful smile on her lips and a sing-song quality to her voice. "Jackson must be pretty special."

Yeah, I silently agree. *That's what I'm afraid of.*

I must be wearing my thoughts all over my face because, slow and careful, Amelia rises. "It's okay to be nervous," she says, gripping my biceps and squeezing. "Just means you like him."

She means well but I still, I grimace.

I like him but I don't want to like him because liking him is scary. Liking him means breaking down the perfect wall around my heart that I've been building for twenty years, specifically designed to ward off men like Jackson. Good men with the potential to destroy me completely.

Kate sighs and nudges Amelia out of the way, spinning me around by my shoulders and taking an entirely different approach. "You are Luna Evans." She shakes me slightly, her no-nonsense, narrow-eyed stare burning into me. "You are beautiful and smart and you make men go all weak at the knees. You don't get nervous. You make other people nervous. So snap out of it."

I can't help but smile. "You know, you're really good at pep talks."

"I know." Kate pats my cheek, equally parts playful and loving. "Now, let's get you ready for your first date, hm?"

17

LUNA

"IF YOU'RE PLANNING to murder me, you left two witnesses back at the apartment who know I'm with you."

Jackson laughs but rumbling down a dark dirt road in the middle of nowhere doesn't seem all that funny to me.

Nice, quiet boy murders the pretty, loud, loose blonde. Sounds like a true-crime podcast.

The hand resting on my thigh squeezes. "We're almost there."

I open my mouth to ask where, exactly, *there* is but I'm interrupted by the truck slowing. Jackson's intent gaze heats the side of my face as my lips part in surprise, eyes wide as they take in the field lit up by strings of twinkling lights casting a dim glow, just bright enough to make out the neat rows of cars stretching towards a giant screen lit up with an old-fashioned film reel countdown.

To be honest, I didn't know drive-in movies were still a thing. But I like it.

I really like it, and as I lace my fingers through Jackson's and turn to face him, I pray my huge grin conveys just how much. He hides his relieved smile by bringing our clasped hands to his lips, leaving them for a long moment as he steers the truck towards an empty spot. He parks in reverse and gestures for me to get out, leading me around to the back.

Undoing the tailgate, he clambers up, movements jerky and

nervous. "I got your cushions," he says, wearing a silly, nervous grin as he holds a hand out to me. "And blankets."

The lump in my throat stings as I swallow, my hand shaking as I take Jackson's hand and let him hoist me up. "I can see that."

I wish I couldn't. I might close my eyes to block the sight because who knew the sight of a truck bed could make a girl so emotional? It's not just pillows and blankets. There's a bag tucked in the corner, Sour Patch Kids and Warheads spilling over the top the same way they frequently spill out of the bottom drawer of my bedside table. A cooler sits beside it and when I crack the top, I find my favorite drinks lurking inside. The warm, fuzzy feeling in my chest officially turns to suspicion when my gaze snags on a brochure advertising tonight's movie and, surprise, surprise, it's my favorite.

I side-eye Jackson. "Who's the rat?"

"I don't reveal my sources."

"So secretive," I tut teasingly, but there's an edge to my voice even I recognize.

Clearing my throat, I adopt a smile that's probably just as awkwardly nervous as Jackson's and sit. He's quick to follow my lead, quicker to pull me closer, sharing his warmth. Always so damn warm.

Our closeness is jarring. Weird because we've certainly been a hell of a lot closer than this before but it's different. More… I don't know. Just *more*, and it gives me this weird plummeting feeling. Like I've been pushed out of a plane and I'm free falling. Like I'm completely out of my depth. I don't like it, not one bit, but I think that where Jackson's concerned, that feeling is never going to be far behind.

Nerves have me fiddling with the hem of my dress. When Jackson lays a blanket over my bare legs, I fiddle with that instead. I don't know how to act. I don't know what to say. God, who would've thought that the best way to get Luna Evans to shut up would be to bring her on a damn date?

I jolt when Jackson slips his hand under the blanket to grip my thigh. "Luna?"

"Hm?"

Warm breath brushes my temple. "I'm nervous too."

"I'm not *nervous*."

I feel his smirk against my skin. "Could've fooled me."

Reeling back, I narrow my eyes at him. "I think I liked you better when you didn't speak."

"I think you're full of shit."

"Wow." I draw back, feigning offense. "You're supposed to be *nice* on dates."

Lips lifted in a smile too cheek and endearing for me to handle, Jackson leans in until his forehead nudges mine. "How would you know?"

Screeching indignantly to drown out my bark of laughter, I shove at Jackson's chest. My attempt to push him away fails before it actually begins; catching me by the wrists, he lifts them to his mouth, his stifled laugh brushing the base of my thumbs as his lips do. "I'm sorry."

I wrench my hands away but I don't get very far, two of mine trapped between one of us and held hostage, clasped to his chest. "I feel like I've been duped," I huff, resigning to my fate and slumping against his side. "You were so sweet before. Is that your ploy? Put on the nice guy act long enough to get the girl?"

"Maybe I am just nice."

"Sounds fake."

"Didn't peg you for a cynic, Luna."

"I don't think a general distrust of men makes me cynical, Jackson."

I regret the words—no matter how true they may be—the minute they leave my mouth and something sad twists Jackson's features. "When I figure out how to earn your trust," he says, kissing my hands again, "I hope you'll let me."

No promises, I say internally, hating myself for it.

On the outside, even though I'm positive he sees right through it, I smile. "You can start by getting me a drink."

Jackson obliges, if a little hesitantly, as though he wants to say something else but thinks better of it. He drags the cooler over, digging inside to retrieve a peach-flavored Crush, and it's ridiculous, how gooey and warm I feel over a man knowing my favorite drink and going out of his way to get it.

The gooey warmness, though, takes a backseat to disgust when I catch sight of the flavor Jackson brandishes.

"Grapefruit?" I hiss, grimacing when he actually swallows the foul liquid. "The worst flavor? Seriously?"

The man has the *nerve* to look indignant. "It's my favorite."

I tut at him as I cradle my much more respectable peach beverage. "This might be a dealbreaker."

The raise of Jackson's brows is nothing short of a challenge. "Oh really?"

"Yup."

A scoffed breath caresses my cheek as he leans in close, his nose brushing mine, his lips hot against the corner of my mouth. My breath catches at the sudden proximity, my stomach fucking somersaulting as he smoothes a hand up my thigh, settling dangerously close to the crook of my hip. "Are you sure about that?"

"Ye-"

I don't get to finish my retort.

Lips capture mine, and I manage to hold off for all of ten pathetic seconds before I kiss him back, not even caring that he tastes like the cursed grapefruit Crush.

∼

I'm barely watching the movie.

I'm way too focused on the man nestled beside me.

At some point, we shifted. Huddled closer together. Me slouched between his legs with his chest warming my back, his big hands rubbing my bare arms and chasing away the cold of the night. His arms crossed over my chest and his chin resting on my shoulder, I'm completely surrounded by the man, and it's an odd yet wonderful thing.

I'd be lying if I said I wasn't a lover of physical touch. I'm all about skin-to-skin contact. I'm no stranger to casual affection.

Just not like this.

I can't recall a time in my life when I was held like *this*.

Gentle yet firm.

Comforting yet alarming.

Safe yet so very dangerous.

I can't tell if it makes it better or worse, how very aware he is of my... strife? Confusion? Complete and utter dating ineptitude?

Better, maybe, because whatever it is, he counters it all with nothing but comfort. A tight grip and murmured words of assurance, regular reminders that he feels just as out of his depth as I do. That he doesn't expect anything from me; he just wants me.

And it does help.

If *distracting* can be considered helping.

When wrapped up in arms like Jackson's, how's a girl supposed to focus on anything else?

The movie all but background noise, I shift to the side, tilting my head back to gaze up at him. "I have a question."

Not at all perturbed by the interruption, Jackson crooks a brow.

"What's your favorite color?"

"Blue."

"That's a disappointingly vague answer for an artist."

The corner of his mouth twitches. "You wanted an exact paint shade?"

I sigh, my eyes briefly closing in a feign moment of disappointment. "You're supposed to say something romantic. You know," I attempt a sorry imitation of his voice, *"light blue, like your eyes."*

Jackson's chuckle brushes my forehead a second before his lips do. "I use a color called Spun Sugar a lot," he says quietly. "It's pale cyan. That's my favorite."

Oh, do I hate just how well that line works.

Blinking in the hopes that'll dispel the fucking hearts swirling in my eyes, I fire another question at him. "Favorite song?"

"Hm." His head hits the cab window he's slumped against, his face scrunching up as he thinks. "I don't know."

I tut. "Another cop-out answer."

Fingers pinch my arm before slipping between us, fishing his phone out of his pocket. "Here." Unlocking it, he opens Spotify and drops it on my lap. "Check for yourself."

One scroll through the only playlist on there–probably the first and only red flag this boy has displayed–shows an eclectic music taste. A little bit of everything. Laughter bubbles up in my throat because when I say everything, I mean *everything*. "Big One Direction fan?"

Face deadpan, he says, "I have four younger sisters. I had no choice."

Four.

Jesus Christ. That's the whole gentleman thing explained. "Your mom must love having so many girls."

In an instant, I know I've fucked up somehow. Something heavy darkens the mood as Jackson tenses, his grip on me loosening just a bit, because I've done what I do best; put my big foot in my bigger mouth. "I'm sorry, I didn't mean to hit a nerve."

"It's okay." Jackson offers me a weak smile before clearing his throat. "She's not in the picture. Neither is my dad."

My mouth opens to comfort him, closing just as swiftly because comfort is not among my specialities and I don't actually know what to say. *'Sorry your parents left you. Hey, my dad left too?'*

Eloquent.

"Favorite food?" I meant to break the tension but God, I think I actually managed to make it a little worse.

Jackson's smile is sad. His eyes are sad. The slump of his fucking shoulders is sad.

"We lived in Boston for a little while and there was this really good Japanese restaurant near our house. My dad took me there when he visited once and I remember being so excited. He didn't get why. When he asked, I said because I'm Japanese, and he just kind of said... *Oh.* Like he'd forgotten. I thought he chose the place on purpose but apparently not."

"Is your favorite food the rat poison you feed to him or something?"

"No," he laughs, a decidedly unhappy noise. "It's the two hundred dollar ramen he let me order because he felt bad."

Never in my life have I wished to be someone well-versed in comfort yet here I am, twice in one night, pleading for just that. All I can think to offer is a brush of my lips against the bottom of his jaw, my hands sliding along his arms so I'm holding him instead of the opposite.

"One more question." I whisper. "How does a first date end?"

Jackson softens, eyes regaining that signature softness. "I bring you home."

"Do you come home with me?"

"Not tonight." Two words kill any inkling of hope. "I walk you to your door, kiss you goodnight, and leave."

"Like a gentleman?" I sigh when he nods, his laugh kickstarting my heart a beat. "But you're at least gonna go home and jack off thinking about me, right?"

He glances at me briefly, just long enough for me to see the wicked smile lighting up his face. "Oh, fuck yeah."

18

LUNA

PROFESSOR JACOBS NEEDN'T WORRY about me corrupting his daughter. Pen is plenty corrupt all on her own. She's a fucking menace. It's been two hours of thwarting her attempts to dance on the bar, confiscating her phone to stop her from drunk texting an ex, preventing her from seducing the scruffy bartender who reeks of weed. And trust me, a girl with tequila thrumming through her veins is no easy thing to wrangle.

I'm not used to this role of mothering friend who prevents others from making fools of themselves. *I'm* usually the drunken fool, Kate the responsible one, and after tonight, I have a newfound respect for my friend. This is *exhausting*.

I'm not saying I've been an angel all night; I've knocked back more than one cocktail and belted Nelly Furtado loud enough to draw glares. But I haven't attempted to put on a Burlesque show or accost any unworthy men like my pretty blonde friend, and I'm careful with my alcohol intake since I don't even really know where we are.

It's an off-campus bar, somewhere Pen frequents with her artsy, slightly pretentious film major friends. A dimly lit, kind of grungy place, all funky decor and overpriced cocktails consisting of liquor I can't pronounce. Lucky for me and my pitiful bank account, Pen insists on paying.

With her dad's credit card.

Because I'm the one who dragged you out, she claims but I know a little something about daddy issues, and tonight, she reeks of them.

"The film industry isn't a reliable career," Pen mimics her father's low baritone, her impression surprisingly accurate. Slumped across from me, she huffs in annoyance, her bangs flying out of place with the heavy breath. "It's so *frustrating.* I don't wanna be a stuffy old lawyer. No offense."

"Hey, I don't wanna be a stuffy old lawyer either." A young, hot, successful one is way more preferable. I think; I'm a little fuzzy on the whole career thing.

Amidst a myriad of grumbled complaints, Pen knocks back her umpteenth drink, slipping from the booth and searching for another the moment the glass is empty. I keep an eagle eye on her as she stumbles her way to the bar.

Only my phone buzzing in my pocket can distract me. It's embarrassing, how quickly I fish it out, how much I deflate when the text is from some random past hookup rather than the guy I actually want blowing up my phone.

It's pathetic, how attached I'm becoming to Jackson. We've talked every day since our date. Seen each other almost every day. I should have gotten my fill by now. Yet the temptation for more is so fucking strong, I can barely hold myself back. Hell, the main reason I came out tonight was to try to prove that I could survive one Jackson-less night. That I'm not completely and utterly under his paint-stained thumb.

As I squint at his contact indecisively, I realize I'm failing miserably.

To somewhat satisfy my Jackson craving, I read over the unanswered text he sent earlier today. The one asking what I'm doing tonight, which I ignored because I knew my weak self would've folded and invited him out in five seconds flat. I haven't gotten anything else from him since, so maybe he's not as itching to talk to me as I am him.

The decision is made for me when a loud, drunken cackle calls for my full attention. Dropping my phone on the table, I glance aside with a groan, already expecting the worst.

It's a welcome surprise when I find my friend not attempting to get topless on the bar. The two guys occupying her are a little less welcome. Pretty good looking guys. Very clean cut.

Not quite my type anymore.

Pen catches my eye and winks before sauntering over, new drinks in hand and new pals on her tail. I'm a little disgruntled, not entirely keen on being a third wheel or having to politely deflect any unwanted advances, but I push it aside, replacing my frown with a polite smile.

Pen introduces the guys as they slide into our booth, one beside Pen and the other next to me, but their names are forgotten within milliseconds. I zone out of their conversation almost immediately, choosing to occupy myself by playing with the straw of my too-sweet fruity drink, avoiding eye contact with my phone, and ignoring Pen and her guy drooling all over each other. I'm seconds away from creating an excuse to bail when a clearing throat catches my attention.

"Sorry for ruining your guys' night."

I eye the guy beside me. Aaron, I think Pen said his name was, looks as unhappy with the new arrangement as I am, and I find some comfort in that. "That's okay."

"You come here often?"

I can't help but laugh. "Was that a line?"

Possibly-Aaron cringes. "Bad?"

"Awful."

Maybe I'm going soft but I take pity on the guy. I indulge in his attempts at conversation and I quickly learn Definitely-Aaron is not all that bad. Sure, he throws the occasional flirtatious comment my way but when I evade them stealthily and politely, he retreats gracefully.

"I'm guessing you have a boyfriend?" At my questioning stare, he shrugs. "Either that or you're just really not interested in me."

"I have a…" I'm not sure what I have. A guy I went on one official date with but have spent almost every waking moment with for God knows how long? How do you describe that? How do you describe Oscar fucking Jackson in five words or less? I sure as hell don't know how to do it without ending up praising the boy to the high heavens for an hour like a blithering, lovesick fool. So, I improvise. "Something."

And that's enough, apparently.

From that point forward, Aaron is nothing but respectful. He doesn't try to hit on me again, and any awkwardness ebbs away until we're actually having a decent conversation.

Pen is taking the opposite approach. She's all over her guy, and he's all over her. A spark of jealousy ignites in my stomach, and I tap my nails against my phone case as if that will summon who I'd prefer to be hitting on me right now.

Get a fucking grip, Luna.

It takes all my willpower to turn the thing off and shove it in my bag.

Out of sight, hopefully out of mind.

"I think my brother and your sister might be in love."

Copying Aaron, I grimace at the couple suddenly sucking face across from me. "She's not my sister."

"Oh?" Aaron's brows rise, his expression genuinely surprised. "You look alike."

A snort escapes me. "Because we're both blonde?"

My new friend's expression is nothing short of guilty. "Maybe."

I'm fucking freezing.

Shivering outside the bar, my thin denim jacket does fuck all to ward off the cold seeping through the holes in my jeans. I could've gotten a ride with Pen and her new beau, but I wasn't willing to subject myself to any more of their fondling. Aaron offered to wait with me but I waved him off since my Uber was ten minutes away.

An inadvertent lie, *was* being the operative word. Twenty minutes later, my driver is in the exact same spot. A few more and I let out a huff of frustration when he cancels out of nowhere.

Cursing loudly, I turn on my heel with the intention of hiding inside while seeking a new ride but a voice more chilling than the wind stops me.

"Having trouble, princess?"

A scowl freezes my face before I even lay eyes on my least favorite asshole. His name tastes like battery acid as I spit it out, "Dylan."

"Miss me?"

"Like a hole in the head," I reply with false sweetness but

complete sincerity. Ignoring his beady, leery gaze as best I can, I shuffle toward the bar door, the handful of words I've wasted on him already too much for my liking.

"Hey, now." He steps in my way. "We're not done here."

"Yes, we are."

He tries to grab me but I see it coming, quickly stepping out of his reach. I know the damage those ugly hands can do, and I'll avoid them at all costs. Even if avoidance earns me anger, snark turning to cruelty as he snarls at me threateningly. "You ruined my relationship."

"You did that all on your own, dipshit."

Unsurprisingly, Dylan's skull is too thick for logic to pierce. "I was good to her and you turned her against me."

Yeah. Because being good to someone always includes cheating and abuse. "You're fucking delusional."

Dylan advances and I'm forced to retreat but I don't back down. I remain straight-backed and glaring because guys like Dylan get a kick of making others feel weak. Like they're less than them. Like he did to Amelia.

His expression shifts again, going from vicious to lewd as he clicks his tongue in annoyance, eyes perusing me slowly. Nausea coils in my stomach, disgusting and dirty, and I tug my jacket tighter around me, hating that there's a man alive who makes me wish I hadn't dressed so revealing.

"Does it ever get boring?" Dylan slurs. "Acting all high and fucking mighty like you're not just a worthless slut who throws herself at anything with a pulse?"

It's not the words themselves that hurt, it never is. It's the intent. The aim to hurt me. The implication that I'm doing something wrong, that I'm somehow less. But punch to the gut they may be, I don't react to his crude words because I know that's what he wants. I won't give him the satisfaction so I ignore the sting of the too-easy slander people are so quick to throw at me in a verbal brawl simply because I'm a woman who chooses to live however the fuck she wants.

He means nothing to me therefore his insults mean nothing to me.

Unfortunately, my lack of a reaction only seems to rile him up. His tone becomes more bitter, harsher, lewder, and his expression matches. "You know, I really try not to take it personally that I'm the only guy on campus you haven't fucked yet."

I balk.

Yet.

Try never.

Try would rather be skinned alive.

Try would rather never have sex again.

Dylan wrongly takes my disgusted silence as an invitation to shuffle closer. "We could change that."

"Eat shit, asshole." Done entertaining this conversation, I shoulder Dylan out the way with as much force as I can exude, flashing both middle fingers as I make a second attempt for the bar's front door. I'm almost home-free when an unwanted stinging pain spreads across my ass cheek.

When I whip around to find Dylan smirking, hand clenched like he's trying to preserve the feel of my skin, I lose it. Closing the distance between with a handful of furious steps, I slap the bastard across the face, hard, before shoving him away. "*Do not fucking touch me.*"

Dylan smirks, hands raised in sarcastic surrender, not the least bit fazed. "You let everyone else."

"Shut the fuck up," I snarl, shoving him again. "I am not Amelia. I don't protect people who don't deserve it so if you ever touch me again, I will sue your ass so fucking fast, your head will spin."

It's a lie. A bare-faced lie. I wouldn't sue him, would never report him, for the same reason Amelia didn't.

No one would believe us.

She's never said it aloud, but I know it's what stops her. She's scared of the backlash, the questioning, the doubt. The assholes who would undoubtedly ask if she deserved it, if she provoked him, if she's lying because he cheated on her and she wants revenge.

I hate that I share the same fear.

On the off chance Dylan is suddenly smart enough to sense my bullshit, I make myself scarce quickly, finally succeeding at escaping into the relative safety of the bar.

Five, ten, fifteen minutes pass before I stop watching the door.

With numb fingers, I fish out my phone, moving on autopilot as I scroll through the contacts. I don't realize who I'm calling until, after a lifetime of ringing, it connects.

"Luna?"

Jackson sounds... off. Tired, understandably because it's late, but there's something else. A lack of the usual stomach-clenching warmth that I've become way too used to.

That I really, really need right now.

"Hi." I cringe at my shaky voice, fiddling nervously with the ring on my finger. An anxiety ring, I think it's called. A thin gold band with moveable beads that I can slide around the metal when I get fidgety or overwhelmed. There's usually something weirdly soothing about the simple action, but it doesn't seem to be working right now.

Background noise seeps through the call, the buzz of a television and a few other grumbling voices, before a door closes and the only sound is Jackson's gruff, concerned voice. "Is everything okay?"

"Yeah." Even I can admit I don't sound convincing. Sucking in a deep breath that stings my lungs, I let it out on a ragged exhale. "No. Can you..." Another deep breath, almost painful, but that could be the ache in my chest. "Can you come get me?"

He doesn't hesitate for a second. "Where are you?"

~

I'm perched at the bar cradling the hot chocolate I coerced the bartender into making when a cold breeze caresses my back. A second later, a hand lands on my lower back, spreading warmth through my body. "Are you okay?"

"I'm fine." I grimace at how curt my reply is but it's instinctual.

The longer I waited, the more I regretted calling him. I feel like a fool. Embarrassed that I let Dylan get to me. Annoyed that I need a man to rescue me like some useless damsel in distress. Frustrated and confused that Jackson was the first person I wanted to call yet he didn't sound all too happy to hear from me. Even more annoyed that, out of everything, that's what I've been sitting here fixating on.

Calloused fingers grip my chin, gently directing my gaze to his. His expression startles me, warm and concerned yet guarded. Too distant, so unreadable. "What happened?"

I attempt a nonchalant shrug. "Just Dylan being Dylan."

Immediately, Jackson stiffens, a muscle in his jaw jumping. His eyes flit around my face, down my arms, over every visible piece of skin. "Did he touch you?"

"Just spewed bullshit as usual," I lie.

"But you're okay?"

"I'm okay."

The grip on my chin tightens almost imperceptibly before dropping. Without another word, Jackson shrugs off his jacket and lays it across my shoulders, cutting off my half-hearted protests with a single look. He holds a hand out to me, something about him warmer but still inexplicably off. Smiling weakly, I slip my hand into his and let him lead me outside.

The drive home is unbearably silent. I wrack my brain trying to figure out how the hell I've managed to screw up, what I've done to piss him off, but when we make it to my apartment, I'm still no closer to an answer.

I make no attempt to move. I don't want to go inside. The girls will know something is up immediately and I don't want them to, especially not Amelia, not when she's been doing so good lately.

My mouth opens and closes as I search for what to say, starting and discarding a dozen sentences before I finally manage to force something out, such a simple request somehow feeling like a mammoth task. "Can I stay with you tonight?"

As soon as I ask, I regret it.

Jackson hesitates, and it's like a slap to the face.

I immediately try to backtrack, shaking my head as I unclip my seatbelt and reach for the door handle. "Sorry, never mind, I don't know-"

Jackson cuts me off by reaching over me and batting my hands away, pulling the ajar door firmly shut. "Of course you can."

My fingers remain hovering over the handle, shoulders tense, body ready to bolt. "Are you-"

"Luna."

"Okay." I sink back into my seat, letting him clip my seatbelt back into place, trying to ignore the way he touches me as little as possible.

I hate this. This is not how car rides between us usually go. There's never distance. I'm always yanked as far as the seatbelt will let me go, one of his big hands wrapped around my thigh, every red light an excuse to kiss me, touch me, thread his fingers through my hair.

This tension is awful, even more so because I can't figure out what the hell is causing it. It only gets worse when we get to his house and I'm greeted by roommates who don't offer me anything more than a curt nod. Cass is absent, leaving just Nick and Ben. The former looks pissed as hell, his expression cold, and the latter avoids all eye contact instead of greeting me with his usual exuberance. I frown, hugging myself awkwardly and letting the smell of Jackson's jacket comfort me, and avert my gaze to the floor as I follow Jackson up to his room.

He's quiet as he gathers up clothes and sets them on the bed, murmuring for me to change before he moves to go back downstairs. I step in his way before he can, my confusion and frustration reaching a tipping point. "What's with the cold shoulder?"

Jackson shifts on his feet. "I don't know what you mean."

"It's like a fucking tundra in here."

Jackson kisses his teeth, looking equal parts guilty and annoyed and something else. I don't like this, not being able to read him, not knowing what's going on. It makes me feel insecure and silly and small, three things I pride myself on not being. "Did I do something?"

I take Jackson's sigh as a yes. He leans against his dresser and folds his arms across his chest, staring at me for one excruciatingly long moment before sighing again. "I told you I don't play games, Luna. If you don't want to do this, I need you to tell me, okay?"

I gape at him like a fucking fish, feeling like I'm missing a giant slab of information, a vital piece of a puzzle. My hands hover in mid-air, half reaching for him, half held up in some kind of surrender. "I'm confused."

"So am I," he exclaims in exasperation, running his hands through his hair before they come to rest at the crown of his head. As he leans back to stare at the ceiling, I try not to stare at the sliver of toned, tanned stomach revealed by his raised arms. I try to patiently wait for him to speak again but God, is it an itchy lifetime before he blows out a deep breath and locks gazes with me again. "Were you on a date tonight?"

"*What?*" A scoff leaves me as I gawk at him. "No! Why would you think that?"

He averts his gaze, choosing to stare at the wall behind my head.

"I saw some stuff. I swear to God I wasn't stalking you or anything, Cass follows that Pen girl and saw some of her posts and he sent them to me."

"What posts?" I ask, already pulling out my phone and opening up Pen's Instagram, momentarily confused because the first thing I see is a picture of me and Pen with the caption '*date night*', and surely that's not what he's talking about.

But as I click through the rest of her stories, my face twists in a grimace.

Okay. Yeah. I get it.

Most of the many, many pictures and videos littering my friend's social media are of me and her. Or her and that guy. But in some of them, I'm with Aaron. Laughing, talking, joking around. In one, he's got his arm slung across the back of my seat as he leans in to whisper something in my ear, and it looks like I'm laughing my ass off at whatever he's saying, although it's way more likely I'm giggling at Pen.

Yeah, that could definitely be misinterpreted.

Pocketing my phone, I look at Jackson with a pleading panic. "I promise, it's not what it looks like. Pen and I were at a bar, that guy started hitting on Pen, I was left talking to the wingman. *Just talking*."

The more I explain, the more his shoulder deflate until he drops his head almost shamefully. He glances up at me through eyes squinted with embarrassment. "Oh."

"*Yeah*." In his defense, it does look bad. If the situation was reversed, I'd react the same. No, I'd react worse. I would've been at that bar within the hour, dressed to the nines and ready to shove all my hotness in his face. I certainly wouldn't have sat at home quietly and let it happen.

"Fuck, Luna, I'm sorry."

"It's okay. A little dramatic but okay."

With a hoarse chuckle, Jackson eliminates the space between, fingers hooking through the belt loops of my jeans, his forehead nudging mine with too light of a touch for my liking. "I don't share," he reminds me, breath hot and words heavy, "I get jealous when I think the woman I like is on a date with someone else, especially when she's been ignoring me all day." A guilty grimace twists my face for a moment before he wipes my expression clean with a swipe of his thumb against my bottom lip. "I get jealous and annoyed and a little upset, and the guys are assholes but they're loyal assholes so they do whatever they just did. I'm sorry we jumped to conclusions."

"You were jealous," I repeat, frowning when he nods. "But you still came to get me when I called?"

"Of course I did."

"Why?"

For the first time tonight, Jackson touches me properly, not just a featherlight, fleeting brush, and the sigh of relief that leaves me is downright embarrassing. Smoothing my hair back, he cups my face with his hands and leans forward until we're sharing air, his breath tickling my lips and his gaze searching for something within mine. "I can't tell if you're purposely being difficult or if you really just don't know what it feels like to be liked."

Probably a bit of both.

"You came because you like me."

A small smile tugs at his lips, his nose gently brushing mine. "Atta girl."

God, I feel ridiculously out of my depth. The way he looks at me, reacts to me, talks to me... It's rattling. Overwhelming. I'm not sure if I like it, but I know I like him and I can't keep almost ruining shit.

Clutching at his wrist, I explain that as best I can. "I've never-" *Had a healthy relationship that wasn't platonic*, I finish silently. "I don't know how to do this."

"I know," he whispers softly, thumb stroking my cheek. "We'll take it slow. Whatever you're comfortable with." He kisses my knuckles lightly, smiling against my skin. "How about we start with just dating? Exclusively."

"I'm comfortable with exclusive," I croak out. More than comfortable. The thought of him going out with or flirting with or even touching another girl makes me a little fucking rabid, actually.

Jackson's answering smile is utterly satisfied, just shy of smug. His grip shifts downwards, one large hand swallowing my neck and tilting my head upwards. I don't get any warning before his lips meet mine with surprising force, drawing a gasp out of me that he takes full advantage of by plunging his tongue into my mouth. It's quick and breathtaking and a little fucking depraved, all clashing lips, teeth, tongues.

When he pulls away after way too short a time, he squeezes my side, fingers digging into the layers of clothes separating me from him. With a groan, he tears himself away from me and heads for the door, leaving me panting in the middle of his room. "Where are you going?"

"Just need to talk to the guys for a second." He pauses at the door and glances over his shoulder, jerking his head towards the bed. "I want you in that bed when I get back."

"Naked?" I grin as his jaw tightens. Rolling my eyes, I sarcastically salute him and shrug off his jacket. "Yes, sir."

Dark eyes gleam, and I half expect Jackson to stalk across the room and kiss me again. But, much to my disappointment, he slips out the door, leaving the door cracked behind him as he disappears downstairs.

A better woman would ignore the low voices drifting upstairs.

I eavesdrop shamelessly.

"Her date didn't pan out?" Nick quips dryly, something undeniably protective softening his snarky tone.

"Cut the attitude." Jackson's stern tone sends a shiver up my spine and God, isn't it a little sick that I wish he was using it on me? "She wasn't on a date, she was with a friend. Not that it's any of your business. Or mine," he grumbles the latter, regret tainting his tone.

The rest of the conversation isn't clear but the reaction to Dylan's murmured name is unmissable. Snarled curses erupt immediately, and I pick out Ben asking if I'm okay, Nick asking if Amelia is, both questions making me smile.

When their voices quieten and footsteps creep my way, I don't linger any longer. I make quick work out of changing into a spare tee and boxers before burrowing under the covers. Only minutes later, warmth engulfs me, an arm encircling my waist as a woodsy scent wafts over me.

I snuggle back into Jackson, sliding my hand into his where it rests on my stomach. Lips press against the spot just below my ear. "Do you want to talk about what happened?"

"No, I really don't." I squeeze his suddenly very tense hand. "It wasn't a big deal. I'm okay, I promise."

Jackson says nothing, just buries his head in the crook of my neck, the arm trapped underneath me curling upwards to lock across my chest and hold me as close as possible.

The sound of steady breathing lulls me to almost-sleep quickly. Just before sleep overcomes me completely, I hear him whisper my name softly. When I hum sleepily in response, his grip on me tightens as his lips kiss my neck.

"You can always call me."

19

JACKSON

I CAN'T STOP TOUCHING her.

Her soft hair, the slender nape of her neck, the dip in her waist. Everything and anything. I've never considered myself a particularly touchy-feely person but I can't get enough of her. I think it has something to do with the fact I can't quite believe that I *can* touch her all the time. That she wants me to.

I get to draw her too. I could draw her all day, and some days I damn near do; one flick through my sketchbook would convince anyone I'm a stalker. Luna doesn't mind, though. In fact, she encourages it. She likes being 'my muse' as she so graciously dubs herself. Not that I care.

She can call herself whatever the hell she wants if the word 'my' sits before it.

'My girlfriend' would be preferable.

But baby steps.

Even right now, when I'm supposed to be studying, I couldn't resist ditching my textbooks in exchange for my sketchbook. Something about her stretched out at the foot of my bed, typing rapidly on her laptop, hair spilling out a messy bun, and glasses I didn't even know she wore until a couple days ago perched on her nose, have my fingers itching for a pencil and paper.

I could sit here all day, perfectly content drawing quietly, if whatever she's smashing away at didn't have her growing increasingly frustrated.

She keeps messing with her fingers, that's her tell. Twisting her ring, bending her pinkies back in some freaky contortionist move, pressing down on her thumbnails.

When I coast my free hand up and down her bare leg in an effort to get her attention, she kicks me away, the crease between her forehead intensifying. I call her name softly and she doesn't even glance up, her glasses crooked as she scrunches her nose in concentration. Tossing my sketchbook to the side, I wrap my fingers around the ankle closest to me and squeeze.

Nothing.

"Luna." She waves me off with a flick of her fingers. "*Luna.*"

Irritated blue eyes meet mine. "What?"

The snapped word trails off in a surprised yelp when I tighten my grip and yank her toward me. Carefully setting her laptop out of harm's way, I scoop her onto my lap. She screeches and claws at me, complaining about needing to finish something, and the only way to shut her up?

Pressing my lips against hers.

I can't help but smirk when Luna instantly relaxes, becoming a ragdoll in my lap. I keep it slow and sweet, much to her disappointment. When I pull away and she whines in protest, I reprimand her by snapping the waistband of her leggings. "What's up with you?"

"Nothing." Just like that, she hardens again. Crossing her arms over her chest, pouting like a child, fingers wildly tapping against her forearms. "I'm trying to work."

My hands close over hers to halt the fidgeting. "You're all twitchy."

Her cheeks flush as she drops her gaze, squirming in my lap. I stifle a groan as her ass continuously brushes against my crotch—intentionally, I bet—and I grip her hips to stop the fucking wriggling. "Tell me what's wrong."

She doesn't. She won't even look at me. Ironic, considering the hell she gave me over eye contact, or lack thereof. Still does, actually; my inability to hold her gaze is her favorite thing to tease me about.

Twirling her hair around my fist and tugging, I force her gaze upwards and give her an *'I know you're full of shit so you might as well spill'* look.

With an indignant sigh, she drops her arms. The muscles in my stomach clench as her fingers find the hem of my t-shirt, brushing my skin as she fiddles with the fabric. "I'm just having a bad day."

"Care to elaborate?"

No, apparently. Luna remains silent as she casts a wistful glance at her laptop. Funny, considering she looked like she wanted to snap the thing in half about five minutes ago.

"Did something happen?" I prompt gently. She shakes her head. "Is it class?" She shakes her head again. "I can guess all day, sweetheart, if you make me."

"I'm not *making* you do anything," she retorts, that signature bratty lilt to her voice.

Unimpressed, I yank her hair again, harder this time. A little shiver wracks her as she crosses her arms again, then uncrosses them and starts twisting that damn ring. When she mumbles something inaudible under her breath, I squeeze her gently. "Speak up, sweetheart."

She scowls at me but it's half-hearted. A beat passes before she repeats herself, barely loud enough for me to hear. "I didn't take my medication this morning."

I pause, making sure my tone is clear and even, before asking, "Medication?"

"I stayed here last night, obviously, and I forgot to bring it."

"You didn't take your medication because you stayed here last night," I repeat slowly, the revelation tasting sour on my tongue. "If you needed to go home, you could've told me."

"It's not a big deal."

"Yes, it is. You can't just skip a dose." I don't know what she takes, but I'm pretty sure nothing allows for a skipped dosage.

Luna bristles, her scowl turning a touch fiercer. "Sorry, *doctor*, when did you get your medical degree?"

"Stop picking a fight."

"Stop acting like I'm incompetent."

I take three long seconds to breathe before saying, "I'm not fighting with you." When she tries to argue, I cut her off. "Shut up before you piss me off, Luna."

Pink lips clamp shut immediately. Strong thighs tense around me, a very different kind of intensity clouding blue eyes. I look away before I get too lost, too distracted. Standing with Luna still wrapped around me, I ignore her squeals of protest as I set her down. Stepping away, I grab my keys off the nightstand, simultaneously tossing her shoes at her. "Let's go."

"Go where?"

"To get your meds."

"We don't have to-" The look I give her puts an immediate end to her weak protest. Without another word but with plenty pouting, she follows me downstairs.

It's not until we're in my car and speeding towards her apartment that she says, quiet and unnervingly meek. "They're for ADHD."

"What?"

"My medication," she repeats, gaze downcast. "It's for my ADHD."

"Oh." I frown as I mentally run through everything I know about the disorder. Not much, and there's a good chance what I do know is rooted in some kind of stereotype. As we pull up outside Luna's place, I make a mental note to research it later. "I had no idea."

"I don't make a habit of telling people." Something about her snarky tone has me suspecting there's a story there, a reason why she made an effort not to tell me. When I glance at her, my suspicion grows. She looks almost embarrassed as she studies my expression, recoiled slightly like she's bracing for something.

Curling my hand around the back of her neck, I massage the tense muscles there. "Anything I can do to help?"

Her forehead creases to match mine, lips parting in a perfect little 'o', and I swear surprise crosses her features. It takes a minute for her to respond, shaking her head slowly.

"You want me to come up?" She shakes her head again, still looking at me weirdly as she gets out of the car and sprints up to her apartment. Barely five minutes pass before she's back beside me, a bag in hand indicating she's staying over again tonight.

I duck my head to hide a smile. I like that she didn't ask, just decided. It means she's comfortable.

Starting the car and peeling away from the sidewalk, I drive with no real destination. Somewhere with food, maybe. It's probably not good to take meds on an empty stomach, and I know damn well she hasn't eaten since breakfast. A meagre breakfast too, considering the food situation in my house is pretty dire.

One hand taps a random melody against the steering wheel, the other resituating itself cupping the back of her neck. "You have a lot of bad days?" I pose the question carefully, not sure if I'm prying. It's clear this isn't something she feels comfortable talking about, but I don't want to just brush over it and have her thinking I don't care.

Luna huffs, bristling. "You mean do I skip my meds a lot?"

I shoot her a look.

Leaning back into my grip, she mutters an apology under her breath. "Not really. It gets worse when I'm stressed or tired or forget my meds. Which I rarely do," she adds the latter in a grumbled rush. "Today's just a combination of all three."

"You're stressed?"

"A little."

"Because of me?" The question comes out before I can stop it. "Because of the thing the other night," I clarify with a wince. I still feel guilty about that, jumping to conclusions and making assumptions like an asshole. And the whole exclusive thing, maybe I pushed too hard. Shoved her into a corner she felt like she couldn't get out of so she agreed.

A pinch to the skin between my index finger and thumb jolts me out of a panic spiral. "No, dummy. Class is stressing me out, not you. The tired thing, though, that is your fault."

I grit my teeth to hide a shit-eating grin.

In my defense, she kept me up last night just as much as I did her.

I intend to retort that but something in my wing mirror catches my eye. At the sight of a familiar building, an idea springs to mind. "You know what I do to relieve stress?"

With a cheeky smile, Luna quirks a suggestive brow.

I roll my eyes. "Not that."

Luna pouts, her shoulders slumping in exaggerated disappointment. "Then what?"

"Just trust me."

"I look ridiculous!"

She doesn't.

She really doesn't.

I don't think a universe exists where Luna Evans could ever look anything other than perfect.

Even with a too-big helmet hiding her pretty face.

I can't decide what I like best; the grey leggings slick against her legs accentuating her ass or the Sun Valley Rays hoodie swamping her lithe body with my number on it or the way she's wielding a baseball bat, fingers wrapped tight around the handle as she swings it testingly through the air.

She looks like a less unhinged but just as hot Harley Quinn.

"Come on!" She calls across to where I stand beside the pitching machine, the remote in my hand poised and ready to fire baseballs at her. She's swinging that bat and posturing around like she knows exactly what she's doing despite the fact we both know damn well that she's never played a day in her life. I tried to coach her a little only for her to laugh tauntingly. "How hard can it be? Ben does it."

I snort; I see her point but Ben is a clumsy fool everywhere but on the field. Luna would probably keel over in shock if she ever saw him play.

"Ready?" I double-check, my caring caution earning a dramatic eye roll in response. Shaking my head and saying a silent prayer, I press a button on the remote and let a baseball fly out.

The whooshing sound of it leaving the machine is drowned out by Luna's piercing shriek of surprise. "What the fuck?" Dropping the bat, she scuttles backwards as the ball whizzes past her, pinning me with daggers. "Are you tryna kill me?"

Drama queen.

"How hard can it be?" I yell back, mimicking her overconfident tone.

She scowls and picks up the bat again, brandishing it at me threateningly. "I didn't think it would be that fast."

Ignoring her whining, I cross my arms and stifle the urge to roll my eyes again. "Go again."

"Does it have a slower setting?"

"*Luna.*"

"Alright, alright," she grumbles, setting her shoulders back and gritting her teeth as she gestures for me to release another baseball. I do, and when the exact same thing happens, I can't hold in my laughter. Her screech is damn near ear-shattering as she flails her arms exaggeratedly. "I thought you liked me!"

Taking pity on her, I pocket the machine remote and jog her way. Positioning myself behind her, I settle a hand on her lower back, the other between her shoulder blades. "First of all, your posture is godawful."

She glances at me over her shoulder, an exaggerated simper on her face. "You say the sweetest things to me."

Ignoring her sarcasm, I grip the cage of her helmet and force her gaze forward again. Kicking her feet further apart, I settle a hand on her shoulder and push down gently until her knees are slightly bent, not too much, just enough. As my fingers skirt down her arms to adjust her grip, she leans back with a soft sigh that I'm almost sure is accidental, wiggling her ass against me in a move that I'm absolutely sure is purposeful. I guide her though a couple of swings, first with my hands covering hers, then with them on her hips, murmuring corrections under my breath.

The third time, I step back and watch her, nodding in approval. "Try again," I call over my shoulder as I jog back to the pitching machine. "Keep your eyes on the ball this time."

This time when a baseball comes flying her way, Luna doesn't flinch. Instead, she swings with confidence, and a loud cracking sound rings through the air as ball and bat connect. Squealing, she drops the bat and bounces toward me, throwing herself in my arms with the excitement of a player who just won the MLB World Series. "I did it!"

I wrap my arms around her, probably smiling just as wide as she is because what the fuck else am I supposed to do when a beautiful, happy woman chucks herself in my arms? "That was good, sweetheart."

"Better than Ben?"

"Could steal his spot on the team out from under him."

Luna scoffs and slaps me upside the head for my sarcasm but she's beaming. Fucking beaming. Beaming and blushing and so fucking beautiful. So horrendously out of my league that I'm not quite sure how I managed to get myself in this position. I'm not going to question it, though. I'm going to hang onto her for as long as she'll let me.

Not literally, though. We look weird as fuck right now, hanging off each other in the middle of the batting cages, and the looks we're garnering are making me want to bury my face in her neck and hide. I allow myself one more moment with her wrapped around me, smothered in her sweet, vanilla scent before dropping her carefully to her feet and nudging her back towards the dropped bat, slapping her ass when she pouts. "Again."

With a wink and a mock salute, she croons, "Yes, Coach."

20

JACKSON

It's pitch black outside by the time we leave the batting cages.

I have to drag Luna out of the place. My little perfectionist was reluctant to leave until she aced her swing, and I wasn't complaining because, shit, she looked damn hot doing it. Only when the employees start shooting me pleading eyes, silently begging me to let them close up and get home, do I force the bat out of her hands and corral her outside.

Her voice carries across the empty parking lot, her excited chatter as warm as her hand in mine as we stroll to my car parked in the furthest, darkest corner. An almost painful smile splits my face at how much she enjoyed something I do, something that's a pretty major part of me.

"Next time, I'm teaching you how to pitch," I tell her as I open the passenger door for her, waiting for her to slide in before jogging around and getting in the driver's side.

Luna's head lolls towards me, smile distorted by her cheek smushed against the headrest, gaze soft and genuine. "I'd like that."

I'm not sure who leans in first.

Probably me.

I just know that one moment I'm staring at her, wondering how the fuck I got so lucky, and the next, blue eyes are reeling me in like there's an invisible string tugging me closer. We meet in the middle, a clash of soft, smiling lips and warm skin.

She's playful tonight. Nipping at my bottom lip, chasing my tongue with hers, gripping my wrists in an effort to keep me at arm's length when I cup her face, stopping me from taking control.

It's a constant battle for control between us, one that I'm determined to win, one that I will win because when I let myself imagine this girl, submissive and willing...

Fuck. Mindblowing.

A gasp escapes her as my tongue lashes against hers, a sound that quickly dissolves into a moan when I bracket her throat and dip her head back for better access. Just like that, she's putty in my hands.

Her squeal rings in my ears as I haul her onto my lap, my shirt bunched in her hands as she steadies herself. Even without the halo and the wings, she's a fucking angel perched on my lap, hair wild and eyes hungry. I waste no time in reattaching our lips purely because I don't have the self-control to not do so. The hand not wrapped around her neck blindly searches for the switch that slides my seat backwards, giving us more room, and avoiding the possibility of Luna's ass jamming against the horn and accidentally drawing more attention than the rapidly fogging windows probably already are.

When we're horizontal, her chest flush against mine and her long legs folded on either side of my thighs, I grasp her ass and push her hips even closer to mine, not wanting a single speck of distance between us, groaning as the heat between her thighs bleeds through our clothes. *Too many clothes*, the devil on my shoulder insists.

In one swift movement, I yank her hoodie up and the straps of her tank, tossing the former somewhere in the backset so I can properly worship the bare tits revealed. Eagerly, I suck a pretty pink nipple into my mouth, lashing and laving at it with my tongue. Her little whimper when I tug it between my teeth sends a rush of heat to my cock, her hands tugging my hair harshly having the same effect.

We groan in unison as her ass grinds against my jean-covered cock, straining uncomfortably in an attempt to bury itself where it wants to be—pure fucking heaven, I just know it.

If her wild grinding is anything to go by, Luna wants the same thing.

Her head falls back as a blissed-out whimper escapes her, depriving me of seeing her face twisted in pleasure but I'm too distracted by her tits to care. Fuck, they look good in those lacy bras she loves but they look even better like this, completely bare to me. So fucking soft and supple and sensitive.

So fucking sensitive.

I bet I could get her off just from nipple play alone. I'm sure as fuck going to try. Not right now, though. Right now, I want to, no, need to, see her face as she comes, to feel her unravel around my fingers.

Releasing her nipple with a pop, I shove her backwards just enough to yank her top all the way off. Her leggings are harder to shed, too tight and not enough room for her to wriggle out of them. Frustrated and impatient, I grasp the seam between my fingers and pull.

Luna gasps and squeals my name as the fabric rips. "Jackson! Those were-*fuck*." Her protests trail off in a stuttered moan, pretty blue eyes rolling to the back of her head as I slip my hand inside her panties.

"What was that?" I taunt, grazing my teeth against her jaw at the same time I graze her clit lightly.

Her reply comes out as a choked gasp. "Nothing."

"No?" Wetness soaks my fingers as I pinch her clit, her body spasming and writhing on top of me. "Could've sworn you said something."

"Nope," she gasps. "Fuck, keep doing that."

Smirking against her neck, I give Luna no warning before ripping her panties off too and spearing her quickly with two thick fingers, instantly welcomed by dripping, warm heat. Desperate cries leave swollen lips as her pussy clamps around me, her hips resuming their erratic grinding. Nails biting into my biceps, her head drops to my shoulder, her breath hot and ragged against my skin.

"Good girl," I rasp, smashing the heel of my palm against her clit. "Ride my fingers, sweetheart."

She does as I say, bucking wildly against me, using me for her pleasure. I drive my fingers upwards, scissoring them inside of her until her entire body is shaking. Her wanton cries are like music to my ears, a particularly loud one almost deafening me when I slide a third finger inside her and she goes *feral*, coming violently and soaking my hand.

I don't stop. I couldn't stop if I wanted to because my hand is doing that thing it does, disconnecting and gaining a mind of their own, except this is so much fucking better than mindless sketching. My sole goal is bringing Luna pleasure, and it doesn't take long to achieve that again, her second orgasm just as violent and dizzying as the first. She takes longer to recover this time, body twitching, head lolling, yet hips still rolling as she fucks herself slowly.

"I want more," she whines breathlessly, pleadingly, her hand purposefully grazing the front of my jeans and making my head swim.

My movements grind to a halt.

I take a good look at my girl, and God, is she a sight. Flushed cheeks, lips puffy and abused, blue eyes hooded but bright. Nipples puffy and tender, wetness coating the apex of her thighs, body marked red from my hands and teeth. A literal wet dream spread open and begging in my lap.

Actual perfection that I reject again. "I'm not having sex with you for the first time in a car."

"Aw," she croons breathily, hips still grinding and trying to coax me into moving, "you want it to be special?"

Kissing my teeth at her attitude, I yank her face forward at the same time I drive three fingers further inside her. "There's not enough room for me to fuck you properly in here."

Her eyes roll to the back of her head, her pussy squeezing with a vice-like grip as I work her slowly. She's so fucking wet and sensitive, it doesn't take long to get her where I want her. The moment I feel her climbing towards her peak, I still.

I pull out of her slowly, smirking when I feel her clamping in an effort to keep me inside her, and bring my fingers to my mouth, taking my sweet time licking the glistening wetness off my fingers as she watches.

So fucking good.

Shifting my grip to her chin, I thumb that bee-stung bottom lip. "I don't want you here. I want you naked in my bed, wet and begging for me all night long. I'm gonna fuck you so hard you won't be able to move without thinking of me for days. I wanna ruin you, Luna, and I can't do that here."

∿

She goes frighteningly still.

Her jaw drops as she gapes at me, and I momentarily wonder if I've gone too far. I start to apologize, silently cursing myself for getting carried away, but I'm cut off with a searing kiss. Suddenly, it's my turn to fucking melt.

Her kiss is more frantic than it was a moment ago, more urgent. She pulls apart from me just long enough to hurriedly yank my shirt over my head, dainty fingers grazing my skin and igniting a fire wherever they touch. Her gaze is scorching as she rakes it over my torso, and I silently thank Coach Kelly for all those obligatory workout sessions.

Luna's tongue and hands wander in tandem, the latter toying with the zip of my jeans. It takes a monumental amount of self control to grab her wrist and stop her. A little self preservation too because I'm so fucking hard that I have a feeling one brush of her fingers will be enough to have coming. God, one *look* from her would probably be enough at this point. "What're you doing?"

She sits back on my thighs, giving me a perfect fucking view of her naked body, a combination of mischief and want glittering in her eyes. "Trust me?"

Slowly, skeptically, a little because I'm intrigued and a lot because I'm a weak man around her, I release her. I let her unzip my jeans, flexing my hips so she can drag them down enough to reveal the tent in my boxers, the fabric so strained I'm convinced it's about to rip.

Sinking her teeth into her bottom lip, Luna scoots forward and lowers herself down, rolling her hips against mine and drawing a groan out of me. The only thing between us is the thin material of my boxers, and that might as well be nothing. I feel every bit of her wet warmth, her clit pulsing as she drags it along my cock. Her breath hitches as she repeats her movements, harder and closer this time.

She drops her head to my shoulder, kissing her way up my neck and catching my earlobe between her teeth, the dangerous lilt in her voice promising all kinds of dirty things. "Is this allowed? Technically, I'm not touching you."

A strangled laugh strains my throat. I answer by gripping her hips tightly and flexing mine up to meet her. We're both wound equally tight, both chasing the same high. My hips pump to meet the roll of hers, every slide and bounce and moan making my stomach tense and my balls tighten.

A voice in the back of my head urges me to shed my boxers and bury myself inside her, but I don't. Not yet. I don't think she's ready for that, for the commitment that'll come with.

We're dry humping like a couple of fucking teenagers, so it seems fitting that I come in my boxers like a teenager too, groaning as I explode, closing my eyes and imagining it's her tight pussy that I'm filling up with my cum. She's not far behind, shuddering and shaking, the sounds leaving her easily classed as heavenly.

A little fucking lightheaded, I struggle to regulate my breathing. I wasn't even inside her and I came harder than I have in my life. And just the thought of being inside of her has my cock hardening again.

Blinking a couple times to clear the blurriness still lingering at the edge of my vision, I glance down at the limp, naked body curled around me. It's amazing, fascinating even, how she goes from this sex confident, erotic seductress to this adorable cuddly girl clinging to me, sighing contentedly as I stroke her hair and kiss her forehead.

"Jackson?" She mumbles, fingers tracing the curve of my jaw.

"Yeah?"

She props her chin on my chest and gazes up at me. "I like you too." Her voice quivers slightly, eyes filled with vulnerability flitting back and forth between mine. "I don't think I've told you that."

She hasn't, but I knew. Actions speak louder than words and all that shit. She might not be good at expressing her emotions verbally, but she's fucking fantastic at expressing them physically. But still, it's nice to hear. "Good to know."

I'm not sure how long we lie there, completely uncaring that we're butt-ass naked in a random parking lot. Eventually, she forces herself into a sitting position, no small amount of satisfaction running through me when I notice her thighs quivering. Her tits brush my chest, nipples still peaked and hard and red, as she leans forwards to rifle through the pile of discarded clothes in the backseat. Only the strongest man would resist molding his hands to them, and I have never claimed to be a strong man.

Swatting me away, Luna sits back with a back. The lusty haze in her eyes is gone, replaced by a hint of annoyance, some shock, and a tiny bit of awe, I think. She frowns as the scraps of black fabric in her hands before narrowing her eyes at me in accusation. "You ripped my leggings."

Smiling with faux guilt—I don't feel guilty in the slightest about destroying the fabric keeping me from the sweet spot in between her thighs—I reach back to grab her hoodie and shove it over her head, hiding her perfect naked body from my greedy eyes. "I'll buy you new ones."

Her pout lessens slightly, the corner of her mouth twitching slightly. "And new panties."

"I'll just rip them too."

"Jackson!"

"Fine." Gently depositing her in the passenger seat, I click her seatbelt into place before smoothing back her hair, letting my hand linger on her cheek. "Whatever you want."

21

LUNA

"Hang on," I mutter beneath my breath, shifting all the books I'm lugging so I can rifle for my phone. Professor Jacobs just *loves* assignments that can't easily be researched online, hence why I'm hoofing it across campus looking like I just swindled a librarian. "Hang on, hang on, *hang on.*"

A harrumphed sound of triumph leaves me as my fingers brush against the incessantly ringing device hidden at the bottom of my bag. Wrestling it free, I don't bother checking the caller ID before pressing it to my ear. "Hello?"

A familiar husky voice greets me. "It's Nick's birthday tonight."

"That's a weird way to say hello."

I can practically see Jackson rolling his eyes, can definitely hear him murmur something about me being a brat. "We're having people over. You're coming."

Planting myself and my horde of books on the first bench I see, I huff a soft laugh. "I am?"

"Yup."

"I think you're supposed to invite me."

"Why would I when I know the answer is gonna be yes?"

"I didn't peg you as the cocky type."

"Confident," Jackson corrects, and I hear his smirk through the phone. "You wanna know why I'm confident? Because you like me."

I groan quietly, instinctively reaching up to swipe at my cheeks as if that will get rid of the pink flush staining them. "Shut up."

I like you too.

Soppy little dumbass.

I should've kicked his ass for ripping my leggings *and* panties, both of them brand spanking new but instead, I fucking simpered at the man, and I'm definitely blaming the orgasms this time. They weaken a girl.

He weakens a girl. Makes me soft. Makes me comfortable. All kind eyes and unconditional acceptance.

Like with my ADHD. I don't tell people because I'm pretty scarred from a lifetime of ignorant dipshits saying I just need to try a little harder, calling me attention-seeking. Looking back on it, I can recall so many times when Eva and Bea would make subtle demeaning comments, both behind my back and to my face, and I put up with it because I didn't entirely disagree.

But Jackson? He didn't even blink. He didn't fuss or fret or look at me differently. He didn't ask any invasive questions. He just quietly, unobtrusively offered his help.

And finger-fucked me into oblivion.

So, yeah. I guess he does have the right to be confident.

"I guess I could make an appearance," I hum nonchalantly, picking at a loose thread in my sweater, hoping he can't hear my ridiculous smile. Honestly, there's no way in hell I'm missing tonight. For one, it's an opportunity to see Jackson and I jump at any and all of those.

But it's also an opportunity to get Amelia out of the house and around people that don't live with her, are kind of related to her, or have enormous crushes on her. It'll be a hard sell considering what happened last time she was there but I'll swing it. She needs it; she's all but wasting away, physically, mentally, socially.

When she isn't in the apartment moping, she's at the gym.

With Nick.

Or at the bookstore.

Where Nick works.

Or at Greenies.

Where Nick just so happens to spend an unreasonable amount of his time.

Another excellent reason to go out tonight; I have lofty ambitions of shoving those two in a room together, locking the door, and throwing away the key until they work off some of that suffocating sexual tension.

I feel like popping popcorn and sitting back to watch the show every time they're in a room together. Dancing around their obvious feelings, her ignoring how he watches her every move, him realizing he's watching her every move and proceeding to pretend he isn't. The poor guy has been thirsting over the girl for as long as Jackson has me, and she's oblivious.

Or at least she pretends to be; I think she knows but she doesn't *want* to know. I don't blame her for being a little hesitant, considering her last relationship. I'd be more surprised if she dove right into something new immediately with no qualms.

Especially considering I think we're both pretty positive that Nick has the ability to ruin her a whole lot more than Dylan ever did or could.

Jackson calling my name softly drags me out of my thoughts. "Sorry. Zoned out."

"Everything okay?"

"Just strategizing how I'm gonna drag Amelia out."

"You better figure it out, sweetheart," Jackson jokes. "It's rude to turn up to a party without a present."

I did it.

I achieved the impossible and got Amelia out of the house.

Unfortunately, my triumph is drowned out by inexplicable, over-whelming nerves. Since the moment I walked through the door, I've been on a constant cycle of wiping my clammy hands against my pants, fiddling with my ring, fixing my hair.

"Shake it off, Lu." I scold myself. It's just Jackson. Sweet, kind, surprisingly bossy, occasionally dirty Jackson.

Just. Jackson.

Yet he doesn't feel like Just Jackson when I catch sight of him across the room, finding him already staring at me.

It's as though the world moves in slow motion and hyper-speed at the same time.

Jackson's soft expression morphs into something a hell of a lot more intense as he scans me from head to toe achingly slowly, his gaze acting like a caress. Something flickers within it when he reaches my heel-clad feet. Stripper heels, Amelia calls them, and I have a sneaking suspicion Jackson might be thinking the same thing.

I bank that thought for later.

One second he's smoldering from a distance. The next, he's looming in front of me, the intensity in his eyes physically knocking me back a step.

I sigh softly when he winds my ponytail around his fingers, using it as leverage to tug me closer so he can kiss the corner of my mouth, my cheek, the spot beneath my ear. His voice is basically a growl, sending a tingle down my spine. "Jesus Christ, Luna."

I'm not one to beg for compliments, but when they're coming from Jackson, it's just too hard to resist. Cocking my head, I smirk and raise a brow expectantly. *Go on.*

Fingers toy with the thin straps of my top, the material like sandpaper against my suddenly sensitive skin. Snapping one lightly, Jackson drawls, "I was wrong."

"About?"

"I think you're the one who's gonna ruin me."

I don't get a chance to reply, or even really process his words, before he's kissing me. Hard but slow. Full of promise but I'm not really sure what he's promising. Giving me just enough to sufficiently fluster before pulling away.

"You're a tease, you know that?" I half-complain, half-snicker as I swipe a thumb across his lips, scrubbing away the pink lipgloss staining them. I resist the urge to tuck his hair behind his ears, because acknowledging the tendrils escaping the sloppy bun at the nape of his neck would mean acknowledging how much I *like* the fucking bun, and that's not something I'm ready to do.

He does the same for me, fixing the smudges he caused, letting his palms linger on my cheeks as he sweeps his gaze over the length of me again. "You are so fucking perfect."

Despite my best efforts not to, I blush something fierce at the compliment I basically begged for yet still sounds so sincere. Briefly, I wonder if I can pass the redness off as a byproduct of the room's heated temperature.

One look at his satisfied smirk and I know I can't.

So, I engage evasive maneuvers. "Wanna dance?"

Our dancing doesn't last long.

The friction between our grinding bodies, the heat of the room, the heavy breaths quickly become too much. I don't know who drags who upstairs, I think it might've been a mutual effort. All I know is a flurry of tangled tongues and wandering hands as we practically fall over each other in our haste to get behind closed doors, and it's a miracle we make it upstairs without breaking our necks.

When my back hits a door, I blindly reach for the handle, twisting it open just in time to get shoved inside Jackson's room. He follows close behind, kicking the door shut behind him with a loud slam.

While I shiver with suspense in the middle of his room, he leans against the wall. Such a casual stance but there's nothing casual about him. He's tense, brimming with barely restrained energy, practically vibrating with need. I'm no better, so wound up I can barely see straight.

For the millionth time tonight, his eyes rake over me. A long, slow once-over that has my skin tingling wherever his eyes land, has me shifting nervously from one foot to another in anticipation, has me clenching my thighs together in an attempt to ease the ache brewing between them.

Jackson catches the movement, and he groans as he scrapes a hand over his face. The sound goes straight to my lower stomach, tightening the muscles there almost painfully, as does his voice when he commands, all growly and downright fucking dangerous, "Strip."

Yes fucking sir.

So quickly I almost get a head-rush, I bend at the waist to unstrap my heels with slightly shaky hands. A grunted sound of protest causes me to stop. When I peek at the stiff man looming in front of me, Jackson shakes his head sharply. "Leave them on."

I drop my head to hide my grin. Suspicions confirmed.

Good thing I wore a skirt.

With a single tug, the ribbon securing it comes undone and the silky fabric pools at my feet. I shed my top at lighting speed, and my chest captures his attention, like I knew it would; at the risk of it being ripped right off my body, I wisely forewent a very expensive bra. When Jackson kisses his teeth, I blink innocently. "Just saving time, baby."

His grunt is less than convinced.

Hooking my fingers under the waistband of my panties, I slowly drag them just a little bit lower. "Keep going?"

My question receives a jerky nod in response. Bringing my hands to my hips, I coast them up my stomach, brushing lightly over my tits before cupping them gently, obscuring them from his view. "You sure?"

"*Luna*," my name on his lips is a groan and a plea and a command, all three wrapped in one word, like he can't decide between them. His next three words, however, are just one; a command, plain and simple, said with so much dominance and raw fucking power I damn near moan. "Keep fucking going."

I don't. I'm playing with fire. I know I am, and I'm going to get so fucking burnt, but I can't help it. It's too easy, too fun, too rewarding to rile him up. Which is why I pour fucking gasoline on the flames, letting out a moan as I slip one hand between my legs. "Or what?"

"Or I'll take them off for you."

"Is that supposed to be a threat?" Because it's not. It's the opposite; it's the goal. I wore my least favorite—but still cute—pair of panties for this very occasion. I'm game, as long as he doesn't, like, rip my heels. I'm not sure if you *can* rip a pair of stilettos but I feel like if anyone can do it, it's Jackson.

Even from a distance, his dark chuckle caresses my skin. "If I take them off, they stay off all night."

"I'm not seeing the problem here."

"If I take them off," he repeats slowly as he closes the distance between us. Dragging his nose up my neck, across my jaw, along my cheek, he inhales deeply, letting out his breath on another low laugh. "*I've* done all the work. You think you get rewarded for being a brat?" Without letting me respond, he wraps his fingers around my throat, grip deliciously restricting. "Do what I say or you're gonna spend all night tied to my bed with my fingers and my tongue in that tight fucking pussy."

"I'm still not-"

"But you won't come. No matter how much you beg or cry or plead, you won't come. Because I won't fucking let you."

My mind eddies of all coherent thoughts. Well, almost all; *where the fuck did this man come from* is a pretty prominent continuous chant. As is *am I ever going to get over this man's mouth?*

It's a threat, a very real one, a painful punishment, yet fear is the opposite of what I feel. A snippet of a vision flashes through my mind, one of me spread-eagled on his bed, thrashing wildly, my legs spread wide with him in between them. Taking and taking and taking but never giving.

It shouldn't sound exciting. It shouldn't sound pleasurable. It shouldn't soak my fucking panties. But it does. And he knows it. His lips curl up in a wicked smile. "But you'd like that, wouldn't you?"

Any disagreement is futile. He sees right through me. He tilts my head back roughly, allowing him more access as he leaves slow, open-mouthed kisses along my collarbone, over the swell of my breasts, so close to...

A loud yell makes us jolt apart. My hands instinctively move to cover my chest while Jackson's relinquish their grip on me. Both our gazes fly to the door as a dull thud echoes through the house and more shouting breaks out.

"What was that?" Jackson doesn't answer my croaked question. Silently frowning, he moves to peer out the window. Whatever he sees has him swearing underneath his breath. Faster than I can process, he scoops my clothes off the floor and tosses them to me. "What's going on?"

Opening the door just enough for him to slip out, he pins me with a stern look. "Stay here," he commands in that arguing-with-me-would-be-a-death-wish tone but it's not the same. It doesn't have that usual sensual ring to it. It's stressed. Angry. Maybe a little panicked.

It's that little bit of panic that stops me from being annoyed when he thunders downstairs, leaving me mostly-naked and dripping wet in the middle of his room.

"What the fuck?" I murmur as I get dressed. In between trying and failing to ignore the incessant throbbing between my thighs and imagining the demise of whoever caused a fight at the most inopportune time, I only briefly contemplate doing as Jackson said and staying here.

Yeah, the whole ordering around thing is strictly reserved for the bedroom.

I'm halfway out the door when the shouting kicks up a decibel. A scream rings out amongst the clamor, and I freeze because that scream, and the desperate shrieks that follow?

They sound a whole lot like Amelia.

22

LUNA

DYLAN FUCKING WELLS.

Spineless son of a bitch. Spawn of Satan. A sad excuse for a man who very soon will be hobbling around campus missing his teeny tiny dick and his grape-sized balls.

I'm fucking fuming. Sitting on the guys' couch, watching my friend shiver and cry and blame herself yet again for that asshole's actions, I am *fuming*. I have been since the moment I stepped outside and found a rapidly growing crowd with a thrashing, crying redhead in the centre. I didn't recognize the guys Amelia clawed at as she tried to get to a bleeding Nick but the piece of shit who gripped her by the back of her dress and tossed her aside like a fucking trash bag? I knew that was Dylan before I even saw his face.

I swear to God, if someone else hadn't beaten me to it, I would've flattened the fucker. Although, I think there might be a long line for that honor, and Nick is currently frothing at the mouth to be at the front.

It hurts to look at him. Like, physically hurts. The sight of his swollen eyes—trained on Amelia since Cass carried her through the door—and bruised skin is giving me a headache. The only solace in this situation is the fact Dylan crawled away with his tail between his legs looking just as beat up, courtesy of Cass, Nick, *and* Amelia. It would've been so inappropriate to start cheering and clapping when she nailed him straight in the jaw, but God, I wanted to so badly. And

174

if the overwhelming shock of the situation hadn't had me glued to the spot, I probably would've.

However, that sense of triumph I felt, the little inkling of pride that flourished, quickly wore off when Amelia crumpled to the floor the second Dylan was out of sight. It vanished entirely when she cringed as I took her hand, and I got that same sick feeling in my stomach that I did that awful night in September.

I silently simmer as I watch my friend fall apart, taking all the blame for something that isn't remotely her fault. I watch Nick comfort her, and can't help but wonder what would have happened if she'd met Nick first, before Dylan ever existed to her.

I would do anything, *anything*, for the ability to turn back time. To go back to the day they met and stop it from happening.

Fingers laces with mine, stopping the fidgeting I didn't even realize I was doing. Glancing down, I find the skin beneath my ring bright red, rubbed raw from twisting too much. A little green-tinged too because the thing cost, like, two bucks from some dingy thrift store.

When I shift my gaze to the hand holding mine, I cringe. They're just bruises. The skin isn't even broken. Jackson doesn't flinch in the slightest when I run my thumb over his busted-up knuckles. He's nowhere near as bad as Nick but still, I hate it.

I hate every mark left on the people I care about by a man I despise.

I can't let it happen again.

I don't realize I'm standing until a sea of furious words spill out of my mouth. "You can't do this again. This is the third time he's hurt you. You have to report him."

A heavy silence settles in the room, tinged with disbelief and a steady thrum of ever-growing anger. Cass is the first to break it, voice a deadly kind of quiet. "The third time?"

Something in the back of my head nags at me to shut up. Insists I'm going too far. But it's drowned out by so much anger and irritation and fucking guilt that I can't hold in my angry, dry laugh. "You think that was bad? Two months ago she came home with a split lip and a concussion after he-"

Amelia cuts me off by hissing my name and my angry gaze flicks to her. Pleading eyes silently beg me to shut up but I can't, I'm too far gone, too lost in a white-hot rage.

Out of my peripheral, I see Cass looking between the two of us slowly. I can see the cogs turning in his brain, trying to piece together the small tidbits of information he's been given. "He hit you?" Amelia promises him he didn't. A lie of omission, a fucking technicality. After everything, she's still covering for him.

"No," the words spill out before I can stop them, acidic and bitter and wrong, "he just slammed a car door in your face."

My lips snap shut a second too late. Too slowly, my brain catches up with my mouth and I deflate. A wave of regret downs out my anger at the sight of Amelia's face, painted with anger, shock, betrayal.

Fuck.

Too far.

Way too fucking far.

"You have no right to tell them that," Amelia seethes and I recoil.

I know. *I know, I know, I know.*

My mouth opens and closes as I search for something to say, my chest aching as Amelia turns away before I can, speaking to Cass in soft apologetic tones.

Like a scolded puppy, I retreat to the sofa, sinking onto the cushions and wishing they would envelop me entirely. Tucking my legs up to my chest and resting my chin on my knees, I cover my mouth with my hand as though that will keep anything else from flowing out.

Fuck.

The next hour passes agonizingly slowly.

Tense and weepy and *awkward*.

Nick fled the room halfway through the retelling of a concise version of events for Kate's benefit—she picked a hell of a party to skip—like he couldn't bear to relive it all. Amelia lasted a whole twenty minutes before mumbling an excuse and following him upstairs, armed with booze, a first aid kit, and a heartbreakingly guilty expression.

It's funny, how earlier tonight, that would've had me cartwheeling in delight. Nick and Amelia, alone in his bedroom, shacking up for the night? Mission accomplished.

Except mission not accomplished because the whole point was to relieve some of that stress weighing Amelia down, not add more.

I stay exactly where I am. Still curled up on the sofa, still wishing it would swallow me whole. I avoid eye contact with everyone—especially Cass because he keeps sending curious, pleading glances my way, and I scared I'll somehow spill more secrets—and selfishly wallow in how fucking awful I feel.

Jackson hasn't left my side, happy to let me hide from the world in the crook of his neck. A hand gently plays with the ends of my hair, the other coasting up and down one of the legs strewn across his lap, squeezing comfortingly every so often. "It's okay," he whispers every so often. "Everything will be okay."

"I shouldn't have said anything," I whisper back, regret burning my throat like acid.

Jackson stays silent. Just keeps stroking and murmuring and soothing, like I'm a child recovering post-tantrum while I twist my ring round and round and round until the friction burns my skin. A quiet plea to stop caresses the top of my head and when I don't, Jackson does it for me. Slipping the ring off my finger and onto his pinky, he frowns as he brings my hands to his lips, blowing gently on the inflamed skin. "I'm throwing this thing away."

"It looks better on you."

The corner of his mouth twitches as he swipes a thumb across my lower lip, the smell of the Arnica I smoothed over his bruising knuckles tickling my nose. "You tryna put a ring on my finger already?"

I pull a horrified face but below it lurks a weak smile. He's good at that, making me smile when I least feel like it. "You throw it away, you buy me a new one."

My grumbled comment earns me an amused eyebrow raise. "Now you're trying to get *me* to put a ring on *your* finger?"

"I hate you."

Still smiling, he leans in, his skin soft and warm as he rests his forehead against mine, gently nudges my nose with his. "Liar."

Yeah. Big, fat liar. But I don't get the chance to deny it because a body throws itself on the couch beside me, making me curl further into Jackson as though he can protect me from what is undoubtedly about to be a verbal spanking.

From the moment Kate burst in the house, I've avoided her. I already know I fucked up. I don't need the lecture.

"Luna-"

"I know," I cut off what I'm sure is a very eloquent reprimand. "I fucked up."

"Yeah, you did." Kate balances out her curt tone with a gentle hand on my shoulder. "But you'll fix it tomorrow."

Instinctively, I go to fiddle with my ring, rolling my eyes when I'm hindered by Jackson's tight grip. Kate zones in our clasped hands, a hint of a smile on her face that she hides with pursed lips. Scooting closer, she casts a cautious look in Cass' direction before whispering, "Did something happen between Nick and Amelia?"

"Your guess is as good as mine."

"I just wonder what set Dylan off," Kate wonders aloud, but we both know the answer.

Nick could've been tying her fucking shoeless and Dylan's reaction still would've been cataclysmic. He doesn't know how to react with anything other than extremity. An outfit he doesn't approve of, a waiter getting his order wrong, a fucking haircut.

Rejection.

He takes none of it. He makes all of it someone else's problem.

And I am so, *so* tired of it being mine.

My second journey upstairs tonight is very different to my first.

No grabby hands or smashing lips, just silence and tension and cautious glances at Nick's closed bedroom door before Jackson shuts his.

I get ready for bed quickly, eager to close my itchy eyes and rest my aching head. Fingers that aren't mine tug my hair free of its constricting ponytail, smoothing out the tangles. and I lean into the touch eagerly. Lips graze my cheek before hands squeeze my shoulders and steer me towards the bed, one pulling back the covers for me to slip beneath.

I do and Jackson joins me quickly, shirtless and his jeans

exchanged for sweatpants, smelling all minty fresh and clean. I'm tugged back against his chest the moment he lies down, engulfed in his arms, limbs all tangled together, his fingers alternating between stroking my back and massaging the nape of my neck. I exhale a pent up breath only to inhale deeply, breathing him in.

I'm exhausted but my mind won't stop racing. I'm desperate for sleep but I can't find it, and not even Jackson's presence has its usual lullaby effect. I can tell he's still awake too, the rise and fall of his chest against my back too erratic. When I toss and turn for the millionth time, he holds me in place. "You'll fix it tomorrow."

A wholly unattractive snort escapes me. "You sound like Kate."

I feel his smile against my skin. "I'm taking that as a compliment."

"You should. She's the only one of us with her shit together."

I envy her for it. I'm not naive enough to assume that Kate has a perfect life, I know she has her fair share of problems. But it's the way she handles them that I'm jealous of. With a grace and clarity and sureness that I could never achieve in a million years. The epitome of control.

I'm the opposite. Rash and angry and impulsive. Incapable of rationally solving something even if my life depended on it. Always opening my big fucking mouth when it's not wanted. My mom blames it on my diagnosis. Kate and Amelia say it's because I'm a Leo. But the scary thing is I'm pretty sure it's just *me*.

"I fucked up," I whisper into the darkness. "I keep fucking up."

Jackson doesn't say anything but I can tell he's listening, waiting for me to keep talking.

"I knew what was happening and I let her stay with him. I didn't do anything."

"What could you have done?"

"Something. *Anything*."

"Luna," Jackson says quietly, coaxing me to face him, a hand on my chin directing my eyes to his. They're alight with a fierce sincerity, an essence of pleading, like he's desperate for me to hear him. "There isn't anything you, or anyone else, could've done."

That's not true. I could've pushed harder. I could've prevented all of this. But he doesn't know that because he doesn't know everything. No one knows everything. No one knows just how much I could've put an end to this. Months ago, before it got so fucking bad.

"He hit on me." The confession spills out, my chest constricting from the weight of it, an automatic wince curling my features.

"The other night?"

"Before that." I swallow down the guilt rising like bile in my throat caused by the secret I buried. "At the end of sophomore year."

The only time, besides the other night, I've ever been alone with Dylan.

The reason I made an effort to never be alone with him again.

What happened in my apartment. The apartment I share with his girlfriend, who was on her way home from work. A place I'm supposed to always be safe in, *my* space.

"He was drunk. Or high. Honestly, probably both. I can't even remember what he said exactly. I brushed it off. I thought I was imagining it or that I misunderstood what he said or something."

My head shakes at my own naivety.

I might not remember what he said but I can still feel the effect it had on me, the revolt that trickled down my spine and left me feeling dirty. Maybe if I'd been smarter and shut it down, it wouldn't have gone any further.

Hindsight. A wonderful thing.

"He grabbed my ass."

Jackson stiffens, and I avert my gaze. I don't want to see the look in his eyes. Pity or disappointment or whatever, I don't want it.

"I pushed him away and he grabbed me again, by my wrist this time." Fucker has a thing for wrists. Words can't describe how ill I felt when I saw those familiar marks on Amelia. "It was so quick. I didn't even realize what was happening until he was trying to kiss me." A bitter laugh escapes me. "He touched my boobs. Fucking honked them like a horny teenager."

I recoiled immediately. Pushed him away. Yelled at him to get his greasy paws off me. I was halfway out the door, ready to intercept Amelia on her way home from work and tell her everything when Dylan's voice stopped me.

"She won't believe you."

I swear I can still hear him sometimes, and my snorted laugh that followed. *"You wanna bet?"* I'd sneered but all my confidence had been knocked in an instant by a snickering laugh and cocky, downright evil smirk.

"He said he'd tell her it was me who came onto him," I croak out, shame coating every syllable. Word for word, I repeat his threat. *"I'll tell her you were desperate and jealous and begging for me. Who do you think she'll believe? Her loving boyfriend or her little whore friend who fucks anything that moves?"*

Jackson flinches and I'm not sure if it's from the words themselves or my tone. Harsh and spitting, mimicking Dylan's that night.

I had flinched too. And I faltered. I believed him. Dylan and Amelia were good at the time, or as close as they ever were to it. Amelia was happy. She was so fucking in love, or at least she thought she was. She *worshiped* him.

So, I stayed quiet. I acted fine when Amelia arrived home barely ten minutes later. I acted fine when Dylan kissed Amelia with the lips he'd tried to kiss me with and grabbed her with the same hands he'd grabbed me with. I acted fine when I slinked off to my room and turned up the music to a thumping volume to cover the sound of me sobbing.

I acted fine when everything went to shit after that.

It was like Dylan just stopped trying, or even pretending, to be a good boyfriend. Amelia blamed herself but I knew it was my fault. I knew it was my rejection, my silence, my cowardice that caused the downfall of the relationship she was desperately clinging to.

I know now that if I'd told Amelia, she would've believed me. If I'd told her, none of this would have happened. Just another one of my shitty calls.

After what feels like an hour of tense silence, I finally muster up the courage to look at Jackson. The hard look in his eyes shocks me a little, such an enormous contrast to their usual warmth. "He assaulted you," he grinds out, a muscle in his jaw jumping erratically. "You're so angry that Amelia didn't report him but you didn't either."

"It's not the same." What happened to me was short, over before I even realized what was happening. It was one time. What happened to Amelia was prolonged and vicious and purposeful. He wanted to hurt her. He just wanted to fuck with me.

Or to fuck me.

"Like hell it isn't," Jackson spits, tone riddled with frustration. He expels a heavy puff of air as he rolls onto his back, his hands leaving me to scrub at his exasperated expression. "Jesus, Luna."

"I'm sorry," I whisper because it's the only thing I can think to say, because I owe someone an apology and she's not here to hear it.

"Don't do that. Don't apologize because he's a piece of shit."

I press my lips together to keep another from spilling out.

Jackson's head lolls towards me, his expression softening, a gentle hand smoothing over the top of my head. "You never told Amelia?"

"I couldn't. I can't. It's too late now, it would just make things worse." And I've already done enough of that. "She'd hate me."

"No, she wouldn't."

He's right, she wouldn't. She's too good, too kind, for that. But I'd hate myself. For really being as shallow and self-absorbed and dramatic as people perceive me to be. For suddenly revealing my own 'assault' at Dylan's hand and stealing the attention away from Amelia. What convenient timing.

Jackson opens his mouth to speak again, maybe to ask something else, but I cut him off. "Can we please stop talking about him now?"

"Can I just say one last thing?"

I nod.

"No one is at fault here but Dylan. Not you, not Amelia, no one but him."

I can't speak past the lump in my throat, so I nod again.

Exhaling deeply, Jackson wraps his arms around me again, crushing me to his chest, holding me like I might disappear. "Fuck, I hate him."

"Join the club."

23

JACKSON

CHIRPING BIRDS, the smell of coffee and a slight pinch in my knuckles wake me up the morning after Nick's disastrous birthday.

Well, that and a string of loud, colorful curses.

My muscles pop as I stretch out, my forehead creasing as I find the spot beside me empty, a warm pillow where Luna should be. Cracking open an eye, I'm greeted by the sight of her naked except for a pair of my sweats halfway up her legs, hissing rapidly into her phone, words unintelligible but irritation evident. I choke on a laugh when she trips over her own feet, only just managing to catch herself before she goes tumbling to the floor.

Luna whips around, scowling something fierce, mumbling something before hanging up. As she chucks her phone aside, she loses her grip on the sweats and they slip down her thighs, momentarily flashing me. "Going commando?"

Her scowl deepens as she fists the loose material in her hands, depriving me of all that smooth, tan flesh. "*Someone* ripped my panties again."

Damn right I did. After everything that went on last night, we were both way too wound up to fall asleep, her with guilt, me with anger. So we took out a bit of that pent-up energy on each other; I've got the scratch marks on my chest and she's got the shape of my hand imprinted on her ass to prove it.

A yawn blurs my vision as I prop myself up on one elbow. "Why the hell aren't you in bed?"

"I have class."

Scoffing, I reach over and grab a handful of her sweats, dragging her towards me. "I don't like waking up alone."

"You're not alone." She rolls her eyes and begrudgingly sits on the edge of the bed. "I'm literally right here."

When she tries to wriggle away, I drop my head in her lap and secure my arms around her waist. She sighs but her hands go to my hair and comb through the knots, slender fingers deftly twisting a few strands into a braid. I let her; if she's messing with my hair it means she's not trying to mess with that damn ring currently turning my pinky finger an interesting shade of green.

"Who were you talking to?"

"Pen, reminding me how late I am for class," she grumbles, tugging my new braid pointedly.

"If you're already late, you might as well stay."

"Nice try." Soft laughter and softer lips brush my cheek. "I have to go."

"Skip it and get your ass back in bed."

She pauses for a second, contemplating, I can tell, and I bury my face in her lap so she can't see my smug smile. When I trace the dimples on her lower back, tickling lightly the way she likes it, she sighs contentedly and flops on top of me. "You're cuddly in the morning."

Ordinarily? No.

With her? Fuck yeah, I am.

Especially after last night. Damn right I'm reluctant to let her go. If I don't occupy my hands with her, I'm pretty sure they'll end up somewhere else.

Like slamming into Dylan Wells' grimy fucking face.

Grunting, I shift onto my side, attempting to drag her down with me. With a whine of protest, Luna manages to evade, wriggling out of my grip and darting for the door.

'I have to go," she calls over her shoulder as she steals a t-shirt and slips on the sliders she's taken to leaving here, simultaneously tying the sweats currently swallowing her slender waist as tightly as she can. "Attendance is part of my grade."

Well, shit. Can't really argue with that. Sighing, I roll out of bed, scratching the itchy scratches on my chest as I amble towards her.

"What're you doing?"

I glance up from yanking a pair of sweats up my legs to find Luna frowning at me. Well, kind of frowning at me, kind of eyeing my cock with too much interest for the limited time we have. "Walking you to class."

Her frown cracks instantly, melting into something softer that she ducks her head to hide, using a sheet of messy hair as a shield, and as much as I want to smile at the effect such a simple gesture has on her, it also makes my chest ache a little too. It's the bare minimum, Common decency, really, yet it surprises her.

That kind of reaction happens a lot more than it should. Our first date, the batting cages, every date after that. I bought her flowers last week, just because, and when she opened the door to find me standing there with a bouquet, she just blinked in confusion and asked if they were for Amelia.

God, I want to punch whoever ruined such simple fucking intimacy for her.

Tugging on a t-shirt, I just watch her fumble around for a second. Taking her meds, twisting the front of her borrowed t-shirt into a knot so it exposes a tiny sliver of midriff, braiding her hair back from her face so it matches mine.

I like every version of Luna but I think this one is the best. Rumpled, disheveled, a touch sleep-deprived. Wearing my clothes. Blue eyes soft and sleepy. Bare-faced except for a few remnants of eyeliner she didn't quite manage to scrub off last night. Cheeks puffy, one a little flushed from sleeping on it all night. Beautiful as always. This Luna is relaxed and comfortable, and I'm pretty sure it's not a side of her she lets many people see.

Maybe that's why I love it so much.

And when she slides on her glasses, it reminds me that she is, in fact, a human being with the eyesight of a mole and not some otherworldly goddess who somehow stumbled into my bed.

Sidling up to her, I lift the glasses from her face just enough so I can swipe away the black smudged beneath her eyes. "Why don't you wear these all the time?"

Luna snorts. "A boy told me once that I look like a porn star with them on. Because, you know, apparently blonde hair, big boobs, and glasses scream porn even on a fifteen-year-old."

Nausea settles deep in my belly at her words, at how casually she says them.

Fifteen. Barely older than my youngest sister. My fists clench at my side, and the face I've been imagining punching all morning suddenly morphs into a faceless, nameless highschooler.

Luna balls my t-shirt between her fists, tutting in mock disapproval. "Stop imagining punching a child."

"Wouldn't be a child anymore now, would he?"

"No," she agrees with an eye roll. "He's probably getting drunk in an STD-riddled frat house. Or watching busty, blonde, visually impaired porn."

God, I can't comprehend how she lets all the shit said about her, said to her, go. How she stands there, cracking jokes and smiling like they don't affect her. If someone said that about Kate or Amelia, she'd land herself in jail defending them. But when it comes to herself? She's so nonchalant it kills me.

Pink lips twist into a pout as she gives me a little chiding shake. "It's okay. It was just some horny teenager."

I grunt.

"I'll start wearing them if that makes you feel better."

It's my turn to roll my eyes. "You should wear them because you're gonna walk straight in front of a bus one day if you don't."

"I'm not that bad."

"You almost walked into a lamppost yesterday."

"I did not!"

"Yeah, you didn't, because I saved your pretty ass."

Luna suffocates a laugh, pretending to scowl at me and failing miserably. I trace the smile she tries to hide with my thumb, grateful for its appearance, however reluctant. I didn't see much of that last night.

It's as though we both have the same thought, both remember last night, both acknowledge the lingering elephant in the room, at the same time. Face dropping, Luna clutches my t-shirt a little tighter, thumbs tracing the neckline.

I bend to brush my lips against her knuckles. "You feeling okay today?"

"I'm good," she lies, smile strained. "I just really want to speak to Amelia."

"You wanna check if she's awake before we leave?"

Luna answers my question by making a beeline for the door, almost ripping it off the hinges in her haste to creep across the hall. She inches towards Nick's room, balancing on the balls of her feet as she stealthily nudges the ajar door further open, both of us wincing when it creaks ever so slightly.

The sight that greets us draws a soft 'aw' noise out of Luna, her bottom lip poking out in a pout, wide eyes glancing between me and the bed. Nick and Amelia lie passed out in his bed, curled up beside each other, heads so close they're sharing a pillow, one of Nick's hands resting on the slender, pale thigh draped over his lower half, the other loosely tangled with hers.

Nick. Cuddling.

Jesus.

It takes a physical effort to restrain myself from taking a picture to tease him with later, or to whip out whenever he denies the fact he's head over heels for the girl. Stopping Luna is even harder; her twitchy fingers are halfway to the phone in her pocket when I stop her. "Don't meddle."

A harsh glare and an elbow to the ribs are what I receive for that intervention. "I'm not going to meddle," she insists, her second lie of the morning. "But this needs to happen. Look at them."

Gripping the back of her t-shirt, I drag her away from the door before she loses her internal battle and goes full paparazzi. "Come on, trouble."

"Spoilsport."

Nick is right.

Lurking outside a lecture hall, a steaming hot chocolate in one hand and a herbal tea that tastes like grass in the other, waiting for my girl who isn't technically my girl, I guess I am pretty pathetic.

Rolling my shoulders as much as the fucking boulder of a bag weighing me down will let me—Luna didn't want to bring her overnight bag to class, so I brought it for her—I blow a strand of hair escaping from my braid out of my eye. I got reamed by the boys when they spotted it this morning; Ben chased me out the door singing the Pippi Longstocking theme song while Cass called me Elsa. Luna flipped them both off, told them to kiss our asses, and reminded them which one of us had a hot, naked blonde in their bed last night.

So modest, my Luna.

When the lecture hall door finally swings open and I catch sight of a tired blonde drowning in oversized clothes, I suddenly forget about the ache in my shoulder, the hair in my eye, and the minor burns scalding my palms. Luna doesn't spot me straight away, too wrapped up in talking to her professor, and even from a distance, the conversation looks awkward and strained.

Frowning, I start towards her but the sudden influx of students pouring into the hallway hinders me. As does the appearance of a different crop of blonde hair.

A girl I vaguely recognize blocks my view of Luna. Smirking eyes, a shade darker than Luna's and a little more green-tinged, scan me slowly from head to toe, making me feel like a mannequin on display.

I clear my throat uncomfortably. "Hi?"

Light laughter escapes the mystery blonde. She waves her hand in the air dismissively, the faintest blush creeping up her neck. "Sorry, that was creepy. You're Jackson, right?"

When I nod, she holds out her hand. "I'm Pen. Luna's friend."

Ah. The infamous Pen.

I shuffle the stuff in my grip so I can shake her hand, but my smile is pinched, my focus elsewhere, straying over her head. "She's fine."

Pen floats into my eyeline again, smirking. "My dad's just a hardass."

"Your dad?"

"Professor Jacobs. He's just chewing her out for being late." A sly expression overcomes her features. "I'm assuming that was your fault?"

I shrug, scratching my head as a little bit of guilt sinks in; I didn't think she'd actually cop shit for being late.

"And I'm assuming you're the reason she looks like that?"

That makes me crack a genuine smile. She really does look ridiculous. The epitome of a walk of shame, minus the shame because she wears the look with pride.

Pen must take my smile as an invitation to chat, because she chatters on and on for what feels like forever but is realistically barely five minutes. I shift awkwardly in place, reshuffling the styrofoam cups in my hands again just because it gives me something to do. It's not that I don't like her; I don't know her. I just want to get Luna and get the hell out of here.

A wave of relief hits me when my girl finally strides over, eyeing the beverages in my hands hopefully. "One of those for me?"

"Both."

Her beam is mega-watt as she plucks the hot chocolate from my grip. "Excellent answer." My newly freed hand goes straight to her hip, clinging for dear life and yanking her closer so I can drop a kiss to her temple. She leans into me easily, a low moan escaping her as she chugs half her drink in one go. "I love you."

All three of us freeze.

A slow, steady blush creeps up Luna's neck as her blurted confession sinks in, eyes wide with something akin to horror as she turns to me. "I did not mean it like that."

Pen's laughter echoes around the hallway, her expression the complete opposite to Luna's; she looks about ready to crack open a bucket of popcorn.

"You didn't?" I can't help but tease.

"Stop it."

"Come on, sweetheart, you're breaking my heart." I get shoved so hard I almost drop her second beverage. Catching her by the elbow, I can't help but kiss the pout off her lips through my laughter. A little rougher than intended, her little slip of the tongue spurring me on, the idea of her loving me igniting something in me that I table for later before it becomes overwhelming.

"Alright, alright. Break it up before I vomit. Or cry."

Luna breaks away from me to thump Pen, who yelps before thumping her right back. As I chuckle at their bickering, I feel the burning sensation of someone staring at us, making me glance up. Pen's dad, Luna's professor, is watching us with narrowed eyes. I offer him a smile, but it fades when he doesn't return it. Mouth set in a straight line, his gaze flits from Luna to Pen, and his expression hardens even more.

Weird.

The sound of Pen calling a goodbye draws my attention away

from the professor just in time to see her racing away from us, presumably off to another class. Luna's cheeks are still tinged red, her chest rising and falling with awkward laughter. Smiling, I sling an arm over her shoulders. "Hungry?"

"Starving."

"You gonna propose to me if I bring you to a drive-thru?" The book in her hand meets my stomach with a thump, drawing a pained huff out of me. "You're violent today."

"You're annoying today," she retorts with an exaggerated sneer.

It's in this moment that I pinpoint why I love seeing flustered, flushed, messy Luna. She's usually always so poised and in control and... I don't know, above me? Not in a bad way. Just that she always seems like she's miles ahead, like she knows what she's doing, what to say, how to act. Or, at least, in the months I was gathering up the courage to actually talk to her, she always seemed like that. And I like that side of her, but I like this side too.

It makes me feel a little less out of my depth.

24

LUNA

EARDRUM-THREATENINGLY LOUD MUSIC echoes off the walls of my apartment, my only company since Kate and Amelia left for Thanksgiving with their families.

I hum along to it, letting it calm me even though I feel the complete opposite; nothing elevates my stress levels quite like packing. I'm powering through, though, because packing means getting out of Sun Valley, and God knows I could use that. With everything happening lately, this city and this apartment have felt stifling.

I fixed the monstrous mess I made. Apologized to Amelia and meant it so very much. *It's not okay but I forgive you,* she'd said and I'd taken it happily because God, it was more than I deserved.

But repaired friendships aside, I still need to get out of here. I'm actually looking forward to this weekend. Not because I love Thanksgiving or anything, Ma and I don't even celebrate it. The extent of our grand plans usually includes a mountain of takeout eaten in our pajamas on the sofa, a cheesy romcom playing in the background as my mom grills me for the latest gossip. That's what I'm excited for; some good ol' normality.

Though, my excitement is slightly tainted as I wonder how the hell I'm going to avoid Eva and Bea for an entire weekend—call me a princess but I've been treated a little too well lately to revert back to dodging thinly veiled insults and silly, childish mean girl bureaucracy. And Owen is a whole other tangled web.

With the blaring music and my full focus on strategizing plans of evasion, I don't hear my phone ringing. It's only when the song changes do I hear it, along with knocking. Ignoring the latter—the tenants of this apartment don't have the best track record with unexpected visitors—I answer my phone. "Hello?"

"Open your door."

The smile on my face is damn near automatic.

I fly to the door at lightning speed. Within seconds of opening it, Jackson's inside and all up in my business. "I've been knocking for ten minutes."

"What're you doing here?"

Large hands settle on my waist. "I'm not gonna see you for four days."

"And a few extra hours was gonna kill you?"

"Maybe."

"Drama queen."

"Stop being a brat and kiss me."

I roll my eyes but oblige because how can I not? Hands tug me flush against him before circling around, pawing my ass. Toying with the hem of the t-shirt riding up my thighs, Jackson pulls back just enough to glance down at my attire. "Is that mine?"

"Yup," I reply, not the slightest bit ashamed.

A pleased noise rumbles in his throat as he tugs on the hem again. A palm slaps my bare skin as he gives me a final peck. "Put some pants on and let's go get some food."

"I can't. I have to pack."

Eyes dart in the direction my thumb jerks, dark brows shooting up when Jackson clocks my overwhelming suitcase. "You know you're only going for a weekend, right?"

"Shut up."

His laughter creates a warm feeling in the pit of my belly that only spreads when he grips the back of my neck and pulls me in to kiss my forehead. "Go pack. I'll cook."

"You cook?"

Modest as always, Jackson just shrugs and ambles into the kitchen, rooting through the cupboards and fridge like he owns the place.

Apparently, he cooks.

Damn it.

~

Jackson is singing.

Like belting at the top of his lungs in that deep, husky voice, swaying around the kitchen brandishing a spatula singing.

I think I'm going to die.

Packing was abandoned long ago in favor of watching him dance around, so fucking cute.

And hot. Very hot.

I know I'm checking him out, he knows I'm checking him out, and yet still, when he suddenly looks up from the stove, I drop my gaze. Grabbing the first piece of clothing I can find, I pretend to inspect it, ignoring the low chuckle from the kitchen.

"Luna?"

I aim for nonchalance as I glance up.

Jackson smirks, leaning against the counter with his arms folded. "You hungry?"

Yup.

Very.

I shrug as I clamber to my feet. "I could eat."

Joining him in the kitchen, I fish out cutlery while he dishes up a portion each of something delicious-smelling—*kare raisu*, he tells me it's called—and carries our bowls to the living room. Halfway through cracking open a couple drinks for us, nose crinkled in disgust as I handle the dreaded grapefruit Crush, my phone chimes from the sofa where Jackson chucked it earlier.

"Can you check that?" It's probably just my mom checking my flight details for the millionth time.

Except the moment I turn around, I know it's not.

Jaw rigid, Jackson grips my phone way too tightly.

I take a cautious step toward him. "What?"

Brown eyes soften when they meet mine. Without a word, he sets my phone on the table, gesturing to it stiffly. Bracing myself for an unsolicited dick pic, I squint at the screen.

The text I find is arguably worse than a random penis.

. . .

Owen: hey sugarplum, see you tomorrow night? Parents are out of town. Need something to be thankful for again ;)

Fuck.

When I automatically go for my ring and come up empty—the little bastard glints at me teasingly from Jackson's pinky—I cross my arms over my chest awkwardly. "I wouldn't have replied," is all I can think to offer.

"I know," is his soft, genuine reply that confuses me because he doesn't exactly look thrilled. I sure as hell wouldn't be.

"You're not pissed?"

"Not at you." Sitting down, Jackson digs into his food with a shrug. When I make no effort to join him, a crease forms between his brows. "Should I be?"

No.

It would be so easy to just say no.

I never did like taking the easy way.

"If I thought you were going home to fuck other girls, I'd probably be a little pissed."

In a split second, something shifts in Jackson. Not in his demeanor; he remains as calm as ever as he sets down his food and leans back, smoothing his hands down his thighs before resting his arms on the back of the sofa. Such a casual stance yet every muscle is tight, every vein pronounced.

It's his eyes that really change. They harden and gleam with someone wicked. It's the tense, dominant power rolling off him. It's his voice as he asks, slowly, calmly, deadly, "Are you going to fuck him?"

Say no, my inner voice begs me. The angel on my shoulder, or maybe my self-preservation skills.

But I can't help it.

I shrug.

Despite the fact I wouldn't touch Owen with a ten-foot-pole anymore, I fucking shrug because provoking Jackson is too damn fun. Too damn rewarding. Which is why I push harder, challenging him and that pesky self-control. "A girl has needs."

Oh, does that work.

In the blink of an eye, Jackson is on his feet and stalking towards me. Predator and prey, he forces me to take a step back, then another and another until my back bumps against the wall. No, a door. My ajar bedroom door. Jackson shoves it open and keeps advancing until my calves hit my bed and I'm forced to sit.

My breath catches in my throat as Jackson towers over me. Goosebumps erupt as his knuckles brush a path down my cheek. "I know what you're doing, Luna."

I grasp my bedsheet with a death grip. "What am I doing?"

I don't get a reply. I get pushed onto my back, the hem of my t-shirt shoved up my thighs before I can blink and for a split second, a crack appears in Jackson's demeanor. Lips curling, he snaps the waistband of my pale pink panties covered in a Hello Kitty print, a stark contrast to the usual lacy numbers I wear. A joke birthday present from the girls that became my favorite comfy pair.

When Jackson chuckles teasingly, I slap him upside the head. "Shut up."

"I like them." He ducks his head, and I inhale sharply when I feel his hot breath through the flimsy fabric. "You wear these for Owen?"

I try to retort but it dissolves into an open-mouthed moan when teeth nip my clit, and already-damp material is only made damper by a teasing tongue. Jackson something else but I don't catch it, too caught up in the zinging sensations shooting up my spine.

All of a sudden, I'm on my stomach, my confused yelp muffled as my face is buried in my bedsheets. The sound morphs into a moan when lips kiss a path down my bare back. Hands are suddenly everywhere, caressing, stroking, slapping, slipping my panties off. Heavy weight hovers over me, hips press into my ass, breath tickles my neck. "I said what needs, Luna?"

I don't reply. I can't reply. I'm too focused on the hard cock digging into me, begging for some attention. And I beg for some of my own, with a low moan and a thrust of my hips.

"You wanna get fucked?" Jackson croons, teeth nipping at my racing pulse point, tough darting out to ease the sting. "You need me to fuck you?"

Like I need oxygen.

When I glance over my shoulder, Jackson is right there, his nose brushing mine, our breaths mingling. "Please."

Calloused fingers graze my skin, sweeping my hair back from my face. "So pretty when you beg."

"*Please.*"

"No." He punctuates the single word with a harsh, stinging slap on the ass. "Maybe when you learn how to fucking behave."

"But-"

The argument I know I shouldn't make but can't fucking help is cut off when rough, demanding hands guide me upright, positioning me on my knees, spreading my thighs. "Up."

I rise up on shaky knees. Without warning, he slides underneath me and tugs me down onto his face, his tongue slipping inside me before I can even fathom what's happening.

My legs give out almost immediately. Falling forward, I clutch the headboard, holding on tight as he fucks me with his tongue. Two fingers spread me open, baring me completely to him, a third joining his tongue and eddying my mind of all coherent thoughts. "*Holy fucking shit.*"

The sounds echoing around the room are obscene. Wet, sloppy sounds. Moans and groans. My neighbor probably thinks I'm making porn but I can't find it in me to care, not when *he's* in me.

So many curses fall from my lips, intertwined with praises to Jackson's name. I find purchase in his hair, tugging hard, and that seems to only spur him on, his tongue and fingers plunging in and out of me just as manically as I'm writhing on his face.

I come quick, so hard I almost pass out. I lose all feeling and control in my legs. I briefly worry I'm crushing Jackson but he seems pretty fucking happy, still lapping away at me like a man on a mission.

I moan, long and pained, as he licks and nips and caresses until I can't take it anymore. I try to rise, desperate for a break, even for just a second, but he just yanks me down again, arms wrapped around my thighs tightly so I can't move, fingers digging into my flesh hard enough to bruise, and I swear I can hear his voice in my ear, a ghost of a whisper from the first night we spent together. *I didn't say you could stop.*

I think I might be sobbing.

Tears of pleasure, that's a new one for me.

My whole body shakes, my insides feel like goo, and my brain is nothing but haze.

By the time he finally relents, I can barely hold myself up. I crumple, literally crumple, as weak as a sheet of paper, when he slides out from underneath me. He moves to hover over me and I watch, an odd combination of dazed and abuzz, as he licks his glossy lips and fingers clean.

Those same fingers wrap around my throat. "You still thinking of fucking someone else?"

"Hell fucking no."

There's a challenge in his eyes, one to counter mine, and even though I don't know what the challenge is, I have a feeling I'm already the loser. Urging me upright, he swaps our places, sitting on the edge of the bed while I kneel on the floor. Leaning back on one hand, the other curls around my chin. "Prove it, sweetheart."

I think I go a bit light-headed with giddiness.

Finally. Fucking *finally*.

Never in my life have I been excited to give someone a blowjob but here I am, all but foaming at the mouth, pathetically eager as I dive for his waistband. I don't bother teasing him. I yank down his sweats and boxers in one swoop, his thick, hard cock springing free.

Honestly, I'm a touch worried about how the fuck all of that is going to fit in my mouth but I'll gladly accept the challenged. I want it inside me, right fucking now.

Fingers comb through my hair, collecting it in a makeshift ponytail. A smug smirk curls the corners of his mouth. "Too much for you, sweetheart?"

Asshole.

I waste no time, as eager to get him in my mouth as he is to be in there. My jaw screams, stretching wide and straining to take him, but I ignore the sting. I take him inch by inch, going slow because I have to, only stopping when he hits the back of my throat.

He's restraining himself, I can tell. Holding back. Letting me set the pace. It's nice and all, but it's not what I want.

All it takes is my eyes flicking up to meet his, my nails scraping his balls lightly, my tongue caressing the underside of his cock, and he lets go. The other side of him takes over. Gritting his teeth, he tightens his grip on my hair to an almost painful degree. His hips piston rapidly, slamming into my mouth brutally, his loud groans filling the room as he hits the back of my throat repeatedly.

My eyes water, I can barely breathe, and it's all I can do to grip his thighs and just hold the fuck on, but I love it. The brutality of it all, the pleasure rippling through his expression, the dirty praises falling from his lips and going straight to my lower belly. I fucking love every moment. I'm dripping wet, my upper thighs soaked with my arousal, and the pulsing between my legs is almost unbearable. When tears start rolling down my cheeks, Jackson falters, withdrawing slightly but when I glare up at him, pinching his thighs, he continues, even faster, even harder.

When his thrusts get sloppier, his cock twitching and swelling in my mouth, I know he's close. Gazing up at him through teary eyes, I squeeze his thigh encouragingly. And then he's coming, spilling down my throat, all but choking me but I swallow dutifully as he groans my name. When he finishes, he pulls out of his mouth with a wet plop, falling back on his elbows with a spent grunt. Head tilted to the ceiling, eyes half-closed, he mutters curses under his breath.

Sitting back on my heels, I struggle to catch my breath, tongue swiping to clean the corners of my mouth. On shaky legs, I crawl onto his lap, smoothing my hands over his thighs. His chest heaves as he tries to recover too, and when I slide my hands up his chest, I feel his heart thumping erratically. Dropping my head to the crook of his neck, I smile. "Too much for you, sweetheart?"

I barely get the comment out before I'm on my back again, his head between my legs, showing me the true definition of *too much*.

I sleep like a log the entire flight.

My throat is scratchy and raw, my scalp aches, and my thighs feel like I've pulled a muscle somewhere, but I swear it's the best sleep I've ever had.

When my mom picked me up at the airport, she took one look at me and laughed. Made a crack about how I need to learn to handle my hangovers better before dragging me to our favorite Nepalese restaurant to fix me up.

I can barely look her in the eye. It's hard to concentrate on our conversation while I stuff my face with dumplings when mere hours ago I was... well, stuffing my face with Jackson. The mere memory of it, the look in his eyes as he unleashed on me, makes me shiver.

"Cold, hun?"

I can only pray I don't look as guilty and flushed as I feel. "It's a bit draughty in here." A blatant lie, and not even a good one. This place is the epitome of cozy, and the *momos* I'm devouring are definitely keeping me warm.

A whole minute of intense perusal passes before Ma smiles, wide and bright and knowing. "There's a boy."

"What?" Even I can hear how horribly high-pitched my voice comes out. "Why would you think that?"

Ma's grin grows. "I don't hear a denial."

"*Ma.*"

"What's his name?"

I drop my head to my hands. "Jesus Christ."

"Funny, I was under the impression he died."

"Please stop."

A napkin snaps in my direction. "Tell me!"

"His name is Jackson, alright?"

"Oscar Jackson?"

I blink, gaping at my mother, partly in horror, partly in confusion. "How the fuck do you know that?"

That bastard napkin comes flying towards me again. "Language!"

Batting her away, I repeat my question. "How the hell do you know who Jackson is?"

"I subscribe to the UCSV Newsroom," she tells me, way too nonchalant for my liking. "Someone there is very fond of the baseball team."

Yeah. I know. Made that comment once or twice myself, perhaps a touch snarkier.

"He's cute, Lu."

I hum a nondescript reply.

"The long hair though?"

"It grows on you."

Ma whistles, loud and teasing. "I need to meet this boy. Must be pretty special if he has you blushing like that."

An accurate observation; I think I've blushed more in the past few weeks than I have in my entire life.

"What about you?" I counter, praying she lets me turn the conversation back on her. It's not that I don't want to tell her about Jackson. I do, I really do, because I have a feeling she would adore him. Actually, I have a feeling most mothers would weep with joy if Jackson was the boy their child brought home. I just don't want to talk about him when I can still feel his hands on my ass and his cock down my throat. "Any special man in your life?"

Luckily, my attempt is successful, and my mother's amused snort tells me all I need to know.

"What about the guy buying all your paintings?"

"The *anonymous* guy buying all my paintings," Ma corrects. "I wouldn't even know *he* was a *he* if his assistant didn't refer to him as *'sir'* all the time."

"That's kind of creepy."

"He's paying me," Ma says, deadpan as he proves I am, in fact, my mother's daughter. "I don't care."

25

LUNA

I DON'T KNOW how I ended up here.

I tried to avoid them, I really did. I made it two whole days without so much as a glimpse of my old friends. But one trip to my favorite coffee shop and I got cornered, and subsequently dragged out for the night.

A club is the last place I want to be. I would much rather be curled up on my mom's lumpy couch gorging on leftovers, maybe with a movie in the background and Jackson on FaceTime.

But either I'm weak or Eva and Bea are exceptionally manipulative because here I am, shotting tequila in a tight dress after providing entirely too small of an argument.

To add fuel to fire, Owen's here. I've kept my distance all night, subtly shimmying away when he dances over or excusing myself to get a drink or darting to the bathroom. I know I can't avoid him forever, and that comes to fruition when we pile into a booth at the back of the club and Owen makes sure to snag a spot beside me.

Dread settles in my stomach as he slinks an arm around my shoulders. "You ignored my texts."

I pointedly shrug him off. "You didn't take the hint."

"Ouch." He presses a hand to his chest, mouth downturned in an exaggerated hurt expression. "Watch the claws, Lu. What did I do?"

When I mentally scramble for an excuse as to why I've done a complete one-eighty and given him the cold shoulder, all I come up with is the truth. Fiddling with the straw of my drink, I cast a nervous glance in the girls' direction. They're not paying us any attention, too caught up in squawking about the latest gossip, but I drop my voice and scoot closer to Owen as a precaution. "I'm seeing someone."

He blinks. "Seriously?"

"Yes."

"You," he repeats slowly, "are seeing someone."

"Uh-huh."

"Monogamously."

A spark of irritation straightens my spine. "*Yes*, asshole."

"Sorry." He holds up his hands in surrender. "Just never thought I'd see the day Luna Evans got a boyfriend."

"You have a boyfriend?"

It's a testament to their ability to sniff out gossip, how Eva and Bea manage to hear the one thing I'd rather they didn't in a rowdy, noisy club. I cringe at their gaping expressions, their jaws practically on the floor. "No, I don't."

"You just said you were seeing someone."

"I am. But he's not my boyfriend."

Eva crooks a snooty brow. "But he's getting all the benefits." I shrug, because how the fuck else do I respond to that? The girls exchange glances before erupting into giggles. "Oh, sweetie. Luna's been Luna'd."

My stomach twists in a knot. "What's that supposed to mean?"

"All that sleeping around and messing with boys' heads was going to catch up with you eventually," Bea explains as casually as if she were talking about the weather, as if what she's saying makes perfect sense, as if she didn't just essentially call me a manipulative slut. "It's, like, karma or something."

No, I feel like correcting her. *This is my karma. Having to suffer in your drab presence.*

Before I can vocalize that, though, Owen butts in. Sporting his peacemaker tone, he shoots me pleading glances, silently begging me to let their snide comments go. "Where is he this weekend?"

I sigh and oblige, if only because denying Bea a reaction is oh-so-satisfying. "He's home. His family's got a ranch up near Sequoia."

One of the girls, I'm not even sure who, snickers. "He's probably rolling around in a barn right now with his childhood sweetheart."

Their laughter rings in my ears as I slump in my seat, fists clenched on my lap. Owen's frown sears the side of my face, his shoulder bumping mine gently. "Guys, come on. Enough."

"We're just kidding," Eva protests with a pout. She rolls her eyes, letting out an indignant huff before pasting on a fake smile. "So, you like him?"

"Of course she likes him," Bea jumps in before I can get a word out. "She turned down Owen."

"Wait until she has a few more shots, she'll change her mind."

They talk like I'm not even here, dig after dig after dig, ranging from how Jackson's cheating on me to how I'll eventually cheat on him. When they start bitterly pondering how Jackson managed to 'break the Ice Queen,' I down my drink and stand. "I'm gonna go."

A chorus of whines break out. "We're joking! God, when did you get so sensitive?"

Gathering my bag and jacket, I leave without so much as a backward glance. As I stomp through the club, my annoyance grows. I'm irritated, less so with what they were saying, more so with the fact that I let them say it. I sat and took it like a little bitch when I should've chucked a drink in their faces.

The sound of my name being called cuts through the ruckus of the club, and I glance over my shoulder to find Owen pushing through the crowd towards me. When he reaches me, his hand lands on my shoulder and squeezes, eyes soft with sympathy. "You okay?"

I nod, already pulling out my phone with the intention of calling a cab to get the hell out of here, bypassing the unopened messages from Jackson because fuck me, those girls got in my head something good.

Owen's hand covers the screen. "Wanna go somewhere?" When I hit him an 'are you fucking kidding me?' look, he clarifies, "I'm not hitting on you. I just don't wanna go home yet. Empty house blues."

Another one of the reasons me and Owen's arrangement has always worked so well, how we always maintained a friendship; we never have liked being alone.

Still, I hesitate.

Sensing my trepidation, Owen nudges me gently. "We've been friends longer than we've been fucking, Lu. I promise I won't try anything."

The hopeful look in his eyes tugs at my heartstrings, and I feel my willpower wilt. "Fine. One drink."

I should've known better.

God, when will I ever learn that one drink is never really just one drink?

One vodka cranberry turns into two, and that turns into three, and then a two-for-one deal on cocktails enters the mix so, naturally, I have a couple of those. I'm not sure when the shots start, and I sure as fuck have no clue how many I consume. I only remember them burning something fierce on the way down.

And on the way back up.

Owen isn't far behind me on the drunk scale, matching me drink for drink like the competitive son of a bitch he is. We egg each other on, try to one-up each other, and it's fun, for a while. We're having fun. Good ol' friendly fun.

Until we aren't.

I forgot that the main flaw in Owen and I drinking together isn't that we might accidentally fall into bed together; it's that we never know when to shut up.

Which is how, less than two hours after I committed to one, singular, innocent drink, I'm hunched in a rickety plastic chair in the emergency room waiting for Owen to get his possibly-broken hand x-rayed.

It was my fault, really. I was the one who spent twenty minutes vomiting up my fucking soul before my equally plastered friend dragged me out of a club bathroom. Unfortunately, I think I could consume all the alcohol in the world and still, the mouthy bitch in me wouldn't shut up; she was certainly alive when some dickhead tried to steal our cab.

The specifics are a little blurry but I think the phrases '*cock-sucker*' and '*shrimp dick little bitch*' might have been used. Whatever I said, it was enough to catch the guy's attention. It all kicked off after that, and before I knew it, I was the one helping Owen into a taxi while he cradled his poor, deformed hand.

Even after all that, I'm still too drunk. My head is spinning, my stomach is rolling, and I swear I can feel the alcohol burning a hole in my liver. Even that antiseptic hospital smell can't cover up the stench of vodka seeping from my pores.

"One drink," I mutter as I slump over in my seat, shaking my head at my own naivety. "Dipshit."

"Talking to yourself, sweetheart?"

Oh, do I hate the hope that flutters in my chest before I recognize Owen's voice.

"Don't call me that," I warn the man ambling toward me, looking just as decrepit and drained as I feel. I cringe at the cast encasing his hand. "Broken?" His sullen nod evokes a wave of guilt. "I'm so sorry."

His not-bandaged hand socks me gently on the shoulder. "Shut up. You didn't break my hand."

I started the fight though, didn't I? Could've kept my fat mouth shut and just let the little bastard take our taxi. But nope. Drunk Luna is just as foolish as Sober Luna. I'm too tired to argue though, so with a resigned sigh, I shakily get to my feet.

Immediately, I regret it. Letting out a groan, one hand goes to my throbbing forehead while the other settles on my churning stomach.

Concern lighting up his face for the second time tonight, Eoin cups my elbow, steadying me. "You okay?"

He is literally broken yet he's asking if I'm okay. I'd laugh if I didn't think it would make me projectile vomit. All I manage is a grunted yes. "Just dizzy."

"You don't look so good."

"Gee, thanks."

"Lu, you're kinda green."

"I'm fine," I insist even as I swallow down the bile rising in my throat. "I just need to sleep."

And fresh air. Fresh air and sleep. And probably another strategic vomit.

On legs that feel like jelly, I take a couple of steps towards the emergency room doors. With each one, my body becomes heavier and heavier until it feels like I'm trudging through mud.

I'm almost outside when my vision blurs and my ears start ringing.

I think someone says my name but I'm not sure. All I know is my legs give out completely, my knees hit the floor with a dull, painful thud, and someone hooks their arms underneath my armpits before the rest of my body follows.

The last thing I think of before my world goes black?

The unopened texts from Jackson sitting in my inbox.

26

LUNA

Dehydration.

Fucking dehydration.

Not alcohol poisoning, not a spiked drink, not even an inconvenient but kind of cool broken hand. Dehydration is what took me out.

Guess when they say not to mix your meds with alcohol, they really mean it.

I'd be embarrassed if I wasn't so consumed with feeling like complete and utter shit.

The hospital didn't even admit me. I woke up in the ER, hooked up to a banana bag. Less than an hour later, they sent me on my way with nothing more than a few disapproving glances. Tail between my legs, I dragged my ass back to Owen's place to pass out because I looked like death incarnate and if my mom saw me, she'd lose her mind. After barricading myself in the spare room and peeling off my clothes, I pretty much fell asleep the second my head hit the pillow.

God knows how many hours later, a quiet voice tries to coax me awake. My brain is too melted to pinpoint it; not even hospital-grade fluids could prevent the massive hangover I feel brewing in my temples. Groaning, I roll away from who I'm assuming is Owen and shove my head under the pillow in an attempt to drown out him calling my name.

Soft laughter and warm breath tickle my bare shoulder. "Lu, wake up."

"Fuck off," I grumble into mattress, wincing at my croaky voice. I reach around to slap Owen away, only for my hand to get caught between two calloused ones.

"Wake up, sweetheart."

I stiffen as the only cutesy pet name I can stand cracks through my hazy, sleepy mind and this time, it's not Owen saying it.

Shifting towards the voice, I crack an eyelid, frowning at the unexpectedly familiar face looming over me. Wondering if I'm still plastered. "What the fuck?"

Looking about as tired as I feel, clad in a pair of crumpled sweats and an equally wrinkled hoodie, Jackson is perched on the edge of the bed. Holding my hand. Stroking my hair.

I'm hallucinating. I'm still completely, incoherently drunk, and I'm hallucinating. That's the only explanation because Jackson is in California with his family, not in New York with me.

Forcing my bleary eyes wide open, I blink in confusion. Each time, I expect him to disappear.

He doesn't.

"What the fuck?" I repeat because they're the only words coming to mind right now. Maybe I'm still asleep. It wouldn't be the first time I've had a vivid dream about Jackson.

But then he chuckles, low and deep and very, very real, and it hits me that Jackson is here.

In New York.

In Owen's spare bedroom.

Despite my throbbing head and the fact that all I want to do is drag Jackson further into bed and curl into his side, I get the overwhelming urge to explain. Explain what happened tonight, how I ended up here. And find out why and how the hell he's here.

When I open my mouth to do just that, though, I'm cut off by a quick shake of his head. Shoving me aside gently, Possibly Fake Jackson slips beneath the covers. When he stretches an arm out towards me, I take his cue, wasting no time attaching myself to his side, burying my head in the crook of his neck, hooking a leg around his, pressing myself as close as humanly possible. Both arms hugging me tight, Feels Real Jackson rubs soothing motions down the length of me, from the curve of my neck along my thigh, and the continuous, monotonous movements do a world of good in lulling me back to sleep.

I fight it off, though, wanting to savor this confusing, but so fucking needed, moment. Two days and I missed him a pathetic amount. I missed the affection, the companionship, but mostly I just missed him. And he couldn't have magically appeared at a better time.

Inhaling deeply, I swear my headache eases as my lungs fill with that familiar spring-like scent. Propping my chin on his chest, I trace the contours of his face with my eyes, noting the dark circles beneath his closed eyes and his even messier than usual hair.

As though he feels my gaze on his face, his eyes flutter open, a lazy smile already tugging on his lips. "You're staring."

"You're in New York."

"I am."

"Why?"

"Figured you could use a hug," is his confusing, entirely too-simple response. When I frown, he adds with a sigh, "Owen called."

That's… interesting. Very, very interesting.

And concerning.

"What did he tell you?"

"Not much." Jackson accompanies what is probably a lie with a kiss dropped to my forehead. "Just that you had a bad night."

"You flew across the country because I had a bad night?"

"I flew across the country because I freaked the fuck out when you weren't responding and then some guy called me in the middle of the night and said you were in the hospital."

An embarrassed wince crumples my face. Making him worry for no good reason is bad enough. Inspiring him to jump on a plane in the middle of the night and fly for five-and-a-half hours to a whole different time zone for no good reason?

Mortifying.

Jackson smoothes out the wrinkles marring my forehead, shrugging like it's no big deal. "You would've done the same."

Except I wouldn't have. The thought never would've crossed my mind. Just another reason why Jackson is infinitely a better person than I am, and another reason why I don't deserve the sweet man lying beside me.

"What about your sisters?" God, they probably hate me. All they had with their brother was a measly weekend and I effectively stole it away.

Fingers graze my upper back, cupping the nape of my neck and squeezing comfortingly. "They didn't need me. You did."

A lump forms in my throat, accompanied by an annoying, unexpected dampness in my eyes. "Stop being so sweet."

"Why?"

"Because I'm hungover and it makes me want to cry."

Laughter washes over me, heartier this time. That big, booming one that I feel in my bones, in my stomach, in my chest, and kind of makes me want to cry even more. Swallowing hard, I discreetly swipe at my eyes and attempt to cover up my embarrassing sniffling with a cough. Still, my whispered 'thank you' comes out entirely too wobbly for my liking.

"I told you," Jackson says gently. "You can always call me. If you need me, I'm there. And if your ex fuck buddy calls me, I'll be there a lot quicker."

He's joking, I can hear it, but nevertheless, I find myself promising, "Nothing happened."

"I know." There's nothing but pure conviction in his voice. "I trust you."

Three simple words yet they carry such profound weight.

Especially after last night.

Even in my drunken haze, the venom Bea and Eva spit my way still consumed my thoughts. They filled me with doubt, made me feel insecure, until I convinced myself that Jackson would agree with everything they were saying.

Once again, I should've known better.

"Are we gonna talk about what happened last night?"

Jackson's careful but direct question has my stomach heaving. Lower the steaming mug of tea in my hand to the bedside table, I twist a piece of still-damp hair around my finger nervously. "Do we have to?"

His mouth says 'no' but his eyes say 'spill it.'

I avert my gaze to the window, momentarily distracting myself with the stellar view Jackson's hotel room has. I was pretty ecstatic when he revealed he's only flying home tomorrow, the same as me, so we get to spend the day together. Not that we're doing much besides lazing around, eating, and sleeping.

A lot of the latter. In a bed so comfortable, there's no way it's not expensive.

This entire hotel reeks of money. All polished marble and big, fancy plants and ostentatious mirrors. I've never felt so out of place than when Jackson ushered me through the lobby, my stunning attire of last night's outfit with Jackson's hoodie thrown over the top and a bird's nest-style bun piled on top of my head attracting more than one disapproving look.

"Are you sure we're in the right place?" I'd whispered, hugging myself tightly when the receptionist's unimpressed gaze fell on me.

Jackson just gave me a brief nod and a reassuring smile before turning to the bitchy receptionist with that smile turned up to megawatt status. He looked almost as run-down and tired as me, just as messy and raggedy, yet somehow, he fit in. All charm and confidence and control. Honestly, his whole demeanor was hot as fuck. I would've jumped him the second we found privacy if I wasn't well aware of my desperate need for a shower. And a toothbrush.

Post-room shower, wrapped in an impossibly fluffy bathrobe, and revived by a gloriously greasy room-service breakfast, I wanted to jump him too. But of course, he wants to talk about last night.

Typical.

Pulling the comforter right up to my chin, I make my best attempt at looking pathetic—not exactly a hard feat, considering my incredibly hungover state—and bat my lashes at the man laying beside me. "I really don't want to talk about it."

"Okay," Jackson says, and I hate him for it. I hate his gentle understanding and his inability to push boundaries and his easy concession because even though it's not his intention—maybe *especially* because it's not his intention—I feel guilty. Hiding things from him makes me feel shitty because he's so fucking *open*.

Which is why, with a huff, I mutter, "The girls said some stuff."

I've mentioned Eva and Bea before, so it's unsurprising when his face screws up. "What stuff?"

I relay every dig they hit me with. All their little, demeaning comments that chipped away at my confidence, my common sense. Reliving the whole ordeal is no less humiliating than actually experiencing it; I can't even look at Jackson.

I don't need to, though, to hear him scoff. "They're full of shit."

Jackson does not like my unconvinced shrug one bit. Two fingers lift my chin, lifting my gaze until it meets his. "They are full of shit," he repeats, enunciating each word clearly and slowly. "I don't care what label we put on it, I'm yours, you're mine, that's it."

Yours. Mine. Two little words with so much weight.

"Lu," he breathes my name softly, his lips so close the word brushes over my own. "I don't know how to make it any clearer that there is no one else I want. I wanted you the first time I saw you in the diner, smiling like butter wouldn't melt. I wanted you when you spilled a drink on me and vomited your guts up yet still looked at me with nothing but confidence. I sure as fuck wanted you when I kissed you for the first time." A featherlight touch brushes my lips, barely even a kiss yet it still steals my breath away. "And I especially want you right now."

"You got a thing for hungover blondes?"

"Nah." His nose brushes mine as he shakes his head. "It's the robe."

I snort and roll my eyes, hoping I play off how fucking ooey gooey his words make me feel even if his knowing smile suggests otherwise.

It fades slightly when, after raking his gaze over me in that way that makes me fidget, his expression sobers. "Luna, I really fucking like you."

Reigning in a grin, I look away because I can't look at him when he's looking at me like that. "You're awfully romantic today."

"I think you're supposed to be romantic when you're trying to ask someone to be your girlfriend."

My fidgeting halts, my gaze flying to his. Words get stuck in my throat, choking me momentarily, but I manage to croak out, "What?"

This time, Jackson's smile is one of utter calm, mimicked in his voice. "I know you wanted to go slow. I know this scares you. But I'm gonna ask you anyway. And if you say no, that's okay. Like I said, labels don't mean shit."

I hate that I panic.

I hate that instead of kissing the life out of him, instinct drives me to scoot off his lap and towards the edge of the bed, fleeing like a fucking startled animal.

I hate that every cell in my body screams at me to run out the door, down the hall, out of this fucking fancy hotel that he's paying God knows how much for because he flew five hours to fucking cuddle.

But then the ring on Jackson's pinky glints in a way that catches my eye. I catch sight of one of my scrunchies around his wrist; he says he steals them because they're better for his hair, but when he was sleepy and sweet and a little drunk once he told me it's because he likes how they smell. Vanilla, or something. I spot the remnants of the pink nail polish still staining his fingernails from last week when I had a bad night and just needed something to do.

Sucking in a breath, I take a moment and just fucking think for a second.

I'm not sure anymore that the little voice telling me to run is instinct. I think it's a habit. Self-preservation, maybe. The 'leave first before they leave you' mentality I've carried around for years.

Jackson doesn't move a muscle. He sits there, watching me calmly, waiting patiently, not an ounce of pressure or coercion, and looking at him, I know I don't want that instinct, or whatever it is, anymore.

I just want him.

Swallowing hard, I summon every ounce of strength I possess. "Go on, then."

Two dark brows shoot up.

"Ask me."

The answering smile I get is nothing short of fucking wonderful. Hands settling on my hips, he drags me back onto his lap until our chests are flush, my arms instinctively going around his neck as he leans his forehead against mine. "You wanna be my girlfriend, Lu?"

A part of me acknowledges how cringy this is. How this would have been a past me's nightmare. But a bigger part of me, a better part, is so happy that it drowns out that smaller part. So, I let my lips tip up in a smile that rivals his, and I let myself be ditzy and swirly, and I let myself bask in the happiness spilling out of him and over-whelming me.

"Fuck yeah."

27

LUNA

My boyfriend is taking me on a date.

Because, you know, I have a boyfriend.

Weird.

I guess I should say my boyfriend is *trying* to take me on a date. I'm wholly opposed to the idea; I would be perfectly happy spending the rest of tonight in this hotel room.

Preferably naked.

Jackson has different, lofty ideas. He glares at me playfully from where he stands in the bathroom, a towel slung loosely around his waist as he rakes argan oil through his wet hair. "Tough shit. We're going out."

I whine as I flop back onto the cloud-like bed I'd rather not leave. The soft sheets tickle my cheek as my head falls to the side, eyes following Jackson as he crosses the room and crouches to rifle through the bag thrown on the floor. "Why can't we just stay in?"

He cuts me an exasperated glance as he swaps his towel for underwear. I'm only human, so of course I stare with a dry mouth at the other tempting reason for us not to leave the room. "Because I wanna show off my hot girlfriend."

That makes me snort. '*Hot,* isn't the word I'd use to describe me right now. '*Hot mess,* maybe. Sighing, I prop myself up on my elbows. "I have nothing to wear." Unless you count my outfit from last night that honestly needs to be incinerated.

"Don't you?"

I like a lot of things about Jackson but the smile he's currently wearing isn't one of them. It's smug, like he knows something I don't, and it only gets worse when he digs around in his duffel a little more and pulls out…

A shopping bag.

A branded shopping bag.

An *expensive* branded shopping bag.

I sit up slowly, eyeing the loot suspiciously. "What did you do?"

"You said you have nothing to wear, right?" Jackson replies all matter-of-factly, like him holding what has to be a couple of grand's worth of stuff is no big deal.

I can't help but blurt, "How the hell do you have so much money?"

Jackson stiffens, and not for the first time with him, I immediately know I've fucked up. "What?" I groan. "What did I say?"

With a too-nonchalant shrug, Jackson says, "Money's a touchy subject."

Of course it is.

I have a knack for running headfirst into those.

"It's my grandparents' money," he continues. "We don't really get along."

Such limited information yet so quickly, I'm getting the picture that there's not much family he does get along with.

"I don't *love* using it." Jackson joins me on the bed, dropping the bag on my lap and a kiss on my cheek. "But I have more than I need."

I could play the abnegator and pretend to be too gracious and altruistic to accept but come on. Who am I kidding? I am a simple, simple woman who fucking loves presents.

"Jackson." I adopt a warning tone when I reach into the bag and pull out a black box, one of those fancy ones tied up with a neat red ribbon. Opening it carefully because the packaging alone is probably worth more than me, a soft gasp escapes me at what I find.

A simple but beautiful satin dress sits folded neatly inside. Pale pink and silky smooth, all thin straps and draped, flowing material. I've heard horror stories about receiving terrible presents from boyfriend but this is perfect, so fucking me, and it only gets better when I find a matching mens shirt tucked beneath.

Somewhere between me lifting the dress to see it glimmer in the light, though, and accidentally catching a glimpse of the price tag, the allure dies.

"I can't wear this."

"Not really giving you a choice, sweetheart."

"It's too expensive." *Way* too expensive. He said it himself, money is a touchy subject. It obviously makes him uncomfortable and I don't want to be a source of that when I don't need to be.

Jackson doesn't share that same mindset. "It's the dress or the robe, Lu."

"If you're spending all this money to get me to put out, it's really unnecessary."

"I know."

"I don't need a fancy dinner, either."

"I know that too." A hand coasts along my thigh, settling high and squeezing. "Maybe I just like knowing the whole time you'll be thinking about me fucking you."

"Stop teasing if you're not gonna deliver." It's half a reprimand, half a plea. I don't think I can handle another false start. Tongues and fingers and lips just aren't cutting it anymore. I feel like an addict, constantly chasing a bigger high than the last, and him dangling it right in front of me is downright cruel.

"I told you, sweetheart. I'll stop teasing when you start behaving." Rough fingers rest on the curve of my neck, stroking the flesh there tenderly, contradicting the roughness of his voice and gaze. "You gonna behave?"

I nod without hesitation, and I get a brush of his lips against mine as a reward.

"Good girl."

～

Dinner lasts a fucking eternity.

I can't stop squirming, wriggling around in my seat like an unruly toddler while the immaculately dressed waitress shoots me the occasional irritated glare.

Honestly, I'm not sure if she's glaring at me because the short dress, high heels, and nervous energy I'm sporting are entirely out of place in a restaurant full of people who look like they know exactly where they belong in the world, or if she's annoyed that my presence means the handsome man opposite me is taken.

Judging by the stars in her eyes and the drool on the corner of her mouth, I'm betting on the latter.

Honestly, I don't blame her. I really don't because Jackson looks *good*. Better than good. A silky, pale shirt clinging to every muscle and complimenting his skin tone, long hair slick and styled, and Jesus Christ, his *hands*. The ring he stole from me isn't alone tonight, and the gold bands accompanying it are doing everything in their power to hold my full attention, battling with the rest of Jackson.

I barely taste whatever the hell I eat, way more focused on the deft fingers tracing circles just below the hem of my skirt. Every so often, he sweeps higher, fingertips grazing my inner thighs lightly but oh-so-fucking-purposefully. Each extra centimeter has me jerking in my seat, once so hard, the fork in my hand clatters to the floor.

Little shit.

I try to get my own back. You know, the classic 'oops, I dropped my cutlery, let me just accidentally brush your crotch on my way to get it.'

I'm barely upright again before a strong hand closes around mine. Even as his eyes flare and his voice drops to that dangerous timbre, Jackson exudes composure. "Keep that up, Lu, and I'll fuck you right here on this table."

I have to clamp my lips together to prevent the embarrassing noise brewing in my throat from sneaking out.

Smirking, Jackson pats my thigh, fingers squeezing tightly and remaining there for the rest of dinner.

He's long since let go but still, as we leisurely stroll the short distance back to our hotel, I still feel his burning, branding touch. It's almost annoying how affected I am by him while he remains unrattled. How he's all calm and collected on our way back to the room while I'm a jittery mess. I keep waiting for his demeanor to shift, for him to pounce like he's been promising, but he doesn't.

A pout forms when we go the entire elevator ride without him making a move, and the longer he goes without touching me, the more pronounced said-pout gets. By the time we get back to the room, I'm a bundle of horny irritation bordering on an almighty tantrum.

The rational part of my brain knows this is his goal, getting me frustrated and using my brattiness against me, but still, I play right into his hand. And he loves it; his self-satisfied smirk proves it.

Once we're back in the room, I'm contemplating whether locking myself in the bathroom would be a step too far when hands on my waist pull me to a stop. Hair swept to the side, lips fall to my neck, kissing softly. "You have a nice night?"

I suffocate my soft sigh. "Mmhmm."

"You didn't want dessert?"

"Nothing that was on the menu."

Jackson releases a slow, low chuckle. "Always so impatient."

"Horny," I correct. "I'm horny, Jackson"

That evokes a real laugh, one that rumbles from his chest and vibrates through me when he drops his head to my shoulder. "Jesus Christ, Lu."

"Just being honest." I shrug his hands off, spinning to face him as I perform a serious act of contortion to unzip my dress. "And, honestly, I'm starting to think you're a fraud."

Jackson's laughter stills, his smirk dimming slightly. "A fraud?"

"All talk, no action."

The smirk disappears. The playfulness ebbs away as dark brows arch slowly. "Is that so?"

I hum nonchalantly as I let my dress fall, feeling his gaze drop to my chest as the material pools around my feet. Jackson's jaw clenches, his tongue running over his teeth, his hands forming fists at his side. "Lu?"

"Hm?"

"Get on the bed."

∿

Anticipation crackles in the room like lightning.

My chest feels tight as I cautiously follow Jackson's command. He stalks toward me the minute my ass hits the mattress, coming to a stop a few feet too far away for my liking. Butterflies erupt in my stomach, and if I didn't know myself better, I'd swear they were nerves.

Luna fucking Evans. Nervous about sex.

Ha.

Jackson's hands drifting to the neck of his shirt grab my attention. He works slowly, the act of him unbuttoning somehow so unreasonably hot. Almost as hot as the way he cocks his head at me, watching me like he knows something I don't. "Lean back."

The sheets fist between my fingers as I rest back on my hands so the man staring at me with so much fucking want in his gaze can get a better view. An invisible coil in my stomach tightens at his slow perusal, trailing from my face, down my chest, settling on my closed legs. His face twists in a disapproving expression. "Spread your legs."

I don't know why, but I hesitate. My thighs clench together, unwilling to part, as if they've forgotten this man has done much more than look before. *Cowards.*

"Let's not pretend you're shy, Lu," Jackson croons, brows pitched high as he stares at me in amusement. There's something else hidden in his gaze though, something softer, and it seeps into his voice, automatically relaxing my limbs and quieting the unfamiliar flutters doing a weird dance in my stomach. "Let me see you."

Slowly, I do as he asks. Immediately, his eyes flicker down, gaze darkening as he practically licks his lips. I damn near do the same thing when he shrugs his shirt off, revealing that tan, lean body. "Remember the morning after Halloween?"

As if I could forget.

"Touch yourself, sweetheart."

The commanding cadence of his voice leaves me powerless to do anything but oblige. My hand slips between my legs, his eyes tracking my every move. God, all he's done is stare at me and fucking chat a little yet I'm wet. Easily, I slip a finger inside myself and brush my clit with the heel of my hand, a small sigh escaping me as pleasure tickles my spine.

A displeased tut interrupts my brief moment of pleasure. "Just one? If you can't handle more than that, we're gonna have a problem."

"You have complaints, you do it yourself," I retort but nevertheless, another finger joins the first. I don't restrain my moan, nor my hips as they buck, the sparks erupting from my core only heightened by Jackson's approving nod.

I don't take my eyes off him as he continues undressing. I don't think I could if I wanted to. I think it would physically hurt to tear my gaze away from the beautiful man looming before me.

And the *sounds*.

I never thought the unbuckling of a belt could be sexy. But as those thick fingers, the rings adorning them earlier missing but mine, slip it from his waist, the sound of leather and metal and jeans scraping against each other is the most erotic noise in the world. That combined with the little grunts of approval, the soft, encouraging words... God, who the fuck needs porn?

When he's finally, blessedly, naked, Jackson fists his cock with a tight grip. One harsh stroke draws a whimper out of me, speeds up my own movements. My supporting arm buckles, and I fall back as the pressure in my lower stomach builds, so close to bursting.

A hand wrapping around mine stops that from happening.

Jackson hovers above me, his hips pressing into mine, nothing stopping his erection from digging into my stomach. "The only person making you come tonight is me. Preferably all over my cock."

My pussy clenches at the thought. "Promises, promises."

I barely get the retort out before a pair of lips crash down on mine, rough and demanding and utterly fucking claiming. A groan rips from my throat, or maybe from his, or maybe it's both of us, as Jackson's lips brutalize mine, stealing every last bit of oxygen from my lungs.

Rough kisses move downwards, teeth nipping the sensitive skin of my neck, no doubt leaving marks because God knows this man loves leaving evidence of his presence.

Not that I'm complaining. Definitely not complaining.

Much to my annoyance, Jackson doesn't linger in any one place too long, showering one area of my body with attention just long enough to have me squirming before moving on and lavishing another. He kisses, no, *worships*, his way down, appreciating every inch of skin until I can't tell if the buzzing is a result of an impending orgasm, or from the weight of this unfamiliar pure and utter adoration.

When he reaches my lower belly, tongue swirling my navel as he kisses the jewelry adorning it, his affection turns softer, lighter, barely touching. "Remember what I said that first night? When you were begging me to fuck you?"

My hands grip his shoulders, nails digging into his skin as I try to urge him down where it's wet and aching and in desperate need of some fucking attention. "You said a lot of things."

I feel his smirk against my skin, feel the laugh he huffs. "I told you I wasn't fucking this pussy until it's all mine. So, who's pussy is this, Luna?"

Defiance, or maybe insanity, controls my mouth. "Mine."

The puff of warm air Jackson expels makes me fucking *whimper*. "Wrong answer, sweetheart."

If he thinks yanking me to the edge of the bed, dropping to his knees, and burying his head between my thighs is supposed to be a punishment, he's dead wrong.

There's no easing me into it. There's nothing slow or steady or hesitant about the way his tongue fucking impales me. Nothing gentle about the hand that clamps on my stomach to keep in my place. He devours me like a starved man until my legs are shaking, my hands are just about ripping his hair from the root, and my back is completely bowed off the bed. In mere minutes, or honestly, maybe seconds, I'm so close, I'm fucking there.

Until he fucking stops.

A needy noise escapes me as Jackson crawls back up my body, pressing glossy lips to mine. "Wanna try that again?" he murmurs with a smirk that I kiss desperately, conveying my begging with my tongue, lips, teeth, silently praying he takes pity on me.

He doesn't.

I slip my hands between us, reveling in his groan when I scrape my nails over the sculpted muscles of his chest before making a beeline for the throbbing spot between my legs, ready to take matters into my own hands before I start crying out of desperation.

Jackson stops me before I even make it to my belly button.

"Nice try." He wrestles my hands away from me, one of his pinning both of mine above my head and rendering them useless. Without warning, he slips three fingers into me, my wetness easily accommodating him as he sets a mind-numbing pace that, if he weren't purposely keeping me on the edge, would break me within seconds.

"So fucking tight, Luna," Jackson groans, scissoring his fingers until I'm shaking like a leaf, the tightness in my stomach borderline unbearable. "You think you can take me?"

Honestly, I'm having my doubts. Just his fingers are creating a hell of a burn. The hard, long, thick thing swinging between his legs is going to feel like a fucking freight train slamming into my vagina.

"I know you can. So come on, baby," he coos in my ear, his breath just as ragged as mine. Removing his fingers, Jackson rises to his knees, the tip of his cock brushing my clit and causing another cry to tear from my throat. As he looms over me, his hands coast up my legs until they rest on my knees, forcing my legs further apart to provide a perfect view of every inch of my body. My thighs scream but the ache is drowned out by a jolt of pleasure as he slides his cock through the warm, wet heat begging for him. "Be a good girl and admit it."

I'm weak. A weak, weak woman whose pride is being controlled by her vagina.

Fuck it. "Please, Jackson. Fuck what's yours."

Before I can even take another breath, he's thrusting inside of me.

Oh, *fuck*.

I don't think either of us breathes as he just about splits me in half, every inch of him *throbbing*. Despite how wet I am, there's a painful stretch but it's overwhelmed by pleasure, so much fucking pleasure that it scrambles my brain.

Jackson's face screws up in pure ecstasy, breath heavy and uneven, eyes frantically flitting between my face and where we join like he can't decide which view is better.

He settles on locking his eyes with mine, bracing one hand by my head and the other on my hip as he surges forward. God, I thought he was all in, but apparently not because suddenly, another couple of inches slip inside of me until I swear he's in my fucking womb.

I can't breathe. I can't think. I don't think I can move, but God, I want to because I need more of this.

"Fuck." Jackson's sudden panicked rasp knocks me out of my haze. "Condom."

Oh, God. *Fuck*.

I *forgot*. I never fucking forget; I'm like a walking birth control ad. *No glove, no love* is my sworn motto yet the idea of pausing this for even a second to be responsible…

"I have an IUD," the desperate, lust-addled side of my brain blurts, "and I'm clean."

"Fuck, Lu." Jackson drops his head to my shoulder, his heavy breathing tickling my neck. I whimper as the subtle shift sends tremors up my spine. If he doesn't start moving, I might actually cry.

After what feels like an eternity, Jackson starts to pull out. Assuming he's going to get a condom, my breath comes out in a big, slightly deflated *whoosh*, cheeks a little flush with embarrassment for being such a horny little bitch.

That is, until he surges forward again, drawing a gasp out of me that he swallows by clamping his mouth over mine, the thrusting of his tongue in tune with the thrusting of his hips, deep and so hard, the headboard rattles. "I've never not used a condom before," he pants. "You make me lose my fucking mind, Lu."

Yeah, well, the feeling is definitely mutual.

I grasp for purchase as he pounds into me, palms coasting along the bedsheets, his broad shoulders, his supple ass. Every rough pump sends a jolt of pain through me, but the good kind of pain. The best kind. The satisfying, rewarding kind that's accompanied by so much pleasure, it's all I can think about. My head falls to the side so I can watch him slide in and out of me, too many inches disappearing and reappearing glossy.

"See how wet you are?" Jackson grunts, watching me watch us. "See how wet I make you?"

If he expects anything more than a moan in response, he must be sorely disappointed.

"Come on, pretty girl," he coos, a hand coasting up my stomach to tweak my nipple. "Let go."

I come with a scream, contorting and flailing beneath him. He coaxes me through it with pretty words, calling me beautiful, perfect, all fucking his, and I'm fucking glowing.

I grapple at his chest, unsure if I'm pushing him away or pulling him closer. "Too much," I choke out when a thumb circles my clit, the words barely more than a moan. "Can't."

Lips graze my wrist, my forearm, anywhere he can reach. "You can take it."

God, I don't know if I can. I'm sweating, shaking, dizzy, and breathless but, fuck, it feels so fucking good.

Jackson doubles down, fucking folding me in half like a pretzel as he hoists my leg up and tosses it over his shoulder. "One more, sweetheart," he coos in my ear. "Give me one more."

And because I am the best girlfriend, I do.

Jackson's thrusts become more frantic, his cock swelling inside of me. I dig my fingers into his ass cheeks, urging him further inside of me, if that's even fucking possible. With a low groan, he shoves himself into the hilt, kisses me, and explodes.

Violent is the only word I can think of to describe us coming together. Sweaty skin and dirty words and bruising grips and clashing teeth. I taste blood as he bites down on my bottom lip hard, or maybe it's me biting him because I don't feel a sting of pain, just waves and waves of brain-numbing euphoria.

I have no idea how long passes before our twitching bodies collapse, Jackson bracing himself on his elbows so he doesn't crush me. When, after a long moment of ragged breathing, he eventually slides out of me and rolls on his side, he leaves behind gaping emptiness and throbbing pain.

Fuck, that's going to hurt in the morning.

Even through closed eyes and a hazy mind, I feel his gaze trained on me. "What?" I half-murmur, half-yawn, the effort of cracking an eyelid enough to make my head hurt.

"Nothing." He swipes a strand of sweat-soaked hair away from my equally sweaty neck. "You just look really beautiful."

I resist the urge to crack a lewd joke about how, yeah, I'm sure I do; exhausted, sweaty, his cum dripping down my thighs.

Instead, I revel in the compliment, let it settle in my chest and taint my cheeks with a blush.

When I can no longer stand the weight of his stare, I force myself to get up and stumble to the bathroom to pee, grimacing with every movement. When I return, I find Jackson sprawled across the bed, still butt-ass naked, eyes closed, arms folded behind his head, face lax in an expression of pure content.

I dither in the doorway, an odd feeling in my stomach as I watch him. This part is weird. The staying. Leaving a bed with every intention to get back in. There's still a teeny, tiny part of me that wants to flee, but I'm self-aware enough to admit that it's the shit-stirring, dramatic part.

As though he senses my presence, Jackson's eyes flutter open, a soft smile already curling his lips. My smile, I like to think of it as. The softer yet brighter version of his normal one that I don't ever see anyone else receive. That perfect, brown-eyed gaze lands on me and my heart throws a damn parade in my chest. "You thinking of running?"

"Maybe."

Jackson snorts. "Get your ass back in bed, sweetheart."

So fucking bossy.

Dragging my feet in his direction, I all but collapse on top of him. He lets out a half-grunt, half-laugh instantly wrapping his arms around me. Hands that were so rough mere minutes ago caress my skin with such gentleness, causing a lump to form in my throat.

They still catch me off guard. The soft touches, the reverent ones, the ones that make me feel as though I'm something precious to be touched. I can't tell if it's weird or sad or pathetic that Jackson is the first guy to touch me like that. To look at me like that. Jesus, to talk to me like that.

I do know, though, that it scares the ever-loving shit out of me.

28

JACKSON

SOMETHING ABOUT STARTING your morning by bending your girl over a bathroom counter just puts a guy in a good mood.

I'm practically whistling and skipping as I traipse around New York following the very detailed list of everything Luna wants for breakfast from her favorite bakery. "I think you bruised my uterus," she quipped when I questioned the need for a dozen varieties of pastry. "I deserve a treat."

I can't argue with that.

Luna was passed out in the bath when I left—she claimed she needed a thorough cleanse before bidding her mom goodbye later— and I'm not surprised she's still there when I get back.

The bathroom is cloudy with steam, so many bubbles piled high I can barely see Luna. Head lolling against the lid of the enormous tub, a scrunched-up towel acts as a makeshift pillow as she dozes. When I bend to kiss her damp forehead, blue eyes flutter open and blink at me sleepily, smiling lips murmuring a quiet 'hi.'

"If those are presents," she says with a yawn, eyeing the bags in my hands, "I'm gonna kick your ass."

I twist one of the bags so she can see the brand of the bakery she sent me hunting for, "So you don't want this?"

She's up and out of that bath so fast, I'm surprised she doesn't slip and crack her head open. Water sloshes over the edge as she clambers out, all but licking her lips as she slips towards me, naked and dripping all over the floor. I steady her before she falls, wrapping a towel around her as she steals the food from my hands. Scoffing one of those weird croissant-donut hybrid things in five seconds flat, she's halfway through the second when she notices the second bag in my hand. "What's in there?"

I toss her a new package of Arnica and she catches it with a grateful groan. I didn't realize I'd been so... rough until I saw the shape of my hand imprinted on her asscheek, matching mottled purple patches marring her inner thighs.

I'd feel bad, maybe, if not for the scratch marks spanning my back and neck.

I shake the bottle of meds I swiped from her handbag on the way in here before setting it on the counter next to the green tea I picked up too. Beside it, I drop my other drugstore purchase.

Luna side-eyes the Plan B pill skeptically. "I don't need it. IUD, remember?"

"Can never be too careful." Especially considering how many times I came inside her last night and this morning. With the way she's been hobbling around, I wouldn't be surprised if we somehow dislodged the fucking thing.

Luna rolls her eyes, bypassing the pill as she swipes her tea. "You just wasted fifty bucks."

"Cheaper than raising a kid."

Narrowed eyes dart around my face, searching and thoughtful. "Fine."

I slump in relief as Luna rips open the packet and pops the pill in her mouth, following it with a long sip of tea. Swallowing exaggeratedly, she sticks her tongue out, moving it around as if to prove she's not hiding the pill anywhere. "Damn." She snaps her fingers sarcastically. "There goes my chance at trapping a rich baby daddy."

"I wasn't accusing you of that," I say with more annoyance, more force, than necessary. Snatching the Arnica from her, I slather some on my hands and crouch down beside her, smoothing the cold cream over her bruised skin.

Two hands land on my shoulders, squeezing gently. "I'm just kidding."

I grunt in response, an uncomfortable feeling creeping up my spine. When she's sufficiently covered in enough cream to heal a corpse, I rise, shucking off her grip. As I screw the cap back on, Luna's hip nudges mine. "What was that?"

"What was what?"

"You went a little weird," she explains softly. "If it freaks you out so much, we can use condoms from now on. I didn't mean to pressure you last night."

"You didn't." I almost fucking came on the spot when she offered up the suggestion. Not a single part of me even considered saying no, not just because of how good it felt to be completely bare inside her, but also because of how good it felt for her to trust me like that.

But then it was over and my head caught up with my dick and all I could think about was what would happen if by some fucking chance I'd just knocked up my girlfriend of all of one day. What would happen if I'd just inadvertently but indefinitely changed, maybe ruined, two lives.

"Then what is it?"

I pause, trying to figure out what to say. I must take too long, because Luna sighs, her slumped posture screaming of disappointment. She still forces an understanding smile, though, before leaving me alone in the bathroom.

I watch her reflection in the mirror, downing her tea and scoffing another pastry before tugging on clothes. She's got that look on her face, the one where she's kind of annoyed or upset but trying not to show it. I fucking hate that look, hate being the cause of it even more.

Luna doesn't look up as I approach, nor when I sit on the bed. She only acknowledges me when I loop my fingers under the waistband of her sweats and tug until she stands between my legs. Straight-backed and arms crossed, she crooks a brow, a silent repeat of a question I loathe to answer.

"My mom had me when she was our age," I start slowly, wincing as that familiar uncomfortable feeling I get when I talk—or think—about my parents takes over. "It was an accident."

An accident that ruined her life, and not a day went by that I wasn't reminded of that.

Quite the accusation to throw at a kid.

To be fair, it's not entirely unfounded. I was the beginning of the end for her. The cataclysmic event that shattered her perfect life, ruined all her potential, stole her youth—all her words. On some level, I guess I understand her resentment.

She always said the girls were accidents too but as I got older, this sneaking suspicion grew that maybe she was full of shit.

You see, when my mom got pregnant, her and my dad were on the verge of splitting. He stayed with her out of obligation. Not to her or me, but to his wallet; my grandmother threatened to cut him off if he embarrassed her by having a baby out of wedlock. So they got married, as quickly and privately as possible, with an iron-clad prenup in place preventing my gold-digging, bimbo mother—my grandmother's words, said loud and proud despite the fact my parents were in the same Ivy League college, taking the same classes —from taking any more from the Jackson family than she already had. And, apparently, after I was born, it was good for a while. They were happy, or as happy as two people with very little in common and even less real love for each other could be.

Maybe my mom figured it was because of the baby suddenly binding them together for life because barely a year later, Lux entered the picture. But if playing happy families forever was her plan, it backfired royally. Trying to keep someone in a relationship going nowhere is hard enough. Bring two screaming, crying babies into the mix?

Good luck.

Everything just gets messier after that. A revolving door of parents and new potential step-parents and nannies. Break-ups that always ended with Mom leaving us on some random family member's doorstep for a few weeks. Make-ups that ended with a new sibling.

When she finally left for good, it was a relief, not having to live with the stifling knowledge of being her biggest mistake, her greatest regret. It's been almost a decade since we've heard from her. I don't even know if she's alive, let alone where she is.

And I don't think I care.

The words spill out easier than I thought they would, coaxed by gentle fingers threading through my hair and encouraging, under-standing eyes. When I'm done, the room settles into silence. Not awkward or uncomfortable, just... heavy. Loaded. Charged with whatever emotion pours off Luna in spades, tell-tale squirming letting me know she's struggling to reign in whatever thoughts are running rampant.

"Whatever you wanna say," I reassure her gently, "you can say it."

"I kinda hate your mom."

"So do I, sometimes. But my dad, my grandparents... they're not exactly easy people to be around. It's hard for us but it was harder for her."

"That's even worse," Luna protests, her nails digging into my shoulders. "She knew they were awful and she still left you with them."

"She didn't really have a choice."

"Why do you make excuses for her?"

"She's my mom."

"She can be your mom and still be a shit person who doesn't deserve you."

"I don't think I have the energy to hold a grudge." It's hard when you haven't seen the person you resent since before you hit puberty. And it's not like I had a bad childhood, exactly. Just a messy one. And out of all of it, I got my sisters. The rest doesn't matter.

Luna shifts, careful as she asks, "And your dad?"

I snort. The man I've seen maybe a dozen times in my life doesn't deserve that title, not even nearly. I used to get birthday cards, but they trailed off when I turned... thirteen, maybe? Not long after Mom left. And I'm the lucky one; you go down the line of sisters and the number of visits dwindle. I don't think he's seen Eliza more than twice, and not since she was a toddler.

Dickhead.

"If it makes you feel any better," Luna starts quietly, entwining our fingers, "my dad's an asshole too. Or, at least I think he is. I'm pretty sure a man abandoning his pregnant girlfriend and not wanting to know his kid would qualify as asshole-ish behavior."

"Think we turned out pretty okay without them."

"Yeah," Luna smiles, "I guess we did."

I had a weird dream last night.

Well, more of a memory than a dream. Presumably brought on by talking about my parents with someone other than my sisters for the first time in... well, forever. Whatever brought it on, when I got home from my impromptu weekend in New York, all but collapsed into bed and drifted off, I was suddenly a kid again.

Twelve years old, freshly abandoned, one of the five newest inhabitants of Serenity Ranch.

The storm raging outside mimics the dark attitude of my grandparents, their arguing almost drowning out the loud cracks of thunder. They're fighting about us, of course, and doing very little to hide it. Not even the pillow held over my head is enough to drown out all the reasons why they should ever have agreed to take care of us. How we're nothing but a drain on them. How Lux is rude and Eliza is too quiet and the twins are too reliant on each other and I look too much like Mom.

Funny how they've learned all this without spending any actual time in our presence.

I jump when my bedroom door creaks open, half expecting my grandmother to storm in and announce I need to leave immediately, storm be damned. Instead, the light seeping in from the hallway illuminates four little figures creeping toward my bed.

I sit up with a sigh. "Can't sleep either?"

"Too loud." Lux climbs up and wriggles in beside me, and the other three follow, Eliza plopping herself on my lap while the twins sandwich themselves in by our feet.

Grace wraps herself around my leg, her head resting on my knee. "They hate us."

"They don't hate us." Hate is a strong word. Heavy disdain might be more appropriate.

Eliza's little face peers up at me, brown eyes wide and confused. "She keeps calling me Elizabeth."

"She calls me Charlotte," Lottie chimes in, and the utter disgust on her face almost makes me laugh. I don't think Lottie even knew her full name until we met our grandparents for the first time and, just like they do know, they insisted on calling all of us by our full names. Apparently, nicknames are too 'common' for Jacksons.

I try so hard to distract my sisters, to block out the yelling, but nothing works. When Eliza's sniffles become too loud to ignore, stifled tears leaving a wet spot on my top, I can't take it anymore.

Quickly and quietly, I usher my sisters out of bed and bundle them up as best I can, shoving hoodies over their heads and too-big sneakers on their feet. When they're sufficiently weather-proofed, I hoist open the window, warm, damp air slapping me in the face.

"What are you doing?" Lux grips the back of my jumper, attempting to yank me back inside when I swing a leg over the window ledge. "Jackson!"

"I'm not listening to that anymore." I nod in the direction of all the freaking yelling before pointedly glancing at our little sisters. Lux follows my gaze, eyes darting from the door to the steadily falling rain to the sad girls peering up at us.

A handful of contemplative seconds pass before she sighs and practically shoves me out the window.

It takes some maneuvering but between the two of us, we manage to maneuver the girls outside without dropping them in the growing puddles of mud steadily growing around me. Before she hops out, Lux passes out a bag filled to the brim with blankets, and I stuff it under my hoodie before the rain can seep through.

Together, we make a mad dash for the old barn a couple hundred feet from the house. Lux and I broke in here on our first night when, after a long day of listening to our grandmother berate our absent mother and her choices and her children, the prospect of staying under the same roof as the evil woman seemed way too stifling to consider.

Empty stalls and eerie silence greet us as we push open the creaky door. As we pile inside, a wistful sigh catches my attention. Pushing back her head to reveal a hopeful expression, Eliza's lips twitch. "Do you think Grandma would buy me a pony?"

My chest hurts as I smooth her hair back from her face. "Maybe."

The little fib is worth it; Eliza skips away with an actual smile on her face.

The second she's out of earshot, an elbow jabs me in the ribs. "You shouldn't lie to her like that," Lux admonishes, scowling at me and looking so much older than eleven.

I elbow her back. "I'm the oldest. I can do what I want."

With the wind howling and the rain pelting loudly off the roof, we settle in the loft of the barn, the five of us drifting off to sleep as we huddle under a mound of blankets, sandwiched together like sardines in a can.

Uncomfortable and damp and noisy because of the rain, but at least we don't have to hear about how awful we are.

At least we're together.

I woke up this morning rattled, disorientated, and inexplicably sad. It was the first time we camped out up there, but it wasn't the last. The girls used puppy dog eyes to convince the ranch hands to help us make the place more comfortable, dragging half the contents of our dusty attic up there. Old mattresses, rotting furniture. There was even a hammock, at one point, before someone swung a bit too vigorously and broke it.

It became our safe spot, the one place on the entire ranch that truly felt like ours.

The first bit of a real home we ever had.

29

JACKSON

"For the last time, Lux, I'm sorry."

An unimpressed huff echoes through my phone. "Apologies don't make the abandonment sting any less."

"You are so fucking dramatic."

"Don't curse at me, Oscar."

"Sorry, *Alexandra*."

"Don't start with me," she warns, the sound of something slamming in the background only emphasizing her bad mood. The same one she's been in since I fled the house at the beginning of the weekend, barely calling a goodbye as I frantically booked a flight.

We don't take well to being ditched, us Jacksons.

"I'm sorry, Lux."

My sister grunts, her sullen attitude prominent even as she asks, "Is your friend okay?"

"My girlfriend is fine."

"Your *what*?"

Exactly the reaction I expected. "My girlfriend."

Complete silence lasts for at least a minute. And then, an ear-splitting shriek full of an insulting amount of disbelief. "*Girls!* Oscar has a girlfriend!"

In a matter of milliseconds, a whole fucking chorus of shouting breaks out, so loud I actually have to hold my phone away from my ear.

Among the cacophony, I make out Eliza's voice. "Is it the blonde girl from Walmart? The one who looks like Barbie? Can we meet her? Oh my *God*, Caroline is gonna freak out."

I don't dare acknowledge the mention of my ex-girlfriend, nor the joy Eliza exudes at the prospect of her finding out I'm in a relationship. "I'll bring her to the ranch sometime."

"Seriously?" Lux snorts while the rest of my sisters cheer. "She doesn't look like a ranch girl."

At midnight in a Walmart, she didn't look like a ranch girl. Imagine that. "She left her cowboy boots at home that night."

"I'm just saying, she doesn't seem like your type."

"Do elaborate."

"She seems a little... abrasive."

Here we go. "Abrasive?"

"I don't know. Extroverted. Wild. Loud."

Like any of those are bad things.

"You just described at least two Jackson women." And, ironically, one of them is her. *Was* her. Before the weight of responsibility chipped away at those particular qualities. "How do you even know this?"

"Eliza found her on social media."

Jesus Christ. "So you, what, scrolled through her Instagram and figured her out completely?"

"Jackson-"

"Speaking of partners, how's Mark?"

That shuts her up, like I knew it would.

"Lux," my sister sighs when I say her name, muttering something about a 'bastard big brother tone,' "I love you and I'm sorry for leaving the other night, but if you wanna talk about Luna, you better fix your tone."

"Fix my tone? You sound like Grandma."

Jesus, of all the fucking things she could've said. "And on that note, I gotta go."

If there's an apology, I don't hear it; I hang up.

It's been a long weekend, and I'm not in the mood.

Something cold and wet nudges my shoulder, and I look up to find Cass looming over me, holding out a beer. I take it from him with a grateful nod, shifting to make room for him as he flops down beside me on the sofa. "Your sisters not happy about Luna?"

I grunt as I take a sip. "I think Lux is just pissed I didn't tell her."

"Lying to your sister." Cass whistles, long and low. "Rookie move."

Yeah, you'd think I'd know better by now.

From somewhere in the kitchen, Ben yells, "Why is Grace asking me for pictures of your new girlfriend?"

"Why are you texting my sister?"

With enough pizza to feed a small army balanced on one hand, Ben joins the party, dropping the food on the coffee table and flopping on the sofa opposite us. "Because we're friends."

A terrifying thought.

Tonight was Ben's idea. Pizza, beer, whatever game is on. He wrote it on the whiteboard on the back of our front door a couple of days ago, with the time and the word 'obligatory' underlined in red.

I don't think everyone got the message.

"Has anyone seen Nick?"

A round of shaking heads.

Ben huffs as he snatches a piece of pizza. "He's being weird, right? I'm not the only one who's noticed?"

"Is he?" Cass frowns. "I think he's just focusing on his fight."

I resist the urge to laugh. Of course he hasn't noticed; they haven't been in the same room together since they got back from Thanksgiving and Nick suddenly developed a habit of making himself scarce whenever Cass appears.

Unless Cass happens to be talking about Amelia. Then Nick will linger, pretending to act uninterested. Only when he realizes I notice him lingering does he make a run for it.

I shake off the thought of my friend's sudden sketchy behavior, distracting myself with pizza. It's not quite as good as the deep-dish from the place Luna dragged me before my flight home, but it'll do. Settling back in my seat, I turn my attention to the game.

My buzzing phone distracts me after only a couple of minutes.

"Let me guess," Cass drawls sarcastically, "Luna?"

"Sisters," I correct him with a grimace. Heckling combined with the unrelenting insistence that meeting my girlfriend is a matter of life or death. And Lux's version of an apology; a text asking how many people she's cooking Christmas dinner for. "They're planning the wedding. Grace is set on the fall but apparently, Eliza thinks Luna is more of a summer bride."

Cass snickers. "My bet's on a shotgun wedding."

"Hypocrite. I'd be more surprised if you *didn't* have a secret child running around out there somewhere."

"I did see a little girl at the grocery store the other day who bore a striking resemblance to you," Ben chimes in, hiding his smirk behind his beer. "She had your eyes."

"Hey, remember when you were homeless and I gave you a room? Remember that, quippy?"

"Shame I'll have to move out soon to make room for the nursery."

We make it halfway through the game before someone knocks on the front door.

"Maybe Nick forgot his keys," Cass suggests , but I doubt it, and I'm right.

It's not Nick I find standing on the driveway; it's a disheveled, glasses-wearing blonde with a stuffed tote bag slung over one shoulder.

I waste no time stooping to kiss my girlfriend. "I didn't know you were coming over."

"Didn't know I needed a formal invitation to see my boyfriend."

It's amazing how one word can have me smiling like a damn fool. Opening the door wider, I nod toward the living room. "We're watching the game."

"Football?"

I shoot Luna a dirty look. "Baseball."

She rises on her tiptoes, kissing me again before strutting inside the house. "My favorite."

"Blondie!" Ben squeals when he catches sight of her, holding his arms out toward her and making grabby hands like a toddler. She bounds towards him, and they hug as though they didn't see each other just last night.

"Oh, Jesus Christ," Cass groans, his head flopping back dramatically. "Are you two joined at the hip or something?"

Luna flicks him on the forehead. "Jealous, Cassie?"

"Yes." Cass deadpans. "I've always wanted my own stalker."

"Enough," I reprimand both of them, gripping Luna by the shoulders and steering her towards the stairs. "I'm separating you two."

"Don't you wanna watch the game?" Luna asks with an evil glint in her eye, clearly more interesting in sparring with Cass than watching any sport.

Cass tuts dramatically. "Ditching us for a girl?"

Tossing up a middle finger, Luna retorts, "Grow some boobs, Cassie. Then maybe he'll love you more."

Cass' enraged huff follows us upstairs. I wait until my bedroom door closes behind me before letting a smug smile break out. "You're throwing that word around an awful lot lately."

"What?" Luna's head snaps towards me, brow furrowed in confusion for a second before realization sets in; *love*. She groans. "I didn't mean it like that."

"Mmhmm."

"Shut up." She shoves me away, all stroppy as she chucks herself and her bag on my bed. A faint blush creeps up her cheeks as she folds her arms and scowls at the wall. "Stop smirking," she orders without looking at me.

"How do you know I'm smirking?"

"I can feel it."

I may or may not purposely crank the smirk up a notch.

"Please," Luna begs, flopping on her back and covering her face with her hands. "You're embarrassing me."

My lips purse in a useless attempt to stop the shit-eating grin. Sitting beside her, I lean over and gently pry her hands from her face, revealing that pretty blush I'm really starting to adore.

She might not mean it like that, but I'm pretty sure that's exactly how it is. It's way too early, but I'm pretty fucking sure. I would challenge anyone to spend time with Luna and not fall in love with her in five seconds flat.

It'll be a long time before she's ready to hear that little bit of information, but it's a good thing I'm patient.

For the sake of her flushed cheeks, I change the subject. "Did you come over for a reason other than aggravating my roommates?"

"I have an art project." Sighing, Luna rolls onto her side, dragging that monstrosity of a tote bag with her. With a comical amount of effort, she wrestles out a thick file, flicking to a certain page before shoving it towards me. A familiar assignment stares back at me.

God, I hated visual journals. Every beginner art class I did freshman year had a version of one, and all of them had these ridiculous, cringe-inducing, and entirely uninspirational prompts. Looking at Luna's list, it seems they haven't changed much. My Greatest Joy, When I'm Alone, My Biggest Fear. One of them is circled a couple of times in bright pink highlighter. "How Others See Me?"

The blush that had just disappeared comes to life again. When Luna offers no explanation, I nudge her gently. "If you want my help, you're gonna have to tell me what I'm helping with."

Another sigh rattles her chest. "We have to do a weekly journal entry. And this week we have to pick from these topics and that," she taps a matching pink nail against the highlighted topic, "is the only one I like. And it made me think of you."

"Why?"

Luna drops her gaze, nose crinkling, voice quiet as she admits, "Because I like how you see me."

Fuck, yeah.

I am definitely in love with this girl.

Instead of telling her that, I kiss her. Soft and slow and silently conveying all the things she is so not ready to hear. I don't, however, manage to resist the urge to tease, "Do you *love* the way I see you?"

I see the thump coming a mile away, and I catch her fist before it hits my bicep. "I take it back." She rips her hand from my grip, cradling it protectively against her chest. "I don't want your help. I'll just fail."

"I'm done, I promise." Wrestling her hand back, I kiss her knuckles. "But I think me drawing you kinda defeats the purpose."

Luna shakes her head, shuffling around until she's sitting cross-legged, her hands flexing and unflexing nervously where they rest on her knees. "No, I wanna draw you. Or, at least, try to draw you."

"I don't think that's right either."

"Shut up. It's my journal."

"And you really wanna draw me?"

"You draw me all the time." Case in point; the pinboard above my desk currently littered with blue eyes and pouty lips and dimpled backs. "Figure it's about time I get my own back."

The concentration face is back, solely focused in my direction, and like I've proved so many times in the past, I'm not strong enough to resist anything she asks of me.

"Okay." One simple word has Luna fucking glowing. "Where do you want me?"

30

LUNA

TEN MINUTES.

Ten minutes and I'm done with this crappy class and crappy semester, and hopefully the immensely crappy mood I've been in. I can admit when I'm being a monster, and for the last couple of weeks, I've been a cranky, snippy nightmare.

But in mere minutes, the cranky snippiness will dissipate because my final exam will be over, Professor Jacobs is going to clap his hands and dismiss us and I will be free for an entire two weeks. Free from this class, and its slightly odd professor that still looks at me funny, forever.

Everyone around me is having the same anticipatory thoughts; the sound of furious writing has dissolved into impatient tapping of pens against desks and huffed breaths and absent-minded doodling. When the bell finally chimes, it's a stampede. I take my time packing up, mostly because I have no interest in being trampled, a little because I intend on keeping the white boots on my feet tread-mark free. I linger until it's safe—for me and my shoes—before getting up, slinging my bag over my shoulder as I dig through it to find my phone.

A good luck text from Jackson sits in my inbox, and it makes me smile. He's put up with me like a trooper. Kept me fed and watered and rested. I'm typing a reply, a handful of steps from freedom, when I get stopped by a hand on my shoulder.

"Sorry," my professor apologizes when I jolt in surprise, quickly retracting his hand. "I didn't mean to startle you."

"It's okay." I force a smile, shifting in place, adjusting my bag just to give myself something to do with my hands. "Did you need something?"

"No. Uh, yes," Jacobs stutters, neck turning an interesting shade of red. "I just wanted to wish you luck. Next year. Next semester."

"Oh." I fight to keep the frown off my face because of all the professors to wish me luck, I wouldn't have voted for Jacobs. "Okay. Thank you."

"You've been an excellent student," he continues, and the lie is as laughable as it is confusing. "And an excellent..." His throat bobs as he swallows. "And a good friend to my Penelope."

And the conversation has officially crossed over to the realm of weird.

"I really enjoyed your class," is the only response I can think of. "And Pen is great."

"She is."

I've never been one for awkward silences so when one ensues, I make myself scarce quickly. The waves we offer each other are even more awkward than the silence.

Not quite as bad as the lingering pat he bestows on my shoulder before I make my escape, but still pretty fucking odd.

I barely make it out the door 1 before I'm sequestered by another member of the Jacobs family. A pair of thin, freckled arms wrap themselves around my middle and squeeze as a head of blonde hair props itself on my shoulder. "LuLu, we're done!" Pen squeals in my ear, giving me a shake for good measure.

I pat the hands resting on my stomach affectionately, my fake smile brightening to a real one. "How'd you do?"

"Good, I think." Pen releases me, only for a moment so she can link our arms, and we walk side-by-side toward the courtyard. "Not that it matters. I'll pull the nepotism card if I need to. What's the point of being his favorite daughter if I don't get any benefits?"

"You're his only daughter."

"That we know of," Pen jokes, wriggling her blonde brows.

I roll my eyes as I laugh. "I'm meeting the girls for coffee. You wanna come?"

"As much as I would love to meet the rest of the famous trio, I have to pass." Pen pulls a face, faking a shiver. "My parents are dragging me to lunch."

"Is that a bad thing?"

"They're fighting," she explains. "There's been a lot of subtle glaring and animosity in the Jacobs household lately."

"That sucks." I aim a very loving elbow at her ribs. "I hope it doesn't ruin your Christmas."

Pen snorts. "My Christmas will consist of me sitting very still and hoping no one notices me so I don't get asked about boyfriends or girlfriends or whether I've considered changing majors yet."

I fake a wistful sigh. "The perfect holiday."

The second I answer my ringing phone, I regret it.

My dear mother, who I only see a handful of times throughout the academic year, begins our first phone call in a whopping two weeks—equally hectic schedules don't allow much time for chit chat—with a demand. Not even a hello. Just a firm, "Invite him."

"No," I reply with as much finality as I can muster.

"Yes."

"*No.*"

"Hey, I'm the mother here and I'm telling you to invite him."

"Well, he's my boyfriend and I'm saying no."

Ma makes a little excited squealing sound, the same one she makes every time I drop the b-word. I thought the poor woman was going to lose her voice the day I revealed the big news. Immediately, she pounced on the prospect of Jackson coming home with me for Christmas, completely oblivious to the fact that he technically came home with me for Thanksgiving. The same as I'm doing now, I turned her down, for more than one reason.

First of all, my mother will no doubt scare him away before he even sets foot in the door. I love her but she's an acquired taste. Like herbal tea.

Secondly, if my mother doesn't succeed in sending him packing, Eva and Bea will. I can picture it now; cornering us unexpectedly and

243

regaling him with tales of my whoring ways. I wouldn't put it past them to have a slideshow prepared. Maybe even a song.

Thirdly, I really don't want to incur the wrath of the Jackson sisters again. I know they were pissed about the whole Thanksgiving thing, despite his claims that his absence didn't matter because they don't celebrate Thanksgiving. But I know that if I had a sibling, I too would hate the girl who interrupted our short, precious time together.

And finally; if I did ask him and he said no—which he would because that boy loves his sisters—I would have a very hard time hiding my disappointment. And my embarrassment.

Which is why, for the millionth time, I let my mom know that, "I'm not inviting Jackson."

"You're not inviting me where?"

My surprised yelp echoes around Greenies' smoking area as I jump and twist awkwardly in my seat to find Jackson lurking in the doorway, stifling a laugh. "What the fuck? You scared the shit out of me!"

"Language, Luna!" Ma shrieks before making that godawful squealing noise again. "Is that Jackson? Can I speak to him? If you won't invite him, I'll do it."

"I'm hanging up now." Whatever protest Ma has is cut off by me doing just that, and promptly turning my phone off so she doesn't blow the thing up.

Us Evans women are nothing if not persistent.

The rusty metal chair I'm perched on creaks as Jackson hooks a hand around the back, dragging it until there's a big enough gap between me and the table for him to squeeze into. His knees knock against mine as he rests his ass on the edge, hands cupping my cheeks as he kisses me briefly. "Where are you inviting me?"

"Nowhere."

Up goes the corner of his mouth. "Sounds fun."

I shrug a non-answer, keeping my gaze carefully averted as I lean around him to grab my lunch. Mac 'n' cheese, an Amelia special, straight from a blue box but as long as it's not fried diner food, I couldn't care less. I'm stabbing at a hefty portion of noodles when my fork gets abruptly snatched away from me. "Hey!"

Jackson hides my lunch behind his back, body-blocking me when I try to steal it back. "Lu."

"What?" It comes out more whine than question.

"Spit it out."

Sighing, I fold like a cheap lawn chair. "My mom wants you to come for Christmas. I already told her no, so don't freak out."

"Why'd you say no?" Jackson surprises me by frowning. "You don't want me to come?"

"No, I do, I just…" I trail off with a shrug. "I didn't think you'd want to."

A sound between a snort and a scoff rumbles in Jackson's throat. "You're kidding, right?"

The shake of my head only serves to deepen his confusion. "I came to New York when I wasn't invited. Why wouldn't I come when I actually am?"

I open my mouth to argue, closing it when I realize… well, there isn't one. It's a valid point. One someone more versed in relationship probably would've come to easily but hey, he can't hold it against me. He knew what he was signing up for. "You really wanna come?"

Not a moment passes before Jackson replies, nothing but sincere. "I'd love to."

"Your sisters won't be mad?"

"Oh, they will be." Mischief glints in his eyes as I groan. "But I know just how to soften the blow."

God, I'm not sure I like his tone. "How?"

Grinning wide, he leans forward, surrounding me with an arm on each side of my chair. "How do you feel about a road trip up north in the new year?"

Shopping for a boy is fucking impossible.

I've never done it before. I've never had to. I've lived a beautiful man-and-boy free life up until this point, and never have I resented that until now.

I'm at a complete and utter loss. Except for the drawing I did of him; I framed it even though it's silly and ugly and absolute dirt compared to his artwork but his face while I was doing it? When I asked him if he could? When he saw the completed sketch and quietly traced the lines with a smile that made my chest hurt? I don't know, I just figured he'd like a copy. If only so he could look at it during times of artistic self-doubt and feel better about himself.

But I'm pretty sure a shitty drawing in a two-dollar frame isn't a present.

"Just buy yourself lingerie and call it a present for him," Kate had suggested on my way out of the door, ready for a frantic last-minute shopping session.

I'd snorted; obviously, that was my first idea. The new light pink set is already in my suitcase. Except I can't call it a present for him when it will most definitely end up being a present for me, especially because said present will more than likely get ripped to shreds and the ripper in question will insist on buying a replacement. Probably a much more expensive replacement made of diamonds or cashmere or fucking gold.

God, I'm dreading finding out what Jackson got me. Amelia joked that it's probably a key to his house. Kate said an engagement ring.

Both are terrifying.

I tried to wrangle it out of him. I used all my best persuasion techniques, most of which involve me on my knees or naked or both.

None worked.

The knowledge that he's going to buy me some perfect, expensive present that will somehow be exactly what I need or want just makes getting him something even harder. I would ask my mom for help, but I doubt she'd know either. I can't ask Nick because he's probably railing Amelia on a plane right now, and Cass is on the same plane completely oblivious to it. And I know Ben well enough to guess he'd more than likely make the same suggestion as Kate.

"Think, Lu, think," I mutter to myself. I know Jackson. I do, I know I do. I might be a little self-absorbed and selfish but I do listen to him.

He likes art. Horses. His sisters. The ranch. Grapefruit Crush. Me.

I know the things he doesn't like too, but I don't think I quite have the skills to pull off an assassination attempt on the eldest members of the Jackson family.

If I was rich like him, I'd say fuck it and fly his sisters out to spend Christmas with us, but alas, I barely have enough money to buy myself a ticket home. The horse thing seems pretty useless too, and the ranch. A six-pack of grapefruit Crush is my panic present. Which leaves me with art.

I let out a disappointed sigh, feeling like a fraud as I whip out my phone and quickly Google 'what to buy your artist boyfriend.' An iPad is crossed off the list immediately; I can't afford it, and he prefers to draw on paper. A picture of a Bob Ross mug makes me snort, and I'm clicking the link to purchase when my perusing is interrupted by a phone call.

"Ma," I groan upon answering. "I can't talk right now, I'm in a crisis."

"Let me guess," laughter rings in my ear, "shopping for the boy?"

She knows me so well. "This is impossible."

"You can't find anything?"

"Nothing good," I grumble, briefly distracted by a hoodie that maybe Jackson would like.

"Elaborate, hun."

"A shitty framed picture and an arguably not shitty Bob Ross mug that is apparently available in three Targets near me."

"Hun, that sounds fine."

"You know, you're not supposed to lie to your children."

Ma snickers. "I'm not lying. It sounds great."

I huff, still not convinced. "It just feels so... inadequate. Like none of it is good enough."

"Luna, is it..." Mom pauses, clearing her throat. "Is it the money thing?"

The money thing. Aka my boyfriend being rich. Disgustingly rich. Maybe a millionaire. Or a billionaire. We didn't iron out the details but it's got to be rich-rich if he can drop a couple of thousand dollars on a dress. Rich enough that anything I buy him will look pitiful compared to whatever he gets me, or whatever he could get himself.

"He's not going to care how much you spent," Ma says gently. "And if he does, he's a piece of shit."

"He's not. He won't care." But I do. For some reason. I don't know, I just want to do something nice for him, for once. Something equally as nice as everything he does for me.

"You shouldn't either."

I know I shouldn't. I know I'm being silly. But I care.

A lot.

31

JACKSON

"I should warn you."

Luna's whispered words bring me to a halt. I glance over my shoulder and find her dithering at the top of the stairwell of her mom's building, staring at the apartment at the end of the hall, nose scrunched and expression pained. I raise a brow, gesturing for her to continue.

"She's going to be excited."

"Okay?"

"Like, really excited." She manages a couple of steps towards me, close enough that I can grab her hand. "And a little forward."

"Apple doesn't fall far from the tree."

Luna's free hand smacks me on the bicep. "If anything she says makes you uncomfortable, just tell her to back off, okay?"

"I have four sisters who live to make me uncomfortable. I can handle your mother."

"Don't say I didn't warn you." Luna rolls her eyes but she lets me drag her down the hall. We stand outside a pale pink door for a grand total of three seconds before it flies open and Luna gets yanked forward, wrapped up in the arms of a woman the spitting image of her. "There you are!"

Jesus. I thought the Jackson genes were strong but the Evans women are carbon copies of each other, both sporting the same mop of blonde hair and bright blue eyes and even brighter smiles, only a few grey hairs and the odd wrinkle separating them. Not that there's many of those to be found; they could be sisters, honestly.

They even babble the same, talking a million miles a minute as they move inside the apartment, Luna's nerves apparently forgotten. As is my presence until Luna's mom's gaze flits my way and her smile widens exponentially. Before I know it, I'm being dragged into a fierce hug too. "You must be Jackson!"

As not-awkwardly as I can manage, I hug her back. "Nice to meet you, ma'am."

The slap on the arm I get further proves that this woman is indeed Luna's mother, as does her scarily familiar tut of disapproval. "None of that *ma'am* crap. It's Isla."

Oh, how horrified my grandmother would be to hear that.

I smile and nod, and Isla slaps me again, a friendly one this time, two palms clapping against my biceps before she drags her daughter toward the kitchen, making a beeline for the kettle. "Where's all your stuff?" she asks, eyeing Luna's lone handbag suspiciously.

Lu slips into one of the bar stools around the tiny kitchen island, fingers drumming against the surface. "Dropped it off at the hotel before we came here.

"You didn't have to stay at a hotel."

"You don't have room for us here," Luna counters, waving an arm around the small apartment. She's not wrong; the one-bedroom apartment barely looks big enough for Isla.

I like it. It's cozy. Everything I want in a home. Lots of distressed wood and bright colors and old, vintage furniture and a myriad of knick-knacks. Photos of Luna and Isla cover every available surface, scattered across coffee tables and bookshelves and hanging off the walls. There's artwork everywhere too on canvases of every size, artists I recognize and artists I don't, Isla's work probably mixed in there too. A loft hangs above us, and I remember Luna telling me her mom turned her old bedroom into a studio when she moved out.

Isla must notice me staring. Pausing her tea-making, she gestures toward the loft. "Make yourself at home, hun."

I only falter for a moment before heading toward the steep wooden staircase. Immediately, I'm assaulted by the smell of paint. Bright natural light pours in from a skylight, illuminating the paint-splattered walls covered in finished canvases. Half-finished ones lean against the walls. A battered easel sits in one corner, a desk beside it, piles of paints and brushes and palettes stacked high.

God, I'd love something like this one day. A proper studio.

Not wanting to intrude on what's so obviously such a personal space, I don't linger long before heading back downstairs. My feet hit the bottom step just in time to hear Luna proclaim a whispered '*oh my god*.' Still perched on a stool, she hunches over the island with her head in her hands, my favorite pretty blush creeping up her neck.

"What?" Isla remarks, a familiar mischief glittering in her gaze. "I'm just saying! I wouldn't want to stay with my mother either if my boyfriend looked like *that*."

"Jesus Christ, Ma." Luna rubs her forehead as she lifts her head, a groan ripping from her throat when her eyes land on me. Following her daughter's line of sight, Isla spots me too. Unlike her daughter, she doesn't look the least bit embarrassed.

"Your studio is incredible," I tell her as I make my way over, coming to a cautious stop beside Luna. I'm not sure how she feels about the whole PDA in front of her mom thing, so I keep my hands firmly by my sides.

That is, until she cozies up beside me, grabs my arm and throws it over her shoulders before shoving her hand in my back pocket.

Isla eyes us in amusement, pure delight in her grin. "Thanks, hun," she responds to my earlier compliment, shoving a mug of piss-yellow, grassy liquid in my hands. "Luna mentioned you're an artist."

I force down a sip of the tea and shrug. "I like to draw. Nothing like what you can do."

"Please, there's no need for modesty in this house." Isla waves off my words and jerks her thumb in her daughter's direction. "This one sends me pictures of your drawings. They're wonderful."

I shoot Luna a look. She offers me a guilty smile. "What? They're of me. Figured I didn't need permission."

Tugging her closer, I drop my lips to her temple. "Sneaky."

"Smart," she corrects.

Isla watches our interaction, hands clasped beneath her chin and an honest-to-God sparkle in her eyes. "I think I've died and gone to heaven."

"Ma!"

"What? I thought you'd never bring someone home. Let me bask in it a little."

"I'm never bringing him back here."

Isla holds up her hands in mock surrender, but the grin on her face doesn't fall.

The conversation lapses into mindless chatter, the two women catching up while I choke down the rest of the tea, Luna watching me knowingly all the while. Since we're not staying here, Isla insists that the least she can do is make us dinner. When she opens up the fridge to start pulling out ingredients, she casts a backwards glance at her daughter.

"Hun, can you drop this over to Mrs Russo?" She brandishes a Tupperware stuffed full of what looks like some kind of pasta. "I told her you'd say hello while you're here, and I promised her my leftovers."

Luna opens her mouth to protest, but it quickly snaps shut when her mom pins her with one of those don't-mess-with-me looks that I think only the Evans women have truly mastered.

Luna turns to me, eyes apologetic. "You gonna be okay here by yourself?"

I nudge her gently toward the door. "Go."

She rises on her tiptoes, pressing a quick kiss to my lips before shooting daggers at her mom. "Behave. *Please*."

Isla slaps one hand over her heart. "Cross my heart and hope to die."

Reluctantly, Luna snatches the Tupperware and ambles out of the apartment, shooting her mother one last warning look before disappearing. When the door closes behind her, Isla pats my arm. "Here, come help."

I round the island to stand beside her, taking the knife she holds out to me. Together, we chop vegetables in silence.

Well, we do for a solid two minutes until Isla sighs and sets her knife down. I knew a 'don't fuck with my daughter speech' was coming but what leaves her mouth? Not quite what I expected. "My daughter is a handful."

Unsure of how to respond, I stay silent.

"She's a handful," Isla repeats. "I know it, she knows it, you probably know it by now. She is not an easy person to know. She doesn't trust very easily or let people in very often and it speaks wonders that you managed it because she makes it hard on purpose. But that tough front she puts on is just that; a front. She hurts just as bad as any of us."

That, I already know.

"You make my daughter happy, but as soon as you don't, we have a problem. You hurt my girl, I hurt you. Got it?"

"Got it." I nod. "For the record, I have no intention of hurting your daughter."

"I know you don't." Isla nudges me, a hint of a smirk on her face. "But I've always wanted to give the whole scary mom speech. How'd I do?"

A laugh escapes me as I go back to chopping carrots. "Shaking in my boots."

~

Luna is still asleep when I wake up on Christmas morning.

Sprawled on my chest like she always is, naked like she always is. I swear the girl can't sleep with a scrap of clothing on.

Tucking a wayward strand of blonde hair behind my girl's ear, I brush my lips against her cheek. "Merry Christmas, sweetheart."

Luna grunts and burrows her face in my chest, clutching me tighter and coaxing a chuckle out of me. "What's that?" I tease, fingers tickling her arm. "You don't want your presents?"

Her head shoots up so fast she almost clocks me on the chin. "I'm up."

Wrapped in the duvet like a burrito, Luna shuffles upright, scrutinizing me as I rifle through my bag. "Jackson," she mutters in warning, cautiously eyeing the multiple gifts I retrieve. I shush her by tossing the first one on her lap, gesturing for her to open it as I stretch out at the foot of the bed.

I purposely started with an easy one but her face still goes a little funny as she unwraps the small parcel to reveal a small box. "To replace the one I stole," I tell her as she lifts the lid and wastes no time slipping the ring inside onto her pointer finger. A simple gold band—one that won't stain her skin green—with a moonstone in the center of a setting shaped like a star that you can spin—so she doesn't rub her skin raw anymore.

That crumpled expression remains even as she holds her hand in front of her face and murmurs, "I love it."

"Good." I toss her another, eager to get this over with because God, I hate giving presents almost as much as I hate getting them. "Next one."

This one, she rips open with a little more enthusiasm, her caution waning ever so slightly. Her laugh hits me right in the chest as a whole bunch of panties rain down on her lap, a mixture of skimpy lacy and comfy cotton.

"To replace the ones I ripped,"" I explain, swatting her away when she flicks the fabric at me. "That one, too."

When she opens the biggest parcel in the pile, I get a faceful of LuluLemon leggings. "This is too much!"

"You're not done yet."

Luna huffs but puts down the present-slash-weapon and reaches for the last one. The only one I'm actually nervous about.

"Don't kill me, okay?"

"Great start." Luna snickers but her laughter abruptly dries up when she opens the slim envelope in her hands. She pulls out the contents gently, hands trembling like she's scared she might ruin them. Her throat bobs as she swallows, her voice a little shaky. "I don't think I can accept this."

"You can," I disagree. "No returns."

"They're-"

"Flexible," I finish for her. Flexible return tickets from New York to Los Angeles, valid any time within the next year. One for her, one for her mom, in case Luna wants to go home or Isla wants to come to us. Whatever they want. "You can use them whenever you want."

"Jackson," she breathes my name like it's a complaint and a praise. "Too much."

"Not enough," I reply, crawling over and flopping down beside her, pressing my lips to her shoulder.

I'd give the girl the fucking world if I could.

Even if the girl very clearly doesn't want it.

With shiny eyes, she pouts. "I don't wanna give you your presents now."

"You already gave it to me." And the now-shredded scrap of pink lace on the hotel room floor was put to good use.

"That wasn't your present."

"Felt like one." As blue eyes roll, I shuffle upright, leaning against the headboard with my hands folded in my lap. "Come on, then. I want my presents."

Every last one of her grumbled protests, I refute. She doesn't seem to realize that I wasn't expecting anything in the first place. That she could get me dirt and I'd be the happiest man alive. That I've never gotten a present that was actually for *me*, that didn't revolve around a price tag.

And a Bob Ross mug with a Target label on the bottom?

That's definitely for me.

32

JACKSON

THE REST of our week in New York is a blur, with Luna in full-on tour guide mode, ushering me around the city, cramming in as much sightseeing as possible. And eating. So much eating. The Evans girls can really pack it away; I have to fight to keep up.

I don't mind any of it. Luna looks so damn adorable, wrapped up in a bright pink faux fur coat and a matching hat pulled low on her forehead, cheeks flushed from the cold, gripping my hand and bouncing on the balls of her feet like an overexcited toddler.

And she looks happy. Really fucking happy. Like, grinning from ear to ear every waking moment of the day. Laughing more than I've ever heard her laugh before. And not the cute little chuckle either, the real cackle that she hates but I love.

It's that laugh that stops me from objecting when she grabs my hand and drags me towards what is quite possibly my worst nightmare.

Give me a seven foot tall horse to ride? I'll do it.

A barn roof needs repairing? Easy.

Strap a pair of skates on my feet and throw me on a patch of ice? It's not going to be pretty. Especially when that patch of ice has what looks like hundreds of people zipping around on it.

"It'll be fun," Luna promises as she drags me towards a stall renting skates.

Fun, maybe. Deadly, more than likely.

I don't complain though; I just grin and bear it.

Luna laces up her skates like a professional while I fumble, all thumbs. She practically skips onto the ice while I shuffle like a newborn deer, awkward as hell. Her skates hit the ice and she's off, gliding around effortlessly, while I can barely manage a single step without risking embarrassing injury. When she does a spinning twirly thing that would've landed me in the hospital, I squint at her suspiciously. "How are you so good?"

Skidding to a stop, Luna shrugs, anything but innocent. "I took lessons when I was a kid. Had a big crush on Tessa Virtue."

"For how long?"

"Five years, give or take." The little shit cracks a smile. "It was more like an obsession."

Of course.

Luna holds her hands out, wiggling her fingers until I take them in mine. Slowly skating backwards, she tugs gently. "Bend your knees a little." I follow her instructions but it does nothing to help the unsteadiness of my skates.

Luna does all the work, pulling me along like I'm a child as I grip her hands for dear life. "Well, well, well." Luna's slightly smug voice has me looking up from the patch of ice I'm staring a hole into. Graceful as anything, she guides us back to the railing, a slender hand on my hip keeping me stable while the other brushes my cheek. "I think we finally found something you're not good at."

"Shut up."

Happiness incarnate, she laughs and brings my mouth to hers, her joy a palpable thing as she kisses me, and I greedily swallow it all.

A loud squeal breaks us apart. "Oh my God!"

Luna stiffens in my arms, and I glance down to find her looking over my shoulder with a rigid expression. Following her line of sight, I find two girls leaning against the railing, gawking at us. "Oh my God," Luna repeats in a monotone voice before pasting on the world's fakest smile. "What're you doing here?"

I'm not sure the girls hear the question; they're too busy staring at me.

"You were telling the truth," one of them says, surprise lacing her tone.

I frown. "Excuse me?"

"We all thought she was lying about having a boyfriend," the other girl chimes in, a smile on her face that's almost as fake as Lu's but decidedly sneakier. "No, sorry. Not a boyfriend. Just a boy. Right, Lu?"

Suddenly, it clicks.

The nasty smiles, the snooty voices, the ability to look down their noses at us despite the fact both Luna and I are taller than them. It's got to be those *'friends.'* The reason I spent Thanksgiving here.

"Eva. Bea." Luna spits through gritted teeth, confirming what I already knew. "This is Jackson. My boyfriend." I notice how she enunciates that last word. I also notice how she clings to my arm desperately. Slipping an arm around her waist, I cling right back, offering the two girls nothing more than a somewhat polite nod.

Polite is not the word I'd use to describe their reactions to me.

Predatory would be more accurate.

I feel like a piece of meat on display as their eyes drag over me, lingering on the arm wrapped around Luna, and on my lips where there are probably traces of her lipgloss. The pair exchange a look that I don't understand but Luna clearly does because she becomes even more rigid, her grip tightening, and I pull her closer. "Hate to rush away so fast," I lie, 'but we've got to go. Lunch reservations."

"Oh, that's too bad." Eva, I think, fakes a dejected expression. "We were hoping we'd be able to get to know you. You know, while you're still around."

I smile, trying not to grit my teeth. "I'm sure I'll be back soon."

"Hm." The one I think is Bea hums, unconvinced. "We'll see."

Yeah, I hate them. I've only known them for a handful of minutes but I hate them. And that's not a word I use lightly, or often.

Five minutes ago, I didn't think I'd be the one dragging Luna off the ice and guiding her towards the nearby bench, eager to change and get the hell out of here. We almost make it, too, but a grating voice and a godawful offer stop us in our tracks. "Hey, we're going for dinner tonight. Why don't you join us?"

"I don't-"

"We insist."

"We have-"

"Luna!"

"Fine!" Luna practically screams as she relents, casting me apologetic eyes.

Those awful girls grin like the cats who got the cream. "Great. We'll see you tonight." Slipping her phone out of her pocket, Maybe Bea holds it out towards me."Give me your number so I can text you the details."

Lu barely manages to contain her snort, and I once again have to tighten my grip on her; this time, to prevent her from clawing Bea's eyes out.

Instead of my number, I give her a dismissive look. "You have my girl's number. Text her."

$\sim$

"We do not have to go."

I shoot Luna a look. Considering we're already standing outside the restaurant, I think it's a bit late for that.

"We could just leave," Luna tries again. "No one's seen us yet."

"If you wanna leave, we can leave." It's an empty offer; I know we're not leaving. Not when there's probably a bet going on us ditching.

Like I knew she would, Luna inhales deeply, setting her shoulders before taking my hand and leading me inside. "We go straight to the bar, okay?" she mutters, anxiously looking around the room in search of her so-called friends. "We go straight to the bar, we take at least five shots, and then we find them."

It's a good plan. Or at least, it would be if there wasn't a fatal flaw. If two of New York's most vapid inhabitants didn't have their eyes fixed on the entrance, spotting us as soon as we appear.

"You came!" Eva and Bea rush towards us, wrapping Luna in a dramatic hug and shooting each other oh-so-subtly surprised glances.

I, unfortunately, get a hug too. An over enthusiastic one that lingers, accompanied by chirping in my ear about how Luna "bagged a hottie.' When they finally let me go, I take a generous step back, purposefully angling myself behind Luna, wrapping my arms around her waist and tugging her back against my chest.

Rude and Ruder pause, their perfectly fake expressions fumbling for just a second before they fix their faces and simultaneously coo over how cute we are.

Again, I find myself thinking about how much I hate them. The way they're looking at Luna, the way they're looking at me, the way they're looking at each other, I hate it. I can't imagine Luna ever being friends with them, ever being like them.

Luna's a lot of things, but mean? Cruel? Duplicitous? Never.

I keep a strong hold on Luna as the girls guide us to our table. We're almost there, just a few steps from the beginning of the end, when she suddenly freezes. Slowly, she lifts her chin to look up at me, a grimace already twisting her face. "I am so, so sorry."

She doesn't get a chance to explain why, and I don't get time to ask. A second later, someone hollers her name. "Luna! There's my girl!"

My girl?

Before I can process anything, Luna is wrenched from my grip and tugged into the arms of someone else. Stiff as a board, she casts a muted smile at the vaguely familiar guy pawing her but he doesn't see it.

He's too busy grinning at me.

"Nice to see you again, Oscar."

It takes me a second to place him.

Owen.

The guy who called me Thanksgiving weekend. Who I only spared a 'quick' hello when he let me into his house before darting upstairs to find Luna.

I probably should've guessed he'd be here. I can easily guess who orchestrated his presence. What I couldn't have guessed though is that he'd be looking at Luna the way he's looking at her right now when I'm standing right fucking here. Not quite as predatory, more appreciative, but still entirely unwanted.

"Damn." He lets out a whistle. "Looking good, sugarplum."

Sugarplum?

Oh, you've got to be fucking kidding me.

I'm about to make a territorial fool of myself when Luna saves me from that fate. She untangles herself from Owen and steps back into my grip, guiding my arm around her waist and squeezing my forearm. "Thanks."

It's quick, the flicker of annoyance, on Owen's face, but I see it. Luna sees it, and she tilts her head back to grimace at me again. Shaking my head—*don't worry about it*—I dip to kiss her before nudging her toward the table.

I feel like I'm putting on a show. All eyes are on us as I help Luna shed her coat and hang it on the back of her chair, as I pull out her chair for her, as she sits and immediately scoots closer to me.

"Sorry," Eva croons a fake apology when I crook a brow at her staring. "This is just…"

"Weird," Owen finishes for her, and any respect I had for the guy, any gratitude I had, disappears into thin air.

I hum a non-response as I slink an arm around Luna's shoulder, my free hand reaching for the menu just as the girl across from me picks hers up. "Wow." Bea fakes a gasp, gaping at her menu with an expression of shock that makes me pray this girl has no aspirations of becoming an actress. "This place is expensive."

Eva follows her lead, just as lacking in thespian abilities as her friend. "Oh God, I didn't realize." She glances at Luna. "I'm so sorry, Lu. I can cover you, if you need it. You too, Jackson."

"That won't be necessary." We talked about this earlier. Luna wasn't happy about it but somehow, I fucking knew something like this would happen. So, when I pull my wallet out, even though she looks less than pleased, Luna gives a confirmatory nod.

"Start a tab for the table, please," I tell the waitress when she approaches, handing over my card. Turning back to the table, I take a moment to revel in the shocked expressions before adopting an easy smile. "Order whatever you want. It's on us."

I didn't think it possible but these people are worse than I thought.

Rude. Vapid. And God, annoying. So fucking annoying.

They're taking advantage of their free meal. It feels like they're testing me, ordering expensive shit and waiting for me to panic. Little do they know, I don't give a shit. For all I care, they can buy the whole damn restaurant if it gets me out of here any quicker.

By the time we make it to dessert, I'm at my wits end, and not because of their overspending or the incessant giggling or the flirty glances. No, it's the endless snarky comments shot at Luna that are testing my patience and the effect they have on my girl.

Every dig has her sinking further in her seat, like she's shrinking as they chip away at her. I try to help, to refute their comments, but they're fucking relentless. Every ten minutes, I whisper offers of faking an illness so we can get the hell out of here, but Luna refuses. She doesn't want to give them the satisfaction. She'd rather just grin and bear it and I have to stomp down the urge to ignore her wishes, chuck her over my shoulder and sprint away, snatching my card at the bar and leaving them with the enormous tab.

They're in the midst of regaling me with some story about a random party their senior year when Eva turns her gaze to Luna, a subtly wicked smile on her lips. "Remember that night, Lu?"

Lu smiles tightly. "Not really."

"Of course she doesn't," Bea chimes in, slapping her friend on the arm. "She went home early that night."

"Oh, yeah." Eva cocks her head, tone thick with innuendo, her insinuation practically slapping me in the face. "Owen did too, if I remember correctly."

It's not like they're implying something I don't already know; Owen and Luna used to hook up, Luna told me herself. But still, I sit a little straighter, tug Luna a little closer, appreciate the hand she rests on my thigh, the drumming of her fingers somewhat soothing.

When no one takes the bait, Eva's face twists in frustration. "You know they used to fuck, right?"

Despite everything, the blurted statement shocks me. It's the most blatantly rude thing anyone's said all night; every other insult was disguised as a joke or a seemingly innocent throwaway comment, moved on from quickly.

Luna's fingers pick up their pace, and I glance over to find her a mixture of cringing and seething. Linking my fingers with hers, I squeeze gently. "Yeah, I know."

"Oh." I daresay Eva looks slightly disappointed not to have caught me off guard with her little attempted bomb. "How about when-"

"You know what," Luna interrupts, downing her drink and getting to her feet. "I think we're done for the night."

"Oh, Luna. We're-"

Again, Luna doesn't let her finish. She strides away without a goodbye, and I'm not far behind. I catch her just as she's pushing outside, my hand gripping her elbow and pulling her to a stop. "Are you okay?"

"No." Shaky hands tuck her hair behind her ears. "I'm fucking pissed."

When I wrap my arms around her, she comes easily, burying her face in my chest. "I'm sorry."

"You didn't do anything wrong."

"This was a terrible idea."

Yeah, I'm not going to argue that.

"I wanted to give them a chance," Luna continues sadly, propping her chin on my chest. "To not be assholes for once. I swear, they weren't always that bad."

"It's okay, sweetheart." Stooping to kiss her forehead, I run my hands along goosebumps arms. "You forgot your coat."

"I can't go back in there."

Another kiss and I release her, slipping off my jacket and wrapping it around her. "I'll get it."

I plan on being stealthy. Hand a waiter a generous incentive to go grab it, linger by the bar, in-and-out in under thirty seconds.

That all goes to shit when a hand caresses my bicep.

"Jackson." Eva appears out of nowhere, pouting when I shake her off and step away. "You don't have to leave."

"Yes, we do."

"*We*," she attempts to coo, but her tone is bitter. "How cute."

My jaw clenches. "Do we have a problem?"

"You probably do." For the first time tonight, that falsely polite expression fades, becoming something borderline vicious as she leans in, voice low and conspiratory. "You know she's only with you for the money, right? Her and her mom are, like, totally poor. She could only go to college because she got a scholarship."

Fucking snob.

I'm saved from answering by the return of the waiter, fluffy pink coat in hand, but it's a brief reprieve. When I make for the door, Eva follows. "She's using you."

"That's enough."

"Come on, you really like that little gold-digging tramp?"

I stop in my tracks, head whipping toward her. "Watch your mouth."

"You know she's cheating on you, right?" God, the glee on her face, the joy she's getting out of trying to ruin someone else, is fucking despicable. "She fucked Owen on Thanksgiving weekend."

I almost laugh right in her face, I really do. Utter amusement curls my mouth upward but Eva's must be too far gone to notice because she continues, "We went clubbing and they disappeared together. No one could get in contact with either of them for, like, two days."

"So?"

Frustrated that I'm not falling for her ploy, a hint of desperation taints Eva's tone as she blurts out, "I saw them together the day after. At a cafe. They looked pretty close. But, hey, what do I know?"

I pause briefly; call it dramatic effect. "You saw them?"

A triumphant smile breaks out across Eva's face. "Mmhmm."

"You saw Luna and Owen together Thanksgiving weekend?"

"*Yes.*" She feigns being annoyed at having to repeat herself. "They were kissing, actually."

"That's weird," I can't help but laugh, "because I was with Luna that weekend. All weekend. In my hotel room. And I'm pretty sure I'd remember if Owen was there."

Her face falls so fast it's downright comical. "I-"

"You're a bitch," I finished for her. "A lying, manipulative, nasty bitch."

"*Excuse me?*"

"You heard me," I reply tiredly because I am so fucking done with these people. "You and your friends are pathetic."

I can't tell if it's embarrassment or anger flushing previously pale cheeks a bright red color, but either way, Eva's face reddens something fierce. "Who do you think you are?"

"Someone you do not want to fuck with." Cocking my head, I pretend to think for a moment. "You go to NYU, right?"

Eva nods slowly, and I let out a thoughtful hum. "My father used to guest lecture there. Regina MacIntyre is the Chairperson, isn't she?"

Bright red fades to slightly green as Eva nods again.

"Hm. I remember her stances on anti-harassment being pretty severe."

"We-"

"Because that's what you're doing. You're harassing her." I lean in, hoping Eva sees every bit of anger coursing through me, and the utmost sincerity in my promise. "And if it happens again, *ever again*, I'm not gonna be quite as nice as I've been tonight. Got it?"

Eva hesitates and I sigh, feigning boredom as I mess with the cuffs of my shirt. "You know, I don't leave until tomorrow afternoon. I'm sure Reggie would be thrilled to have an early lunch with her old colleague's son."

It's audible, the sound of Eva's swallow, more so than the quiet, begrudging, "got it."

Kissing my teeth, I frown, angle an ear toward her. "What was that?"

"I got it," she repeats through gritted teeth and I smile.

"Good." Heading toward the door again, I wait until I have one foot outside before calling over my shoulder. "I wish I could say it was nice meeting you but I'm a really bad liar."

Luna's laughter echoes around the hotel room. "You did not say that to her!"

"I did."

"You called her a bitch?"

"More than once." And she wholly deserved it.

"Do you really know the chairperson of NYU?"

"I met her a couple of times when I was a kid." At a baseball game me and my dad bumped into her and her son, and my dad introduced me as his nephew.

Tossing away the towel she's using to dry her hair, Luna flops on the bed beside me, propping her face in her hands and gazing up at me. "I think you're my new hero."

I haul her onto my chest, the soft material of the hotel robe she's oh-so-fond of tickling my bare chest, and drop a kiss on the top of her damp hair. Forehead nestled in the curve of my neck, lips graze my collarbone. "Thank you for doing that."

"You don't need to thank me." I sat there and let them talk shit about her for too long; putting one of them in their place was necessary for my own mental health.

Angling her head to stare up at me, Luna swallows. "Jackson?"

"Yeah?"

"I think I love you."

For a moment, not a single thing passes through my brain. Another moment before I clear my dry throat. One more before I rasp my only coherent thought, "You think?" Luna's hum is shaky, as shaky as my hands as they smooth slow, calming circles over her back. "Why do you think that?"

"Need me to stroke your ego, baby?"

One serious utterance of her name is all it takes for Luna's bravado to falter. Teeth nibbling on her bottom lip, she thinks for long enough to test my patience. And all she manages to come up with? "You're nice to me."

"You think you love me because I'm nice to you?" I try and fail to hide my amusement, and get thumped as a consequence. "I'm sorry. I'm not laughing at you, I swear. I just think you need a little more reasoning than that."

Luna pauses, and I can practically see the gears whirring in that pretty little head of hers. "You make me feel nice. Safe. I don't know, seen or heard or whatever. You respect me and you protect me and you stick up for me. You know all my favorite things and you're sweet to my friends and you make my mom really happy. And you make me really happy. *And* you're nice to me."

A warm feeling erupts in my chest as the words sink in. "Those are pretty good reasons."

Cheeks pink, she shrugs.

"Luna?"

"Yeah?"

I bend so my lips hover over hers. "I know I love you."

For the split second it takes her to hide it, I see that terrified look in her eyes. "Really?"

"Really."

The first sniffle, I dismiss as being my imagination. The second one makes me frown. The third, I panic a little, alarm shooting through me at the sight of shimmering blue eyes, a single tear tracking a path down her cheek.

I've never seen her cry.

I'm not sure anyone has.

Wiping the tear away with my thumb, I cup her cheek, keeping my touch and tone gentle. "Why are you crying?"

"Because you love me and I can't say it back."

"You'll say it when you're ready."

She lets out a watery laugh. "Sounding awfully cocky again."

Leaning forward, I brush my lips against hers. "Just confident."

33

LUNA

Everyone is happy.

It's weird.

Every single one of us being so completely content is downright weird. Kind of unnerving, too. I feel like I'm waiting for the other shoe to drop, for something to shatter our perfect little world. But I try not to dwell on that feeling of impending doom too much.

After a relatively rocky Christmas and New Year, the world has righted itself and Amelia and Nick are in an actual relationship. A somewhat secret one, but a relationship all the same. Kate and Sydney are as sickeningly happy and perfect as always. Ben's standard setting is happy so no surprises there. Cass has been in a perpetually pleasant state since he walked into his house months ago and found Amelia lounging on his sofa, so again, no big shock.

And I have Jackson.

The boy who loves me.

The first of his kind.

He's not shy about dropping those three little words and every time he says it, my stomach swirls with a mixture of guilt, nerves and excitement. He doesn't seem to care that I can't say it back. But I do. I want to say it, I really do. But I don't want to say it when I'm not sure. I need to be sure. I want the first time I say those words to someone other than my mother or my friends to be real. I want to completely mean it with everything in me.

He deserves for me to mean it.

I can only pray he sticks around long enough for me to figure it out.

Sighing, I roll over in bed, his bed, trying and failing to get comfortable. Unfortunately, it's hard when you're slowly freezing to death. I swear the heating in this house is permanently on the fritz. I usually use Jackson as my main source of heat but he's missing this morning.

Actually, he's been missing every morning this week; long, early pre-season baseball practices are my nemesis. I'm excited to see him play and all, but waking up alone on deathly cold mornings is simply not worth it.

I groan when my alarm goes off, reminding me that I should get up soon. I'm supposed to be meeting the girls, but I want to say bye to Jackson before I leave. Maybe squeeze in a quickie too, if I'm lucky.

A little hopeful rush of excitement creeps up my spine when the bedroom door creaks open, only to be dashed by Ben's head peeking around the door. He's got his hand over his eyes, squinting through his fingers, an almost fearful expression on his face. The poor boy accidentally walked in on me naked one time and he hasn't quite been the same since. "You decent?"

For once, yes; if Jackson can't keep me warm, his hoodie is the next best thing. Lifting the duvet just enough for Ben to slip in, I pat the space next to me. "Get in."

He doesn't hesitate, dive-bombing onto the bed, shivering as he snuggles under the covers. "Fucking hell, it's cold."

Grumbling in agreement, I hook my legs around Ben's and yank him closer so I can steal some of his warmth. "Skipping practice?"

"Nah, we finished half an hour ago," he murmurs into my chest as he uses my boobs for a pillow. "Your boyfriend should be back soon. Think he went on a Starbucks run."

Yeah, I may have threatened bodily harm if Jackson didn't return home with a piping hot beverage and a muffin in hand. In my defense, he knows better than to wake me up at the crack of dawn, even if it was for a kiss goodbye.

Hooking my arms around Ben, I give his back a soft pat. "How's life, Benny?"

"Good," he murmurs against my chest. "Busy."

I huff. You can say that again. I barely see the kid during the week. He's always running between class and practice and God knows where else. I suspect there's a secret man in the picture, but for such an open person, Ben tends to keep his love life pretty much on the down-low. I can never quite manage to pry any juicy gossip out of him. That doesn't stop me from trying though. "Too busy for a boyfriend?"

"Someone has to keep up the single legacy around here."

"Come on." I pout. "Not even a hook-up?"

"I hook up. I just don't broadcast it like you freaks. Some of us are classier than that."

That makes me snort. "If you're not too booked and busy today, me and the girls are going to brunch."

"I have plans." How surprising. "But I'll keep you company before your UberEats delivery arrives."

We get halfway through an episode of Gossip Girl before Jackson finally appears. The sight of us curled up in his bed, his laptop propped up between us, makes him pause for only a moment before he shakes his head with a laugh.

Crossing the room, he drops a kiss on my forehead and sets what looks like a hot chocolate and a blueberry muffin on the nightstand before flicking Ben's forehead. "Stop groping my girlfriend."

Ben pats my chest. "But she's so comfy."

Jackson rolls his eyes as he starts undressing, dropping his bag on the floor and stripping off his sweaty t-shirt. "Unless you wanna see my balls, Benny boy," he says as he starts to tug down his sweats, "get out."

Ben's face twists. "Ew. Gross." Kissing my cheek, he flees the room as fast as his long legs will carry him.

The moment the door closes behind him, Jackson's naked and coming at me for a real kiss. "I'm not sure how I feel about coming home to you in bed with another man," he teases, nipping at my bottom lip playfully. Laughing, I hook a hand around his neck but he slips my grasp. "I gotta shower. Wanna join?"

Casting a glance at my phone, a groan escapes me. "Can't. I have to meet the girls soon. If I'm late, they'll kill me."

His lips puff up in a cute pouty face but he doesn't push. Pecking me again, he heads for the bathroom, giving me a spectacular view of his ass. That thing really is a work of art, adorned with blank ink high on one cheek. I've noticed it before but I've always forgotten to ask about it. Or, more specifically, I've been too distracted by the rest of his nakedness to care enough to ask. "Hey, what does that mean?"

Jackson freezes. A moment passes before he glances over his shoulder, feigning ignorance. "What does what mean?"

I give him a weird look. "The ass tattoo."

"Uh, nothing."

Hm. Suspicious. "It's an ex-girlfriend's name, isn't it?"

"God, no."

"Then what is it?"

There's a long, long pause in which his face contorts in quite possibly the most uncomfortably flustered expression I've ever seen before he sighs and relents. "It's Nick's name."

I blink. My gaze flickers between his completely serious expression and his ass. "Babe, I think that's worse than an ex-girlfriend's name."

"We were drunk!"

"*We?*" I gape. "Nick has your name?"

His grim expression is all the confirmation I need.

"Oh my God." I can't stop laughing. I might actually die of laughter. Imagining a smashed Nick and Jackson stumbling into some random tattoo parlor and cementing their friendship in the form of matching tattoos on their fucking asscheeks has me falling onto my back and clutching my stomach.

God, I wonder if Amelia knows about this. I hope not, if only so I can be the one to break the news.

I attempt to sober up, propping myself up on my elbows, lips quivering with the effort of holding in my laugh. "Be honest with me. Are you in love with Nick? You can tell me, I promise I won't tell anyone!"

"I hate you."

Cocking my head, my lips pull in a smug smile. "Liar."

Jackson softens. "Yeah."

Partner-free days are decidedly rare lately.

Even today hasn't been completely devoid of significant others; I spent the morning with Jackson, I'm pretty sure Nick is waiting impatiently in Amelia's bed, and while Kate might pretend she's so much better than us, I know for a fact that she has plans with Sydney later this afternoon.

But for now, for once, it's just the three of us. I invited Pen but again, she rain-checked; apparently, shit really hit the fan at home over the holidays and she's still suffering through the aftershocks. I'm yet to get the details on that one, but I'm sure I'll wrestle them out of her at some point.

Honestly, a girl's day devoted to pampering was desperately needed. After all the excessive drinking and eating I did over the holiday season, my skin is screaming for a facial. My nails were looking pretty desperate too, considering how many layers of nail polish I painted on and picked off over the course of a week.

Snapping a picture of my new pretty blue manicure, I send it to Jackson, hurriedly putting my phone away when I catch Kate smirking at me. I aim for nonchalance as I raise a brow and sip on the mimosa I ordered with brunch. "What?"

"Nothing," she sings her reply. "Just remembering the days when relationships made you gag."

Up goes a perfectly manicured middle finger in my friend's direction. Kate just smiles while Amelia catches my hand in hers and studies my fresh nails, running a thumb over the pale blue polish. "Since when do you like blue?"

I snatch my hand away. "Since always."

Kate snorts. "Since she got a boyfriend whose favorite color is blue."

"Not everything in my life revolves around a boy, Kate," I chide, tutting dramatically.

But she's totally right. I definitely picked blue because it happens to be Jackson's favorite color. And him happening to like the feeling of long nails scratching his back might have something to do with the longer-than-normal length too.

Judging by Kate's knowing look, she's already guessed as much. But, she drops it, instead focusing on the elaborate, mouth-watering menu laid out on the table in front of us.

I got to do the same, but my phone buzzing in my pocket distracts me. Leaning back slightly in my chair, I sneak a glance, expecting a reply from Jackson. Instead, a different name lights up my screen.

Nicolas Silva: Make sure she eats.

A second later, another message pings through.

Nicolas Silva: Please.

A soft 'aw' sound leaves me as I twist my phone so Amelia can see the screen. Amelia frowns for a moment before her eyes focus on the screen and her frown fades to a soft smile that she tries to hide behind an eye roll. "I swear, that boy is obsessed with my calorie intake."

"I think it's cute," Kate coos. "He cares about you."

"Hm." My brows shoot up. "*Cares.* Is that the word we're using?"

A light pink flushes Amelia's pale cheeks. She pokes me with one of her freshly pointy nails. "Don't start."

I drop it, but only because the waiter appears to take our order and my growling stomach overrules how much I enjoy embarrassing my clueless red-headed friend. Without sharing my intentions with the others, I decide to take a leaf out of Ma's book, ordering a bit of everything to share. When Amelia makes a face at the sheer amount of food I'm ordering, I nudge her pointedly. "Come on. Daddy's orders."

A dramatic shiver wracks her body as she pulls a face. "Please stop."

"What? You getting all hot and bothered?"

"Enough!" The poor girl turns the same shade as her hair as she waves her hands frantically, as if to ward off my playful words. "Order whatever you want. I don't just care. Just please stop talking."

I just grin, patting my friend's bright red cheek. "Good girl."

34

LUNA

I'M SHITTING MYSELF.

Every mile closer we get towards Jackson's sisters, the worse I feel. Dread, anticipation and nerves twist in my stomach, causing an odd combination of 'I might burst into tears' and 'I want to vomit.'

Usually, I don't give a flying fuck what people think of me. It's a well-documented fact that I am who I am and most of the time, I don't care what kind of opinion people might have about that.

But these people are different. They're important. I want them to like me. I *need* them to like me. However, something deep in my gut tells me this weekend isn't going to work out in my favor.

Like I said before, everything is too perfect lately.

Something has to give.

Curled up in the passenger seat of Jackson's truck, trying and failing to focus on whatever song is playing on the radio instead of the negative thoughts buzzing around my mind, I've convinced myself that this weekend is going to mark the end of our weird, wonderful happy streak.

And because I'm not one to wallow alone, I make sure that Jackson is well aware of my fears.

"They're going to hate me."

Like he has for the entire drive, Jackson insists otherwise. "No, they're not."

I don't believe him. Sisters never like the girlfriend. Especially when the girlfriend is a loud, promiscuous blonde who repeatedly steals their brother away for the holidays. Especially when it's *me*.

I don't have experience with siblings, but I do have a history of being considered generally unpleasant by parents. Owen's parents never liked me. Kate's parents think I'm the devil reincarnate, their words verbatim. Hell, even my own dad didn't like me enough to stick around. Amelia's dad and Ma are the only exceptions to the rule, and one of them is bound to me by flesh and blood so does it really count?

So, yeah, I don't exactly have high hopes that Jackson's family is going to fall in love with me on sight.

Jackson takes one hand off the steering wheel and settles it on thigh. "It'll be okay."

Somehow, I really, really doubt it.

My nausea increases tenfold when the ranch comes into view, bathed in wintery, early morning light, looking like a fucking painting come to life. I would admire its beauty, if I wasn't so laser-focused on the four distant figures lingering outside what I'm assuming is the main house.

God, I really think I'm going to be sick.

The truck rolls to a stop, and Jackson gives my thigh another pat, shooting me an encouraging smile before getting out. He waves to his sisters as he jogs around to my side, opening my door for me. When he offers me a hand, I'm glad; without it, my shaky legs might've given out.

The Jackson siblings' reunion is like something out of a movie. It's as though they move in slow motion as they bound towards each other, all happy faces and excited greetings and big hugs. The blatant affection, the love, is downright palpable in the air.

Me? I trail behind, dithering on the sidelines, feeling awkward as fuck and weirdly jealous at the display. Not because I'm not a part of it but because... I don't know, I just don't have anything like that. Amelia and Kate are the closest I have to sisters, and I was pretty much an adult when I met them. I wish I'd grown up with what Jackson has, with siblings that double as best friends.

And, when all four Jackson women notice me at exactly the same time and four heads whip my way and four pairs of eyes begin their scrutiny, I kind of, terribly and selfishly, wish Jackson hadn't.

All I manage to offer is the world's most pitifully awkward wave.

Great start.

The youngest of the four is the first to take pity on me. My shopping cart surfer friend greets me with just as much enthusiasm as she did her brother, not hesitating to chuck herself in my arms. "Luna! I'm so glad you're here!"

I knew the little brawler would be the most likely candidate for the only Jackson sister to like me.

When Eliza steps back, Jackson takes her place, slipping an arm around my waist, his hip bumping mine gently. I look up just in time to catch Jackson mouthing a 'thank you' in his youngest sister's direction.

The other three—or two, actually, considering Lottie has already slunk off somewhere, flaming hair nowhere to be seen—aren't quite as welcoming. They're not rude or anything. Well, Grace isn't; she's just quiet, I think, like Jackson.

Lux, however, is another story. A frowning, sullen story.

As we walk inside the house, I catch Jackson digging her in the ribs and whispering what I'm assuming is hushed reprimand. Eliza must notice it too, because she casts me an apologetic glance and links her arm through mine. "She's not as scary as she looks. Promise."

One out of four.

Not bad.

He's trying to kill me.

Jackson is absolutely trying to kill me. He even laughs when I say as much, the mischievous grin on his face only confirming his nefarious intentions.

"You'll be fine."

I snort, and when the monstrosity next to me snorts too, I reign in a flinch. The big bastard can probably smell fear.

"Are horses supposed to be that big?" Surely not. It must be some kind of super-breed because the thing is fucking massive. As tall as

Jackson, maybe even taller, and ripped. Can a horse be ripped? Because this one is. I'm also not sure if a horse can be pretty, but the beast kind of is. A sleek black coat from head to hoof, so shiny that it glints in the sun.

Pretty, muscly, scary bastard.

"This breed is," Jackson answers my somewhat rhetorical question, giving his big friend a pat.

Clyde.

Clyde the horse.

Clyde the Clydesdale, to be specific. Eliza named him, she told me proudly. She also told me that he's the newest rescue Lux saved from a hoarded situation; she does that a lot, I learned. The youngest Jackson showed me pictures of what Clyde looked like before they cleaned him up, and it gave me a newfound kind of respect for this place, and the horse.

But, no matter how beat up the poor guy may have once looked and how that may have tugged at my heartstrings just a little, it did not make me sad enough to find him any less terrifying.

"I'm not riding that."

"You'll be perfectly safe."

"How the fuck am I even supposed to get up there?"

Jackson gestures to a step ladder perched nearby.

Crap. "I can't do it."

"Yes, you can." He hooks a finger around the belt loop of my jeans —extra tight because apparently friction and horse riding don't mix— and tugs me forward. "You told me you wanted to learn."

"I told you I wanted to learn how to ride a *horse*. That's not a horse."

"Come on." Jackson yanks me closer, bending until his lips hover over my fluttering pulse. "Please. For me?"

A soft sigh escapes me, my hands going to his hips to steady myself. "You're playing dirty."

Teeth graze my skin as he chuckles. "Is it working?"

"Absolutely."

The beam Jackson graces me with is worth the possibility of death, as are the three little words he whispers in my ear.

The hollow thudding sound of Jackson tapping the bottom step of the ladder with his palm echoes around the barn. He holds the other out toward me, an expectant stare on his handsome, manipulative face. Whispered, calming words, escape him, and I honestly can't tell if he's talking to the horse or me.

Clinging to Jackson's hand, I set one boot-clad foot on the ladder. He refused to let me ride in Converse. I bargained for a pair of cowboy boots but apparently, ranches don't actually stock those in surplus.

Heartbreaking.

"Put your foot in here." Jackson guides my sole to rest in the stirrup. "And grab this." He taps the raised lip at the front of the saddle before squeezing my thigh. "Put your weight on this leg, swing your other one over, and put your other foot in the other stirrup."

Yeah. Okay. Sure. Easy.

Gripping the saddle for dear life, I do as he says. It feels like I'm hovering in mid-air forever, one leg cocked as I balance precariously before I plop down on the saddle, earning myself another brush of soft lips. I wriggle in my seat until I'm comfy, following every instruction Jackson gives me—straighten up, sit back a little, adjust my grip. When he's happy, he takes a step back, giving a little triumphant nod. "Told you. You're a natural."

"At sitting down?"

He rolls his eyes as he strides towards his own horse. God, there's something really fucking hot about a guy getting on a horse that smoothly. And those jeans. Extra tight, like mine. Thank God.

He takes a moment to steady himself, a long moment in which my eyes are solely trained on his ass, before glancing over to me. "Ready?"

I smile, pressing my heels into Clyde's side like he instructed me to earlier, and he smiles too. "Ready."

I am never getting on a horse ever again.

I don't care how much Jackson kisses or begs.

Muscles I didn't even know I had ache. My thighs and ass burn. My inner thighs are peppered with nasty bruises, and they weren't even worth it because they didn't involve me getting railed into next week.

Don't get me wrong, I had a good time. We rode to a quiet creek on the edge of the property and it was beautiful. We had fun. It didn't hurt when I was riding. But the second I got off Clyde—the cause of my suffering—my legs all but gave out. Jackson had to practically carry me back to the house.

I sent up a silent thank you when his sisters were nowhere to be seen to save me the embarrassment of them catching me being escorted inside by their brother but I'm not quite as lucky when night rolls around. I catch them exchanging amused looks when I limp into the kitchen, only Eliza offering me any sympathy.

Dinner isn't too bad. A little tense, but I think that's mostly due to Lottie's notable absence. At least I hope that's why Lux is glaring at her dinner plate, and that it's her sister's head she's imagining smashing it over, not mine. But despite the empty chair and Lux's less than stellar mood, I would even go so far as to say dinner is nice.

Eliza vanquishes any chance of any awkward silence, chattering on and on about anything and everything. Even Grace breaks out of her shell with a little coaxing from her brother, and I learn Jackson isn't the only athlete in the family; Grace is apparently some kind of soccer prodigy. It's amazing how much she brightens up when the topic of conversation rolls around to the most recent match her team played; throw a few compliments her way and she beams something fierce.

By the time we're finished eating, I can confidently say that I've won over another member of the family and honestly, I'm feeling pretty fucking proud of myself.

"What're you smiling about?" Jackson murmurs as he stands, leaning over my shoulder so he can grab my empty plate and stack it on top of his.

I tilt my head back, directing a smile up at him. "Nothing."

He gives me a weird look but returns the smile before carrying our plates to the sink. I watch as his gaze flicks to the fridge, zeroing on a piece of paper stuck on by a magnet. Ripping the paper off, he brandishes it at Lux. "You made me a list?"

"After your little Christmas holiday, I thought you'd be all nice and refreshed and ready to work."

I can't help but notice that there's a certain amount of bite in her voice. Jackson must notice too because he shoots his sister daggers, followed by an apologetic look cast my way. I shake my head and wave him off. I reckon I'm owed a little snark.

Sighing, Jackson reads over the list. "The stall doors in the barn are broken again?"

Lux nods. "Fred's gotten out twice."

Beside me, Eliza nudges my arm with her elbow. "Fred's mine. He's really smart."

"He's a pain in the ass," Lux corrects with an eye roll. "Can you fix it please before I wake up with a horse trying to get into my kitchen again?"

"Got it, boss." Jackson fake salutes his sister as he saunters towards the front door, nodding me over. When I get within earshot, he whispers, "You okay if I ditch you for a bit?"

Fisting my hands in his shirt, I shrug. "I'll survive."

"You sure?"

"Go." I shove him away. "You're making me look weak."

He takes a minute to survey me before nodding, dropping a long but still entirely too quick kiss on my lips before heading out the door.

"Wait, I'll help!" Eliza yells, scampering after him, bidding me a shouted goodbye as she barrels past me. When I turn around, I find Grace has suddenly disappeared too. A sense of dread hits me when I realize I've been left alone with a pile of dirty dishes and Lux.

Shit.

It seems Lux realizes the same thing because suddenly, she looks a million times tenser than she did a moment ago. In an effort to keep my hands still, I cross my arms over my chest, clutching my elbows tightly.

"Dinner was great," I offer, cringing before the words even leave my mouth fully. "I wish I could cook."

Lux doesn't respond beyond a dismissive noise. When she gets to work scrubbing the dishes piled in the sink, I try again. "Can I help?"

"I got it."

Thinking third time's the charm, I reach for one of the dishes nearest to me. "Come on, it's the least I can do."

"I said I got it," Lux snaps, ripping the dish from my grasp like I might steal the damn thing.

Frustrated, I press my lips together, hands curling into fists at my side. "Okay." A small huff forces its way out as I turn to leave, taking all of a handful of steps before deciding against it. Spinning on my heel, I plant my hands on my hips. "Actually, it's not okay."

"Excuse me?"

"You don't like me." Lux opens her mouth, to protest or agree, I don't know but either way, I don't let her. "I get it. That's fine. I'm loud and abrasive and wild and pretty and apparently, that makes me a terrible person. Whatever. That's your opinion."

Lux at least has the decency to cringe.

Yeah, Jackson warned me all about that particular phone call on the drive up here. He wanted me to be prepared, and I'm grateful for that, but I kind of wish I could've just floated into this whole messy situation blissfully unaware.

"You don't have to like me, but you could at least try to be civil. Because despite what everyone seems to think, I'm not going anywhere. I really, really like your brother. And he lo-" Shit, I still stumble over that word. "He really likes me. And I want you to like me because you mean the world to him but if you don't, I can live with that. But I need you to at least tolerate me. For his sake."

I don't have the energy to say anything more, nor do I have the energy for her to shut down my plea, so I don't wait for a reply. Like a coward, I high tail it out of there, scurrying towards Jackson's room as fast as my legs will take me, briefly considering locking the door behind me.

I try not to feel dejected as I pad towards Jackson's bathroom, shedding clothes behind me, praying the hot water is enough to soothe my muscles and my head. But I can't help but feel as though Lux is the one member of the Jackson family that I'll never win over.

And that fucking sucks because I'm pretty she's the most important one.

~

Hours later, I'm the only one left awake in the house.

Jackson warned me that ranch work tires a person out. I just didn't think he meant 'dead-to-the-world-by-9PM' kind of tired.

After an hour of tossing and turning and trying so hard to achieve the stellar knockout sleep Jackson is getting, I give up.

Jackson's bedroom door closes quietly behind me as I creep towards the kitchen. I potter around as quietly as I can, silently cheering when I find an unopened box of green tea hiding in the back of a cupboard. Jackpot.

I'm pouring hot water into a mug when the sound of creaking hinges startles me and I almost spill boiling water down my arm. Spitting out a curse, I whirl around just in time to catch a head of dyed hair sneaking in the front door.

Lottie doesn't spot me straight away. She's too busy giggling and whispering over her shoulder to the boy hot on her tail.

How interesting.

Leaning against the counter and cradling my mug, I clear my throat as loudly as I dare in the otherwise quiet house. "Should've used the window."

Lottie drops the boy's hand like it's fire, eyes wide and surprised as they land on me. "Shit."

"Lottie, right?" I quirk a brow. "I'm Luna. We didn't get to meet earlier."

She says nothing, the expression on her face a cross between anger, relief, and whatever you call an expression that indicates you want the ground to swallow you up.

Taking a loud slurp of tea, I nod my head towards the poor cowering boy. "Who's your friend?"

"None of your business."

I whistle, the corner of my mouth twitching upward. "Attitude? Really? That's how you're deciding to play this?"

Lottie scowls.

"Okay then." I set down my mug. "I can take a hint. You'd prefer to introduce him to your brother, right? I'll go get him."

I have no intention of actually getting Jackson—mostly because I'm not sure I could rouse him from his coma—but apparently I'm a better actor than I thought. I barely take a step towards the hall before I'm body-blocked by Lottie.

"Don't. Please." God, I don't think I've ever heard that word sound quite so impolite.

I feign a thoughtful expression. "Yeah, I think it's a bit late for guests too. You wanna see him out, or should I?"

Oh, Lottie's got the whole pissed-at-the-world thing down to a tee. Her scowl would've knocked me on my ass back in the day, before I became accustomed to bitchy teenage girls. She keeps on scowling as she ushers the boy—who hasn't said a word this whole time but has been staring rather intently at my boobs—out the door.

I can tell she wants to slam it behind him but she doesn't. Probably because it would wake up her siblings, and God forbid anyone else gets dragged into this. When the boy is safely out of earshot, she turns to me, scowl intact, voice a perfect hiss. "That was so fucking uncool."

I can't help but laugh. "What, did you want me to hand out condoms?"

"You could've just minded your own damn business."

"Or I could've woken up Jackson and Lux. Come on, you got off easy."

"Shut up."

"Hey," I stand a little straighter, squaring my shoulders. "Watch it."

"Who do you think you are?"

"A girl who'd prefer not to have to bail her boyfriend out of jail when he gets arrested for murdering an innocent boy."

"You're a bitch."

"Must be something in the air."

I didn't think that scowl could get any more intense, but hey, it does. Steam might as well be pouring out her ears as she narrows her eyes, something almost cruel glinting in them. "Figures. Oscar's last girlfriend was a bitch. Makes sense the rebound would be too."

I have to make an effort not to visibly flinch. *Rebound.* That's arguably worse than being called a bitch. Actually, scratch that. It's definitely worse.

As if she senses she's hit a sore spot, Lottie's lips tip upwards in a wicked smirk. "You didn't know, did you?"

I don't say anything.

Lottie snickers, waving her hand in the air. "He's been in love with Caroline since he was thirteen. They get back together every time he comes home. If I were you, I wouldn't get too comfortable." Still smirking, she pushes past me and heads towards the stairs. "And next time, instead of getting involved in my business, just shut your damn mouth."

What a little *shit*. I've half a mind to yank her back here by her swooshy little ponytail but I reign myself in, letting her stomp upstairs like the monstrous brat she is. I copy her just a little, a stomp to my step as I head back to Jackson's room.

If she thinks I'm keeping her secret after that little performance, she's dead wrong.

I hate that doubt makes me hesitate before climbing back into bed with Jackson. He stirs, rolling towards me and reaching out lazily, half-open sleepy eyes blink at me. That same little seed of doubt prevents me from cuddling up to him. Instead, I perch on the edge of the bed.

Jackson frowns, gaze darting from me to the space between us. "Where'd you go?"

"Couldn't sleep," I tell him, pulling my knees up to my chest. "Full disclosure, I may or may not have just caught Lottie tryna sneak a boy in."

That wakes him up. He groans in annoyance as he rolls onto his back, swiping a hand across his eyes.

"I kicked him out, and I talked to her. One wild child with behavioral issues to another. Or I tried to, at least."

Jackson props himself up on his elbows. "Did she say something to you? Is that why you're sitting all the way over there?"

And he calls me dramatic; *all the way over there,* aka a handful of inches away. "She just mentioned someone called Caroline."

Jackson stiffens. *Bad sign.* "Caroline's my ex."

"Ah." So that much is true.

"Who I've talked to maybe twice since we broke up before college."

"*Ah.*"

"Sweetheart, what exactly did Lottie say?"

"Doesn't matter." Mind put to rest, I snuggle up beside him.

Jackson sighs, head hitting the pillow with a dull thud. "I'm gonna kill her."

"Go easy on her." When Jackson frowns down at me, I add, "She's obviously acting out for a reason. She's probably sad or hurt about something."

"She doesn't seem sad or hurt."

"Sometimes it's just easier to be angry." What's that phrase? Hurt people hurt people?

Something tells me that's the epigraph to Lottie's life.

35

LUNA

Okay, so maybe I like the fucking horse.

He's kind of hard not to like. Like a puppy. A very overgrown puppy. A gentle giant. Despite my adamance that horse-riding is not for me, Jackson somehow managed to coax me back up there. I blame that smile; when he bears those pearly whites at you, it's impossible to say no.

Anyway, I got back up on the horse and it was like Clyde knew how much pain he caused me. The whole trail ride, he ambled gently along like he was making an effort not to jostle me. When his equine friends sped up, he ignored them and continued his slow plod. He kept tossing his head to the side, as though he was glancing over one massive shoulder and checking on me. And when we returned back to the barn and I slid off him, grimacing as my sore feet hit the solid ground and my thighs screamed, Clyde stuck to my side like he was holding me up, his mouth nuzzling my shoulder.

He still scares the ever-loving shit out of me but he's growing on me. I'm a little resentful that it took less than a weekend for him to break me like a little sappy bitch but whatever.

Clyde likes me too, Jackson said so himself. Apparently, the big guy is not easy to win over, what with his history and all. But the beast whinnies something fierce and stomps around in his stall every time I enter the barn, which I took as code for 'I want to murder her' but Jackson claims means the opposite.

He also claims I've found my soulmate in horse form; inscrutable, a little bratty, and needy as hell. He got kicked in the shins for that one. By me, not the horse.

Although, if Clyde is as enamored as Jackson claims, maybe I could arrange that.

Today has been good. Better than yesterday, sibling wise. Grace and Eliza have fully given themselves over to the Luna agenda, and any lingering awkwardness or animosity that may have existed yesterday between us has completely dissipated.

Lux hasn't exactly gone out of her way to be nice to me, but she hasn't purposely been mean either. She's been civil. Tolerant. Just like I asked her to be but I'm still a little disappointed; I didn't expect us to crack open a bottle of wine and braid each other's hair or anything but... I don't know. An actual conversation would've been nice.

Still, it's better than the current situation with Lottie, although that's not exactly hard. I probably shouldn't have ratted her out but what can I say? Petty bitches bring out the kindred petty bitch in me. And I didn't exactly want to return the trust Jackson's shown in bringing me here by lying to his face and pretending nothing happened.

Jackson didn't explicitly tell me that he had a talk with Lottie, but I can assume as much. It's the only reason I can think of why a teenage girl would be spending her Saturday mucking out stalls, surrounded by shit, while the rest of us have a relatively relaxed day. Maybe I'd have it in me to feel guilty if the little shit's words from last night weren't still floating around my head, or if she didn't keep shooting me murderous looks every time I wander into her line of sight.

Her scowl burns into the back of my head as I make my way into the house, fucking dying to clean myself up a little after a morning spent on top of a horse and helping out around the ranch. It's amazing how fucking dirty you get here. I swear I've barely done anything yet there's dirt under my nails, on my face, in my hair, caking my boots.

Leaving the dirty boots on the porch, I pad inside the house on socked feet. Everyone else is still outside so I take a moment to just admire the place. I really, really like this house. It kind of reminds me of Ma's place, way more expensive but just as chaotic.

Jackson's artwork is everywhere, and some of Eliza's too; one of the many things I learned in the last day or so is that Eliza is a little art nut too, just as talented as her brother. The fridge is covered in a myriad of post-it notes and schedules and permission slips to sign. Homework is strewn across the kitchen table. I almost trip over a stray soccer ball more than once. Thrown over the back of the sofa are a bunch of wooly blankets that are softer than anything I've ever felt in my life; shocked doesn't even begin to describe the emotion I felt when I learned Lottie was the one to knit those.

The spawn of Satan is a knitter. You learn something new every day.

I'm washing the morning's grime off my hands when a picture on the windowsill catches my eyes. A complete family picture, the only one of its kind in this house, as far as I've seen. All five of the Jackson kids—Eliza is just a lump in Jackson's arms—and four adults I'm guessing are their parents—God, Lux is her mom's double—and grandparents.

Everyone looks fucking miserable. The whole photo reeks of tension, so immensely different from every other picture around the house.

"It's for show." I jump at the sound of Lux's voice, spinning around just as the screen door slams shut behind her. She's staring at the photo too, a slightly pained expression on her face. With a strained sigh, she tears her gaze away from the photo and trains it on me. "Our grandmother pitched a fit about there not being any family pictures so we put that up just to pacify her."

I back up a step, resisting the urge to hold my hands up in the air like a thief trying to prove their innocence. "I didn't mean to snoop."

Lux shrugs. "You weren't. Not like it's hidden away." Tossing me a dish towel for my wet hands, Lux gently nudges me aside, flicking on the sink to rinse her own hands. "It's awful, right?"

"What?"

"The picture." A grimace twists her face. "We look ridiculous."

"You look sad."

"Observant."

"For a dumb blonde?" I wince as the sarcastic words leave my mouth before I can stop them. "Sorry."

"Don't be." Lux takes the dish towel from my hands. "For the record, I never called you that. I would never."

"Thanks, I guess."

Lux doesn't reply. Leaning around me, she simultaneously flicks the kettle on and reaches into the cupboard above us to retrieve a couple of mugs. "You want coffee?"

"No, thanks. I don't drink coffee."

"Shit, yeah. Tea, right? We're not big tea people around here but I bought a box in case you wanted some."

A little surprised that the tea I drank last night was her doing, I offer her a smile. "I found it. Thanks."

Lux nods as she potters around the kitchen, pulling out stuff for lunch, and I excuse myself, making my escape to Jackson's room. I don't make it far though before Lux stops me. "You wanna help?"

I hesitate for a moment, briefly contemplating saying no just to be petty. I quickly decide against that idea and nod, cautiously moving to stand beside her. "I feel like I need to warn you though, my mom nicknamed me Fire Hazard when I was five."

Lux shoots me an amused look. "Five?"

"I was very advanced."

She chuckles softly as she points me towards a chopping board and sets me to work slicing tomatoes. We work in silence, the only sound the hissing of the bacon Lux is frying. Might not be too friendly but the girl can cook. I'm still drooling over dinner last night, only aided by the sight of Lux slathering butter on thick slices of home-made bread and toasting them off.

She hands me lettuce to rinse off and I do so dutifully, my gaze drifting out the window to where Jackson, Eliza and Grace are messing around outside. A smile tugs at my lips as I watch him grab a sister under each arm and whirl them around, the girls' squeals wafting inside.

"You want me to get them?" I ask, glancing over my shoulder at Lux and finding her already staring at me.

"No. I..." She shifts, crossing her arms over her chest. "I'm sorry about yesterday. I was having a bad day, I took it out on you, and I shouldn't have done that."

Lux pauses briefly, breathing deep before continuing. "I love my brother. He's my best friend but I have to share him a lot, and the little piece of him I get just got smaller. I didn't handle it well and I'm sorry."

Well, damn. I wasn't expecting that. "I appreciate the apology," I say slowly, receiving a brisk nod in reply. "For what it's worth, I get it. You're just looking out for him."

"He's spent his entire life protecting us," Lux confirms what I already suspected. "Figure the least I can do is return the favor."

Before I can reply, the front door creaks open again and Jackson strides in, starting to call my name but trailing off when his gaze lands on me. He freezes in the doorway. Brown eyes dart frantically between me and his sister, body tense like he's bracing for the worst. "All good?"

Smiling, Lux knocks her elbow against mine, subtly rolling her eyes at Jackson's display. "All good. Luna's just helping me make lunch."

Weirdly, her soothing words do nothing to minimize Jackson's alarm. Instead, it increases as his frantic gaze bounces around the kitchen, checking for damage. "Please tell me you didn't let her anywhere near the stove."

Asshole.

$\sim$

A weekend is all it takes for me to fall in love with Serenity Ranch.

There's something about this place. It's so… peaceful. Clean. Quiet. I feel like I can actually hear myself think for once.

I could do without the occasional waft of horse shit but otherwise, perfection.

Another thing that's perfect?

My boyfriend.

I would probably be content to sit on the porch watching him muck around all day. One, because him messing with his sisters is fucking adorable. Two, because for the love of God, *those jeans.* They're definitely coming home with us. There's no chance that I'm leaving those babies here to collect dust.

As though sensing me watching him, Jackson turns my way, eyes locking with mine and lips tipping up in a smile. I stand as he breaks into a jog towards me, letting out a whistle that makes me laugh and blush simultaneously. At his prompting, I do a spin, my skirt flaring out around me, and he whistles again as he gets an eyeful of bare thigh. One hand lands on my waist and tugs me towards him. The other pinches the hem of my skirt, rubbing the soft material between his fingers. "Ready?"

I have no idea what I'm supposed to be ready for—I just got orders to be waiting at a certain time—but I nod.

Showering me with words and looks of approval, Jackson tugs me towards the battered old truck parked outside the barn. We pass Lux on the way, who tosses him keys and a warning look. "Please bring her back in one piece."

The *her* in question? The truck Lux bestows an affectionate pat upon as Jackson opens up the passenger door. "I will," he promises, kissing his sister's cheek and ushering me inside the truck at the same time. "Don't wait up."

As Lux and the ranch recede in the rearview mirror, I turn to my chauffeur. "So, where are we going that we can't take your truck?"

"Some of the roads around here are a little rough. This one can take the beating better."

"That didn't answer my question."

He shoots me a boyish smile. "I know."

Little shit.

I learn very quickly that he was right about the roads. If you can even call them that. They're more like organized trails of dirt. Overgrown, rocky trails of dirt that rattle us around mercilessly.

But the view is so worth it. Wherever he's taking me, the route is scenic as fuck. Sun on the verge of setting casts a golden light over everything, glinting through gaps in the trees towering on either side of us. I get a sense of deja vu as we drive, reminded of our first date. This time, though, when we steer away from the treeline and exit into a clearing, there's no movie screen waiting for us. No, there's better.

We emerge onto some kind of viewing point, a rocky outcrop jutting out over miles of lush land. A small gasp leaves me as I sit straighter in my seat, leaning forward slightly so I can get a better look at the view stretched out before me. "Where the hell are we?"

"The border between Serenity Ranch and the national park." Jackson glances at me, amusement lighting up his face. "Pretty, isn't it?"

I snort. Pretty doesn't quite begin to cover it. Fucking beautiful. Idyllic, lush, picturesque, all those words and more. Green, so green.

Ridiculously green. And vivid, like a painting. God, it almost hurts my eyes.

Not for the first time, I wish that I was an artist like my mom or Jackson just so I could view this place the way they do, so I could go home and recreate the scene before me with nothing but my mind as a reference, like I know Jackson will probably do. He'll probably stay up all night perfecting it, and wake up tomorrow covered in green paint that always manages to transfer onto me.

I'm so entranced that I don't even notice we're moving until the view is ripped away from me as Jackson throws the truck in reverse and swings around. "Hey!"

"Wait a sec." He laughs at my impatience. Putting the truck in park, he gets out and circles around to open my door and hoist me out. Once again, he's pulled out one of his bed of the truck tricks; a familiar stack of blankets and an array of snacks wait for us as we clamber up. We have actual food this time, presumably cooked by Lux. I crack open one of the thermos' tucked into a carrier bag and get a whiff of tea, the other one letting out the delicious aroma of hot chocolate.

It's weird how after everything he's done for me, I still get over-whelmed. I'm still surprised when he does something nice, when he makes an effort, when he remembers little things like the fact that I fucking like tea. I don't know if that's something I'll ever get used to, being cherished. I'll try though.

His choice of activity for tonight also surprises me. When he said date night, I assumed a restaurant, maybe a movie. "Not that I don't love it," I start as I sit cross-legged in the bed of the truck, accepting the blanket Jackson tosses at me. "But why'd you bring me here?"

"It's my favorite place on the ranch," he explains simply. "The girls don't come up here because the drive is shit. It's kind of the only place that feels like mine, you know?"

I don't know because I don't think I have a place like that but I nod anyways.

"I used to come up here when it all got too much and I just needed a break from everyone."

My heart cracks a little imagining a younger Jackson trekking up here all on his own just to get a little peace. Looking out over the expanse of green, I rest my head on his shoulder. "I love it."

Lips brush my temple. "I love you."

"I love you too."

I swear to God, the entire world freezes.

I didn't mean to say it. It just… slipped out. Naturally. Comfortably. So quietly that for a second, I'm not sure Jackson heard. I'm not sure it actually came out. For the longest moment of my life, he doesn't react, further reaffirming my suspicions that I said those three little words in my head. That I said them and meant them for the very first time and it didn't actually happen.

But then he breaks out into a smile that rivals the view and before I know it, I'm in his lap and he's kissing the life out of me, hard and claiming, leaving me gasping for air when he pulls away. "Took you long enough to figure it out."

36

LUNA

It's like I blink and sophomore year is over.

It's been a chaotic semester, to say the least. With everything that happened with Amelia and Cass and Dylan and the accident... Yeah, it's safe to say that we're all glad that summer has finally rolled around.

I've got grand plans to spend the entire thing at Serenity Ranch. I was a little hesitant at first when the opportunity was first presented —I usually spend half of summer break working and the rest of it in New York—but Ma and Jackson joined forces and insisted.

And because Ma's paintings have been selling pretty steadily lately so money isn't as much of an issue, and because I'm physically incapable of saying no to my boyfriend, I relented. I'm glad I did because God, am I excited. Jackson is too, as is at least one of his sisters; I've been getting ecstatic messages from Eliza for weeks.

I've been back to the ranch a few times with Jackson over the last few months. My visits are frequent enough that the kitchen cupboards now have a designated tea section and everyone has started referring to Clyde as my horse. I even managed to earn myself a pair of cowboy boots. It makes me all fuzzy and tingly just thinking about it. It feels like I've been accepted into a club, indoctrinated into the tight-knit Jackson family and I fucking love it.

A knock on the door distracts me from my daydreams about summer. An excited squeal escapes me as I rip the front door open and reveal my mom on the other side. She squeals back, embracing me in a solid hug, squealing again when I slap her on the arm. "I was supposed to get you from the airport!"

"My flight landed early and I knew you wouldn't be ready." Ma eyes my robe and slippers combo pointedly. In my defense, her flight wasn't supposed to land for another half an hour. And I was only going to leave another fifteen minutes after that because God knows she likes to dawdle.

Regardless of her spending a needless, extortionate amount of money on a taxi, I'm happy to see her. By some grace of God, our schedules finally aligned and a free weekend opened up for both of us so, at long last, Ma used the tickets Jackson got her for Christmas. The sneaky bastard bumped her up to first-class too without either of our knowledge, which probably explains why Ma looks all refreshed and glowy and not at all like she's just spent half her day traveling.

"Where's the boy?" Ma asks as she sets her bag down, peering around the tiny apartment like Jackson might be hiding in some nook or cranny.

"At the stadium. He's got a game tonight." The game might be hours away but Jackson's pre-game ritual starts early. Like Cass does that weird hand signal thing with Amelia, Jackson has his own routine. I'm not exactly a fan of spending practically an entire day apart, but who am I to mess with his mojo?

Eager blue eyes dart to me. "Are we going?"

"Obviously." I've yet to miss one; if Jackson's at that stadium, chances are I am too. The games are long and boring and the weather is inexplicably always either freezing cold or boiling hot, no in between, but I still go.

The incentive lies somewhere in those tight pants and flexed muscles, and in the afterparty—win or lose, I always get well and truly fucked. In the locker room, under the bleachers, in the parking lot. You name it, I've probably been railed there. Something about the game just gets the boy pumped, and I am more than willing to be the thing on which he takes his energy out on.

Banishing any and all thoughts of those particular extracurricular activities, I rush to exchange my robe for jeans and one of Jackson's Sun Valley Rays hoodies. Shoving my feet into shoes, I grab my keys and purse off the kitchen counter. "So I was thinking lunch and then a walk around campus before the game?"

"Sounds good." Ma links her arm through mine. "Can we go to that Green place?"

I internally roll my eyes. *Greenies.* "Absolutely not."

"Why not?" She whines. "I wanna see where you work."

I take a moment to imagine my poor mother being subjected to the greasy cesspool of disease and drunk college students that is Greenies. Tugging her out the door, I pat her arm pacifyingly. "No, Ma. You really don't."

For once, I won an argument against my mother.

I managed to convince her that Greenies wasn't the way to go. Instead, we had a nice lunch not surrounded by drunk, leering idiots. In the relative peace of a local cafe, we caught up on each other's lives.

Aka I got battered with questions about Jackson and college.

Mostly the former.

The campus tour commenced after lunch and quickly became a lot more detailed than I intended it to be. Ma forced me to show her pretty much every room I've ever had a class in, and she insisted we have a sneaky look around the art department too.

We're almost home free, so close to being out of the building without incident, when we turn a corner and smash face-first into someone. Two someones, actually. I break out in a smile as I recognise the blonde who collided with me.

"Hey stranger." I pull Pen into a hug that she returns eagerly. I offer Professor Jacobs a polite smile that he doesn't return because he's too busy staring at something beside me. I ignore his weird expression and focus on my friend. "It's been a while."

"Sorry." Pen grimaces. "I've been busy." It sounds like a lie, a loaded one. Code for *'remember when I told you Christmas was a shit-show? Well, the effects are still lingering.'*

I never did get the details on what happened, and I don't think now is the time to push, so I settle for making introductions. "Pen, Professor Jacobs, this is my mom." I expect my mom to jump in, insisting she be called Isla like she usually does, but she stays eerily silent. When I glance her way, her appearance coaxes a frown out of me. She's white as a sheet and rigid, looking like she's seen a damn ghost or something. "Ma, you okay?"

It takes a hard nudge until she snaps out of her daze. Shaking her head once, she adopts a fake bright smile. "Yeah, hun. You ready to go?"

"Uh, yeah." I give her a weird look before turning to Pen. "We're going to Jackson's game, you wanna come?"

"I-"

"No." Jacobs butts in before his daughter can answer. "She can't."

Steam pours from Pen's ears as she scowls at her father. "Dad."

"Penelope, no."

"Why not?" Her dad simply answers with a shake of his head, but neither Pen nor I miss the way his eyes frantically dart to my mom. If I didn't know any better, I'd swear there was fear lurking in his gaze. And something else.

Something that looks an awful lot like recognition.

As she glances between me, my mom, and her dad, it's like something clicks in Pen's head. All of a sudden her face drops and she turns as white as Ma. "Oh my God." She breathes out shakily. "It was her?"

"Penelope." Jacobs clasps his daughter's shoulder tightly only to be knocked away, abrupt distance put between them. "Not now."

"Oh my God, it was." Tears blur her eyes, wide with shock, tinged with disgust. "I think I'm gonna be sick."

"What's happening right now?" No one answers despite the fact it feels like everyone knows what's going on but me. Ma says nothing but her gaze says everything. Apology. Guilt. "Ma, what the fuck is going on?"

Pen's entire body shakes as she turns to me, as does her voice. "My dad cheated on my mom when she was pregnant with me."

"Penelope, don't," Jacobs rasps at the same time Ma chokes out a plea.

Pen doesn't listen to either of them. "He had an affair with a student."

Remember that moment I was talking about?

The one I was waiting for?

Where the perfect, happy little life I've been living suddenly gets ruined?

A twisted feeling deep in my gut is telling me that moment has arrived.

I choke on my next words. "Why are you telling me this?"

"Because I think twenty years ago my dad fucked your mom." A bitter laugh escapes Pen as my world attempts to crash down around me. "Or should I say our dad?"

I laugh. I actually laugh. Because my brain can't comprehend what she's saying, can't label it as true, convinced Pen's just been drinking the conspiracy theorist Kool Aid or something.

But then I look at my mom.

I look at Professor Jacobs.

I catch the look they share, one that definitely does not scream strangers.

And suddenly I think that I'm going to be sick too.

I'm drunk.

I have been for a while.

A month, give or take.

A month since the bombshell of the century was dropped on me. A month since my life imploded. A month since I stumbled into a bar with Pen, with my sister. A month since I started going there almost nightly.

It's the only thing that helps drown out that gut-wrenching conversation playing on a reel in my head. The only thing that over-whelms the image of my mom's face as the awful truth came to light.

And *her* face. Jacobs' wife. My stepmother, technically. The woman whose life, marriage, heart, I had a role in destroying.

I had to meet her. I had to sit there and listen to my mother apolo-gize, listen to Jacobs' bullshit explanation, listen to her fucking weep. She was heartbroken. Destroyed by the knowledge that her husband had, *has*, a child with someone that isn't her, by my existence.

And Pen.

Really? You look alike.

It's laughable now, remembering the interaction that seemed hilarious to me at the time but now feels like the universe was mocking our ignorance. Toying with us. Dangling the truth in front of our faces but never quite letting us see.

My sister.

The daughter he wanted.

I was never supposed to exist. He paid my mom to get rid of me, for her silence. Gave her a fat wad of cash and said 'take care of it.' He just assumed she did, never took the time to check. He didn't care enough to check if he had another daughter wandering around. I don't even blame him.

Get rid of the secret love child made during an illicit affair with a student or ruin the family you actually want and your reputation?

Not a hard choice.

Isla Evans didn't agree.

She kept me, obviously. Fled the state with me growing in her belly. Florida, that's where I was conceived. Where I would've grown up. Where Pen would've grown up if I hadn't turned her life upside down too. I wonder if Ma would've settled in New York if she'd known the man she was running from ended up only a state over, hiding in Boston from the secret life he led.

I have grandparents in Fort Lauderdale. Two sets. Neither of them knew I existed. Or know. I'm not sure. I doubt my mom or Jacobs wanted to call and drop a twenty-year-old dirty little secret on their elderly parents.

I always thought my father was the bad guy. And he is. He's a cheating, lying dick.

But now my mom, the woman who raised me, my fucking hero, is the bad guy too. The other woman. A liar.

And me. The other child. Made of lies and deceit.

A mistake.

The apartment is quiet as I stumble inside, the key sounding way too loud as it scrapes in the lock. The girls are probably out. I think they're avoiding me lately and I don't really blame them. I'm like a ticking time bomb always on the verge of going off. I snap and I push and I make sure it's impossible to be near me because it hurts to be around them.

And it works for everyone except him.

I smell him before I see him, as weird as that sounds. Fresh and clean and like home. Guilt curdles in my stomach because I don't deserve for him to be here, waiting for me, perched on the edge of my bed with that damn look on his face. Knowing and sympathetic and sad.

Looking at him hurts.

I've been treating him like shit and I know it. I haven't told him what's wrong. I don't want to. I don't want to tell anyone. I don't want to be any more of a burden. There are four people in the world that know what I am, that look at me through a different lens, and I can't take anyone else.

"Where were you?" His voice is so soft, so gentle, so fucking careful.

Mine is the opposite. Harsh and cutting and so uncaring despite the fact my heart feels like it's cracked in half. "Out."

"Where?"

There's nothing judgemental in his voice, nothing accusatory, only concern, and yet I snap anyway. "You're my boyfriend, not my warden."

"Luna, please." He sounds tired. So tired. So sad, too. And I'm the source of it.

Luna Evans; the endless source of pain and sadness. Great.

Huffing out a sigh, I kick off my heels and toss my purse on the bed. "I was out with Pen, okay? Is that a crime?"

"I was worried."

He's always worried and I hate it. I can't breathe knowing the dark circles under his eyes are because of me or that he didn't go home for the summer because I couldn't bear the idea of dragging down the atmosphere of Serenity Ranch and he didn't want to leave me alone.

"I called you."

"I saw."

"You didn't answer."

"I was busy." Busy drinking in silence with Pen because she's the only person I can bear to be around.

Jackson huffs in frustration. "Jesus fucking Christ, Lu."

There it is. The breaking point. I push him on purpose, waiting for the moment he stops being sad and starts getting mad. It's easier to deal with him being mad. Because I'm mad, so fucking mad, and someone else being mad too just makes me feel that little bit better.

"I barely see you, Luna. You ignore my calls, you ignore me. I don't know what the fuck I did wrong."

Nothing. Absolutely nothing. He is perfect and I am awful. The only thing wrong is me.

When I make no effort to reply, his jaw tenses, irritation flaring in his eyes. "I can't keep doing this."

"I get it, Jackson. I'm a terrible girlfriend."

"Yeah," he snaps, brown eyes aflame, "right now, you are."

It's the truth, we both know it, but hearing him say it still sends me reeling, my head snapping back as the ugly truth slaps me in the face and riles my anger. "Okay, then. Maybe I shouldn't be a girlfriend anymore."

Silence settles, my words hanging heavy in the air between us.

"Is that what you want?"

No.

I say nothing.

I don't mean it.

He says nothing either.

I take it back, I take it back, I take it back.

Slowly, Jackson gets to his feet and crosses the room towards me. Rough hands cup my face, forcing my gaze from his chest to his face. "If you want me to stay, I need you to tell me."

Not a single word leaves my lips.

It'll be easier this way, I tell myself. If he walks away because I pushed him. If he walks away before I hurt him. If he walks away because I told him to and not because he wants to.

Utter defeat twists his face and crushes my chest. "Okay," he breathes shakily, dropping his hands. "I'm done fighting with you, Lu." My eyes drift shut as his lips brush my cheek for what I can't help but think is the last time. "Please take care of yourself."

I keep my eyes screwed shut as he walks away, leaving my heart on the floor behind him.

AFTER

It might take a year,
it might take a day,
but what's meant to be will always find a way.

PLAYLIST III

Billie Eilish - TV
About You - The 1975
Too Well - Reneé Rapp
The Gold - Phoebe Bridgers
More Fun To Miss - Daisy Jones & The Six
Back To December - Taylor Swift
Dunno - Mac Miller
Liar - Paramore
ceilings - Lizzy McAlpine
Big Black Car - Gregory Alan Isakov

37

LUNA

"Fuck."

The guy underneath me grunts as I climb off him and flop in the passenger seat of his car. I only take a second to regain my breath before I start fixing myself up; I want to get out of here before the foggy windows start drawing attention.

And his heavy panting is starting to annoy me.

A welcome lick of cold January air cools my sweaty skin as he momentarily gets out, presumably to dispose of the condom. When he settles beside me again, slamming the door behind him, I wince.

Too loud. Too much attention-drawing potential.

A hand paws the back of my head. "Did you come?"

I hum a yes. I did, I guess. He does always make me come, he's nice like that, but it's just that.

Nice.

Nothing earth-shattering but I think nice is kind of what I need. Nice is easy not to get attached to.

When I first landed a job working as an assistant in a law office, I didn't pay attention to anyone but my boss. I didn't want to. I was too wrapped up in my head, in making sure I didn't fuck up another part of my life. It was a miracle I even got the job, a fact I'm well aware of. But somehow, I did, and God knows I didn't want to do anything to mess it up.

But then the months passed and I got comfortable. Comfortable enough to look up from my desk every so often, and he caught my eye. He was charming and handsome and safe because nothing beyond the physical stuff attracted me to him

And that's what hooking up with him has always been. Purely physical. Scratching an itch. Sporadic. No emotions attached at all. Most of all, completely casual. Honestly, the guy could disappear tomorrow and I might not even notice.

But I'm not quite sure he's gotten the memo.

"You wanna grab dinner?"

I grimace as I button up my shirt. "I have plans."

"Oh." I hate that he sounds disappointed, as if he doesn't know the score by now. When the opportunity arises, we bang. We don't linger, we don't go out. That's it. "Another time?"

"Probably not," I can't help but be honest as I open the passenger door, swing my legs out and slip on my heels.

Before I can escape, he latches onto my hand. "I'll see you Monday?"

"Mmhmm." I hum noncommittally, flashing a blank smile, shaking his hand off me and hightailing it away.

The parking lot is empty, my car and his the only ones remaining. Unsurprising, considering it's a Friday night and work ended hours ago. I stayed longer to finish up a few things, he did too, one thing led to another and now I'm late for the plans I actually wasn't lying about having.

I'm in for an ass whooping and the weak orgasm wasn't even worth it. Didn't take the edge off like I hoped it would.

I practically throw myself into my car, eager to escape the cold. Flicking down the rearview mirror, I grimace at my appearance. Smeared lipstick, smudged mascara, hair mussed. Smoothing the freshly dyed brown looks back into a ponytail, I fish a makeup wipe from my purse and scrub my face clean. Not like I'm trying to impress anyone where I'm going.

For a moment, I simply stare at my reflection in the small mirror. I find that I've been looking at myself differently lately. I used to always see my mother's face staring back at me. Used to assume all my traits were from her since we looked so similar.

But now I look at him and I look at Pen and I see all these similarities and I wonder if me and my mom are really as alike as I thought we were. I wonder if things had been different, would people have compared me more to him or to her.

It hurts my head to think about all the what-ifs.

Pushing away those thoughts that tend to plague me lately, I flip the mirror up and plug the address into the GPS even though I know it off by heart by now. I just wish I didn't so I pretend I don't. Grasping the wheel tightly, I pull out of the parking lot and start towards the hell that has become my regular Friday night.

God, I need a drink.

~

I hate this house.

I hated it the first time I came here and I hate it six months later. I hate it even more when there's a rental car parked outside like there is tonight.

The only thing I don't hate is the familiar fake redhead leaning against her car.

"You're late," Pen chastises the moment I'm within earshot.

"I know. I'm sorry."

She surveys me as I walk towards her, her eyes narrowing in suspicion. "You missed a button."

Glancing down, I swear when I find the top button of my shirt unbuttoned, revealing a little too much bra than is appropriate for 'family' dinner. I hastily button it up while avoiding Pen's gaze.

"You were having sex."

God damn it. "I was not!"

"You have sex hair."

My hand flies up to fix my ponytail. "Shut up."

"The guy from the office again?" Pen presses as I push past her, jabbing my elbow in her side on my way.

"I don't want to talk about this."

"Ew, it was." She wrinkles her nose in disgust. "I hate that guy."

"You don't know that guy."

She levels me with a look. "He thinks breakfast is a protein shake and a wheatgrass shot. I hate him on principle."

I snort at that. She's not wrong. I fell asleep at his place by accident once, a big mistake that I regretted pretty hard when the morning after, I discovered his version of breakfast in bed was just as Pen says. I gagged as I forced down that godawful shot, closing my eyes and daydreaming of croissants. I swear, I tasted grass for a week.

"It's not serious." I tell Pen, and I mean it. It will never be serious. I don't want that. I...

I just can't.

Pen shoots me a sad look, her hand wrapping around my arm and squeezing. "I know."

"There you girls are!"

We both jump at the sudden voice screeching down the driveway, gazes flying to the woman standing in the doorway. Pen and I paste on smiles and hurry toward her.

"Hi, Mom," Pen greets with a kiss on her cheek and a fierce hug.

I keep a bit more of a distance. My hand lifts in a weird wave that Pen snorts at. "Hi, Mrs Jacobs."

Her smile noticeably dims as it flicks to me but still, she tries. She always tries. Wary but welcoming.

She pats my shoulder as I pass her on the way inside, and that familiar wave of guilt crashes over me. I still feel it every time I see the woman. It hasn't lessened over time. I've just learned to deal with it, just like how she's learned how to deal with me.

The hand on my shoulder tugs a little, stopping me from following Pen further into the house. I glance back at Mrs Jacobs. "Your mother's here," she tells me carefully, barely containing her wince.

A wince that I copy. "I know. I saw the car outside and assumed."

"Okay." A comforting squeeze. "I just wanted to warn you."

I offer her as real a smile as I can muster. "Thank you."

Six long months and I still haven't gotten used to the feeling that hits me when I walk into a room and find my mother, my father, and my sister all sitting together. It's an indescribable emotion, one I feel way too fucking often. This awful combination of confusion and hatred and guilt and... grief, I guess. Grief for the perfect, happy life I lost.

It's like one day I woke up and I was someone else. I was still a daughter but someone else's daughter. Someone's step-daughter. Someone's sister.

I'm kind of grateful for that last one because at least there's someone in the world who has some semblance of an idea of what the fuck is happening.

My cheeks hurt from how hard I force a smile. Briefly glancing at my mom, I nod. "Ma."

She perks up the moment I look her way, her smile almost as fake and bright as mine. "Hi, hun."

I have to look away, noticing Pen purposely sit on the sofa next to Ma so I don't have to. I whisper my thanks as I sit on her other side.

"Luna."

"Professor Jacobs."

His expression twists to one of exasperation.

The man has tried, God has he tried, to get me to call him by something but I refuse. It's too casual and he's not casual. He's not my friend. He's not my dad. He was my professor and now he's the guy who fucked up my life. Who fucked up multiple lives. All because he couldn't keep his dick in his pants.

He's barely even a person to me.

This whole arrangement was his idea. He claimed he spent twenty-one years not knowing me and he didn't want to waste a single one more. I refused, at first. I was adamant that I wouldn't play happy family.

It turns out the Jacobs men are just as stubborn as the Evans women. He pleaded. He begged. He offered money and cars and countless other shit that I didn't want or need. I would've said yes just to stop all the fucking incessant bribery and begging, but in the end, it was Pen who convinced me to.

She always went because she didn't want to leave her mom alone with him, and she'd come home after so fucking miserable and drained. So, I agreed to this whole bizarre thing because maybe if I was there it would be just a little better for her.

Drinks, as always, are the most tolerable part of the evening, mostly because they involve me and Pen subtly trying to outdrink each other while our father stares at us, disapproval evident but not enough balls to call us out. Ma, when she joins us once every couple of months for God knows what reason, alternates between casting pleading glances my way and apologetic ones towards Mrs Jacobs while quite skillfully ignoring Professor Jacobs.

By the time we move to the dining room—because of course they have a big, fancy dining room—I'm usually swaying on my feet a little. Tonight is no different. Except tonight, it seems like someone in this family manages to find their courage because Ma catches me by the elbow the second I stand.

"Lu." She tugs me to face her. "Hi."

I swallow hard and force a smile. "Hi."

The awkwardness kills me. It genuinely feels like a knife to my gut. I can't think of a single previous time in our life when it's been awkward between us. But I guess everything has to turn to shit eventually.

"You look good, hun." *Better than the last time I saw you.*

I hear those unspoken words, loud and clear, and barely contain a scoff. Of course I look better than the last time she saw me. A corpse would look better.

I can admit, I was a fucking mess, and not the hot kind. The first few months after the big news dropped, I was a liability. Drinking myself half to death, barely eating, barely moving. Finding out my mom's a homewrecking liar, my dad's a cheat, and my sister had been sitting beside me in fucking class for half the year... It was a lot.

Add in the breakup that cracked me in half and I was basically a shell of a person.

I was drowning and I refused to let anyone help. I think Pen was the only person I spoke to for most of the summer, and that was only because I had to. Hard to ignore the person you live with.

Then junior year started and I got a colossal kick in the ass. The first month or so of college, I was still a moping mess, skipping classes, most of the time not on purpose but just because I was too out of it to remember they were even on. And then I got an email informing me my scholarship was at risk. Even in the state I was in, I had the good sense not to fuck with the one thing shining any bit of light in my life.

So I got out of bed, rolled into a much-needed shower, and wised the fuck up because no fucking way was I going to throw my life away because of a lying, cheating, scumbag of a man.

I sorted myself out. I processed the Jackson-sized hole in my life the proper way; by getting new piercings and dying my hair and hiding the box of his things under my bed, out of sight but never quite out of mind. I got a job. Two jobs, actually, because Greenies fired me and even though the place was a steaming pile of shit, they paid well. The couple of nights a week I managed to pick up at a bar not far from campus weren't quite enough to survive, and then the office job opportunity fell in my lap, so I took it.

I got it together. It was hard and the last thing I felt like doing, or even wanted to do. But I did it.

"I don't leave until Sunday," Ma continues, reminding me of her presence. I wince, already knowing what she's going to say. "Can we do something tomorrow?"

"I can't." Her face falls. "I have homework to catch up on and I work tomorrow night."

She arches an unconvinced brow. "The office is open on a Saturday night?"

I'm a little surprised she knows about the office job considering I sure as hell didn't tell her about it but I shake it off. "No. My other job."

"Two jobs, Lu?" Ma shifts in place, crossing her arms over her chest in an oh-so-motherly way. "Hun, if you need money-"

"No." I butt in before the offer can fully leave her mouth. "I don't want your money." Not when it's *his* money.

Surprise surprise, not only is Professor Jacobs my secret father, but he was also Ma's secret buyer. I don't believe Ma when she says she didn't know it was him. I don't believe anything she says anymore.

Without letting her get another word out, I walk towards where Pen is lingering, waiting for me. She offers me an encouraging smile as she links her fingers through mine, squeezing me tight when I give her the 'I'm okay' nod.

I am okay. I've been okay. I'm always okay.

I just want to get through this night, get through this dinner, so I can go home and forget these people exist for another week.

Dinner lasts a fucking eternity.

By the time we get through dessert, I'm ready to pull my own hair out. It's just so awkward. So uncomfortable. So tense. Everyone is on edge, always. No one really talks because no one really knows what the safe areas of conversation are. It's all 'how's work?' or 'how's college?' or 'my, it sure is cold outside.'

All of it is nauseating.

The peaceful quiet of my dark apartment is like a warm hug when I finally, *finally*, shoulder the door open. I'm alone tonight since Pen's staying at her boyfriend's place. Needed the comfort after the dinner from hell, she'd told me.

I get it. I need comfort too. I just find it in different ways. Like meaningless hookups and bottles of wine and family-size tubs of ice cream. Tonight, I'm going for the latter.

My two-year roommate stint with Kate and Amelia ended pretty soon after the Evans-Jacobs family meltdown. Sydney moved in with us that summer, and while I love the girl to pieces, the apartment felt too full when all I wanted was to be alone. Especially considering Nick spends most of his time there, him and Amelia shoving all their happy, lovesickness down my throat. God, and then there were all the memories to deal with.

Pen was looking for a roommate since she couldn't stomach being under the same roof as her father. I had to get out of the apartment, so I got the hell out of there.

Shutting and locking the door behind me, I kick off my heels and hurry through the modest-sized two-bedroom apartment, eager to get out of my clothes. I lied earlier, about all his stuff being hidden under my bed. I couldn't part with the clothes. They're just too damn cozy not to use. And sometimes, if I concentrate hard enough, I swear I get a faint whiff of that fresh, spring smell.

It's probably a little masochistic considering how much my chest aches, how I get this tingly feeling behind my eyes whenever I slip the familiar Rays hoodie over my head, but I'm a weak woman. I can't resist.

My phone buzzes just as I'm fishing an extra-large tub of mint chocolate ice cream out of the freezer. I smile at the message from Pen checking if I got home okay. Flopping on the sofa, I type out a reply with one hand, digging out a spoonful of ice cream with the other.

At least there's one good thing in my unexpected new life. Honestly, I don't know what I would've done if I didn't have Pen. I would've lost it a hell of a lot worse. I've got a sister. A half-sister, technically, but I dare anyone to try to say that to our faces. Not that anyone knows or anything because we've kept our dysfunctional family secrets to ourselves, but still. For all intents and purposes, Pen is my sister.

I'm scrolling mindlessly through Instagram when I see it. My throat gets clogged, my head goes all fuzzy, I get warm all over. Ben's on one of his posting sprees again, as he usually is on a night out. I knew they were going out. Either he or the girls always make an effort to invite me, no matter how many times I turn them down.

I just can't bring myself to do it, and the reason is staring me in the face right now.

It's nothing dramatic. It's literally just a picture of him but I swear to God it hurts.

I've mostly gotten over that whole self-loathing phase that plagued me for a couple of months. It doesn't pop up as often as it did, just the occasional time when I catch Mrs Jacobs looking at me a certain way or when I see the strain between Pen and her dad.

It always, without fail, reappears when I see him. Because out of everything, that's the thing I hate myself most for. Ruining that.

I stare at the slightly blurry photo for longer than is considered normal before switching my phone off and tossing it aside. Eventually, after a gallon of dairy and a couple of hours of indulging in self-hatred, I doze off, curled up on the sofa with the TV playing low.

All alone, just like I made sure I would be.

38

JACKSON

"Fuck."

I swear as a jagged piece of wire slices my palm open. Bright red blood pools in the centre of my hands, dripping off the edges and splattering on the grass, some of it hitting the toe of my boots. Another curse leaves me as I fish a rag from my back pocket, the wound smarting as I wrap the material around my hand.

Getting injured is a hazard of the job. I've gotten a million new cuts, scrapes, bruises, and scars in the last six months, since I made it my mission to fix every single thing wrong with this damn ranch.

The coat of paint the barn needed? Done. The broken fences on the western edge of the property? Fixed. Every bit of old, rusty equipment that Lux insisted could be restored? Basically brand new.

It's safe to say I've been keeping busy. Or as Lux says, annoying the shit out of her. You'd think she'd be happy about how much time I've been spending at home; any spare time I have, I make the drive.

It's easier to pretend here.

The moment I clamber up the porch steps and set foot in the house, Lux's glare finds me, gaze immediately flicking down to my shoddily wrapped hand. I swear, she's like a bloodhound, able to sniff out wounds from any distance. "Oh, for the love of God."

In the blink of an eye, she's fishing out our well-used first aid kit, huffing as she gestures for me to sit at the table. "You're a fucking disaster."

A hand slaps me upside the head when I quietly quip, "You say the nicest things to me."

"What was it this time?"

"Barbed wire."

Lux wrinkles her nose. "Nasty."

Nasty, indeed. "Hurts like a bitch."

"Good." My sister tosses the bloody bandage in the trash. "Maybe you'll learn to be more careful."

My eye roll becomes a wince when Lux douses my hand in antiseptic without warning, the stinging sensation making my whole hand tingle. *"Fuck."*

"It's deeper than I thought," Lux tuts, bringing my hand to her face to get a better look, fingers gently probing the edges of the wound. "That's gonna scar."

I groan in anticipation; I know what that means.

Lux smirks as she clambers up onto the kitchen counter, rummaging around in the upper cabinets until she pulls out a half-empty jar. My nose crinkles at the sight of it, as if I can already smell the contents; the most godawful, supposedly medicinal blend of garlic,honey and God knows what else. It smells like shit, it burns like hell, and if Lux makes you choke down a teaspoon of it dissolved in water disguised as some kind of fucked up tea? Good fucking luck.

Our mom swore by the stuff. It was one of the few parental things she ever did, slapping that shit on every bruise or skinned knee in sight. Apparently, the habit stuck because now Lux keeps a jar stored away for the same reasons. Last summer, it was full and relatively untouched. The big chunk of it now missing is my fault, and my fault only.

We both cough as Lux twists open the jar and the potent smell attacks our eyes. I contemplate fleeing before the shit can take root in my hair and pores but Lux wraps an iron grip around my wrist. Dumping a scoop on my palm, she disregards my whines of protest, spreading it around until the cut is completely covered before wrapping clean gauze around my hand.

Sympathy? None to be found.

A look that screams 'that's what you get for being a reckless dumbass?' Plentiful.

Letting the stuff do its thing, Lux moves to the sink, slathering her garlicky hands in soap and scrubbing hard enough to rub her skin right off. "You could've cut your finger off."

"You would've sewn it back on."

The joke earns me a dirty look. "You have to be more careful."

"Yes, mom."

A wet hand hits me upside the head, again. "I'm serious, Jackson. There's enough shit going on around here. I don't need a maimed brother to add to the list."

"It's sweet how much you care," I coo, rising to tug on my little sister's braid with my good hand. "But I'm fine. I can take care of myself."

A snort escapes her as she swats my hand away. Drying her hands, she lands against the counter, still sporting that disapproving expression as she cocks her head. "I'm worried about you."

"You don't need to be." At her knowing look of disbelief, I sigh. "It's been six months, Lux. I'm fine."

She snorts again. "Fine. Yeah. That's what you are."

"Hey, you got broken up with too. You don't see me smothering you."

"You don't see me practically killing myself fixing this place," she shoots back. Shifting in place, she waves a dismissive hand in the air. "And Mark didn't break up with me. It was mutual."

Mutual, my ass.

Mutual breakups don't lead to you crying so hard, you vomit. I heard her, every day straight for a damn week when she locked herself in her room and wouldn't talk to anyone. That doesn't exactly scream *mutual* to me.

It might be hard to tell, but it's been a rough few months for the Jackson family. Two pretty fucking colossal breakups that left the eldest siblings out of commission. The twins started college and moved into dorms which sent Lux into even more of a tailspin. Lottie is still a nightmare, or at least according to Grace she is. Eliza hates school and she won't tell either of us why.

But we've managed. We pushed on. We got over it, kind of.

I just keep reminding myself that I'm almost home free. One semester left and I'll have graduated. A few months until I can get the hell out of Sun Valley. Until I can come home, something I never thought I'd wish for when I left.

"Have you talked to her?"

Lux doesn't even mention her name but I still tense, still feel that tug in my chest. "No."

Lux huffs. "Have you tried?"

I shake my head.

"Have you even seen the girl?"

I shake my head again. Not quite a lie but not quite the truth.

In the beginning, I steered clear. She made it obvious she didn't want to see me—or hear from me or talk to me or be around me—so I obliged. I went two, maybe three, long fucking months without seeing her once.

But it's hard to avoid someone completely. Especially when you're used to constantly seeking them out. I started getting glimpses of her again, her disappearing around corners, spotting her across campus. Not enough yet too much.

She dyed her hair. A light brown threaded with highlights that catch in the sun. She looks healthy. She looks happy, which fucking kills me as much as it pleases me. She's doing better than I was, than I am, and that's all that should matter to me but the selfish little asshole nagging at the back of my mind hates it. Wishes she was as much of a mess as me. Wishes she felt as fucking lost as I did, as I do.

But apparently not.

And I'm fine with it, really. If she's okay, I'm okay.

Really.

I hate this house.

I remember last year when I loved it. When it seemed light years ahead of our previous house because the floors weren't rotten and the walls didn't have mold.

If I'd known what would happen, I never would've resigned the lease.

All these months later and there are still little bits of her everywhere.

I still find herbal tea hidden in the kitchen cupboards. Blonde hair everywhere, stuck to my clothes, little strands in my hairbrush. Some of her clothes and a toothbrush tucked in one of my bottom drawers that she either doesn't remember leaving here or doesn't care enough to get.

But some things's continued presence is my fault. The framed drawing on my desk that I couldn't bring myself to trash. I took down most of my drawings of her because keeping them up felt creepy, but a pair of sketched blue eyes still lurk. That godawful Bob Ross mug contains an array of paintbrushes, and the handmade one from Isla still holds my morning coffee.

Yeah, I'm a weak man.

I'm contemplating just how fucking weak I am, alternating between staring at that fucking mug and the half-done drawing on my lap that has unconsciously started to bare a resemblance to her, when my bedroom door flies open and three bodies pile into my room.

"Get up," Nick demands, snatching my sketchbook from my hands and tossing it aside. Ben goes straight to my chest of drawers and yanks them open so he can rifle through my clothes. Cass dramatically shoves the shit piled up on my desk aside and sets down a bottle of alcohol and four shot glasses.

Fucking hell, it's like they rehearsed this.

"What is this?" I regret asking the question before it's even fully out of my mouth. My friends collect at the foot of my bed, peering down at me, and suddenly I feel like a kid in trouble. Is this what Ben feels like when we gang up on him?

"This is an intervention," Cass states, folding his arms over his chest and hitting me with a hard look.

Oh, Jesus Christ.

First Lux, now the guys. I can't catch a fucking break this week.

"Guys…"

"No." Nick holds up a hand to stop whatever excuse I'm struggling to come up with. "We're going out."

"I really don't-"

"Don't want to let your best friends down by being a buzzkill?" Ben finishes for me with not quite what I was going to say. He presses a hand to his chest, his lips jutting out in an exaggerated pout. "Aw, Jackie. I'm so glad we're on the same page."

Little shit.

I don't notice Cass pouring shots until he's holding one out to me, the potent smell of straight vodka ticking my nose. "We've let you mope, buddy."

"For six long fucking months," Nick mumbles under his breath, earning thumps and disapproving glares from the other two. "What? He's been living his little vow of silence and celibacy for too long. It's not healthy."

"Yeah, because you wouldn't be any less pathetic if Amelia broke up with your sorry ass." Cass winces the moment the words leave his mouth, shooting me an apologetic glance. "Sorry."

I just roll my eyes.

Silent, maybe a little.

Pathetic, probably.

Celibate, not exactly. It's just been a dry spell, with a brief interlude somewhere around my birthday, I think. I thought it would help but it just left me feeling nauseous and empty with my sheets stinking of an unfamiliar perfume and my favorite shirt stained with an awful shade of orange lipstick.

It's just... I haven't changed. One heartbreak didn't suddenly arouse an urge for meaningless hookups. I still want a bit of substance or stability or fucking feelings or whatever.

Even if it is kind of terrifying that, out of everyone, the romantic status I envy the most is Nick's.

How times fucking change.

With a sigh, the already-on-the-route-to-engagement man sits down on the edge of my bed. "I have to tell you something."

"Don't," Ben butts in only to be ignored.

"She's seeing someone Jackson."

Oh, how I wish he wasn't close enough for mishearing him to be an option. "What?"

"We *think* she's seeing someone," Cass corrects, shooting Nick a scowl. "I was dropping Amelia off at Luna's new place a couple of months ago. Some guy was leaving her apartment."

That means nothing. She has a roommate.

As if sensing my thoughts, Cass continues, "Amelia said Pen's got a boyfriend. It wasn't him."

Okay.

It still doesn't mean anything. He could be anyone. A friend. A delivery man. I don't know, a fucking electrician.

A hand lands on my shoulder. Ben offers me a soft, sad smile that has me bracing for more. "Cass and I drove past that new office she's working at a couple of weeks ago. She was with the same guy."

Something about the way he says it, the way he averts his gaze, tells me that *she was with the same guy* is code for something worse.

Okay.

Fine.

She's seeing someone.

That's okay. It was bound to happen, sooner or later. Maybe I was hoping for later but whatever. I don't care. I shouldn't care. I'm not allowed to care.

Fuck it.

Rolling back my shoulders, I snatch the shot Cass is still holding out of his hand. Without second-guessing it, I knock back the foul-tasting liquid. Shoving the empty glass back towards Cass, I get to my feet, slapping my hands against my thighs. "First round's on me."

39

LUNA

YOU'VE GOT to be fucking kidding me.

Six months. Six whole months I've managed to avoid him. I developed some killer leg muscles from taking the long way everywhere so I wouldn't cross paths with him. I avoided my usual routines because they were his routines too. I stopped seeing my friends because they're his friends too.

All that useless, wasted effort, just for him to casually stroll into my new place of work.

You have *got* to be *fucking kidding me.*

The universe is messing with me again. We're not anywhere near any of the usual campus bars or his place or the baseball stadium. There's no reason for him to be here. There's not even a reason for me to be here; my shift ended half an hour ago. But an unexpected rush hour hit and I couldn't just leave.

If I wasn't in the middle of pouring a pint, I'd duck and crawl my way out of here. Instead, all I can do is angle myself accordingly and pray the big guy waiting for his beer hides me from view.

It doesn't work.

It's like Jackson walks in the door and his gaze immediately gravitates towards me. That shouldn't be such a surprise; it always used to be that way. I don't know why I thought that, despite everything, that would ever change.

He stops in his tracks, the person behind him bumping into his back. Ben, I realize. Oh God, all four of them are here, the whole fucking gang. And by the looks on their face, they're as shocked to see me as I am to see them. Cass leans forwards to whisper something in Jackson's ear, probably an offer to leave, but he's not listening.

He's looking right at me. Surprise flickers across his face, quickly followed by confusion. Then those dark eyes I got so used to seeing every day rake over me, long and slow, hot and oh-so-fucking familiar. Something flares in them as his jaw locks, his hands fisting at his sides so hard the veins in his arms pop.

I'm half convinced he's going to stalk over and... I don't know, do something.

But he doesn't. After the longest moment, his expression clears and he looks away like I'm not even here.

Despite myself, my shoulders slump. I deserve that, I guess. No, I don't guess; I know. I was a bitch to him. To everyone, really. To be honest, it's a miracle the girls even still attempt to be friends after the summer from hell.

The guys, I'm not so sure about. Ben, I talk to all the time because once you've got that kid in your orbit, you're never getting rid of him. But Cass and Nick... I haven't talked to, not since it all went to shit, through no fault of theirs. I was the one to pull away. I was the one who needed the space, so I took it.

And I have no idea how they feel about that.

Lucky for me, though, I have a feeling I'm about to find out.

I'm so focused on Nick's surly approach, I don't see the girls lurking behind him until they're right in front of me.

"What the hell?" A tiny, ineffectual fist meets my bicep as Amelia leans across the counter and socks me. "Since when do you work here?"

I shrug, using the guy still waiting for his beer as an excuse not to answer.

Out of the corner of my eye, I see Amelia deflate. I see the big, bronzed hands that curl around her shoulders and squeeze, and I see the bug-eyed look she shoots Kate. *Your turn.*

The other best friend I've gotten exceptionally adept at neglecting sighs. "I texted you."

"My phone is off." As it tends to be these days. Don't have much use for it. "What can I get you?"

"Seriously?" Kate shakes her head and scoffs. "You can't even talk to us for two seconds?"

"I'm working."

"You can take a break," Amelia coaxes gently, hiding her annoyance better than Kate does.

"Do you want something or not?"

Disappointment. Sadness. Anger. All palpable emotions leaking from my friends doing their very best to crack the cold front I'm trying so hard to maintain.

The latter is mostly Nick, pouring off the man in waves, all of it directed at me. Squeezing his girlfriend again, he gently pushes her towards the table the others have occupied. She doesn't protest, and that's what gets me.

I spent a long, *long* time willing Amelia to start using that flimsy backbone of hers.

And I hate that she doesn't use it on me.

The moment her and Kate are out of earshot, Nick is leaning in. "You don't talk to them like that."

Silently, I brandish a middle finger.

Nick laughs, a cold, empty sound. Arms folded on the counter, he bends down, looking genuinely curious in a way that's kind of terrifying. "When're you gonna stop, hm? When they all hate you? Will that be enough?"

It takes half a dozen swallows before the pesky lump in my throat lessens enough for me to spit, "Fuck off."

"Breaking Jackson's heart wasn't enough, you gotta wreck Amelia's too?"

"Fuck *off*, Nicolas."

"You think she deserves that?" Nick cocks his head, all challenge and no sympathy. "You think any of us deserve that?"

No. Of fucking course I don't.

But I don't know how to do anything else.

"Aw, Nicky." I fake a pout, pressing a hand to my withered little heart. "I didn't know you cared so much."

I don't, I wait for him to say. That's the answer I expect, the one I deserve, the one I want because it's the only thing I can handle.

I can't take the sad, pitying frown I get instead. It's gone quick, replaced with that typical Silva pissed-off-ness, but the effect of it lingers like a fucking splinter in my chest. Nick slaps his palms against the counter once, not aggressive, just final. "Don't come near our table unless it's to apologize," he says before stalking off.

I have half a mind to leap over the counter and initiate something very similar to a schoolyard brawl; partly because I hate him telling me what to do, mostly because I hate the fucking truth bomb I didn't need. Luckily for Nick and his disturbingly pretty face, I'm distracted by someone grabbing my elbow.

Quickly forgetting Nick–or, at the very least, shoving him to the back of my mind–I focus on the short brunette peering up at me, hazel eyes rife with stress. Gideon's not a regular bartender here, she just has the great misfortune of living upstairs with her son and helps out when we're in a pinch. Judging by the look on her face, I suspect tonight wasn't meant to be one of those nights.

Which is why when she asks me to stay an extra hour, just until the rush dies down, I can't bring myself to say no. Especially with those fucking doe eyes gazing pleadingly up to me; it would be like saying no to Bambi.

"Blake with his dad?" I ask, referring to her four-year-old son.

Gideon pulls a face. "No. He bailed again." Frustration has my co-worker slamming a glass down on the counter with a bit more force than necessary. "I had to get a sitter."

Her tone makes me wince. It's not the first time I've heard of Blake's dad being a deadbeat. He's come in here a couple of times, and the guy reeks of bad news. Every time I see him and his greasy hair and sneering face, I wonder how the hell he managed to seduce someone as sweet as Gideon, who is quite possibly the reincarnation of Tinkerbell. She reminds me of Ms Honey from Matilda, which is fitting because, by night, she might be a bartender, but by day she teaches second graders. I just know there's a whole horde of seven-year-olds out there completely in love with this woman.

"If you ever need help," I start, leaning around her to snag a bottle of rum off the shelf. "I'm a pretty good babysitter." A lie but I suspect it's seriously bad karma not to offer a Disney princess disguised as a single mom help if she needs it. I've never babysat in my life and I have a feeling Gideon knows that so I tack on, "and I'm cheap."

Shooting me a grateful smile, Gideon bumps my hip as she

squeezes past me, calling over her shoulder on her way to the opposite end of the bar. "I'll keep that in mind."

~

Time goes quick when you're up to your eyeballs in shots and beers
and intricate cocktails that make me want to slap my past self in the
face for ever ordering.

It's a blessing in disguise, really. Being busy is better than being at
home contemplating my shitty existence. Being busy is fun when I'm
working with Gideon; watching this tiny, sweet little woman shooting
down men left right and center and handing them their drunk asses is
a fucking sight to see.

Being busy makes avoiding people who are very hard to avoid a
little easier.

I did as Nick asked. I haven't gone to their table. I haven't served
them at all; I don't know if Gideon has a sixth sense or something but
anytime one of them approaches the bar, she suddenly appears and
attends to their alcoholic needs.

That doesn't mean I haven't had one eye on them all night. It
doesn't mean I haven't noticed Jackson is practically glued to the
table, as are his eyes. Or that every time a new round is needed, the
girls are the ones to come up and order.

It doesn't mean I've managed to ignore just how much a hot
commodity my ex-boyfriend and his friends are.

Whatever. None of my business.

I'm pulling what is probably my hundredth pint of the hour when
a hand squeezes my shoulder and Gideon's brunette head knocks
against mine. Smooth as anything, she takes the half-full pint from
my grip and nudges me aside, seamlessly transferring control of the
tap to herself. "There's a guy over there asking for you."

Breath catching, I falter for the briefest second before following her
line of sight. A weird mixture of relief and disappointment floods me
when I find my favorite baby-faced blond beckoning me over with
two fingers.

"Luna," Ben coos when I'm close enough, dragging me halfway
across the bar to plant a kiss on my cheek, the alcohol on his breath
making me scrunch my nose. There's a hint of an apologetic edge to

his smile when he pulls back and reminds me that, "We didn't know you worked here."

If we did, we wouldn't have come, I hear him say silently.

I wave him off. "You need something?"

Ben rattles off another round of the usual, and I wince at the addition of shots. Sambuca, to be specific. So it's one of *those* nights.

As I shuffle around the bar making their drinks, I indulge Ben in the conversation he's trying desperately not to make awkward but it just is, to some extent. It's hard for it not to be when there's definitely two pairs of eyes watching us. Maybe three. I can't quite bring myself to check.

"What happened to Greenies?"

"I got fired." Apparently, not turning up to three shifts in a row is frowned upon. Who knew? "Months ago."

Weirdly, surprise lights up Ben's face. I assumed someone–namely the girls–would've told him, or he would've figured it out on his own. At my questioning glance, Ben shrugs. "We haven't been there in a while. Since…"

Since I screwed up our perfectly nice friend group by stomping all over his best friend's heart.

Yeah. I got it.

It looks like on top of everything else I messed up, I also cost Greenies some of their best business.

It's probably bad, how much that little tidbit of information thrills me.

"Are-"

I interrupt what's sure to be another question with an answer neither of us actually care about. "Do you guys have, like, a roster or something? Can I expect Cass to come over next and have a crack at me?"

Ben has never been one to take my shit, and he certainly doesn't now. "I came to order drinks, Luna. And not with a side of bitch."

I squint at him. "Call me a bitch again and I'll spit in your beer."

Ben squints right back. "Help me carry these over and I'll take it back."

"You know I can't."

"Luna Evans," Ben gasps dramatically, eyes wide and a hand flattened over his heart. "Are you *scared*?"

"Fuck off."

"That shit doesn't work on me, Blondie." Ben's gaze flicks to my hair before he corrects himself. "Or Brownie, I guess. Cute, by the way."

"Thanks." I set the last drink of his mammoth order down on the counter with a definite thump. "Are we done now?"

"Nope." Picking up the bare minimum of two measly drinks, Ben takes off at the speed of fucking light, shouting over his shoulder, "Thanks for the help!"

Panic claws its way up my throat, no matter how hard I try to fight it. Every curse under the sun leaves my mouth as I fill a tray with the remaining drinks, frantically glancing around for Gideon or the other useless dipshit who works here but of course, they're nowhere in sight.

'Fuck," I mutter as I hoist the heavy tray up, my near-to-snapping wrist the least of my problems. "Fuck, fuck, *fuck*."

I can do this. I can march over there, drop off these goddamn drinks with a goddamn smile on my face. I can wait until after my job is done before shoving my head in the nearest toilet and spewing the knot of anxiety in my stomach.

My attempt at confidence, valiant as it was, dies the moment I approach the table and the rapid conversation quietens. When my shaking hands cause the glasses to clink together as I set them down, I internally curse myself.

Come on, Lu. Get it together.

Cass, bless his little soul, is the first to greet me. An awkward side hug, a kiss to the top of my head, and a mumbled 'hello' but a greeting all the same. It's better than the daggers I get from Nick; intimidation tactics don't usually work on me but Jesus Christ, when it comes to protecting Amelia, the guy is terrifying.

"I'm sorry," I whisper to the redhead keeping her green-eyed gaze firmly on the rum and coke I slide her way. I repeat the sentiment as I set a glass of wine in front of Kate. "I'm really, really sorry."

Grasping the stem of her glass, Kate chugs half the liquid in five seconds flat. "Gonna have to be a bit more specific, Luna."

"I can't." I can't do so many things. Talk about it, think about it, look at them, be around anyone without fucking resenting them for their carefree happiness. So, so many things.

I don't have to see it to feel their disappointment. It clings to me like a shitty, unwanted second skin, like a thin layer of dirt impossible to shower off.

And it only worsens when I risk an upward glance and find the biggest reason for my shaky hands already looking right at me.

It pleases me, just a little, that Jackson's smile is as dodgy and pained as mine. "Hi."

God, I missed his voice.

I missed his face.

If I thought seeing a random photo online of him hurt, seeing him in person, up close, has nothing on that. It's *aching*, how fucking beautiful he is. His hair is still long, thank God. When I dyed mine, this weird intrusive thought popped into my head out of nowhere, so concerned that Jackson did a similar breakup makeover and chopped off all his hair. I'm glad to see I didn't fuck him up that badly.

By some miracle, I keep my composure as I dole out Sambuca. "Want me to leave this here?" I joke with Ben, laughing when he nods greedily, making grabby hands at the bottle. "I'll start a tab."

Handing over the goods, I start to walk away when a hand on my arm stops me. I swear to fucking God, I know it's him before I even turn around. Some things, some touches, you just never forget.

A flush creeps up my neck as I step away so his hand falls, treating it like a hot poker; painful to stay in contact with for too long. "Everything okay?"

Jackson holds up his other hand, showing me the card slotted between his fingers. "For the tab."

I take it carefully, a shiver creeping up my arm when his fingers brush mine. A small smile pulls at my lips when I spot flecks of paint on his fingers, an expression that's replaced by a concerned frown for the gnarly looking cut marring his palm. It takes a physical effort to resist the urge to ask him about it. "Thanks."

Jackson just nods. As if he can't help himself, his eyes linger on me, and I stand there silently, unprotesting, as they roam, his gaze covering every inch of me and leaving warmth wherever they land. It could be a moment, a minute, or even an hour before he clears his throat again and turns around rapidly without another word, snatching his drink off the table and taking a long slug.

Well. That went better than expected.

After dithering for an embarrassingly long second, I slope back to the bar where rapping knuckles catch my attention. Gesturing to the barstool across from her, Gideon shakes her head. "Sit. You're done for the night."

I hesitate, even as my tired feet and even tired mind scream their thanks. "You sure?"

"We can handle it." Gideon jerks her head towards the third bartender working tonight, some guy named Rick that is so useless, I honestly forgot he was even here. It appears that in every bar you work at, at least one staff member has to be good-for-nothing. Hence why I don't really want to leave Gideon working on her own.

But in the end, the weak woman in me prevails. My reluctance dissipates when Gideon slides a blessedly overfilled glass of red wine toward me. "You look like you need it."

I sigh as I slip onto the barstool, grabbing the glass with as much eagerness as Ben grabbed that Sambuca bottle, knocking back at least half of it in a millisecond.

"So," Gideon rests her elbows on the bar, voice just above a whisper, "who is he?"

I avoid eye contact. "Who is who?"

"Seth Clearwater over there."

I snort. "Did you just make a Twilight reference?"

A dishtowel whips me on the arm, accompanied by a pair of narrowed, accusatory eyes. "Don't avoid the question."

The humor in the air fades as I squirm in my seat. "Just an ex."

Gideon hums thoughtfully, her voice low and teasing. "Doesn't look like just an ex."

"Gid, please."

"Fine." She holds her hands up in surrender. "I'll stop. But I'm just saying, if he was, like, fifteen years older, I would be all over that."

I blink at her. "You're only four years older than me, Gid."

"I like 'em grown."

"You like old men."

"Silver foxes, honey," Gideon corrects in her low, southern drawl. "You want a refill before I get back to work?"

Without hesitating, I shove the glass back to her. "Keep 'em coming."

40

JACKSON

I REGRETTED GOING out the moment that first shot burned my throat.

Hell, I regretted it seconds after we left the house.

I definitely fucking regretted it when we walked into a random bar and the first person I saw was the bartender. The very reason I was out in the first place.

If I thought the Greenies uniform was bad, it has nothing on this. Short denim skirt, a cropped black t-shirt, fucking miles of bare, tan skin. A few strands of hair secured back in a loose braid, the rest flowing around her shoulders. She looked fucking phenomenal blonde, but shit, she might look even better brunette.

I didn't think that was possible.

Luna being here, looking that fucking good, contributed to me getting drunker than I intended to, than I wanted to. The first couple of rounds, I knocked back quick because I felt like I needed them, like I needed to keep myself busy to stop myself from doing something foolish like marching over there. I thought it would calm me down. Would dull the... whatever the fuck I felt when I walked through those doors and saw her.

Instead, the excessive alcohol just amped up all those ideas and chiselled down my willpower not to do them.

I probably should've left. A smarter person would've left. But I never claimed to be smart so I stayed. Planted myself at this table, one hand gripping the side of my chair like that might keep me in it, and proceeded to drink myself silly until maybe, *maybe,* I could forget she was here.

It probably would've worked if she hadn't done the exact same thing.

Her shift must've ended not long after we arrived because she's gone from being behind the bar to sitting at it. For the last hour or so, she's been knocking back a stomach-churning combination of red wine and vodka shots, alternating between laughing with the pretty brunette bartender and making friends with the pair of guys huddled beside her.

The round she dropped off at our table was the last I indulged in. After that, I was too busy staring at her to drink. Too busy staring at the dickheads crowding her. Too busy tensing every time they inch closer.

It seems like the more I sober up, the drunker she gets. I can tell when she starts tipping towards the sloppy end of the scale because she gets louder, starts slipping off the barstool, starts slowing down. I bet if she turned around, her eyes would be hazy, half-shut in that way they tend to go when she's had too much, and her cheeks would have that familiar rosy flush I love.

Loved.

Whatever.

"You're staring," a voice slurs as an arm snakes around my shoulders, shaking me playfully.

I jerk an elbow back into Nick's stomach. I'm not staring. I'm just... checking on her. Making sure she's alright. Keeping an eye on her drink since she clearly isn't.

Nick doesn't seem to get that. "Just go talk to her."

"I did talk to her."

"You call that talking?" Nick snorts. "You said one word and then gazed lovingly at each other for ten minutes."

"Leave him alone." Cass loops an arm around Nick's neck and yanks him away from me. Nick shrugs him off, shoving his future brother-in-law away from him with a roll of his eyes. When the two of them inevitably start bickering over nothing, like usual, my gaze strays back to Luna.

I don't like what I see.

She's facing me now, back braced against the counter. She's not looking at me though. The guys on either side of her have her full attention. Have her laughing, head thrown back and eyes closed so she doesn't see the look the creeps share.

Nothing but fucking predatory.

The bigger of the two rests a hand on her thigh and leans in to whisper something in her ear. She laughs again, louder this time, before almost falling on her face as she hops off the barstool. When both guys steer her toward the door, I'm on my way over there before my mind can catch up with my feet.

I don't stop until I'm right in front of her. Almost in slow motion, her head tilts back to look up at me, blue eyes widening a fraction. They widen even more when I ask, "You okay?"

The guy gripping her waist scoffs. "She's good."

I don't waste my energy acknowledging him. "Luna, are you okay?"

She doesn't respond. Just blinks. Just stares at me with this weird look on her face like she's not sure I'm actually here. God, she's so fucking out of it.

I have to grasp my temper with two hands when the guy squashes her against the side of his body, coaxing a wince out of her. "I said she's fine."

"I wasn't talking to you."

His friend barks out a laugh. "What are you, her boyfriend?"

"No." Luna beats me to answering, her voice so slurred I can barely make out the words. "Not my boyfriend."

Her words, truthful as they are, are like a punch to the gut, an unwanted reminder that we're not together and she's seeing someone, but I shrug it off.

The guys huff simultaneously. "Listen, back off. She wants to come home with us. Don't you, babe?"

The look on Luna's face says the opposite. "I-"

"We're leaving." The handsy one tries to drag her away but she wriggles from his grip. She stumbles, managing to take a single step away before the other guy links a hand around her bicep and tugs her towards him. "Come on, you said you wanted to have some fun."

"I-" Luna frowns. "I wanna go home."

"We'll take you home."

Over my dead fucking body.

"Luna." Her gaze flicks to mine. I hold out a hand towards her, hoping no one notices it shaking. "C'mere."

Relief is too small of a word to describe what floods me when she takes a wobbly step my way. A soft hand slips into mine, nails painted a pearly purple color digging into my skin as she clings to me. Another step forward and her forehead meets my chest, voice muffled. "Make them go away."

My shoulders relax as she slumps against me, a ragged breath leaving me. I wrap an arm around her waist, erasing that dumbass' touch, holding her tightly against me. Fixing a glare on those guys, I jerk my head towards the door. "Find your fun somewhere else."

"Hey-" They step forward, furious gazes flitting between me and Luna.

The second he does, I feel a presence on either side of me, Nick and Cass' shoulders knocking against mine. In one smooth move, they've shoved both of them backwards, Nick snatching Luna's things while Cass angles himself slightly in front of us. "Fuck off."

For a long moment, the pair survey us, probably weighing up whether or not starting something is worth it, before eventually ambling off. "Fucking cocktease," one of them grumbles as he stomps away.

Jackass.

Luna tenses in my grip, nails digging into me harder. When my thumb rubs soothing circles across the sliver of bare skin above the waistband of her skirt, she relaxes slightly, letting go of my hand to grip my shirt between her fists.

"I didn't do anything," she murmurs into my chest, voice thick with frustration. "They said they'd walk me to my Uber. I thought they were nice."

My hand instinctively goes up to cup the back of her head, my arm tightening around her, my chin resting atop of her head. "You're okay."

I have to fight to keep the anger from my voice. I'm pissed. Pissed at the two jackasses who tried to take advantage of her. Pissed that apparently, no one else in this damn bar noticed it happening. And yeah, I'm a little pissed at her too, for wandering off with them. The last one might not be rational, or my place, but I can't help it. She knows better than that. She's smarter than that.

Lu doesn't move as I drop my hand to take her stuff from Nick, who's watching me with careful, cautionary eyes. Ben's appeared now too, peering around an equally concerned looking Cass to try to get a look at Luna. "She okay?"

Without moving her face from my chest, Luna nods at the same time I do. Dropping my head so my lips are level with her ear, I ask quietly, "You want me to call the girls?"

She shakes her head.

"Pen?"

"She's out." Propping her chin on my chest, tired, slightly dazed eyes stare up at me. "Will you take me home, please?"

It's another one of the things I know I definitely shouldn't do, yet I find myself nodding anyway.

She falls asleep in the back of the Uber.

Like passed out, dead to the world kind of asleep.

Before, I wouldn't have minded. I'd probably laugh a little, maybe snap a picture to send to the girls or use as blackmail. It would be fine if her head wasn't in my lap, her knees pulled up to her chest as she curls up almost completely on top of me, one arm wrapped around my thigh as she hugs it to her. Even asleep, I'm half convinced she's trying to kill me.

When we pull up outside her place, I squeeze her shoulder gently, whispering her name. She barely even stirs. Squeezing her a little harder, I give her a shake. "Lu, you gotta wake up now."

A quiet groan leaves her throat, vibrating up my thigh. "Don't wanna."

She protests further when I open the car door, sliding out from underneath her and exiting the car. Offering the driver an apologetic smile, I half-drag, half-carry Luna out after me. "Can you walk?"

She takes one step and confirms the answer is a resounding 'hell no.'

A squealed laugh escapes her as I scoop her up with a sigh, cradling her in my arms and starting towards her second-floor apartment. She wastes no time getting comfortable, apparently completely unphased by being carried up two flights of stairs by her ex-boyfriend. Awkwardly opening the front door when the keys I wrangled out of her purse, I side-shuffle my way in, careful not to bang her head against the doorframe.

It's nice, this new place of hers. Bigger than the old one, despite the fact there's only two of them living here. That makes sense though, I guess, considering Pen's dad is some hotshot lawyer-turned-professor. The guy probably bought this whole damn complex for his precious daughter.

I open the first door I see and luck must be on my side because it's definitely Luna's bedroom. It's almost identical to her old one, the same fluffy rug on the floor, the same soft, pink blanket tossed haphazardly across her bed, the same pictures and posters decorating her wall. It smells the same too. Vanilla.

But that might just be the girl curled up against my chest.

Gently, I set her limp form down on the bed. With a sigh, she curls up into a ball. She doesn't react, or even open her eyes, as I pull her feet onto my lap and ease her shoes off, or when I leave the room to go rummage around in the kitchen for some painkillers and a bottle of water.

I, however, definitely fucking react when I return to her room and find a half-naked, wobbly girl struggling out of her clothes. There's a split second when all I see is tan skin and lacy underwear before my mind catches up with my eyes and I avert my gaze to a safer area, like her face. She's managed to wriggle out of her skirt, kicked it halfway across the room too, but she's gotten herself caught up in her t-shirt. It would be a laughable sight, if not for the half-naked thing.

Or the ex-girlfriend thing.

Or the her being drunk off her ass thing.

"Jesus, Lu." I sigh as I walk towards her. Tapping her shoulder so she stops wriggling, I guide her free from the tangled mess she's inexplicably created. When I pull the shirt over her head, I'm greeted by the sight of dishevelled hair and flushed cheeks. A lazy smile pulls at her lips as a giggle escapes her, accompanied by a slurred 'whoops' that draws a matching smile out of me.

I don't know if it's the smile or the laugh or just fucking her, but a moment of weakness hits me. I find myself reaching up to smooth down her hair, to tuck some of the wild strands behind her ears so I can see her face properly. And then, on their own accord, my hands move to cup her face, just for a second, just long enough that the warmth of her cheeks soaks my hands. Long enough that she leans into me, letting out a tired, content hum as her eyes drift shut.

She's seeing someone.

I drop my hands like she's burned me.

Abruptly taking a step back, I clear my throat, looking anywhere but at her. In an effort to busy my wandering hands, I turn on my heel and head for her closet, on a mission to find her pajamas. She used to keep them in the bottom drawer so I check there first, and I'm right. An array of neatly folded pajamas stare back at me.

My pajamas.

The soft t-shirts and sweats I wore whenever I stayed over. A couple of my hoodies, including a Rays one that I thought I lost at practice. Even a few pairs of boxers that I'm positive are mine.

I don't let myself think about it too much, don't let my brain read into it. I just grab a t-shirt and slam the drawer shut. Out of sight, out of mind.

"Here-" I start to say, mouth snapping shut when I turn around and find Luna with her back to me. A groan attempts to rip from my throat as her hands curl behind her, reaching for her bra strap, fingers struggling to undo the clasp.

Her little whine of annoyance has me shifting in place, as does the pouty look she shoots me over her shoulder. "Help?"

Yup. Definitely trying to kill me.

Draping her pajamas over my shoulder, I make my way towards her on legs almost as wobbly as hers. My hands shake as I reach up to undo the clasp, a lump forming in my throat when the straps fall down her shoulders. As quickly and as painlessly as possible, I help her change, very much trying to ignore the soft thud of her bra hitting the floor and my knuckles brushing against smooth skin.

Another content sight leaves her when I help her under the covers and she snuggles up to her pillow. She huffs as her hair falls in her face so I snatch up a stray scrunchie sitting on her bedside table and pull her hair back in a sorry excuse for a bun. That lazy smile returns as she reaches out to pat my hand softly. "Thank you."

"That's okay."

A frown creases her face as she reaches up and tugs on a strand of my hair, confirming that maybe I'm not the only one with wandering hands. "You didn't cut your hair."

The almost bewildered expression on her face makes me smile. "Did you want me to cut my hair?"

She scrunches up her nose in distaste. "No. Never."

"Okay." A laugh tickles my throat. "I won't."

My answer must please her because she drops her hand, still smiling as her eyes drift shut. I wait a minute before carefully getting up to leave, making sure the water and painkillers are easily accessible.

I've one foot out the door when her quiet, sleepy voice stops me.

"Where're you going?"

I stop in my tracks, turning around slowly. Propped up on one elbow, she's staring at me, looking the epitome of confusion. Like she can't possibly understand why I'm leaving. "I gotta go home, sweetheart."

Her frown deepens. "Can you stay for a bit?" Even in her drunken state, she must notice the hesitation on my face. "I don't like sleeping alone."

And if that doesn't just crack my chest wide open.

I can't say no. I physically am incapable of saying no. When it comes to her, I always have been.

I'll just stay until she falls asleep, I reason with myself as I walk towards her again, shoving off my jacket and toeing off my shoes.

She asked me to stay. I'd be a dick to say no.

If Amelia or Kate asked, I'd do it for them.

Someone has to make sure she doesn't choke on her own vomit.

Those are the reasons I convince myself are true as I settle on the bed beside her, almost hanging off the edge in an effort not to touch her.

I'm just being a good friend.

41

JACKSON

I FUCKED UP.

I don't mean to stay.

I fully intended on waiting until she fell asleep and creeping out.

But I just can't bring myself to.

I just lie there, wide awake with my eyes trained on the girl curled up beside me, half making sure she doesn't choke on her own vomit, half relishing in something I've ached for for six months.

Fuck, I've missed this. I've missed this so much it hurts. We're barely even touching, just her knees brush my side and her forehead rests on my shoulder, but it feels like she's everywhere.

At one point in the night, she wakes up. Her eyes flutter open, a crinkle forming between them as she frowns when my chest is the first thing she sees. Her whole body goes rigid, regret and horror written all over her sleepy face. She raises her gaze slowly, eyes half-closed in anticipation.

I wait. I wait for her to swear and shout and kick me out.

But she doesn't.

Instead, her expression softens. Any ounce of worry is washed away and replaced by pure relief. Without saying a word, she drops her head to the crook of my neck and wraps an arm around my torso. Hooks a leg over my waist and she wriggles closer until she's all but lying on top of me. Out cold again in less than two minutes.

My arms twitch at my side, begging to pull her even closer. I shouldn't. She's not in her right mind. She doesn't know what she's doing.

I. Shouldn't.

But I do.

I can't help myself. My arms have a mind of their own as they snake around her waist, hauling her the rest of the way on top of me, that familiar, comforting weight spreading warmth throughout me.

And I fall asleep.

The next thing I know, I'm blinking awake, squinting against the bright light flooding the room, briefly very confused. Wondering if I dreamt the last few months.

And then the sleep fog coating my mind clears and it all comes flooding back.

Just for a moment longer, I let myself revel in her clinging to me before I carefully slide her off of me. Not careful enough; I freeze when she makes an annoyed grunting noise and jerks awake.

Confusion flashes in a blue gaze when Luna finds me hovering on the edge of her bed. Something else flickers there too, something I can't put my finger on, before she wipes her expression clean. Propping herself upright, she drags a hand down her face. "Did we fuck?"

Her harsh tone makes me wince. "No, we didn't *fuck*."

"Then why are you here?"

The cold detachment in her voice, on her face, pisses me off but I'm too tired to fight with her. I can't.

Sighing, I give her the short version of the story. "You got too drunk last night so I brought you home."

"My knight in shining armour," she grumbles sarcastically under her breath. Yawning loudly, she stretches, her t-shirt riding up her thighs and catching her attention. She stares at the material for a moment, a hint of a blush coloring her cheeks but it fades as quickly as it appears. "If we didn't fuck, why am I half-naked?"

"Blame yourself for that."

Her nose scrunches, and I can't tell if it's out of embarrassment or regret or maybe both. "Great."

"Be happy it was just me and not the two creeps you tried to leave with." Fuck, I regret that as soon as I say it.

Luna frowns. "What?"

"Nothing. Never mind." I get to my feet quickly, suddenly struck with the need to get out of here. She doesn't remember any of last night. That's fine. It's probably for the best. If she remembered asking me to help her, asking me to stay, relying on me, it would only make things worse.

A mixture of confusion and frustration creases Luna's face for a moment before she adopts that infuriating indifference. Sitting back on her heels, she crosses her arms over her chest. "So. That's what happened."

It's my turn to be confused. "What?"

"I tried to leave with someone and you got jealous. Had to whisk me away, right? Save me from my whoring ways? No one's allowed to touch what's yours?"

"Jesus... no, Luna." I gape at her, not quite believing what's coming out of her mouth. The jealous part, yeah, a little; no one wants to watch their ex-girlfriend get chatted up right in front of their eyes. But if she'd been sober, if those guys hadn't been creeps, if she'd actually wanted to go home with them, I wouldn't have stopped her. It's not my place.

But saving her from her whoring ways? Fuck off with that shit.

She's pushing me again, fishing for an argument that I really don't want to give her. Shaking my head in frustration, I snatch up my jacket and shove my feet into shoes. "I'm leaving."

"Yeah, you're good at that," she snarls at my back.

Fuck this.

"Okay, enough." I whirl around, pure anger directing me back towards her. "Don't you fucking dare. I didn't leave."

"I-" She tries to butt in, probably with another snarky comment but I don't let her.

"You shut me out. You wouldn't talk to me, you barely even looked at me. For a month, Luna, I tried to help you and you refused to let me in. I had no idea what was going on with you. What was I supposed to do? Wait around until you decided I deserved your attention again?"

My yelled words hang heavy in the air. I watch as Luna deflates, her defiance and snark evaporating as her shoulders sink. I wait for her to say something. Anything. Prove me wrong for thinking she just didn't want me around anymore.

She says nothing.

I'm halfway out the door when she finally manages to get a word out. "Jackson."

Glancing over my shoulder, the sight of her genuinely makes my chest ache. Sitting there with her hands folded in her lap, fingers tapping against each other, hair falling out of that shit bun I did and spilling around her shoulders. Peering up at me and chewing on her bottom lip, she looks so lost. So sad. So small. "I-"

Hope flutters in my stomach as she opens her mouth to speak. As quickly as it springs to life, it dies when she suddenly shakes her head. Straightening up, her face hardens again and I want to fucking scream with frustration.

"Thanks," is all she says. That coldness is back, her nonchalant tone of voice sounding like she couldn't give less of a fuck. "For bringing me home."

"You're welcome."

She hesitates for the briefest of moments before jerking her head towards the door. "You can go now."

Pursing my lips, I nod, hurrying out of there without another word, all but ripping the front door off the hinges in my haste to get out of there. Brisk morning air slaps me in the face as I step outside. Resting my hands against the railing across from her door, I lean against it for a moment, dropping my head and taking a few deep breaths. I let the coldness of the metal seep through my clothes, the equally cold air calming me down.

"Fuck."

∼

By the time I get home, it's the afternoon.

I walked; I needed the fresh air, needed the time alone to just... think.

Plus, my phone died sometime in the wee hours of the morning and I doubt Luna would give me a ride.

A groan escapes me when I push open the front door and find the boys waiting for me in the living room. It seems the intervention portion of this weekend wasn't exclusive to last night. Immediately; the questions begin.

"What happened?"

"Is she okay?"

"Did you fuck?"

Cass gets thumped for that last one. He yelps, scowling at me as he rubs his arms. "What? You need a good fuck."

"She was drunk, asshole."

"Not last night, obviously." Cass shoots me a 'duh' look. "But look me in the eyes and tell me nothing happened this morning."

I look him dead in the eyes. "Nothing happened this morning."

Ben cackles loudly, reaching over to slap Cass in the chest. "Pay up, bitch."

Pouting, Cass huffs dramatically as he pulls a couple of bills from his wallet and begrudgingly tosses them at Ben.

I gape at the pair in disbelief. "You guys bet on us hooking up?"

"*They* bet." Nick rolls his eyes. "I stayed out of it, like a normal person."

Unbelievable.

Shooting the pair a dirty look, I head for my room. "Hey!" Ben protests. "Tell us what happened!" A round of boos follows me up the stairs as I flash them my middle finger.

As I kick my bedroom door shut behind me, I shed my clothes from last night, eager to get them off and myself in a shower. I need to rinse off the smell of booze from last night. And the smell of vanilla. Quickly stopping to plug in my phone to charge, I hightail it to the bathroom.

Steamy warm water greets me like an old friend. I stand under the hot spray, face tilted upwards, washing away the evidence of last night. I didn't realize how hungover I feel until right now.

Worrying about Luna, being mad at her, apparently has the same effect on me as adrenaline. A safe distance away from her, I feel like I'm fading now. A headache is setting in, I'm starting to get the shakes, and my eyes ache from a sleepless night.

Yeah, going out was a really fucking terrible idea.

When my fingers start pruning, I reluctantly shut the water off. Wrapping a towel around my waist and using another to dry my hair as I exit the bathroom, I almost have a fucking heart attack when I find Ben sitting on my bed, chowing down on a bowl of cereal. Seemingly unphased by my half-naked appearance, Ben gestures towards my desk. "I made you breakfast."

Sure enough, there's a matching bowl of cereal sitting on the wooden surface, accompanied by a tall glass of orange juice and a mug of what smells like coffee. "Couldn't have bought me something nicer with that twenty bucks you won?" I joke, taking a long slug of coffee instead. Extra strong, just what I need.

"Fifty, actually," Ben corrects with a smug smile. "So nothing at all happened?"

"Nothing at all happened," I confirm, and not for the last time, I have a feeling.

"But you stayed over."

"She was out of it. I didn't want to leave her alone."

Ben's little hum implies he doesn't believe me but I ignore him. Instead, I check my phone, frowning at the sight that greets me. A few messages from the boys asking if I'm coming home aren't anything weird. A couple from Amelia checking if Luna's okay, easily explainable by Nick letting her know what happened. No, it's what must be at least a hundred missed calls from my sisters that worry me.

Dialling Lux's number quickly, my fingers anxiously drum against the desk as I wait for her to answer. Panic floods me immediately when instead of a 'hello,' I'm greeted by the sound of muffled crying. "Lux?"

"Jackson," is her whimpered reply. "You need to come home."

"What happened? Is someone hurt?"

Ben's alarmed gaze flicks to me, his eyes wide and questioning. *Is everything okay?* he mouths at me.

I don't know, I mouth back. It feels like an eternity passes before Lux finally replies, her voice shaky as she drops an entirely unexpected bomb.

"It's Mom."

42

LUNA

I SHOULDN'T BE HERE.

I feel weird being here.

He won't want me here. He doesn't want to see me. After the way I treated him a few days ago, there's no way he's going to be happy when I rock up at his home.

But I couldn't not be here. After everything he's done for me, I couldn't just... not come.

His mom fucking *died*.

So, I donned the only somewhat conservative black dress I own and suffered through the long drive to Serenity Ranch, deja vu hitting me when I felt like vomiting the whole time. We skipped the service but judging by the number of people pouring out of the main house, we make it just in time for the reception.

The fidgeting I've been doing the entire drive here amps up a notch as the six-seater we rented rolls to a stop and my friends pile out. I, however, stay exactly where I am, too busy convincing myself of all the terrible ways this will go wrong to move.

Again and again, I twist the ring on my forefinger. The one he got me. I don't wear it usually anymore. The sight of it makes me sad but I sucked it up and slipped the thing on today. A peace offering, of sorts. Me trying to convey that I'm not here to pick a fight or cause trouble.

And maybe, I just missed wearing it and I like having an excuse.

Blowing out a sharp breath, I force myself out of the car. I barely have my feet on solid ground before Kate is taking one hand, Amelia grabbing the other. "You okay?"

I'm not the person she should be asking that but I nod anyway. They offer wary looks but when I nudge them forward, they follow the guys toward the house.

I, again, hang back a little. Just so I can soak up being back in this place again after missing it for so long. And God, did I miss it.

Jackson himself is nowhere in sight but his sisters are. I watch from the relatively safe distance of the bottom porch step as my friends embrace the grieving girls, unsure how or if I should greet them. I've almost convinced myself to join them when Eliza's teary gaze flicks to me and I freeze.

She doesn't hesitate before running down the steps and throwing herself in my arms, knocking the breath out of me. Instinctively, my arms sneak around her back and hold her tightly. "I'm so sorry, Eliza."

She sniffs loudly, head buried in the crook of my neck. "I missed you."

Fuck, she might as well have punched me right in the heart. Tears tickling the back of my throat, I return the sentiment. "I missed you too."

So much more than I ever thought I would.

When she pulls away, I grasp her by the shoulders, holding her still so I can just look at her for a second. God, she looks so much older. I can almost hear the arguments that must have been had in this house about the light brown streaks in her dark hair and the new jewel sparkling in her nose, another couple decorating her ears. She must be, what, almost sixteen now? Jesus. "You punch anyone lately?"

Despite the tears staining a path down her cheeks, Eliza snorts a laugh. "No one who didn't deserve it."

"That's my girl."

The youngest Jackson attempts her brightest smile. My hands drop as she maneuvers to my side but the connection is quickly replaced by one of hers slipping into mine as she drags me inside.

Within seconds of entering, Grace is at my other side, wrapping an arm around my waist to give me a brief side-hug. Even Lottie offers a stiff nod of acknowledgement before dropping her watery gaze to her shoes.

They're putting on brave faces but, God, they look crushed. I know none of them were close to their mom—I don't think Eliza even remembers her all that much—but, like Jackson told me once, she was still their mom. She was still a part of them, however fucked up that part might have been.

Jackson said something to me before, how he doesn't have the energy to hold a grudge, how she had her reasons and sometimes, he could understand them. It looks like the girls have adopted that same mentality.

I brace for impact when Lux floats into view, half expecting, I don't know, a punch to the face, maybe. It's safe to say I'm surprised as fuck when instead, she nudges her sisters aside and wraps her arms around me. "It's good to see you."

"Is it?" I joke before I can stop myself. Thankfully, I receive a snotty laugh in reply.

Lux pulls back, one curled up fist meeting my shoulder in a playful punch. "Yeah, it is. He'll be glad you're here."

"I'm not so sure about that."

Red-rimmed eyes roll. Eliza clinging to my arm, Lux gripping the other, I'm guided into the living room.

It's almost instantaneous, how I find him. Tucked away in the corner, surrounded by our friends.

With an unfamiliar pretty girl glued to his side.

A carefully manicured hand wraps around Jackson's bicep, big doe eyes blinking up at him. When she rises up on her tiptoes to whisper something in his ear, he barely seems to hear her, just gracing her with an absent smile before shaking her off.

Eliza lets go of me to run up to him, and I watch as he crushes her to his side. My stomach drops when she pokes and says something to him, my whole body tense when she points my way.

His gaze flickers to mine and whatever semblance of a smile he was faking, it drops. I expect the worst as he says something to the people surrounding him and strides towards me. I would step back, would maybe flee the scene, if his sister didn't have a death grip on me. His last few steps are cautious, almost disbelieving. He nods and smiles at his sister first but his eyes are back on me in a second.

"You came."

I hate how surprised he sounds.

Because I have no idea how to respond to that, I just nod. *Obviously* seems a touch too sarcastic given the circumstances.

I barely even notice Lux dropping my hand and disappearing into the crowd. I'm too focused on watching Jackson take another step forward, close enough that I have to tip my chin up. Close enough that if his hair weren't tied back, it would probably fall forward and tickle my cheeks. Close enough that I could reach out and grab his hand, easy.

I don't.

My gaze drops momentarily, needing a minute to right myself because, after all this time, he's still so fucking disorienting to me. I hear him clear his throat, see his hands flex at his side. "How are you?" he rasps and I almost laugh.

"I think I'm supposed to ask you that."

"I'm fine."

He doesn't look fine. He looks exhausted. Stressed. Handsome in his suit but nothing like my Jackson.

Painfully aware of everyone watching us but pretending they're not, I shuffle forward, lowering my voice. "I'm so sorry, Jackson."

He lets out a heavy breath, surprising me by reaching out to take my hand. "Thank you for coming."

I squeeze his hand. "Of course."

It could be a minute, it could be an hour, but his gaze remains locked on mine for what feels like forever, stealing my breath from my lungs, before it reluctantly shifts to something behind me. When his eyes return to mine, there's something apologetic lurking in them. "I have to talk to some people."

I force myself to drop his hand even though I really don't want to, force myself to take a step back. "Go."

"I'll find you later?" He doesn't sound too sure, like he's expecting me to flee the moment he turns his back.

I hope my firm nod is as reassuring as my words are meant to be. "I'll be here."

~

I'm chugging red wine like it's going out of style.

Despite being so uncomfortable I could cry, I stayed. Partly because I told him I would, mostly because Eliza would probably rugby tackle me to the ground if I tried to leave. And also because my ride is Nick and I don't think he, or any of the others, have any plans of leaving soon. I heard whispers about staying overnight, which makes me want to vomit and weep at the same time because I can't help but think of how different everything was the last time I spent the night.

I don't blame them for not wanting to leave. Even under the circumstances, it's hard not to get roped into the allure of Serenity Ranch. The boys have been here before, but it's Kate and Amelia's first time, and they looked just as entranced as I always have been. I think it helps Lux, having something to do in showing them around, giving her regular spiel, talking up the place she worked so hard to make as amazing as it is.

I haven't talked to Jackson since he hurried off. I haven't had the chance; he's being pulled in every direction, talking to everybody in sight. The whole socializing thing is wearing him out, making him miserable, I can see it in his face. He looks like he could use a drink. And a nap.

And maybe surgery to remove that girl that's been clinging to him all afternoon.

Caroline.

When Eliza spilled who she was, it wasn't too hard to gather that she's not happy about her presence. Neither is Lux, if the sketchy glances she keeps shooting her brother's ex are anything to go by.

God, the girl is all over him. Groping him like we're at a club, not a funeral.

That might be the slightly tipsy side of me talking but still.

Ugh.

When the sun starts going down and the temperature drops, an itchy feeling overwhelms me. Everyone who was lingering outside piles into the house, and I hate it.

Outside, I can deal with, but inside is just… too much.

Watching Caroline fucking fondle Jackson is something I prefer to observe from afar. Or not at all.

No one notices me slipping away. Like I always used to whenever I came here, I naturally gravitate towards the barn. A neigh greets me as I shoulder the heavy doors open, and I smile as I approach the beast calling out to me.

"Hey, buddy," I coo quietly as Clyde rattles the stall door gently, whinnying happily when I run my fingers through his soft mane. He tosses his head, knocking it against mine and I laugh as his soft coat tickles my skin.

Big flirt.

"He missed you."

I jolt as I spin toward the ajar barn door and find Jackson leaning against it, watching with a soft smile. Clearing my throat, I return my attention to my monstrous friend. "I missed him too."

If someone had told me a year ago that I'd feel a genuine longing ache in my chest for a creature that gave me thigh burn and a bruised ass, I would've laughed in their face.

"You can take him for a ride, if you want."

Clyde and I snort in unison. Raising a brow at Jackson, I gesture at my dress. "Not exactly dressed for a ride." Besides, me riding off into the sunset during a funeral is a touch dramatic, even for me.

Jackson's gaze burns into me as he agrees with a brisk nod.

I avoid looking at him, focusing on the hand stroking Clyde. "Is it okay that I came?"

Out of my peripheral, I see him take a couple of steps towards me. "Why wouldn't it be?"

"I didn't think you'd want to see me."

"I always want to see you."

My head jerks up so fast I almost give myself whiplash. "What?"

Jackson shrugs nonchalantly, as if what he just said is nothing. Narrowing my eyes, I scan him quickly. Swaying a little, looking a touch more dishevelled than he did when I first arrived, eyes red-rimmed but I don't think it's just from crying. "Are you drunk?"

Cracking a boyish smile, Jackson holds his forefinger and thumb a small distance apart in the universal sign for 'just a little bit.'

"Jackson…"

"My mom is dead, Luna. I'm allowed to have a couple of drinks."

Those blunt words shut me right up. "I'm-"

"Please, don't say you're sorry." The stall door next to Clyde's groans as Jackson leans against it, shoving his hands in pockets. "I'm so fucking sick of people saying they're sorry."

I snap my mouth shut.

"She was in Michigan," Jackson says after a beat of silence. "This whole time, she was in Michigan." He kicks at the ground, a sarcastic laugh leaving him as he shakes his head. "I dunno, I just thought if you abandon your kids so you can live your own life, you'd go somewhere cooler than Michigan. Europe, maybe. Or Japan. Her mom still lives there."

"You ever meet her?"

"I don't think she even knows we exist."

This would be a great moment, I think to myself, *for empathy.* To tell him I can relate to that. Family not knowing you exist.

I don't.

"You know I didn't know I was Japanese until I was seven? No one thought it was important to tell us." His laugh, God, his laugh, so bitter and hurt it hurts me too. "I heard her talking in a foreign language on the phone, I asked what it was, and she said Japanese. And that was it. That's all she ever gave us."

I don't reply. I wouldn't know what to say. All I can do is listen.

"I hate that I care enough to hate her."

Fuck, and don't I understand that too.

Jackson's gaze flicks upward, landing on me, and I shift under the weight of its intensity. An involuntary shiver shoots up my spine when he takes a step forward, hands outstretched ever so slightly. "I'm gonna hug you now, okay?"

I'm pretty sure it's a rhetorical question because the words barely leave his mouth before I'm enveloped in a strong pair of arms, the smell of hay and horse mixing with fresh grass and spring and a hint of booze.

I don't give myself time to overthink it. I just wrap my arms around his waist, wanting to cry at how my body melts, comfortable for the first time in months. Except for a few days ago when I woke up with him in my bed, before the panic and the gut-wrenching sadness set in, and I chose to be angry instead of relishing in it.

I hate that this moment of pure content is happening because

something horrible happened to him, but I don't think about it
right now.

I'm just thinking about him, hugging me like his life depends on it,
and me hugging him right back.

43

LUNA

"You're Luna, right?"

I tense at the sound of a sugary sweet voice that I've only heard a handful of times yet I already hate. I especially hated it when it echoed around the barn earlier calling for Jackson for some reason or another, interrupting whatever moment he and I were sharing.

The sense of deflation I felt when he dropped his arms and stepped away from me as quickly as possible still lingers.

Forcing a smile, I look at Caroline where she lurks in the doorway of Jackson's bedroom. I didn't mean to come in here; I got sidetracked on the way to the bathroom. The door was ajar, and I couldn't help myself. I had hoped for a moment alone but apparently, that was wishful thinking.

The ex-girlfriend of my ex-boyfriend steps forward. "I'm Caroline." *Oh, I know.* "Jackson's... friend."

My hand twitches at my side, itching to slap that look off her face. All coy and demure and *friendly.*

That might be the red wine talking.

I hate how comfortable she looks as she saunters into his room and perches on the edge of his bed, smoothing her hands over the bedsheets, looking like she belongs. Looking at me like she knows everything. "It must be weird for you to be here."

"Probably about as weird as it is for you."

"Oh, it's not weird for me. I'm practically family."

I resist the urge to snort. Yeah, I highly doubt the actual family members would agree with that statement.

Unperturbed by my lack of reaction, Caroline continues, "It's just so awful, what they're going through."

I hum my agreement. Maybe if I don't make conversation, she'll just go away.

Again with the wishful thinking.

"I came right over here as soon as I heard. Jackson was a mess, the poor thing. Just cried in my arms for days."

She's fishing for a reaction, I can tell by her voice, but I refuse to give her one. Fisting my hands at my side, I smile through gritted teeth. "It's nice that you were there for him."

God, I fucking hate that smile of hers. "Well, we have history, you know. A lot of it. I knew he'd want my comfort."

Not just comfort. *Her* comfort, specifically. Like only her comfort would help him.

Bitch.

I'm about to excuse myself before I do something like, I don't know, throw her out the window, when a dramatic huff steals my attention. "You're still here?"

Because the atmosphere wasn't awkward enough, Lottie chooses this moment to darken the doorway, arms folded and that seemingly permanent grimace on her face. I assume the teenage angst is directed at me until I realize that scowl is solely focused on Caroline.

The latest object of Lottie's wrath adopts a gritty smile. "Of course I am."

"Why?"

God, I want to laugh. Turns out, Lottie's shitty attitude is pretty damn hilarious when it's not directed at me or anyone I actually like.

Caroline's fake smile tightens. "C'mon, Lottie. I'm just tryna help."

"Whatever." Lottie rolls her eyes. "Jackson's looking for you."

Caroline brightens as she gets to her feet, hastily heading for the door only to be body-blocked and scoffed at. "Not you." Humor glitters in light eyes as Lottie jerks her head towards me. "You."

Oh, now I *really* want to laugh.

It's not a competition but *ha. I win.*

Brushing past the pair and wondering how long it'll take before the scratching and hair-pulling begins, I hurry down the hall. Most people have cleared out by now, and it's only my friends and the family left gathered in the living room, squashed on the sofas.

It looks—and sounds—like, everyone is following Jackson's lead and getting a little toasted. Even Eliza's cradling one of those barely alcoholic wine coolers, and looking nothing short of delighted about it. When she catches sight of me hovering in the doorway, she lifts the bottle in greeting, waving it excitedly and wiggling her brows. Beside her, Lux flicks her arm and rolls her eyes, toasting me with her bottle of water.

Jackson is alone in the corner, sprawled in an armchair, a beer in hand and his head resting in the other as he silently watches everyone. He smiles softly as I approach, no hesitation in how he wraps calloused fingers around my wrist and tugs until I'm settled on the arm of the chair. Shifting awkwardly, I clear my throat. "You were looking for me?"

He hums quietly, messing with the rings adorning my fingers. "Everyone's staying the night. Are you okay with that?"

Even if I wasn't, I don't really have a choice; my ride is curled up on the sofa, his girlfriend in his lap and the youngest Jackson chatting his ear off about photography. But really, I don't mind.

Not that much.

My knee knocks against Jackson's. "I'll sleep in the barn with Clyde."

That coaxes a laugh out of him, a large hand enveloping my knee and squeezing.

I'm painfully aware of how close we're sitting. And the longer we sit, the more the night goes on, the closer we get.

At one point, Jackson shifts my legs so they're draped across his lap and scoots me closer until my ass sits on his thigh.

I blame my lack of protest on the wine.

After his third beer, his head lolls, falling to the side and settling in the crook of my neck. It's instinct that has my hand reaching up and twining in his hair, fingers burying in the silky strands and stroking the way he used to like. Still likes, apparently, if the pleased rumble in his chest is anything to go by.

I could blame the wine again for my own head falling forward and resting on top of his. I could also blame it for my free hand creeping towards the one of his that rests on my thigh and lacing our fingers together. And I could definitely blame it for lulling me to sleep, and not the soothing strokes he rubs along my skin.

I'm not sure how long I doze for. I just know that the next time I open my eyes, I'm being cradled in a pair of strong arms. Blinking away the sleep, Jackson's face comes into focus just as he sets me down on a soft surface. His bed, I realize, the knowledge bringing a whole horde of butterflies to life in my stomach. "What're you doing?"

"Go back to sleep," he shushes me gently. Too sleepy to protest, I let him ease my shoes off, let him tuck me under the covers. Tucking my hands under my face, I curl up in a ball, relishing in the comfortable warmth.

"Where are you sleeping?" I ask through a yawn. My face twists in a grimace when he points at the floor. That doesn't seem right. "The sofa?"

"Taken," he tells me as he arranges a couple blankets in some poor excuse for a bed.

I don't know if it's the drunk side of me or the desperate, needy side but something makes me scoot over as far as I can without falling off the edge of the small bed and pat the empty space I make. Definitely drunk but maybe needy and desperate too, Jackson doesn't protest. He just flops beside me, his head lolling towards me, his eyes trained on mine.

For the second time today, he shocks me by saying exactly what's on his mind. "I miss you."

A lump forms in my throat. "Jackson..."

"I know," he says softly, a rueful grin on his handsome, tired face. "I'm not allowed to. But just lemme pretend for a sec."

Pretend. Pretend everything's okay. Pretend everything's normal. God, that would be nice.

I choose to, once again, blame the wine for the way I inch closer to him, not stopping under my chest is flush against his side and my head rests on his shoulder. "Okay."

It's a bad habit we're creating, this falling asleep in each other's beds business.

I think my body knows it too, because it wakes me up at the crack of dawn and doesn't let me go back to sleep. The sun is barely up when I slip out of his bed, stopping to switch his alarm off on the way out my door because I have a feeling sleep is not something he comes by often these days.

Padding down the hallway, I make a pit stop in the living room to steal a blanket, careful not to wake any of the bodies passed out there. No one stirs as I wrap the blank around my shoulders and creep outside, even when the screen door squeals loudly.

A chilly, morning breeze caresses my bare legs as I slump on the porch steps. I'm still wearing my dress from yesterday because apparently, asking for a change of clothes is where I draw the line. Hugging the blanket tighter around me, I breathe in the brisk but fresh air.

I sound like a broken record but God, I missed this place so fucking much. I missed the feeling I get whenever I'm here. All I've wanted the past few months was the peace I associate with Serenity Ranch and I couldn't get it, and it was my own damn fault. And as good as it feels to have that now, I'm already dreading leaving and not knowing if I'll ever be back again.

When the door creaks open behind me, I brace for Jackson. I only relax slightly when Lux appears in my peripheral, swaddled in a blanket too, a mug cradled to her chest and another held out to me.

I accept the drink, the heat of it seeping through the ceramic into my cold hands, the steam warming my face and carrying the scent of green tea. "Is it poisoned?"

Lux's elbow meets my ribs as she sits down beside me. "Drama queen."

I say nothing, just elbow her back. We huddle together, sharing warmth as we sip our tea in silence. After a while, I feel Lux's gaze on the side of my face, so eerily similar to the way Jackson stares me down. "You look like shit."

"Gee, thanks," I respond wryly. "You always were my favorite."

She doesn't entertain my attempt at comic relief. "Seriously, Luna. You look miserable."

"Yeah, well. Makes sense."

"Luna," she starts, soft and unoffending, "what happened?"

I know what she's referring to and it makes me itch. Just thinking about the whole ordeal last summer fills me with an icky mixture of embarrassment and nerves and guilt and utter fucking disgust that I'm even involved with it, and with how I lashed out after I found out. "I don't wanna talk about it."

"Lu-"

"Hey, it's me who should be checking up on you," I interrupt, nudging her knee with mine. "How are you doing?"

I send up a silent thanks when Lux sighs and lets me change the subject. "It's weird. Like, I knew she was never gonna come home but now it's because she can't and not because she doesn't want to. I don't know how to feel about it."

"I think that's normal."

Lux shrugs. She sniffs, voice thicker and quieter than it was a moment ago. "I feel like I don't care as much as I should," she whispers. "I never really counted on seeing her again so, like, what's the difference?" Another sniffle, and I pretend I don't see the tear slipping down her cheek. "And I have so much other shit to worry about right now, it just... God, I sound awful, but it doesn't seem all that important."

Wrapping my hand in hers, I squeeze tightly. "I'm really sorry this is happening to you."

"Yeah, me too." Shaking her head and straightening up, Lux wipes her face before turning to me and pinning me with a look that, honestly, scares me a little. "I need to go somewhere later and I want you to come with me."

"Okay?"

"No one else knows."

A bad feeling settles in my gut. "Are you sick or something?"

The laugh she lets out is bitter. "Something like that."

I wait for what feels like a lifetime before she sucks in a deep breath, something that looks a lot like fear flickering in her brown eyes. "I'm pregnant."

～

"They definitely thought we were a couple."

Lux takes her eyes off the road for a split second to shoot me a look. "They did not."

"Did you see how that creepy receptionist looked at us? He definitely did."

"He was looking at *you* because *you* look like *that*."

I snort. "What's that supposed to mean?"

Lux shoots me another look. "You're hot, Luna. The creepy man thought you were hot."

"Sounds like you want us to be a couple."

My comment earns me a slap on the arm, but it's worth it. It makes Lux smile. She's been a jittery mess since the appointment.

When I woke up today, I really didn't think my morning was going to be spent at a clinic two towns away staring at my ex-boyfriend's sister's ultrasound. I thought she was joking when she told me, I really did. I thought it was payback or something.

Like, ha ha, here's your karma for hurting my brother in the form of a fucking heart attack.

But no. She was deadly serious and she proved it; I couldn't argue with the blurry black and white blotch squirming on the ultrasound technician's screen. Or the small bump rounding her stomach. I can't believe, with how close the Jacksons are, that no one's noticed that thing. She claims I aided in helping to hide it; apparently, Jackson's been too distracted to pay much attention to her. She waved off my apology; she's not ready for him to know anyways.

The only person who knows besides me is the father, and according to Lux, he's doing his best to pretend he doesn't know. I offered to slash his tires but Lux declined.

I might just do it anyway.

"I need someone neutral to know," was her reasoning for telling me. She needed to tell someone who it doesn't directly affect, I guess. Someone who wouldn't freak out like she knows Jackson and her sisters and, Jesus Christ, her grandparents will. I'm happy to be that person, if it makes things a little easier for her. I'm happy to hold her hand at an ultrasound and suffer the leers of pervy receptionists and kind of lie to a bunch of people I care about.

She's growing an entire person in secret. The least I can do is be a shoulder for her to lean on. Or cry on. Or an ear for her to bitch to.

I'm sucking down the dregs of a strawberry milkshake—one of four Lux ordered because she claimed we needed a cover story but really, I think she just wanted McDonald's—when we arrive back at Serenity Ranch. Both Lux and I's faces screw up when we see everyone gathered outside. It looks like they're loading up the rental, getting ready to leave.

Lux's car has barely rolled to a stop before Jackson is jogging our way. A frown on his face, he opens Lux's door and leans inside. "Where did you two go?"

"Out," is Lux's simple reply.

"We got food," I blurt out quickly, holding up the almost empty paper bag as proof.

Before Jackson can question us further, Lux shoves him aside so she can get out of the car, mouthing a 'thank you' my way when he's not looking.

I do the same, planning on scurrying towards the girls and using them as cover, but a tall body in my way stops me. "Hi," Jackson greets me, an intense, unnerving look on his face.

I swallow hard. "Hey."

"You were gone when I woke up."

I don't like waking up alone.

I slap that ghost of a voice out of my head quickly, before I do something silly like cry. Instead, I shrug, aiming for nonchalance and hoping it hides how much sleeping in a bed with him messes me up. "I'm an early riser these days."

He snorts in disbelief before his eyes narrow. "You turned off my alarm."

"Thought you could use the sleep."

Crooking a brow, he leans against the car, arms folded. "That your way of telling me I look tired?"

"You look fine."

"Fine? Hurting my ego, sweetheart."

"Fishing for compliments, baby?"

I think we both realize what we're doing at the same time. The joking around. How close we are. And it's simultaneous, how we snap out of it, both take a big step back and awkwardly clear our throats.

Fuck, we're so bad at this.

Scratching the back of his head, Jackson clears his throat again. "I'm staying here for the rest of the week but I'll be home on the weekend. Can I, uh, see you, or something? On Friday maybe?"

Shit.

"I have plans," I reply awkwardly, hating how quickly his face drops. "A dinner thing."

"Oh." Something like realization crosses his face, and I don't like that I can't understand what it means. "Okay."

Hating how quickly things became uncomfortable, I jerk my thumb towards our awaiting friends. "I have to go."

"Yeah. Of course."

He joins me as I walk towards the truck, holds the door open as I climb inside, both pointedly ignoring the inhabitants watching us like we're a fucking soap opera.

"Thanks for coming," Jackson says to everyone, but he's staring right at me. Still stares when he closes the door. I swear, even when we're driving away, his gaze somehow stays trained on me.

Only when the ranch is out of sight do I feel myself relax. With a sigh, I slump in my seat.

"Luna?"

My head rolls to the side to face Ben, and I almost groan at that sneaky little look on his face. "What?"

"Where did you sleep last night?"

44

JACKSON

"Lux!"

"I'm coming!"

When five minutes pass and her bedroom door stays firmly shut, I pound my fist against the wood. "Lux, I swear to God!"

An annoyed groan sounds from within. "I said I'm coming!"

"They're almost here!"

"Jesus fucking Christ, Oscar." The door swings open, revealing my swearing, glaring, furious sister. "Happy?"

"Took you long enough."

Bony elbows catch me in the stomach as she pushes past me. "I was getting dressed."

I eye her outfit skeptically. She's wearing the same dress she always does, one of the ones that hang in her closet specifically for these visits, but with a huge chunky cardigan over the top. I wince before the next words even leave my mouth. "She's not gonna like the cardigan."

Understatement; she'll hate it. It's homemade—a Lottie creation from back when she liked us enough to make us things—and it looks like it.

Lux shoots me a dirty look. "She can kiss my ass."

God, she's in a fucking mood lately.

Following my stomping sister into the kitchen, I find the rest of them gathered around the kitchen window, watching our impending doom inch its way closer, the atmosphere chillingly somber.

It says a lot, really, that a visit from our grandparents harshens the mood more than burying our mother did.

They didn't show up to the funeral. It was too short notice, they said. But they sent their condolences, of course, in the form of fat deposits in each of our bank accounts. I don't know why I was even surprised. They're too busy for holidays and birthdays and graduations; why would the death of the mother of their beloved grandchildren affect them any differently?

Something about their visit today feels… off. Worse than usual. For starters, both our grandparents are making an appearance; it was our grandfather that called. So, when two doors open instead of one, I'm not surprised.

But when a third does, my heart drops.

When I recognize the person getting out of the back seat, it fucking burns.

"Is that-"

I cut off Grace's shaky question. "Go upstairs."

"What-"

"All of you, upstairs, now."

I don't wait to see if they listen to me. The screen door slams off the wall as I throw it open and storm outside, porch steps groaning beneath my feet as I barrel down them. "Get the fuck out of here."

"*Oscar.*"

I ignore my grandmother's shrill, indignant voice. My gaze, my attention, all of my fucking anger is focused on the younger man cowering behind his parents. "Leave, right now, or I swear to fucking God-"

"Oscar, stop." I flinch when he says my name, hating how it sounds coming out of his mouth. "I'm just here to pay my respects."

Bullshit.

Paying your respects would involve having respect. He didn't respect her, he didn't love her, he didn't even fucking like her. This, showing up almost a week after the fact, is fucking disrespect. "Consider them paid. Now, leave."

For the first time in his pathetic little life, Oscar Jackson Senior stands his ground. Stands straight-backed, hands fisted at his sides, face serious.

God, he looks just like Lottie.

"I want to see the girls."

Over my dead fucking body. "No."

He actually has the audacity to look offended at my refusal. "They're my kids."

"The fuck they are." He gave away that right, literally and figuratively, a long time ago. He threw it away, threw us away, like we were nothing. He never earned that right.

I did.

"*I* raised them. Not you. Not them." I gesture towards my grandparents before stabbing a finger at my own chest. "*Me*. They're my fucking kids and I'm telling you to stay the fuck away from them."

"Oscar Jackson, you watch how you talk to your father," Grandma hisses, her face red with a mixture of anger and embarrassment.

"He's not my anything."

"Lower your voice." All three of them glance anxiously around the ranch. Like paparazzi are going to erupt from the treeline and discover that, shock horror, their beloved, charismatic, oh-so-progressive politician-turned-philanthropist is actually a massive jackass with five illegitimate children he abandoned over a decade ago. It would ruin his career, if that happened. *We* would ruin his career.

Hence why our grandparents pay us off and keep us hidden away on the ranch.

"Fuck you," I spit at the woman who has caused me and my sisters so much fucking pain.

There must be something in the air because for once, my grandfather finds his voice. "You will not disrespect your grandmother like that."

I laugh in his face. "Fuck you, too."

"*Oscar.*"

I ignore my father's voice, instead sweeping my arm in the direction of their car. "All of you, leave."

My grandmother narrows her eyes, turning up her nose at me. "You can't tell us to leave. This is our land."

"How much do you want for it?"

The words come out so quick I barely register that I'm saying them. I think, for quite possibly the first time in her long, miserable, life I've rendered my grandmother speechless because she gapes at me for a moment before choking out, "What?"

Can't back down now. "How much is it gonna take for you to leave us alone?"

She scoffs, regarding me with utter condescension. "You couldn't possibly afford it."

Clearly, they've lost count of all those deposits. "Try me."

They blurt out a number and I almost laugh; God, they really have no idea how much this place is worth. "Done."

"Wait-"

"And you're gonna transfer legal guardianship of the girls to me."

"What-"

"Send me whatever the fuck I need to sign and I'll sign it. Now, get off my ranch."

I think it's the shock that has them leaving without protest. They amble towards their shitty little car, casting stunned glances over their shoulders, hopefully setting eyes on me for the last time. Before he shuts the door behind him, my father casts me a look, a long one that I guess is supposed to be meaningful, supposed to convey something to me but all it does is make me hate him a little more.

Fucking coward.

It's only when they're completely out of sight that I let myself breathe. I pretty much crumple in half, my palms resting on my knees as I suck in a breath. A hand curls around my shoulder. Dazed, my gaze drifts to my side to find Lux staring wide-eyed up at me, face pale and mouth slightly ajar. "What did you just do?"

"I have no idea."

A week later and I still have no idea what I've done.

It happened a lot quicker than I thought it would. Actually, I didn't really think it would happen at all. I anticipated a fight. I didn't expect them to send the paperwork over before the weekend was even done. A couple of signatures and a check in the mail and that was it.

They must have been more eager to get rid of the place than I thought.

Or, more likely, eager to get rid of us.

Whatever. It's no skin off my back. The place is mine.

Serenity Ranch is mine.

Well, technically mine. Really, the place has always been Lux's, in the way that counts.

I thought she was going to kill me, when I actually went through with the sale. At first, she got angry, berating me endlessly about how reckless I am. Then she got all weird and soppy and cried while hugging me and thanking me for making them leave. And then she got angry again, at our dad this time, cursing his name and calling him every derogatory name under the sun.

He tried to call. Or at least I assume the random numbers blowing up my phone, the girls' phones and the ranch's landline have all been him. I ignored every single one, made sure the girls did too, and blocked any number I didn't recognize.

He doesn't get to do this. He doesn't get to miss our entire lives and then suddenly show up when we're all grown, after the hard part is done. After Lux and I did the hard part for him. He doesn't get to be some sick consolation prize. Like, hey, you lost one parent, but here's a backup.

I got paranoid that he would turn up again unannounced and get to the girls this time so I packed them up like I wanted to do the second the funeral finished and carted them all down to Sun Valley for a couple of days. Lux put up a bit of a fight—she acts like the place will sink into the ground if she leaves it—but the others were more than happy. Even Lottie. The guys didn't mind letting them stay with us, thank God. Nick's hardly ever here anyway so I stuck the twins in his room and let Eliza and Lux have my room while I took the couch.

My friends each had their own different reactions to finding out about what I'd done since they'd last seen me. Nick barked out a laugh and clapped me on the back, snickering under his breath as he wished me luck. Cass smirked and asked if this means he gets a discount in the guesthouses now; Lux responded with a scoffed 'hell no.' Ben just blinked at me and said, "Are you still rich? Or are you normal like the rest of us now?"

I just laughed.

We haven't really been doing much the last few days. We've just been... dealing, I guess. With everything that's happened. I had a game earlier today, so I brought them to that. It felt nice having someone cheering in the stand for me again. I missed that.

They leave sooner than I'd like—Lux had some appointment she needed to get back for—and the second her car disappears from sight, I start wishing I'd gone out after the game like the guys did.

The house feels too quiet, too empty, and as I laze on the couch, it hits me that this is the first time I've been alone since everything happened. The first time I've had a second to think. To process, or whatever.

I don't like it. I don't really want to. What's done is done, I can't change it, and if I have to think about my fucked up family for one more second, I might lose it.

But my mind won't let me not think about it. It keeps straying to the day of the funeral, easily one of the weirdest days of my life. It felt so wrong. Like nothing that was happening was real. Like I wasn't actually there, just watching from afar. All these people were in my house, people who didn't even know my mom, they just came for us, her kids.

I hated it, the crowd and the attention, but I was grateful for it at the same time. I'm glad the girls have a support system since I can't be there all the time. At least, not until after I graduate.

It's ironic that the one bright spot in my day came in the form of someone who makes my chest ache every time I look at her. I knew the others were coming but I didn't think she would. I didn't realize how much I wanted her to, how much I needed her to, until she was in my living room and my knees almost gave out at the sight of her.

It was weird, how normal everything felt. How easily we fell back into that familiar pattern. Sad too, because I had this voice in the back of my head constantly reminding me that it was only temporary. That much was proved when I woke up the next morning and found a cold, empty spot in my bed.

Pathetic, really.

At my own mother's fucking funeral and all I could think about was her.

No wonder I drank myself silly.

My phone buzzes in my hand, and I grimace at the message from

Cass asking, no, *telling* me to join them. I don't really want to. I'm not sure I'm in the mood to be around drunk people, especially the baseball guys.

But I'm definitely not in the mood to be alone.

With a groan, I mutter a 'fuck it' and scoop my keys up off the kitchen table, texting Cass back with one hand and pulling the front door open with the other. I don't realize there's someone standing on the other side until I almost knock them down.

A surprised shriek echoing in my ears, I reach out to stabilise whoever the hell I almost flattened, getting a handful of soft skin as I yank them forward. When the scent of vanilla tickles my nose, my face falls in a frown.

"Luna?"

45

LUNA

I DON'T KNOW why I'm here.

Dithering at his front door, hopping nervously from one foot to the other, a lukewarm casserole dish, the only thing keeping me warm. I left my jacket at the Jacobs' place, and despite the freezing temperature, I was too chickenshit to go back and get it. I'll get it next week.

Or any other Friday night until my death, probably.

Silver lining; the food at their place is always good. So good that my mouth waters every time we sit at the obnoxiously large dining room table and Mrs Jacobs brings out dish after dish of heavenly food. She must notice how quickly, and gratefully, I scoff it all down because she always loads me up with leftovers. Hence the chicken casserole in my hands and the half of an apple pie stuffed in a Tupperware container weighing down my tote.

Food. That's why I'm here. You're supposed to bring grieving people food, right? That's a thing.

A sympathy casserole and pie.

That's why I'm here.

That's what I'm telling myself as I'm hyping myself up to knock when the door suddenly opens. A shriek escapes me as I'm almost barrelled over, a rough hand latching onto my hip preventing what would've been a very messy fall.

"Luna?"

Oh, fuck my life.

Pasting on my smile, I force my gaze to meet Jackson's. "Hi." At his questioning frown, I hold up the dish. "I brought you food."

Slowly, his gaze drops from my face to my slightly pathetic offering. "You brought me food?"

I nod.

"You cooked?"

A flush creeps up my cheeks. "Well, no. Someone else made it. I'm just, uh, delivering it."

Confusion creases his face but he takes the dish regardless. The keys in his hand jingle as he does, drawing my attention to them. "Oh shit, were you on your way out?"

"Kinda, yeah."

"Shit." I take a step back. "Sorry. I'll just go."

"Hey, wait." Before I can get too far, Jackson loops a hand around my wrist. "Don't. I didn't really wanna go out anyways."

I hate the sprig of hope that blossoms in my chest. "Yeah?"

Smiling gently, he nods. "Yeah."

"Okay."

"You coming in?"

I hadn't planned on it—at least not consciously—yet I find myself nodding. And when I step across the threshold, I'm caught between relief and regret.

Being back here feels... weird. Nostalgic. *Sad.*

So many memories, not enough emotional strength to process them all.

Thankfully, Jackson doesn't notice my misty-eyed reminiscing; he's already halfway to the kitchen. "You mind if I heat this up now? I haven't eaten yet."

"Go for it." Grabbing the other Tupperware from my bag, I follow him into the kitchen, dropping the container on the counter and sliding onto a barstool. "I have pie too."

He eyes the food with raised brows. "Who made all this? Your mom in town?"

I barely manage to contain my wince. "No. Pen's mom." Instinctively, my thumb goes to the ring on my forefinger. Still the one Jackson got me. I never took it off after the funeral.

Must've forgotten.

Jackson notices too, his eyes burning into the jewellery, his grip on the spoon scooping casserole into a bowl tightening. Coughing, I tuck my hands under my thighs, out of either of our sights. "I had dinner there tonight."

Jackson tears his eyes away from my hands, or more specifically my thighs, I guess, and nods jerkily.

"That's where I was last Friday night too," I add. The night he asked me to do something and I blew him off.

For a moment, he freezes. Seems to think hard about something, brow furrowed, and comes to some conclusion that has him blowing out a breath. "You eat there a lot?"

Oh, if only he knew. "Kinda."

He wants to ask more. I can see it on his face. But he restrains himself, busies himself heating up dinner. Silence settles, heavy and confused, only interrupted by the low buzz of the microwave. I'm worrying my bottom lip to the point of bleeding, gaze fixed on a random spot on the counter, when Jackson eventually sighs.

"Lu, why are you here?"

My gaze snaps up to his. "I had leftovers."

He doesn't look convinced. "Why are you really here?"

I don't know. "I wanted to make sure you were okay."

That scrutinizing expression softens. "I'm okay."

"I'm glad."

The microwave beeps loudly but Jackson doesn't move. "You could've just called."

I don't have it in me to admit that I deleted his number. Or, more specifically, Pen did. Those first couple of months, when I wasn't doing so well, I sometimes tried to call him when I was drunk. Hid my number and left voicemails I never sent. Pen got annoyed, said it wasn't fair to Jackson. She transferred his number to her phone, deleted it from mine, and told me if I really wanted to call him, I could. When I was sober. All I had to do was ask.

I never did.

Exhaling hard, I slowly admit, "I wanted to see you." The tiniest twitch tightens his jaw. "I feel like we left things on a weird note last week."

"You mean when you left me alone in my own bed?"

I choke on my next breath, wincing and already preparing an apology before I look up and realize he's joking. Shoulders slumping in relief, I cough out a weak, breathy laugh. "We shouldn't have done that."

Another twitch, his hand this time. One finger drumming steadily against the countertop. "Probably not."

"Or any of the other stuff."

The tapping stops. One dark brow arches. "The other stuff?"

"All the touching and shit." *The couple-y shit,* I say in my head. Me sitting in his lap and playing with his hair and him touching my waist, hugging me, missing me. "We can't do that. It's too... confusing."

I watch as his hands form fists, the muscles in his arms prominent as he tenses. His eyes burn into me, their intensity making me squirm. "What are you confused about, Luna?"

Internally, I snort. Where do I start? Literally everything in my life right now is confusing, him all too often being the pinnacle of it. Because I can't quite find the courage to put that into words, to tell him everything, I shrug.

Terrifyingly slowly, Jackson rounds the counter, coming to a stop right in front of me. I have to crane my neck to look up at him, throat bobbing as I swallow hard. With him so close, it's suddenly a lot harder to breathe, to think, to keep my hands firmly cemented underneath my thighs. Giving me all the time in the world to evade, he raises a hand, cupping the curve of my neck.

"I wasn't confused," he says. "All the *touching and shit* wasn't confusing to me."

I almost fall off the stool.

"Jackson," I croak.

"Tell me to stop and I will."

Silence. Complete and utter fucking silence.

He's the one who lowers his head towards mine, but I'm the one who kisses him.

~

The second our lips touch, a jolt of electricity shoots up my spine, one that I feel in my fingertips all the way to the tips of my toes. On their own accord, my hands bury themselves in his hair, pulling him closer to me, and I echo the groan he lets out.

Fuck, I missed this.

He kisses me like he never stopped. Like there isn't a huge gap between this one and the last. Like I'm still his, and it hurts just as much as it heals.

As quick as he descended, Jackson suddenly pulls back. Pouting, I chase after him, but I'm stopped by the grip he has on my neck. "Fuck," he curses quietly, scrubbing his free hand over his jaw.

"What?" I don't quite manage to keep the whine from my voice.

"We can't."

I swear to God, I almost cry. Hands fisted in his t-shirt, I try and fail to tug him back to me, groaning when he stays a solid arm's length away from me. "Why not?"

"You're seeing someone."

"What?" I jerk back, gaping at him. "No, I'm not. Why would you think that?"

"Cass saw you and him."

"Me and who?"

Jaw tense, he all but spits, "Some guy at your job."

Oh.

Fuck.

I'm going to kick Cass' ass.

"I'm not seeing him. We're just..." *Fucking*, I say only in my head but I have a feeling he catches my drift.

The grip on my neck tightens. Brown eyes flash as he runs his tongue over his teeth. My breath catches as his grip slowly, achingly slowly, circles around to entrap my throat, the lightest of pressure making me go a little dizzy with anticipation.

And then he's kissing me again. Harder this time. Full of purpose with none of the hesitation there might have been a minute ago. Almost brutal but I take it all more than willingly.

I squeal in surprise when I'm suddenly lifted up, my legs instinctively wrapping around Jackson's waist, my hands clutching his shoulders. Jackson swallows the noise, not once letting his lips leave mine as he walks us to the living room. Collapsing on the couch with me straddling him, I whimper when our hips align perfectly and I feel his cock, thick and long and fucking *hard*, straining against his jeans. Unable to resist, I grind against him, coaxing a groan out from his lips.

In a flurry of frantic hands, my dress is lifted up and over my head, tossed across the room. His shirt follows, as does my bra, leaving me bare except for the lacy panties I thank God I put on earlier. I barely feel the chill in the air, too consumed by the warmth of his bare chest beneath my palms and the hard grip he has on my hips as he guides my movements.

Warm, soft lips stray to my neck, my collarbone, my chest. Kissing and licking and biting, no doubt leaving marks in their path and making the sensation a million times better, knowing this is real and not another weirdly sad dream. My nails dig into his shoulder, my head thrown back as he licks up the column of my neck. I'm so caught in the feeling of having him pressed to me, underneath me, all over me that I barely notice when his little touches stop.

Blinking a couple of times to clear my head, I look down at him with a frustrated frown. "What? Why'd you stop?"

Jackson doesn't lift his gaze from where it's trained on my chest, tongue tracing a swollen bottom lip. Slowly, those big fucking hands cup my boobs, thumbs brushing over my nipples, circling the silver jewellery piercing them. His eyes are practically black when they flick up to my face, his voice ragged and strained as he asks, "What the fuck are these?"

The corner of my mouth quirks upwards. "Piercings."

He gives me a look that screams 'watch it' and has me glowing inside because, fuck, I missed that look too. Mostly because it usually means I'll get it later and *I want it*. "When?"

"A few months ago." About the same time I dyed my hair.

Another pass of his thumbs has me squirming, my stomach clenching as I rock my hips, searching and desperate for friction. "Do they hurt?"

"Not anymore."

"Thank fuck," is all he mutters before his lips wrap around one hard nipple, teeth grazing the sensitive peaks, tongue lashing against the metal. Fingers roughly tweak the other one, and fucking hell, I'm a goner.

I'm a mess of whimpers and moans, crying out his name and practically tearing his hair out at the root. The constant attention from his hands and tongues combined with his hips thrusting up to meet my rocking ones, the rough material of his jeans brushing my swollen clit... fuck, I can't it.

The orgasm catches me by surprise, so much so that I couldn't hold it off even if I wanted to. My cries echo off the walls, stomach tensing as my pussy clenches around nothing, pleasure ripping through me so hard and fast, it would've sent me to the floor if I wasn't already sitting.

Only when the fog in my head clears and my breathing regulates do I notice Jackson's actions have come to an abrupt stop. "Did you just-"

"Shut up."

My flushed cheeks only make him smirk harder. With a groan, he buries his face in my neck, nose brushing my jaw as he inhales deeply. "Fuck, sweetheart, I barely even touched you." Ragged breaths heat my neck, his tongue lashing against me as he sucks on the sensitive patch of skin beneath my ear. "You needed me that much?"

Yes.

Yes, I did.

God, I really fucking wish I didn't find that smug look on his face as hot as I do.

"You're an ass," I breathe, the words half-whimpered as his hand smoothes over my hip, palm coming down hard on my ass. Yeah, *fuck*, I missed that too, and he knows it. When I jerk against him, an involuntary moan escaping me, he just laughs before claiming my lips again.

"You're fucking soaked for me, Luna."

It's not a question. Just a statement. He just knows. And he's spot on too, because I am. I'm fucking dripping, probably leaving a wet patch all over his jeans. I'm so turned on it's painful yet so fucking welcome because I can't remember the last time I felt like this.

Correction; I can't remember the last time I felt like this with someone that wasn't him.

I don't even have it in me to be mad when I hear the tell-tale sound of ripping fabric as he tears my panties from my body. In fact, I cry out in relief because not long after, a finger drags through my pussy, teasingly circling the bundle of nerves crying out for him. I buck my hips, so ridiculously desperate to get him inside of me but he's not giving in.

Using his grip on my neck, he drags me forward, lips barely brushing mine. "Tell me you want me."

I don't even hesitate. "I want you."

"How much?"

"So fucking much." More than I want air. Or ice cream. Or wine.

His satisfied smile tickles my skin. "Good girl."

My head drops to his shoulder, muffling a cry as two long fingers thrust inside of me easily. I forgot fingers could feel so good, so full. Fuck, I forgot *foreplay* could feel this good. When his fingers retract only to drive themselves in harder, farther, scissoring inside and stretching to the limit, my teeth clamp down on his shoulder to hold in my scream.

He doesn't let my head stay buried in his neck for long. Holding my head upright, he makes sure my eyes are on him while his are on my frantic hips, his thrusting fingers, the heel of his hand grinding maddeningly against my clit. He's met with little resistance when he adds a third, and when he ducks his head to worship my chest again, it's not long before I'm coming around him again, writhing and convulsing on his lap as I chant his name. His name leaves my lips on a sob, a plea for him to stop or maybe a demand for him to never stop ever again.

"One more, sweetheart." In a tender move that so contrasts the harsh way he's assaulting my pussy, his free hand smoothes my hair away from my face before cupping my cheek. "I wanna see you."

A long, low moan rips from my throat as he curls his fingers, stroking just the right spot to have me soaking his hand for a third time. His eyes stay trained on me, never leaving my face once, and I have to close my own because it's too fucking much.

It feels like an age passes before I finally come down from the high. Or highs. It goes on for so long, I can't tell where one ends and another might start. It's almost embarrassing how loud I whimper, how empty I feel, when he pulls out of me, bringing his hand to his mouth and licking his fingers clean. Mine go to his waistband, rising up on shaky knees so I can tug the material separating us down.

I'm tired, blissfully worn out, but I want, I need, more.

His cock slaps against his stomach as I pull him free from his boxers, painfully hard and leaking from the tip. I wrap my fingers around him and he twitches in my hand, my pussy clenching in response as I imagine him twitching inside of me.

Yeah, I most definitely fucking missed that.

Like he did to me, I kiss from the corner of his mouth to his neck, grazing my teeth along his jawline. "Please, Jackson." I squeeze his cock and he groans. "Please, fuck me."

It's like a flip switches.

His body tenses, his hand wrapping around my wrist and tugging, his voice almost pained as he murmurs, "Stop."

I snatch my hand back like he's burned me. Sitting back on his thighs, I frown. "What's wrong?"

He avoids eye contact, staring at a spot behind my head, and I feel the need to cross my arms over my bare chest, to make myself a little less vulnerable. Especially when he says, "We can't."

I groan. Not this again. "Jackson, I swear to God, I'm not seeing anyone. I-"

"For fuck's sake, Luna, I don't wanna fuck you."

It's not his words that have my head snapping back. It's his harsh, sharp tone. The confusing anger. The regret lurking in his eyes.

Mistake. That's what his face says.

Mistake, mistake, mistake.

The back of my throat itches as I scramble off his lap, diving for my dress and yanking it over my head, snatching my bag off the floor and barrelling for the door before he even stands up. "Lu, wait."

Embarrassment and the sting of rejection fuel my movements as I wrench the front door open. I jump when it slams shut again, Jackson's hand coming down on the wood so hard, it groans. "Luna, I didn't-"

"Please," I croak out. "Please just let me leave before we do anything else I'll regret."

The tense, huffed breath he lets out tickles the back of my neck. My nails dig into my palms as the arm beside my head retracts slowly. The second it disappears from my peripheral, I'm out the door and stumbling down the drive.

I think he calls after me again but it's blocked by the sound of my car door slamming shut and the engine sputtering to life, tearing out of that place so fast I'm surprised my wheels don't let out a Fast and Furious worthy squeal.

I wait until the house is safely out of sight before I let a tear slip out.

46

JACKSON

Fuck.

I can't stop staring at the door Luna just slammed shut. The one she ran out of with tears in her eyes and hurt heavy around her.

What the fuck did I just do?

My head drops back against the sofa as I let out a frustrated groan. If my dick could groan, it would. I'm fucking rock hard, and no amount of slow breathes or thinking of turn-offs is going to calm it down. Not when it knows it was a handful of pumps away from coming all over Luna's stomach and tits. Or inside of her.

Fuck.

I half-shudder, half-wince as I tuck myself back in my jeans, purposely avoiding looking at the wet spot staining the front. God, I'm not even sure if it's from me or her. Both, probably. Mostly her though, if the way she soaked my fingers is anything to go by.

Don't fucking think about it.

I'm in the kitchen washing my hands and staring aimlessly at the food she brought like a fucking weirdo when I hear the front door open. Momentarily, I hope it's Luna returning so I can explain myself but my hopes are dashed when Cass' voice rings out, "Jackson?"

"In here," I call back, angling myself behind the island so that fucking wet spot is hidden from the view of the three guys crowding the kitchen doorway. All three of them eye me with various degrees of suspicion and smugness.

"Do you have something to tell us?" Ben asks slowly.

They know.

I don't know how but they so fucking know.

Instead of admitting it, I feign ignorance. "No."

His eyes scan my bare chest and narrow. "You sure?"

"Mmhmm."

"Then why is there a bra on the living room floor?"

Shit. Slumping against the counter, I cradle my head in my hands, an indistinguishable noise leaving me.

"Please tell me it's Luna's."

I grunt, offering Ben half a nod.

"And the nail marks on your shoulders?"

Another curse escapes me as I glance at my arms. Shit, she got me good.

"Fucking finally," Ben literally squeals, and I peek up to find him doing a unabashed happy dance. Cass is smiling too but Nick, he's frowning, eyes too knowing for my liking.

"You don't look very happy about it."

Ben ceases his celebrations, fist reaching out to jab Nick's bicep. "Why do you have to ruin everything?"

"What? Look at him." He gestures towards me. "That's not the face of a guy who just banged the love of his life."

Squinting, Ben surveys me before reluctantly nodding his agreement. "What happened?"

"I fucked up."

"What did you do?"

There's a brief pause as the words get stuck in my throat. Scrunching my nose, I swallow hard. "We were," I cough, "hooking up. She was about to... you know, and I stopped her. She freaked and left."

Confusion mars my friends' faces. "She freaked out because you stopped her?"

"I told her I didn't wanna fuck her." Yelled it, more accurately. So much harsher than I intended.

Silence.

For a solid minute, maybe two, there's nothing but silence. I avoid looking at the guys but I can easily picture what I'm sure are horrified expressions.

"Please tell me you didn't say it in those exact words."

I wince, and when I finally look up, they're wincing too. "Jesus fucking Christ, Jackson."

"She's naked in your lap with her hand around your dick and you yell 'I don't wanna fuck you' in her face?" Cass blinks at me. "Is your dick still attached to your body?"

Groaning, I scrub my hands over my face. "I didn't mean it like that."

Fucking *obviously* I didn't mean it like that. I meant I didn't want to *just* fuck her. I didn't want to hook up and then have her run off in a panic immediately after. But I was frustrated and wound up and it just came out wrong, so fucking wrong.

"We know you didn't," Nick reassures me, shooting Cass a side-eyed glare. "Because we know you're still in love with the girl. She doesn't know that."

I grunt. "When did you become the love expert?"

Nick grins. "Practice."

I wanted to go after her but Nick wouldn't let me.

"Let her calm down," he'd said. "Go rushing after her when she's not ready and it'll only make it worse. Trust me."

Because the guy is one of the only people I know in a solid, steady, healthy relationship, I took his advice. It was probably the right call, too. I know my girl. When she's upset, she snaps. She pushes. So I stayed away.

I'm still staying away, a few days later, when I'm trudging out of class and a loud, extremely pissed-off voice hollers in my direction.

"Hey, shithead!"

I barely get the chance to turn around and check if I'm the shithead in question before something whacks me on the arm. Glancing down, I almost laugh when I see the weapon of choice is a sparkly purple spiral notebook with the words 'it's nice to be nice' printed across the cover.

I definitely do not laugh when I look up and find an angry former-blonde-but-currently-redhead scowling at me. "Pen?"

The notebook attacks again. Another wallop stings my arm, but not quite as much as those accusing eyes do. "What the fuck is wrong with you?"

"Hey, enough." I snatch the offending stationary from her grip, holding it up and out of reach when she tries to grab it back. "What the hell is your problem?" Huffing, Pen crosses her arms like an indignant toddler, muttering something inaudible but definitely insulting under her breath. "Speak up, Pen."

"I was rooting for you, you know," she spits out, and I recoil at not only the venom in her tone, but the underlying quiver, the hint of sadness. Disappointment. "I thought you were a nice guy. But when my s-" She clears her throat. "When my roommate comes home crying her eyes out with half her clothes missing, I'm gonna assume it's not because she spent the night with a nice guy."

"Pen, I didn't-"

"*I don't wanna fuck you?* Are you kidding me?"

I wince. Yeah, I'm definitely not living that down anytime soon.

"Did you get off on it? Embarrassing her like that? What, was it payback for her breaking up with you? Do you know how long I've been trying to..." She doesn't finish her sentence, letting out a groaning, shrieking kind of a noise and slapping my arm again. "I can't fucking believe you!"

"Stop it!" I bat her hand away when she goes for me again. God, for such a slight little thing, she packs power behind her punch. "Can you let me talk?"

Pen narrows her eyes and pouts but nods stiffly.

Puffing out a breath, I shove my hands in my pockets. "I didn't mean for it to come out like that." Snorting interrupts me, blue-green eyes rolling, reminding me so much of the friend she's currently defending. "God, you and her are way too alike."

Pen stiffens. This weird look overcomes her for a moment, lips parting as if she's about to say something before she shakes her head. Her hand lifts, gesturing impatiently for me to continue. "I don't have all day, farmboy."

Letting the sass slide, I tug Pen towards an alcove in the hall so we have some semblance of privacy. "I don't wanna just hook up with her, Pen. I... That's not what I want from her. That was never what I wanted from her. And I didn't want to have sex with her when it would mean something different to her than it does to me."

The indignance narrowing her eyes goes nowhere. "And how do you know what it means to her?"

My head cocks to the side as I give Pen a look. "She broke up with me, Pen." She didn't, doesn't, I don't know anymore, want me. Not the way I want her.

"Not because she-" Pen cuts herself off again, looking like she's one word away from stamping her feet like a tantrum-throwing little kid. Sucking in a breath, her expression softens a little. She does this little anxious glance around before stepping closer, her voice no longer at a deafening decibel. "Look, something monumentally shit happened last summer and she didn't take it well. Her breaking up with you had nothing to do with *you*."

I find that hard to believe. I was there. It felt a whole lot like it was because of me.

Pen must recognise the skepticism on my face because she sighs. "She was a wreck, Jackson. Breaking up with you wrecked her. More than the shit thing that happened that I'm not gonna tell you about because it's not my place, so don't ask."

She looks nervous as she tugs her bottom lip into her mouth and crosses her arms over her chest. "I shouldn't even be telling you this but she cried for, like, a month straight. And she started drinking. Like, a lot. I thought her liver was gonna crap out at one point. I was genuinely terrified to leave her alone in case I came home and found her in a pool of her own vomit."

A knot of worry forms in my chest as that horrific image flashes through my mind. Fuck. "I didn't know that."

She offers me a sad smile. "Of course you didn't. She wouldn't let you."

I hate that. I hate that so fucking much. And I'm angry, so fucking angry that whatever happened, she felt the need to deal with it alone instead of letting me, letting anyone, just help her.

"It was bad, Jackson. And I'm not saying it was all because of you, because the thing-that-shall-not-be-named played a part, but more often than not, it was your name she was sobbing." Pen pauses, a crease forming before her brows. "She loved the fuck outta you, Jackson, and it makes me sad that you seem to think she didn't."

I open my mouth to reply but nothing comes out. I don't know what to say. It's not that I don't think she loved me. I know she did.

It's more that I don't think she loved me quite as much as I love her. Whatever Pen might be telling me now, I saw Luna on campus looking completely unaffected while I constantly felt like shit. And, well, maybe that reaffirmed that belief a little.

And I'd take that, her not loving me as much, any day over everything Pen just told me being true.

"I know it was her choice but losing you fucking destroyed her, Jackson. And if you think for one second that you don't mean anything to her..." Pen sighs and shrugs. "Well, then maybe you don't know her as well as you think you do."

With one final sad smile, she walks away, leaving me with a head full of words, none of them making a whole lot of sense.

47

LUNA

IT'S BARELY the afternoon and I'm already done with today.

Everything is going wrong. Class ran late so I was rushing to work. I had to change in the car and ended up with ripped tights and a missing button on my shirt. I did a coffee run and got a couple of orders wrong, my least favorite mistake because the office assholes never fail to make me feel like an insipid fool when I mess up.

Like I need any more of that lately.

An almighty sigh leaves me as I plop down on my desk chair, the wheels creaking as I spin. It's the first time I've sat down in hours because it's just been one of those days; everyone has needed something and I have had to provide it.

I relish in the silence of my office—well, my repurposed storage closet—but unsurprisingly, it doesn't last long. Whoever raps their knuckles against my ajar door promptly ruins my break, and to make matters worse, the last time I saw the man lurking in the doorway, I was in the driver seat of his car.

More specifically, bouncing on his dick in the driver seat of his car.

I've managed to avoid him since but I guess all good things must end. Hiding a grimace behind a forced smile, I try not to sigh. "You need something, Paul?"

Taking my question as an invitation, my semi-regular hookup strolls into the room and sets a plastic takeaway cup on my desk. "Brought you lunch."

A protein shake.

Lunch.

"Thanks but I already ate." Not quite a lie. I did eat.

This morning.

But I'll take starving to death over something green and chunky any day of the week.

Undeterred, Paul perches on the edge of my desk. "I haven't seen you in a while."

Purposely so. "I've been busy."

"You busy tonight?"

No. "Yes."

"Oh." He pulls a disgustingly cutesy pouty face. "Maybe next week?"

All I offer is a dismissive smile before gesturing towards the neat stack of papers in desperate need of photocopying and pointedly eyeing the door. "I'm kinda busy right now too."

"Right." Paul nods stiffly and nods, making sure to nab my so-called lunch offering before leaving. I swear he even slams the door a little behind him.

Men.

I allow myself a brief moment to release some frustration—otherwise known as silently screaming at the ceiling—before I compose myself, focusing on the task at hand.

Or I try to, at least.

I've barely gotten to my feet, papers in hand, when I'm interrupted by my phone ringing and promptly sent back to my ass.

Jackson.

Jackson is calling me.

I know because in a moment of weakness after the funeral, I snuck his contact from Pen's phone. I figured I'd shoot him a text. Check in. I would've saved myself a whole lot of trouble if I had instead of turning up at his doorstep.

I don't want to answer. I really don't want to talk to him. Even thinking of him makes my skin itch with embarrassment, picturing that look on his face when he yelled at me.

Like he'd just made the worst mistake of his life.

Rolling my shoulders back, I decline the call. Barely a minute passes before a text comes through.

. . .

Jackson: Answer the phone, Luna.

Bossy little shit.

I ignore the text, making sure it comes up as read though because I'm petty like that. Thirty seconds later and another call comes through, and I ignore that too. The moment it rings out, another text dings.

Jackson: sweetheart please. I just wanna talk to you.

Goddamn it. Fucking *sweetheart.*

The next time he tries, I give in with a sigh and a snapped, "What?"

No greeting, just a rushed, slightly panicked. "Are you home?"

"Nope."

"When will you be home?"

"I don't know." A lie. A couple of hours, tops.

"Tonight?"

"I don't know." Another lie; I plan to be home all night.

"Lu," he laughs my name, annoyingly unperturbed by my snippiness. "please. I need to talk to you."

"We're talking now."

He kisses his teeth, and it's genuinely infuriating how the smallest of noises can have me squirming in my seat. "In person. I wanna see you."

I wanna see you.

A brief image of the last time he said that flashes through my mind. When he had his fingers inside of me, a hand bracketing my throat, his hard cock grinding against me, lips and teeth leaving marks everywhere. Marks that are still there, a filthy reminder.

I shake that picture away real quick, crossing my legs to ease the quick-growing ache between them, resisting the urge to rub at the healing purple bruises still marring my chest.

Something in my gut tells me he must be thinking the same thing because when he speaks again his voice has got that husky quality, the one that sends a rush up my spine. "I'm coming over tonight."

It's not a question. It's a statement. No room for argument, and when he adds, "I'll bring food," I'm not sure I want to argue.

I'm so, so tired of arguing.

A handful of seconds is all I manage to hold out before sighing. "Fine."

I hear his smile as clearly as if I could see it. "See you tonight, sweetheart."

God, I'm going to regret this.

I'm wrapped in a towel, soaking wet hair dripping on my bedroom floor, when the doorbell rings. Letting out a curse at Jackson for constantly being so annoyingly on time, I hastily throw on a pair of pyjamas and shove my arms into the sleeves of my robe. Combing my fingers through my hair with one hand, I open the front door with the other, already prepping some snarky comment to greet Jackson with.

Except it's not Jackson I'm greeted by.

"Ma." I make no effort to hide my surprise. She shouldn't be here; in Sun Valley nor at my apartment because I sure as shit never forwarded her my new address.

Ma offers me a wonky smile, awkwardly adjusting the strap of her handbag. "I wanted to see you."

"How do you know where I live?"

"You're my kid, hun. Of course I know where you live."

I don't know what to say to that so I just nod. A painful couple of silent minutes pass when I stand with the door barely open, like I'm guarding the apartment against her, while she dithers awkwardly an arm's length away, before I sigh. "Do you wanna come in?"

When she nods, I reluctantly step back and wave her in. She brushes past me, hands twisting nervously as she surveys the apartment. "This place is nice."

"Yeah." Considering how much Daddy Dearest is paying for it, it better be nice. Morally opposed to taking his money as I am, when

Pen asked me to move in, I couldn't say no. She didn't want to live alone, and I had nowhere else to go.

Plus, every so often, when we're feeling particularly sour about the situation, we run up the electricity and water bills on purpose.

"Is Pen home?"

"She's out." Staying at her boyfriend's for the night, which works out well; if Jackson makes me cry again, at least there won't be any witnesses this time. Pen was downright murderous the other night, spewing vicious threats and colorful expletives that, if I wasn't already completely sure, would've definitely convinced me of our blood relation.

Speaking of... I glance at the clock on the wall. Almost seven. "Did you need something? I have plans."

Ma's face twists into a half-wince, half-grimace. "I want to talk to you, Luna."

Yeah, well, get in line.

"So, talk."

"Luna, enough. Stop with the hostility, please."

"I'm not being hostile. I just don't have time for this."

Ma sighs. "I'm worried about you, Lu."

"I'm fine."

"You're not fine." There's a snap to her voice, an extra bit of fire in blue eyes. "Almost drinking yourself to death isn't fine. Almost losing your scholarship isn't fine."

"That's none of your business." God, I have no idea how she even knows about any of that.

"It is my business, you're my kid."

I snort.

"And Jackson..."

I swear to God, at the mention of his name, the hair on the back of my neck stands up. Like a fucking dog with raised hackles. "Don't talk about Jackson."

"You and him broke up and you didn't even tell me. Your dad told me."

"He's *not* my dad."

A dad gives you rides to school. A dad makes silly jokes and embarrasses you in front of your friends. A dad doesn't make your chest hurt and your head ache and cause bile to crawl up your throat and a ball of self-hatred to settle deep in your gut.

A dad is around longer than a few fucking agonizing months.

I don't understand why she doesn't get that.

"Hun, I know this is hard-"

"This isn't hard." I can't help but laugh at the absurdity in that one little word. "This is fucking unbearable."

Being around her, being in that house, God, even being around Pen sometimes is unbearable. That's another thing I don't understand, how everyone else seems to be able to handle it yet I can't.

How *she* seems to be able to handle it. How I'm the one fucking dying under the weight of this guilt when she's the one who messed up. How he keeps his house and his wife and his reputation while everyone else suffers.

I just don't fucking get it.

"How can you sit there in a home that you ruined and act like everything's fine? Do you even understand how fucked that is?" My voice cracks as I blink back tears. "Did you even apologize for what you did? Do you even regret it at all?"

"Of course I don't," Ma answers without hesitation, her voice and expression soft as she reaches for me. "It gave me you."

"That's a bullshit answer." I step out of her arm's length. "It's like you don't even care. You're so fucking selfish."

"Lu-"

"Get out." She doesn't move. She just stands there, staring at me, mouth a little slack jaw like she can't believe what I'm saying. "*Get out.*"

Achingly slowly, she turns around, walking towards the door at the same pace, glancing over her shoulder all the while like she's waiting for me to ask her to stay.

I don't.

I wait until the door shuts behind her before I let the tears stinging my eyes fall. They stream down my face as I collapse on the sofa, falling faster and faster the more worked up I get. My head falls in my hands as my entire body starts to shake.

I'm so fucking sick of this. The fighting and the anger and the guilt and the fucking secrets. I can't do it anymore, I can't deal with the bullshit. I need it all to fucking stop, just for a minute.

A moaning, wail of a noise escapes me when there's another knock on the door. I try to ignore it but it's unrelenting, a steady rapping of knuckles. When the doorbell goes, I almost scream. Assuming it's my mom coming back for round two, I rip the door open, ready to yell or scream or just fucking cry, I don't know.

Even through tear-blurred eyes, I can tell it's definitely not my mom.

The sight of Jackson standing there, a plastic grocery bag in one hand and a bouquet of flowers in the other, only makes me cry harder. Pink and blue flowers. Pink and blue fucking flowers with a white ribbon securing the stems. I'm not even crying anymore, I'm sobbing, weeping, wailing, whatever the step above just crying is, and it's so fucking absurd that *flowers* are what's sending me over the edge. Shaking my head, I try to slam the door. "Please, just leave."

I shouldn't be surprised that he does no such thing.

Instead, he pushes the door open, forcing his way inside as I cover my face with my hands, like I'm trying to hide the tears. Over the sound of the godawful noises escaping me, I hear the door click shut before fingers wrap around my wrists and gently tug my hands away from my face, replacing them with a new pair. I keep my eyes squeezed shut but, God, I can just picture his face, concern lighting up those brown eyes. Concern I don't deserve, not from him, concern I can't breathe under the weight of.

"What's wrong?"

I try to say 'nothing' but it ends up as another wail that hurts my throat and my head, the noise muffled as I'm cemented against a hard chest. "You're scaring me, sweetheart."

"Please don't call me that." I can't take him calling me that.

Jackson walks us backwards until my calves hit the sofa, pushing me gently to sit. He crouches in front of me, one hand smoothing up and down my thigh while the other guides my head to rest in the crook of his shoulder. "You're okay."

I'm not sure how long we stay like that, him providing gentle touches and soothing words while I snot all over him. Long enough for me to gas out, I guess. For my tear ducts to dry up. Until I manage to pull myself just a little bit together, uncurling my fists from where they're fisting his t-shirt and un-plastering myself from him.

Red-hot embarrassment creeping up my cheeks, I slump back,

swiping my palms over my eyes. "Sorry," I mumble, cringing at my raspy voice.

He dismisses my apology with a shake of his head. "What happened?"

"Nothing."

"Lu, c'mon."

I tug my legs out of his grip, tucking them underneath me. Cautiously, he stands and sits beside me, a carefully calculated distance away.

"Luna, please. Tell me what's going on with you." When I remain silent, he adds, in that soft, kind, fucking concerned voice, "I'm worried about you."

"I never asked you to be."

"That's not how it works." His head shakes, frustration brewing. "I just wanna help."

"I didn't ask for that either." My hands rake through my hair as I stand again, arms spreading wide and gesturing at nothing. "I didn't ask for any of this."

"For what, for me?" Jackson challenges, rising too. "For me to love you? My sincerest fucking apologies."

"This isn't about you."

"Then why am I the one that got hurt?"

"*You* got hurt?" A bitter laugh escapes me. "I met my dad. I met my fucking dad and it turns out he is just the asshole I thought he would be. Worse, actually, because I never imagined him having a pregnant wife. For *months* I sat in a classroom staring at my father and I didn't know. I befriended my fucking sister and I didn't know. My parents are a pair of cheating liars and *I didn't know* so tell me again how *you're* the one who got hurt."

Jackson freezes. He tries so hard to stifle his reaction but complete and utter shock is hard to hide. I can practically see the cogs in his head turning, retracing the last year and slowly piecing everything together, and I see the exact moment it clicks. "Professor Jacobs?"

I nod, barely.

My name leaves his mouth on a long, breathy exhale and I bristle at the pity it holds. "Don't." I step back, hands outstretched like that could possibly keep him away. "It's fine. I'm fine."

"You don't have to lie to me, Lu."

My eyes squeeze shut again. There's a headache building behind them, and I don't know whether it's from crying or if it's because I'm just so fucking tired. "Okay. It's not fine." I'm not fine. "It's fucked. It's so fucked up that it makes me sick thinking about."

"That's why you have dinner at the Jacobs' house."

"Yup."

"And Pen is…" *your sister.*

"Uh-huh."

"And that's why-" Jackson cuts himself off, like he can't bring himself to say it, and he doesn't need to.

That's why you broke up with me.

I hear it loud and clear.

My chest aches as I hum a yes.

"Jesus, Luna." His voice drifts closer and I squeeze my eyes shut tighter. "Why didn't you just tell me?"

"I didn't tell anyone."

"The girls don't know?" When I shake my head, I hear his sigh, feel his frown. "Why?"

Opening my eyes, I can't help but laugh at the confusion on his face. "Because I'm fucking *embarrassed*, Jackson. I hate what they did and I hate that I'm a part of it. Pen can barely look her dad in the eye because of me. Her mom cries all the time because of *me*."

"Not because of you," he argues. "It's his fault. His responsibility, not yours."

"Stop." I back up another step. This is exactly what I didn't want. People telling me how I should feel, trying to rationalize and logicize. I don't want to be rational, I don't want to be logical, I want to be fucking *angry*. "You don't get it."

"Really?" It's Jackson's turn to laugh. "I don't get fucked up parents? *Really?*

"It's not the same."

"No, it's not, but I still fucking get it, Luna." He closes the distance between us so fast, I don't get the chance to retreat. Nor do I manage to duck when his palms cup my face, no avoiding brown eyes holding mine hostage. "When are you gonna get it in your head that you don't have to deal with shit alone, hm?"

"When are you gonna get it in your head that we're broken up?"

His flinch is only a split second but in my head, it lasts an eternity.

An apology sits on my tongue but I can't bring myself to say it. When his hands drop, I can't bring myself to admit I miss them. And when he turns away, I can't bring myself to tell him not to leave.

Luckily for me, he doesn't.

I blink, confused, as he instead of hightailing it out the door like he should, he heads to the kitchen, one hand flicking the kettle on while the other retrieves two mugs. "What're you doing?"

"Making tea."

Making tea.

He's making tea.

"You're not leaving?"

"I promised you dinner."

"And tea is dinner?" I quip, despite the fact that for many weeks post-Jackson, tea was the only dinner I could stomach.

Setting the grocery bag I forgot he had on the counter, he starts pulling out ingredients. "I'm making ramen."

For fuck's sake. I hate when he plays dirty like this, and cooking is fucking filthy.

Especially ramen. Once upon a time, he made it for me all the time. He was so appalled when he got me eating the two-minute stuff from a packet, he started stocking my fridge with the stuff.

Between him and Nick, we could go weeks without cooking.

Against my better judgment–or maybe in complete tune with it–I follow Jackson into the kitchen. I hoist myself onto the counter farthest from him, hands tucked beneath my thighs. "That'll take a while."

"Good," is his firm reply. "Plenty of time to talk."

Yet talk, he doesn't do.

He just silently cooks and I don't know if it's a torturous punishment, payback for being a bitch, or if he's giving me a second to breathe.

Actually, that's a lie. I know.

I might be pretending I don't because it's just a little easier that way but I know.

Not until a mouthwatering smell floods my apartment, a broth bubbles on the stove, does he turn to me wearing that overly serious expression I used to poke fun at, once upon a time. "I'm sorry about the other day."

It's instant, the flush of heat that envelops me, an interesting, regrettable mixture of embarrassment and lust because that is exactly what thinking about The Incident incites. "We don't have to talk about this now."

"That's why I came over," he reminds me, abandoning his cooking and moving to stand in front of me. "I didn't mean for what I said to come out the way it did."

"It's fine."

"It was mean and it upset you so it's not fine."

I say nothing, too focused on watching his hand sliding up my leg until it rests dangerously high on my upper thigh. A finger hooks beneath my chin, tilting upwards and directing my gaze to his.

Brown eyes burn into me, alight with that damn intense look that does weird things to my stomach. "I don't think of you as some hookup or a meaningless fuck. That's what I was trying to say. That's what I would've said if you hadn't run off. Nothing has changed for me, Luna. When something happens between us again, it's not gonna be a one time thing."

When. Not if.

When.

Something lodges itself in my throat as he bends until we're eye level, one dark brow crooked. "Got it?"

All I can do is nod.

"I'm sorry for upsetting you."

Again, a weak nod is the extent of my capabilities.

The corner of his mouth quirks up as he makes a pleased noise. Before I can blink, he drops his hand and spins around, returning to his meal-in-progress with a carefree whistle.

Me? I'm still focused on that one word.

When.

48

LUNA

DURING THE MANY philanderous years of my life, I've become an expert in sneaking out undetected.

A new challenge for me, though?

Sneaking out of my own apartment.

I had no intention of falling asleep while Jackson was still here. Definitely not with him beside me on the couch. And I certainly didn't intend on waking up with soft, steady breaths tickling the top of my head, my face buried in his chest and his in my hair.

It wouldn't have been so bad, really, if he didn't have a hand shoved down my pajama shorts. It could've almost passed for a friendly nap, like one I would take with Amelia or Kate or Ben, if his other hand wasn't curled around my back and copping a handful of sideboob. Everything would be fine if I wasn't wrapped around him like a monkey, hands creeping under his t-shirt to press flat against his bare chest and steal some of his warmth, my face buried so deep in his neck, I'm surprised my face isn't imprinted there.

I swear, I've never moved faster than I did scrambling the hell off him.

By some miracle, Jackson didn't stir. He pouted and he frowned and he wriggled around a bit but he remained blessedly asleep, oblivious to my absence.

Turns out, that wasn't the triumph I took it for.

Because now, I'm standing at my front door, staring at the unconscious boy on my sofa, wondering what the fuck to do with him.

I can't just… leave, can I? That feels like a step too far, even for me.

I'm pondering my limited options when my phone rings. Swearing, I wrestle it from my pocket. Averting my gaze from Jackson as he finally awakens, I frown at his sister's name lighting up my screen and hit the answer button. "Hello?"

The panicked voice that greets me is most definitely not Lux's. "Caroline?"

In my peripheral, I watch Jackson jerk upright. Waving until I reluctantly swing my gaze his way, he mouths *Caroline?*

Mimicking his look of bewilderment, I shrug.

"This is weird," Caroline voices my sentiments exactly, "but Lux told me to call you."

If alarm bells weren't already ringing, they sure as hell are now. "What happened?"

Caroline's deep, shaky breath scares the ever-loving shit out of me. "She was in the shop picking out flowers for the guestroom and I told her to let me help but she refused and she fell. Kind of bad."

"Is she okay?" Three words have Jackson's confusion shifting to alarm, and I hold up a hand in the universal silent command for *hang on a fucking second before you lose it.*

"I'm driving her to the hospital now." Muffled sounds of protest break out in the background that Caroline ignores. "She, uh, says you know."

Oh, fuck. "Is the baby okay?"

"I think so. She's acting like she's fine but I think she's in real pain."

"Okay." Fuck. I rake a hand through my hair, grimacing at the tangles I find. Guess that's what I get for sleeping on it wet. "Okay. Tell her we're on our way."

"We?" Three voices echo.

"Yes, *we,*" I reply with a sigh. "I'm with Jackson now, we can be there in a few hours. What hospital are we going to?"

A slight kink in her voice, Caroline relays the name as I snatch my keys off the counter, and I've barely hung up before Jackson's on me. "Who's in the hospital?" he demands, stealing my keys, holding the front door open for me, and ushering me outside in one smooth second.

I wait until we're a safe distance away from any stairs that shock could possibly send him tumbling down before replying. "Lux."

Jackson stops in the middle of my building's parking lot. "What happened?"

"She fell or something, I don't know the details."

I watch as panic settles into every facet of Jackson's being. He pales. His eyes become unseeing. His chest rises and falls unevenly, breaths ragged, and God, if it was possible for your heart to break more than once, mine would.

"Hey." I loop my fingers around his wrist and shake gently. "She's fine. And we're gonna go make sure, okay?"

Jackson doesn't protest when I wrestle my keys from his clenched fist, nor when I guide him to the passenger side of my car. He remains silent, staring at my dashboard with a listless frown, as I stab Serenity Ranch's address into the GPS.

It's not until we're on the road that his head jerks toward me. "Wait, did you say baby?"

∿

"Alexandra Winona Jackson."

Jackson's enraged voice bounces off the hospital walls, steam practically pouring from his ears as he barges into Lux's hospital room.

I'm sorry, I mouth at her as I scurry in behind him. *I'm so sorry.*

"You're *pregnant*?"

Lux and I wince simultaneously.

"I'm sorry," I repeat. "So sorry."

I didn't mean to tell him. The baby thing just slipped out and then, when he pushed, I couldn't exactly lie. Just like he couldn't exactly help himself from making me pull over, swap seats, and attempt the world record of 'number of speed limits broken in one trip.'

"Don't apologize." Jackson shoots me a withering yet weirdly hot look that very much contradicts his claims of not being mad at me for withholding vital information.

His expression softens momentarily when he turns back to his sister, reclined in a hospital bed, some kind of monitor strapped to her stomach, ankle wrapped up in a bandage and propped on a pillow. "Are you okay?"

She waves him off. "I'm fine. Just a sprained ankle." A hand goes to her stomach, smoothing over the round bump that's significantly more prominent than the last time I saw her. *We're fine*, she seems to say.

"Good." Jackson nods stiffly, crossing his arms over his chest. "Because I'm gonna kill you."

"Oscar, relax."

He ignores her. "Actually, no. I'm gonna kill him."

"*Oscar.*"

"I swear to fucking God, Alexandra, he's dead. Is this why you guys broke up? Did he get you pregnant and then break up with you? Fucking asshole." He's pacing now, creating a draft in the room as he storms from one side to the other, wild-eyed and red-faced, hands braced on his hips.

He pauses at the foot of the bed, grasping the footboard with white-knuckled hands. "How long?"

Lux shifts, her eyes almost apologetic as they flutter towards me for a moment. "Almost five months."

"Five?" Jackson gapes at his sister before side-eyeing me. "And you knew?"

"Not for five months." *Only for, like, one.*

Jackson kisses his teeth. "Oh, well, that's okay then."

"I told her at the funeral," Lux chimes in. "She took me to an appointment the day after."

"I fucking *knew* you two were being weird."

Cautiously, I sidle up behind Jackson, resting a hand on his shoulder. "Calm down. You're gonna pop a blood vessel."

I get another one of those looks but beneath my palm, his shoulder slackens. Breathing deep, steadying breaths, he perches cautiously on the edge of the bed, gaze straying to the stomach swollen with his niece or nephew. "You're pregnant, Lux."

"I'm aware."

"A baby. You're gonna have a *baby*."

Lux hums, absentmindedly rubbing her stomach, the faintest of smiles curling her lips up. A smile that's wiped the moment Jackson asks, "Mark knows?"

Her mouth flattens in a straight line. "Mark knows."

"And?"

"And nothing."

"I'll kill him."

Lux rolls her eyes. "Your girl already offered to slash his tires."

That earns me an appraising look from Jackson, one big hand wrapping around my thigh and squeezing. I bump him with my hip, my hand returning to his shoulder, briefly swiping through his hair before I can stop myself. Lux watches us with a knowing smirk that I choose to ignore. "You hungry? I can run out and get you something."

She straightens up, her face brightening. "Would you mind?"

"Not at all." I hold my hand palm up towards Jackson. He rummages around in his hoodie pocket for a moment before he drops my car keys in my waiting hand. "McDonald's?"

Lux presses a hand over her heart, bottom lip jutting out in a pout. "You might be my new favorite sister."

Red stains my cheeks as I bark out a nervous laugh.

I don't let myself overthink her words, even when Jackson squeezes my thigh again with a smile on his face. I also don't overthink it when he grips me by the chin and drags my face down to his so he can kiss me. Definitely no overthinking happens when his lips brush over my cheek too, his thumb swiping over the warm, tingling spot they leave as he murmurs a 'thank you.'

I'm barely out the door before I hear Lux explode into giddy laughter. I don't stick around to eavesdrop on what she says—I have a good enough imagination to figure it out on my own—I just hightail it to the parking lot and, again, definitely do not overthink a thing.

Every person I pass shoots me a weird look when I re-enter the hospital almost an hour later, balancing at least half of McDonald's menu in my arms.

Lux didn't specify what she wanted, so I got a bit of everything, purposely not using the credit card Jackson snuck into my back pocket at some point before I left. I may not be loaded, but I can swing a takeout.

I've almost made it to Lux's room sans any food-related casualties when a quiet voice calling my name stops me in my tracks.

Dithering at the end of the hall, fingers playing with the hem of her pretty sundress, Caroline smiles nervously. "Need help?"

"Hi." No matter how exceptionally hard I try to keep surprise from my tone, I don't quite manage it. "I didn't know you were still here."

She shrugs as she tucks a lock of dirty blonde hair behind her ear. "I didn't wanna leave until I knew she was okay."

Huh.

That's… nice.

"She's good."

"Thank God." Genuine relief washes over Caroline's features. It surprises me; the last time we met, concern was not something she showed readily.

Not as surprising, though, as what comes out of her mouth next.

"My mom died when I was a kid," she blurts out of nowhere, catching me so off guard I almost drop one of the bags clutched in my hands. She saves it before it slips from my grasp, tucking it beneath her arms as she chews on her bottom lip and shifts awkwardly. "I don't remember a lot about her but I remember the funeral. My dad was…" Something dark crosses her expression before she shakes it off. "He wasn't fully there, you know, so it was kind of just me handling everything."

"I'm sorry," I say quietly, and I mean it. I can't imagine a kid dealing with all of that alone.

"I remember wishing that I had someone there to help me. So at Jackson's mom's funeral…" She trails off, shrugging as a sad smile pulls at her lips. "I know I came on too strong but I was trying to help."

The animosity I feel towards her fades a bit at the genuine concern splashed across her face.

"I'm not a fool, okay? I know he doesn't…" She swallows. "I know he doesn't love me." Something about the look on her face, or maybe the crack in her voice, squeezes my heart. Her head drops, hair acting like a shield, probably to hide the way her fingers come up and quickly swipe beneath her eyes. "I just saw the way he was looking at you and I got jealous and mad so I was rude to you." She shakes her head, a little hiccuped laugh leaving her as she brushes her hair back and says, almost to herself, "We were together for four years and he never looked at me like that."

Well, fuck.

How am I supposed to blame a girl for that when, honestly, if the roles were reversed, I can't say that I wouldn't have reacted the same?

"You know, I thought I was gonna marry him. When I was eighteen, I truly believed he was it for me. And Serenity Ranch... It's the only place that's ever felt like home to me. I just have a hard time letting that go."

That, I can understand. Six months without the place felt like a lifetime.

"I'm not tryna excuse my behavior, I'm just tryna explain it. And apologize for how I acted. I swear I'm not some mean girl, I just don't think before I speak sometimes and everything comes out wrong."

Something else I can't really have against her because, shit, do we have that in common.

Nodding towards the door, I ask, "You wanna come in?"

"I've gotta get back to the store." At my questioning glance, she adds, "I work at the florist in town."

Of course she does. She looks exactly like the kind of girl who spends her days surrounded by bright, pretty flowers. I can just picture her in some kind of greenhouse, elbow deep in dirt yet somehow completely clean, flowers just sprouting to life wherever she looks.

Fucking living sunshine.

Waving goodbye, Caroline starts towards the exit. Before she can disappear from sight, I call after her. "For the record," she glances over her shoulder questioningly, "I think if you told Jackson all that, he'd understand."

A laugh shakes her shoulders. "I know. That's exactly why I haven't." She cocks her head at me, a genuine smile playing across her lips, and God, when she's not being all bitchy or fake, the girl is so pretty it almost hurts my eyes. "It's infuriating, how nice he is, right?"

I laugh too, my smile matching hers. "The worst."

49

JACKSON

OF ALL THE ways I pictured today going, this was not a scenario I anticipated.

I stare at Lux.

Lux stares at me.

Every so often, my gaze flicks to her belly and a wave of nausea washes over me.

Lux is going to be a mom. My little sister is having a baby. I'm going to be an uncle.

Jesus.

My head spins as I mentally compile everything I need to do to baby-proof the ranch and wrack my brain trying to figure out how the hell I missed this. She didn't drink at Mom's funeral but I thought it was just her being responsible. She's been tired lately but that's hardly anything new. That godawful cardigan she wore the day Dad showed up should've been a dead giveaway something was up; she would never subject herself to Grandma's scrutiny without a valid reason.

God, I feel like a dumbass.

"Are you mad at me?" Lux interrupts my internal spiralling, two protective hands on her stomach like she's shielding it from me.

"No." I sigh. "I'm not mad." Not at her, anyway. Hell fucking yeah am I mad at the steaming pile of shit that knocked her up. Now seems like a terrible time to whip out an 'I told you so' but I always knew he was good for nothing. "I'm just surprised."

"You and me both," Lux mutters beneath her breath.

"Do the girls know?"

"No."

"When are you planning on telling them?"

"I was planning on seeing how long it takes them to notice," she jokes, or at least I think it's a joke. "I don't think Lottie will until there's a screaming baby keeping her awake."

That drags a laugh out of me. She's probably not wrong.

She adds, "I'll tell them. I was just... waiting a bit. Until I absolutely had to." A foot nudges my thigh. "Until I told you."

I nudge her back. "Why did you take so long?"

Lux drops her gaze, nose scrunching. "I didn't want you to be disappointed in me."

Ah, fuck.

Standing, I gesture for Lux to scoot over so I can stretch out beside her, slinging an arm across her shoulders and dragging her close. "I could never be disappointed in you."

"I'm not gonna fuck it up. I won't be like Mom."

Heart? Breaking. Chest? Hurting. Temper? Flaring just a touch.

I clutch my sister a little tighter. "I know."

"He's not gonna turn out like us."

"I think we turned out pretty okay." I hum, reaching out to gently poke her belly. "It's a he?"

Lux nods, rubbing her stomach fondly and jerking an elbow into my side. "What do you think of Oscar Jackson The Third?"

"Call him that and I'm kicking both of you off my ranch."

My sister barks out a laugh. "Have you told her about that yet? Buying the ranch?"

"Luna?" The look on her face screams *duh*. "No."

"You probably should. When you marry the girl, the place will be half hers."

"You're getting a bit ahead of yourself." A lot ahead of herself. We're not even back together but when I tell Lux as much, she snorts.

"So she just drove across the state before the sun was up for fun?"

"That was for you, not me."

Another snort. "And what were you doing at her place so early?"

"Sleeping."

"In the same bed."

"On a couch, actually." I'd planned to bring her to bed when she fell asleep but I was so comfortable, I passed out before I could.

"Oh, yeah, that makes a difference," Lux drawls sarcastically. Shaking her head, she laughs under her breath. "Not together, my ass."

I kiss my teeth in mock annoyance. We're not together, and I don't exactly have high hopes of us getting back together either, considering everything she has going on. I doubt that's what she wants right now. I'm still trying to wrap my head around everything she told me.

A lot of information, a lot to process, in less than 24 hours.

"Speaking of the ranch," I deftly change the subject. "I'm gonna look into hiring some more help for you."

If Lux's crumpled expression doesn't tell me exactly how she feels about that suggestion, her mouth does. "I don't need a babysitter, Oscar."

"I know that, Alexandra. But you can't do everything you're doing now and take care of a kid." *Wanna bet?* her face screams, and I roll my eyes. "You're already spread too thin."

"I have help already."

Yeah, the presence of Dipshit and Dumbass doesn't exactly soothe my worries.

"It's a big ranch, Lux. You need more than two people helping to run it." A dozen would be preferable. Plus an assistant to help with the business side of shit. But baby steps.

She's still making that face so I poke her again. "Just let me help you."

Lux regards me for a long moment before sighing. "*Fine.* But I get final say on who you hire."

"Deal."

They discharge Lux not long after Luna returns.

She was a menace to get out of the hospital; making a fuss over the wheelchair they insisted she use, protesting like a brat when the doctor put her on bed rest for forty-eight hours, scoffing obnoxiously when I was told to keep an eye on her. The whole drive home, Luna and I were graced with her '*I can take care of myself*' spiel.

She wouldn't let me help her up to the house. But when Luna sidled up to her and extended an arm, she took it without protest and hey, I'm not going to complain as long as she's accepting help from someone, even if an alliance between them does scare the ever-loving shit out of me.

With the twins at their dorm and Eliza still at school, we successfully get Lux in bed without any questions and only minimal complaint. I get shooed from her bedroom the second she's tucked under the covers, claiming she had a busy, early morning before sarcastically asking if she's allowed to nap without supervision.

At least, I think as I close the door behind me, *I know why she's been such a fucking grouch the past few months.*

I've just barely stumbled into my own bedroom, intending on following my sister's lead and passing out for a while, when I hear the telltale snick of the front door opening. Wholly concerned it's Lux sneaking out to do some shit she absolutely should not be doing, I slope outside with a groan, stepping foot on the porch just in time to catch a flicker of light brown hair disappearing into the barn.

Luna leaves the barn door ajar behind her. Enough that I can peek inside without alerting her to my presence. I can watch with a soft smile as she greets Clyde with a scratch between the eyes and a hearty pat to the side before scampering up the shoddy ladder of the loft I didn't know she knew about. By the time I make it out there, she's climbed out the window onto the overhang I'm suddenly very glad I fixed up last summer. Knees hugged to her chest, she tilts her face toward the sky, squinting at the soon-to-be-setting sun.

"Little early for star-gazing."

She doesn't jolt at the sound of my voice, and I have to wonder if she knew I was steps behind her the whole time.

When I settle beside her, legs swinging over the edge, she scoots closer, leaning her weight against my side ever so slightly. "You okay?"

I hum an affirmative noise.

"Are you mad I didn't tell you?"

"No." At first, maybe a little, but I was quickly overwhelmed by feeling grateful that Lux could at least tell someone. And maybe a little selfishly happy that she chose Luna, of all people, to confide in. "Thank you for taking her to that appointment."

"It was kind of cool," she whispers, tilting her head toward me, showing me the smile gracing her lips. "I saw it wriggling around in there. Size of an avocado, the tech said."

"You saw *him*." I squeeze her hip. "Lux said it's a boy."

"Really?" Her smile brightens. "Aw. You get a nephew."

You do too, I resist the urge to say.

Now who's getting ahead of themselves.

"Are you okay?" I throw her own question back at her. "After last night." When she does nothing but nod, I tug on the ends of her hair. "Words, sweetheart."

She makes an indignant little noise and scowls but it's half-hearted. "I'm good." A manicured hand, nails a rare light blue, slips into mine, another wrapping around my bicep as she completely slumps against me. "I'm glad you know."

Leaning down, I nudge her forehead with mine until she tilts her face upward, allowing me to brush my lips over the corner of her mouth. "I'm glad you told me."

"I'm sorry it took so long."

"Stop apologizing," I mutter, kissing the other side before settling over her lips. My hand cups her cheek as I kiss her properly, soft and slow, in no rush to do anything but revel in the feel of her lips against mine. She sighs into my mouth, indulging me for entirely too short a time before pulling back.

Her voice is quiet, her expression so unfamiliarly unsure, her bottom lip trapped between her teeth as she asks, "Jackson, what're we doing?"

"You tell me."

A brief pause passes before she swallows and says slowly, carefully, "It feels like we're back together."

I don't want to ask because God, do I fear the answer, but I do anyway, my voice embarrassingly croaky. "Do you want to be back together?"

For an agonizingly long time, Luna doesn't reply. When she does, it's so quiet I have to strain to hear her. "Yeah." I literally go limp with relief. "But I'm scared I'm gonna mess it up again."

Yeah, that makes two of us. I'm scared fucking shitless but for different reasons. It's scary how much of me belongs to her. How much of me is affected by, controlled by another person. But honest to fucking God, I wouldn't change it for the world. She fucking owns me and I don't give a shit.

I rest my forehead against hers. "You won't."

She peers up at me, a soft, kind of frightened look in her eyes. "You can't say that."

"Just did."

"*Jackson.*"

"*Luna.*" I mimic her tone, adding an extra whine to it, pulling a reluctant smile out of her that I can't help but kiss. Gripping the nape of her neck so she can't go anywhere, I murmur against her mouth, "I'm not gonna rush you. I'm not gonna push you to do anything you don't wanna do. I'm just gonna tell you that the way I feel about you has never changed, not once. And if you try to push me away again, I won't let you. I know better this time. I'll fight like hell because I fucking love you, Luna."

As the words leave my mouth, Luna's eyes clamp shut, and I can't tell what that means. If she's steeling herself to shoot me down or trying to hide tears or just needs a minute to think.

Whatever it is, it lasts longer than a minute. It feels like an eternity. Goddamn forever passes before, eyes still shut, her mouth opens. "I don't know if I can do it again."

Heart stilling in my chest, my voice is barely a whisper. "Love me?"

"Lose you."

"Did you hear what I just said, sweetheart?" A stroke of my thumb against her cheekbone coaxes those baby blues to open wide. "I'm not going anywhere, and I'm not letting you."

Doubt still clouds her features, and I get it. I really, really get it. I don't hold it against her, not even a little, as I carefully pull her onto my lap and kiss the top of her head. "I got you to trust me once, Luna. I can do it again."

50

LUNA

I'M RUNNING LATE.

I have fifteen minutes to get to the Jacobs' place but considering I'm shoeless, pantsless, and only have mascara on one eye, there's no way I'm making it.

You'd think after so many weeks, I would've found a way to not be late for these damn dinners.

To be fair, it's not entirely my fault. It was late when we got back from the ranch, and I went straight to the bar for a late shift *and* I stayed later than usual because some assholes decided to be obnoxious and hassle us long after closing time. And then today, I had a shit ton of college work to catch up on and I had to go to the office for a couple of hours and on top of all that, I missed a few doses of my meds—it's not like I had the time or the wits to grab them before racing to the hospital.

What's that saying? When it rains, it pours? Well, yeah, the last few days, it has definitely poured.

For the first time since I started going there, the days I spent at the ranch weren't entirely tranquil. I love Lux, I really do, but God, she was a nightmare—and that's coming from me. She only got worse when Grace and Lottie came home, the former turning up out of her mind with worry about being summoned home mid-week while the latter...well, she arrived pissed as hell, probably because Lottie is perpetually pissed. And she was most definitely *not* as delighted as her sisters to find out about her nephew.

She just sat there silently, sullenly, while the others celebrated, and then stormed out when Lux tried to talk to her. Grace tried to go after her but got a door slammed in her face, Lux cried which made Eliza cry which pissed off Jackson and...

And it was a mess.

Never did I think I'd be glad to swap Serenity Ranch for Sun Valley.

Well, I was glad until Friday rolled around.

By the time I locate my pants and finish my make-up, Pen is blowing up my phone with all the ways I'm dead to her. Snatching my keys and handbag off the counter, I hop to the door, wrenching it open with one hand and slipping my heels on with the other. A yelp of surprise leaves me at what, or rather who, I find lurking in the hallway.

Jackson is wearing a shirt. And a blazer. And slacks. And those dressy shoes he used to wear when he'd take me to an obscenely fancy restaurant.

What the fuck?

"What're you doing here?"

Amusement brightens his face. The fist that was poised to knock unfurls and drops to my hip, pulling me close so he can kiss my temple. "Hey. Am I late?"

I blink up at him. "For what?"

"It's Friday, right? You're having dinner at the Jacobs' place?"

"Uh, yeah."

"Cool." Jackson tugs me outside, stealing my keys and locking the door behind me. "You mind if I drive?"

If he notices me staring at like he's grown two heads, he doesn't comment. "You're coming?"

"If that's okay with you."

He... he's coming to Friday night dinner.

I will not cry.

Pressing my lips together, I nod. My knees wobble as I follow him to his car, my grip on his hand vice-like. Ring-adorned fingers are cool against mine, and when I glance down and catch sight of the familiar battered one adorning his pinky, my eyes burn.

I will not cry.

It's not until he clicks his seatbelt–and mine–into place that I feel like I can talk without bursting into tears. "You don't have to come."

"I want to."

I pull a face. "I think you're gonna regret it." When Jackson makes a dismissive noise, I squeeze the hand that quickly settled on my thigh. "I'm serious. It's bad, Jackson. Like, stab-yourself-in-the-eye-with-a-fork bad."

"That's why I'm going."

"Shit, baby, I knew you were kinda a sadist but this is a bit much."

I get a pinch and a side-eyed withering look for that one. "I'm going for you, brat. Thought it'd be a little better if I was there." Jackson shifts to face me, head cocked, almost daring me to disagree. "Unless I'm wrong?"

I only hesitate for a second.

"You're not wrong," I confirm quietly, lacing my fingers with his and bringing his hand to my lips.

Definitely not wrong. If there's anything that can get me through this shitty night, it's Jackson. The thought of asking him did cross my mind but... I don't know. He's got a lot of shit going on. I didn't want to burden him with anything else. And he pledged his fucking love for me and I… well, didn't, I thought it would be selfish of me to ask.

A silly thing to think, obviously.

The moment Pen spots Jackson through the windshield, she screams.

"Thank the fucking Lord." Her half-groan, half-squeal rings in my ear as she yanks open the passenger door and drags me into her arms. Cheek smushed against mine, she squeezes hard enough to make my lungs scream. "I knew you'd get your head out of your ass eventually."

Rolling my eyes, I pinch my sister on the side. She slaps my hand away and pinches me right back, shoving me halfway up the drive-way, kicking at my ankles like the overgrown child she is. I hook an arm around her neck and drag her after me, ignoring her screeching about ruining her hair.

The sound of laughter from behind causes us both to pause.

Glancing over our shoulders, we find Jackson watching us with a smile. "What?"

"Nothing." His lips twitch. Wrapping his arms around me from behind, he leans down until his breath tickles my cheek, his lips just grazing my skin. "The fact that there's two of you in the world is terrifying, you know that right?"

I elbow him again, twisting my head so I can kiss the smile curling his lips as Pen shouts for her parents.

"We're in here, honey!" Her mom hollers back.

And just like that, the mood sobers.

Both Pen and I go straight-backed, the smiles dropping from our faces. Both my hands clutch one of Jackson's in a death grip. He kisses my temple once, twice, three times before following Pen into the living room, dragging me behind him.

Pen makes a beeline for her mom, kissing her cheek and completely ignoring the man beside her. "Mom, this is Jackson. Luna's boyfriend."

I don't correct her.

And even if Jackson didn't return Mrs Jacobs smile–the same one she always graces me with, a little wary but bright and genuine and so damn kind–and hold out a hand to shake before I could get a word out, I don't think I would.

"Nice to meet you, ma'am," Jackson greets smoothly, and in the blink of an eye, Mrs Jacobs' wariness disappears. "I hope you don't mind me intruding like this. Lu mentioned how good your cooking is and I couldn't stay away."

I resist the urge to snort. Fucking charmer.

His words, and his smile, work exactly as intended; Mrs Jacobs is all but simpering for the guy. "Any friend of Luna's is always welcome here. Right, Robert?"

Robert doesn't look like he agrees.

Stony-faced, Professor Jacobs reeks of disapproval as he stares my boyfriend down. A sentiment Jackson is more than returning; he offers the older man nothing more than a nod and a curt, "Sir."

Jacobs doesn't like that. He stands, demanding a handshake too and cutting me a disapproving look. "A little notice would've been nice."

"Robert," his wife chides him, earning her some side-eye too.

Before either can say anything else, another voice chimes in. "Jackson?"

Ma dithers in the living room doorway, surprised confusion all over her face, and I tense at the sight of her. I didn't think she'd be here. I wasn't prepared for her to be here. After the other day…

Jackson squeezes me a little tighter. His smile dims a fraction—for my sake, I'm sure—as he greets Ma. "Nice to see you, Isla."

She returns the sentiment but her eyes are trained on me.

I look anywhere but at her.

Clearing her throat, Mrs Jacobs paints on a smile and ushers us all into the dining room before the tension suffocates us all. Jackson doesn't let go of me once, not even when he pulls out my chair for me and we sit down, not even when food starts being passed around.

"So," Mrs Jacobs starts, a delicious smell wafting towards me as she hands over a platter of whatever meat she's prepared tonight. "You go to UCSV too?"

Jackson takes the platter with a grateful smile, serving himself and me as he nods. "Yes, ma'am. I'll be graduating this year."

"Exciting." Mrs Jacobs smiles. "Do you have any plans after graduation?"

"Not yet."

Professor Jacobs snorts, earning daggers from his wife, his mistress, and both his daughters.

Jackson doesn't falter for a second. "I was thinking of moving back home for a while. My sister's having a baby and I wanna be there to help out."

"That's very admirable of you," Mrs Jacobs coos. Ma nods in agreement while Pen shoots me an 'aw' look, pouting and fluttering her lashes dramatically.

The only one not impressed? Professor Jacobs. "And home is where?"

"Up north. My family has a ranch near Sequoia National Park."

"A ranch." Professor Jacobs kisses his teeth. "That's… quaint."

Quaint. A compliment, under any other circumstances, but from his mouth, it's like a curse. I glare at him. "It's beautiful. And very successful."

"I never said it wasn't, Luna," Jacobs replies in that tone I fucking hate. The one that makes me feel like a silly little kid, like I'm about two feet tall. He uses the same one on Jackson, and I hate it even more for that. "What do you do on this ranch?"

"Lots of things." I see the slightest tick in Jackson's jaw. "Weddings, corporate retreats, things like that."

"And your parents run all this?"

And there it is.

The Achilles heel that has Jackson stiffening.

"No, sir," he coughs out after a moment too long. "My sisters and I do."

"Your sisters?" A noise of utter condescension leaves Jacobs as he shakes his head. "Well, how nice."

"*Robert.*"

"What?" Jacobs flashes innocent eyes at his wife. "I'm just making conversation."

"You're being rude," Mrs Jacobs says carefully, quietly.

Her husband scoffs loudly. "Am I not allowed to get to know my daughter's boyfriend?"

No.

No, he is absolutely not.

Before I can say as much, he continues, "I'm just confused, Luna. I was under the impression you two broke up."

"I was under the impression you were a faithful husband but hey, look, here I am."

The words come out before I can stop them, and I regret them as soon as they leave my mouth. Not because of how Jacobs' face flames —God knows I revel in that—but because of how Mrs Jacobs deflates. Pen rests a hand on her mom's shoulder, mouthing *what the fuck?* at me, and I'm going to apologize. I swear, I'm going to. *Sorry* is on the tip of my tongue, ready to be said.

But then Jacobs opens his fucking mouth.

"You will not talk to me like that, young lady," he barks like has any kind of authority over me, and fuck me, does that grind my gears. As does the way he rears upright in a weak attempt at intimidation, one hand slamming palm-down against the dinner table and making everyone jump.

That whisper of an apology dies a fiery death.

"I can talk to you however I want."

His neck flushes a bright red. "You're under my roof."

"Because you bribed me to be here." *Because your daughter, and your wife, need me as a buffer so they don't claw their own eyes out.* "Trust me, I would very much prefer to be anywhere else."

That red broaches his jaw, spreading up his cheeks as his hands curl into pitiful little fists. "Watch your attitude, Luna. I tolerate a lot from you but after everything I've done for you, you will treat me with a little respect."

"Everything you've done for me?" I scoff. "Are you fucking kidding me?"

"I pay for your apartment," he spits. "I pay your college fees. You wouldn't even be in college if it wasn't for me."

It takes a moment for his words to sink in.

For their meaning to become clear.

I think it hits all of us at the same time. What, exactly, he just admitted to. The gravity of his words. What they imply.

I'm the first one to break it, croaking out a quiet, "What?"

Jacobs blinks. He clears his throat loudly, equal measures aggressive and embarrassed. He sits back in his seat, bracing his hands on the arms of his chair—I think it's an attempt to hide the fact they're shaking.

It doesn't work.

He coughs again, and I get the feeling that's the only reply I'll get.

So, I try again.

"I have a scholarship," I say, "so what the fuck do you mean you pay my college fees?"

He flinches, and whether it's from the shrillness of my voice or the decibel or maybe the language, I don't know, but still, he doesn't answer. He won't look at me. He won't look at anyone.

Especially not his wife, shaking beside him.

"Robert?" she whispers and he visibly shrinks. "Did you know about her?"

"Of course not," he replies quickly.

Too quickly.

"You're lying." Pen gapes at her dad, so much emotion on her face it's hard to pinpoint just one. "You're fucking lying."

"Language, Penelope."

The room fills with the screeching sound of wood scraping on wood as Pen shoves her chair back and stands. "Tell the fucking truth."

Jacobs says nothing but that's okay.

His wife speaks for him.

"You made a donation to the university," she says quietly. "Three years ago, you said you made a donation."

Something painful lodges itself in my throat. "My scholarship is privately funded."

A whimpering crying noise comes from the opposite side of the table as Mrs Jacobs covers her mouth with her hand.

Warm breath caresses my ear. "I think we should leave."

I ignore Jackson, voice cracking as I ask, "How long?"

I don't expect an answer but I get one.

Or rather, Ma gets one.

Jacobs turns to face the woman he got pregnant, his expression so plain, his voice so matter-of-fact. "The day you went to the clinic, I followed you. To make sure you..." He trails off but I think we all hear the end of his sentence anyway.

To make sure she got rid of me.

"You left without even going inside." A tendon in his jaw jumps. "I saw your name on her application and I knew."

His gaze flicks to mine and the cool uncaring in them hits me right in the stomach. "The moment I saw you in my class, I knew you were my daughter."

51

LUNA

THAT FAMILIAR, utterly overwhelming feeling of helplessness looms, constricting my chest and threatening to sweep me off my feet. If it weren't for the hand flush against my lower back, it probably would.

The owner of that hand is what guides me to stand, or more like yanks me to my feet. Pen does the same to her mom, hauling her out of her chair. Professor Jacobs rises, reaching for his wife but she jerks away from him.

"Jennifer, please."

"We're leaving," Pen snaps without looking at her dad, her full focus on her shaking, quivering, crying mother. "You are un-fucking-believable."

I knew you were my daughter.

So, he wasn't living one life for twenty years. He was living two.

You know, I think maybe, very deep down where the little girl who longed for a dad lives, I held out hope that one day, we'd work this out. Not become a happy family or anything but a tolerable one. One that you can have dinner with without feeling like you're choking.

Now, as I begin to understand just how much hatred the human body can handle, that hope dies.

And I think it dies in Mrs Jacobs too.

With a deep, bone-chilling sigh, she stares down her husband with teary but determined eyes. "I want a divorce."

Jacobs gapes at her. "Jen, you can't be serious."

Oh, but she is. She might be sad and crying and heartbroken but God, she's angry too, and everyone in the room can see it but him. Her gaze flicks to Ma and the anger softens, or maybe it just... changes. "I knew about you," she reveals softly and Ma winces. "I knew about all of you."

All of you.

She knew about all of them.

Judging by the look on her face, Ma most definitely didn't.

Mrs Jacobs barely gives us a chance to recover from that bomb before she continues, "You weren't the first but you were the last. I never questioned why until now." Her eyes land on me, and I swear I see humor flicker in them. "You scared him into fidelity, obviously."

Out of the corner of my eye, I watch Pen crumple. I see her angry mask shift just enough for hurt to shine through before she fixes it. I hear what she hears; I was enough for him to clean his act up, but she wasn't.

Mrs Jacobs notices it too, and when she regards her husband again, all that anger comes rushing back tenfold. "I stayed with you because I was young and naive and I had nothing. I wanted a nice, stable life for my daughter so I stayed." She wraps an arm around Pen. "I will regret that for the rest of my life."

With one last anger-filled glare, she turns on her heel and stalks out the room, Pen right behind her. I hear their footsteps retreat upstairs and then the sound of a door slamming, and I swear I don't imagine a frustrated yell.

Professor Jacobs tries to follow them but Ma, quick as a flash, gets in his way. "You knew," she spits. "This whole time, you knew."

"This is your fault," he spits back, fingers wrapping around her bicep and yanking her close. "If you'd just done what I asked and gotten rid of it-"

A cracking sound splits the air as Ma's hand meets his cheek. "She is my daughter." Her fury is palpable, like something charged in the air as she slaps once more for good measure. "You told me you wanted to know her. You told me if you'd known, you would've helped. My gut said you were lying but I gave you the benefit of the doubt because I actually felt guilty for keeping her from you. But you are just as despicable now as you were twenty years ago."

"And what does that make you?" Jacobs snarls. "I didn't force you to do anything. You were more than willing like a little-"

"Don't finish that sentence." For the first time since we walked into this damn house, Jackson leaves my side. He shoves Professor Jacobs back, knocking his hand off Ma and nudging her towards me. "Lay a hand on anyone in this house again and I swear to God, you'll regret it."

Without taking his eyes off Jacobs, Jackson fishes his keys out of his pocket and tosses them towards me. "Take your mom and wait in the car, Luna."

"What're you doing?" I don't think he's going to beat him up—that's not really his modus operandi—but if he does, I really want to see that. Hell, I think we all want to see that.

"Just making sure Mrs Jacobs gets her stuff and leaves in peace." When I don't move, Jackson's gaze flicks my way. "Ten minutes, sweetheart. I'll be right there."

Reluctantly, I go, tugging my mom along behind me.

We're both quiet as we get in Jackson's car, both releasing pent-up breaths in unison, both slumping in our seats. I eye my mom in the rear-view mirror. She looks exhausted, about a decade older than she did earlier this evening.

When she catches me staring, she musters up a weak smile. Leaning forward, she smoothes a tentative hand over my shoulder. "Are you okay?"

I nod, although I'm not sure how much truth there is in it. "Are you?"

Just like she didn't question my slightly deceitful nod, I let her one slide, and silence settles between us as we alternate between staring at each other and anxiously peering at the house, waiting for the front door to open.

Ma breaks the silence. "I didn't know she was pregnant."

"Please don't-"

"No. I need to tell you," she interrupts me firmly, determinedly. "When I first started seeing him, I didn't know Jennifer was pregnant. I knew he was married but he told me he was leaving her, and he gave me no reason not to believe him. He stopped wearing his ring. There was no sign of her in what I thought was his apartment, no clothes, no photos, nothing. There were no photos of her in his office. We went out in public. The only time he hid me was around campus and I thought that was because he was a teacher and I was a student. When I found out, I left him, but it was too late."

She looks... pained. Like what she's telling me is causing her actual physical harm. I want to comfort her, maybe take the hand practically super-glued to my shoulder but I don't. I just... can't.

Ma's grip on me tightens, her free hand coming up to swipe beneath her eyes. "I was twenty years old and in love and I made a mistake. I know that. But if I never made that mistake I wouldn't have you so I mean it when I say I don't regret it. I hate that I hurt people and I hate that it's made you see me differently but I don't regret it." Fingers graze my cheek, so much sincerity and hurt shining in her eyes that it hurts my chest. "I am so, so sorry that I hurt you, hun. I never wanted to."

"I know." And I do.

"I love you."

Ever so slightly, my head tilts so my cheek leans against the hand on my shoulder. "I love you too."

Whatever moment we're sharing is interrupted by the front door opening. Three people spill out into the night, laden down with boxes and bags. Pen dumps her portion of the load in her car before jogging toward us. I crack my door and drag her half-inside, enveloping her in a tight hug. "I'm so sorry, Pen."

Pen pulls back and glances over at her mom quickly, a tight smile pulling at her lips. "We're better off without him."

I squeeze my sister's hand. "Is she staying with us tonight?"

Pen shakes her head. "I'm taking her to a hotel. I'm gonna stay with her tonight. I..." She sucks in a shuddered breath. "I don't wanna be in that apartment tonight. Or ever again."

Yeah, me neither. If I could burn the place down without consequences, I probably would. But I don't think either of us can afford to live anywhere else. "We'll figure it out."

"We will," Pen agrees with a firm nod. She offers my mom a brief word of goodbye before kissing my cheek and scampering off. Just as she gets into her car, Jackson slips inside his.

Instantly, a hand curls around the nape of my neck. "You okay?"

I don't answer his question, mostly because I don't really hear it.

My mind is wholly occupied by the hand gripping the steering wheel. "Why are your knuckles all red?"

The epitome of calm, Jackson shrugs. "He tried to stop them from leaving."

"So you *punched* him?"

"I told him to leave them alone. It's not my fault he didn't listen."

I blink at him. In the backseat, Ma blinks at him too. We make eye contact in the rearview mirror and for a brief moment, we simply hold each other's incredulous gazes before Ma bursts into laughter. Practically doubled over, she claps Jackson on the shoulders and gives him a shake. "Oh my God, I would've paid to see that."

Me, I have a different reaction. Some part of me is laughing. Some part of me thought those exact words.

But most of me is thinking, feeling, doing just one thing.

Jackson frowns at me as I get out of the car. He keeps frowning through the windshield as I round the hood of his car, and then through the driver's side window as I pull open the door. He stops, though, when I lean in and wrap myself around him as best I can. "I love you so much right now."

"Yeah," Ma agrees, shooting me a careful but wry grin. "What she said."

Jackson must be able to tell that I don't want to go home because after we drop Ma at her hotel, he starts towards his place without a word of discussion.

Grateful for the change of location as I am, it makes me a little uneasy. I haven't been there since we got back together, the couch incident notwithstanding. I'm not in the headspace for the guys or the girls or the questions; I just want to go to bed.

And again, I question Jackson's mind-reading abilities because when we pull up outside the house and I take a second too long to get out, he regards me with a soft, knowing smile. The hand gripping my thigh moves to undo my seat belt before snatching up my handbag. "No one's home."

Relieving information, yes, but I still exit the car with some hesitance. "I don't have my stuff."

More than I want a bed, I want a shower. I want to cleanse myself of this fucking day. I want to use my silly overpriced shower gels and lather my hair in a mask and brush out all the knots that have surely formed from countless times raking my hands through my hair in frustration.

A warm hand settles on my lower back and urges me up the driveway. "You have stuff here."

Just for a single step, I falter. "I do?"

"I didn't throw anything out."

Why, oh why, does such a simple thing as him not throwing out a few ragtag bottles of toiletries cause such an ache in my chest?

Sniffing quietly, I hug his arm to my chest and follow him inside, not letting go until we're in his room and he has to physically shake me off with a chuckle. He disappears into the bathroom, and the sound of the shower turning on has my skin prickling in anticipation.

The cold bites at me as I strip off, leaving everything in a pile on the floor but the steam already filling the bathroom warms me quickly, hot water presumably cranked up to the max, just how I like it.

Crouched in front of the sink, Jackson rifles through the cabinet underneath. He hums a satisfied noise when he finds whatever he was looking for, rising with his haul and setting it down with a flourish. "Think that's everything."

A myriad of junk messies the counter. *My* junk, all the little knick-knacks I left here on the off-chance I craved a very specific fragrance of body butter or the hair ties always littering the bottom of my handbag suddenly disappeared or if I stayed over longer than intended—which I always did—and needed contact solution and my spare bottle of medication. "You kept this shit?"

Lips graze my bare shoulder. "I kept all your shit."

"Why?"

"For when you came back and started using it all again."

Don't cry. Do not cry.

Hands land on my hips and guide me into the shower. It feels like all the energy literally leaves my body as the hot spray hits me. I would probably crumple to the floor if an arm wasn't banded around my waist, holding me upright. Fingers begin combing through my hair and I lean into the movements, yet another sigh escaping me.

Jackson brushes my hair to one side, kissing the bare skin revealed. "Tired?"

"Exhausted."

Gentle kisses move to my jaw. "You wanna talk about what happened?"

"Not even a little bit."

Jackson chuckles against my skin, and I can't help but turn my head to capture the noise. He kisses me back way too gently for my liking. I wriggle in his grip until I'm facing him, linking my hands behind his head, nipping at his bottom lip, trying to encourage him, but he maintains his annoyingly slow pace, countering my frustrated groan with a laugh.

Pulling away, he pecks the corner of my mouth. "Stop tryna seduce me. I just wanna kiss you."

"That's boring."

Another laugh, and a hand claps down on my ass. "Tough shit."

Ignoring my whine of protest, he spins me around. I hear the sound of him popping open a bottle before his hands are on me again, all soapy and slippery this time. He coasts them over my stomach, up my sides, carefully avoiding all the places I want him until I'm squirming.

When a noise of disappointment rumbles in my chest, I feel his smile against my neck right before two large hands suddenly cup my tits, squeezing just enough to have my stomach clenching. His thumbs flick over my nipples, making me gasp, as his teeth catch my earlobe.

One hand continues teasing while the other heads down, trapping itself between my thighs as he cups my pussy. "I haven't been inside you in seven months, Luna," he rasps in my ear. "Call me selfish but when I fuck you again, I wanna be the only thing on your mind."

A groan rips from my throat as his fingers tease but they're gone before I get any real action. I groan again, for different reasons, as he goes back to washing my hair like he said nothing at all, leaving me conflicted over whether I want to fuck him or murder him.

My pout is short-lived, gone before it's truly formed, chased away by a whisper against the curve of my neck. "Did you mean what you said earlier?"

Turning in his arms, I coax his face out from where he's attempting to hide it in my collarbone. I take my time dragging my gaze over his features, relishing in having him so close, so personal, again. I note the shadow of vulnerability in warm eyes, and it urges me to recite my own words from what feels like so long ago, even if repeating them scares the shit out of me, "You respect me. You protect me. You stick up for me. And you're very, very nice to me. Even when I don't deserve it."

With every word, Jackson straightens. His face brightens. *He* brightens, every inch of him, and I greedily soak up the glow. "That's a very long way to say 'yes.'"

"I think you deserve the long way."

52

LUNA

I AM NEVER GOING to find somewhere to live.

Apartment hunting in this city is useless. Everything is too shit or too expensive or too far away from college and it fucking *sucks*.

We need to get out of that damn apartment. Like, literally need to get out. It seems Daddy Dearest has changed tactics; he went from blowing up Pen's phone with desperate pleas for forgiveness to threatening to cut her off.

She thought he was bluffing.

The notice of eviction we got in the mail last week begs to differ.

When the month is up, we will literally be homeless.

With a groan, I flop on Jackson's bed, body barely hitting the soft mattress before a hand strokes my hair. "No luck?"

I snort. *No luck* is an understatement. *Luck* has never touched the last place we viewed, a studio owned by a creepy old guy who thinks bunk beds, a single armchair and a toaster oven qualifies as *fully furnished*. "We're so fucked."

"You'll find something."

God, I wish I had Jackson's optimism. "Pen is gonna have to live in a hotel room with her mom for the next however many months until the divorce is final and I'm gonna have to go back to New York and move in with my mom."

There's another chuckle as a heavy weight settles over me, Jackson's hands sneaking under my back and his head resting on my chest. Lips kiss the swell of my breast, then my collarbone before nuzzling the crook of my neck. "What about Kate and Amelia?"

"That wouldn't work." They'd be more than willing to take me in, I have no doubt. They were pretty devastated that I moved out in the first place. But there's no room there for Pen. Shit, there's barely room for me. And, honestly, it would be weird, me living there again. Not only because I'd be in the middle of two disgustingly in love couples, but also because... I don't know, it feels like I've outgrown that place, I guess. Like the me who lived there isn't me now.

Jackson props himself up on his elbows, one of those serious, intense expressions on his face. He tangles a hand in my hair, thumb swiping my cheek, the corner of his mouth tipping up as he swallows, almost nervously. "Move in here."

I almost choke on my breath. "What?"

"Move in here," he repeats, a little steadier this time.

I blink. "Here?"

His smile grows, head dropping so his lips can brush my cheek. "Mmhmm."

"With you?"

"Technically with Ben." I roll my eyes as he tugs on my hair, rising to look me in the eyes again. "Nick and Cass are moving out after graduation. I'm keeping my room here but I'll be back at Serenity most of the time. There's more than enough space for you and Pen."

"Are you serious?"

Jackson hums. "You'd be doing me a favor, really. I wouldn't have to worry about you living in some shithole and I wouldn't have to feel bad about ditching Ben."

"You'd really want that? Me living here?"

Duh, says his face.

"I'd be here all the time."

"You're here all the time anyway," he counters. "And that's kinda how I prefer it."

I chew on my bottom lip as I mull it over. It would be kind of ideal. It's close to college. It's close to both my jobs. I know the rent is dirt cheap because the landlord is some sweet old lady who was mesmerized by her four handsome tenants. And I like this house. It's cold and it always smells like beer and boy and paint but it's nice.

And it comes with Ben and room for my sister.

It's not like I'm moving in with Jackson, I rationalize with my quickly overthinking brain. He'll be at home helping Lux and the baby most of the time. We'd be more like... occasional roommates. Maybe it would help with missing him, being here. I'm trying not to dwell on the fact he's leaving soon, I really am, but it's always in the back of my mind.

"Fine." One word has him breaking out in this big ass smile that makes my heart thump a little faster. "But I'm buying new furniture. I refuse to sleep in a bed that Nick or Cass have been in." Or use their desks. The couch will probably have to go too. *Definitely* the kitchen counters.

Honestly, every surface in this entire house probably needs replacing.

Jackson laughs. "You won't need to, sweetheart. You can stay in here."

"But this is your room."

"Yours, if you want it." He must see the hesitation on my face because he sighs. Sitting up, he drags me with him, one hand settling low on my back, the other cupping my neck as my legs wrap around his waist and my arms go around his neck. "I'd prefer it. Keeping my bed warm and shit."

Yeah, who the fuck am I kidding? I'd prefer that too.

"Are you sure?" I ask one more time, ignoring how he rolls his eyes. "You can't take it back once I say yes. You'll be stuck with me."

The corner of his mouth twitches. "Are you saying yes?"

"Yeah." He tries to kiss me but again, I dodge him. "If Pen says yes too."

Jackson grins, big and bright. "I already talked to her. She's taking Nick's room."

"You are such a fucking sneak." I try to slap his arm but he catches my hand, wrapping it in his fist and holding it to his chest. His third attempt to kiss me is successful, his smiling lips catching my pouty ones as he lowers me onto my back again. He keeps me flush against him, hand cupping my cheek and tilting my face upwards, gaining better access as he coaxes my mouth open with his tongue.

A moan vibrates through as his hips grind into mine, trapping me between him and the bed in the best way possible. My heels dig into his ass as I urge him impossibly closer, lifting my hips to meet his as he kisses me harder, his grip getting rougher.

A hand on my thigh hoists my legs higher, opens my legs wider before skimming along my upper thigh, inching towards the spot between them that throbs for him. His hips grind again, drawing a whimper from me as his hand gets closer and closer until...

"Jackson!"

His screamed name does not come from my lips.

The sound of thumping does not come from his headboard repeatedly hitting the wall as I wish it did.

It comes from his bedroom door, from the force of someone's fists thundering against it.

Jackson and I break apart with simultaneous groans, his murderous expression mirroring mine. "What?" we snap in unison.

"Get your dick out of your girlfriend for two seconds and come help us set up!"

I take it back. I don't want to move in with Ben. I want to murder Ben, the little cockblocking shit.

Jackson's forehead drops to my chest as he groans again. "You can't do it without me?"

"We need those muscles, big boy!"

Even pissed off and horny, Ben's dramatically husky holler still makes me laugh. The moment ruined, I push on Jackson's shoulders until he rolls off of me. "Go. I have to get ready anyway."

A third groan and a brief moment of rearranging below the belt later, Jackson rises from the bed. "I'll be right back," he promises before sloping towards the door and ripping it open. Ben is waiting for him, a shit-eating grin on his face. He pumps his brows twice at me, dodging my boyfriend when he goes to thump him. He shoves Jackson down the hall and disappears after him, barking out orders about how furniture needing to be moved, orders that end in a pained yelp as Jackson apparently succeeds in his second attempt to punch him.

The sound of their bickering doesn't let up, even as they trudge downstairs. I flop back on the bed again, smoothing my hair from my face and letting out another laugh.

Yeah, it's good to be back.

~

It feels weird to be back at one of the boys' infamous house parties.

Like I've been teleported back in time.

I find myself thinking about the first time I was here, before I knew any of them and God, it feels like a fucking lifetime ago.

Unlike that night, I don't have to practically bulldoze my way to the kitchen, elbowing horny men out of my way. Instead, I have my own personal bulldozer in the form of a large, slightly overbearing, very scowly boyfriend. Jackson shoves his way through the crowd for me, clearing a space at the kitchen island for me too, and even sneaks an unopened bottle of vodka from one of the upper cabinets. A second later a carton of cranberry juice appears too.

"For me?" I simper dramatically, a hand pressed to my chest. "You really do love me."

I almost spill the drink I'm pouring when a hand comes down hard on my ass. One arm flailing behind me to slap whatever body part I can reach, the other reaches for a couple of shot glasses. I pour one for myself but when I hold the other out to Jackson, he declines. "Not drinking?"

Snagging a beer, he shrugs. "Not a lot."

"How come?"

"Can't take care of your drunk ass if I'm drunk too, can I?"

I snort. "I can take care of myself."

"Oh, I know." Something dark and fucking dirty flashes across his face as he steps closer, forehead dropping to nudge mine. "I've seen it myself."

When I sock him in the ribs, he chuckles lowly, shifting to whisper in my ear. "Can't do all the things I want to do to you if I'm drunk, Luna. Or if you're drunk."

I set that shot down on the counter so quickly, it sloshes all over my hand.

I discard my other drink too, leaving my hands free to slink around his waist and settle in the back pockets of his jeans. Propping my chin on his chest, I crook a brow. "Oh yeah?"

He hums a response, the noise vibrating through me as he kisses the corner of my mouth.

"Jesus Christ, get a room."

Despite the intrusion, the familiar voice has my lips curving upwards. Twisting in Jackson's grip, I grin at an approaching Pen. A condition of me coming tonight was that she come to; I wanted her to finally meet everyone, and she needed to get out of that damn hotel room. After the latest blow-up with her dad, she tried to pull a me and hole up in there. Refused to talk to anyone, broke up with her boyfriend, all that fun stuff.

Luckily for her, I inherited all the stubbornness in the family so it only took a day to coax her out of there.

My sister lands a noisy kiss on my cheek, doing the same to Jackson before brandishing a bottle of booze in either hand. "I come bearing gifts."

"I like her." Cass joins us, smirking as he surveys Pen and her loot. When his gaze lingers a moment too long, my eyes narrow. I'm about to warn him off when I'm distracted.

"Hi, stranger," Amelia coos in my ear as she rips me from Jackson's grasp and into her own. Kate does the same, holding me by the shoulders and scanning me in a quick once-over as if checking I'm all in one piece. "We didn't know you were coming tonight."

I shrug, feeling weirdly timid under their excited gazes. A presence appears at my back just before a hand slides up to cup the nape of my neck, fingers squeezing gently, comfortingly. The girls' smiles brighten to practically blinding potential. "You guys are back together?"

My nod of confirmation is needless considering how Jackson dips to kiss my cheek, how his hands sneak around my waist to rest low on my stomach. A round of happy, squealing noises echo around our little group, even the boys contributing to the celebration. Amelia shoots me a wink before her face settles in an exaggerated frown, her elbow jutting back towards the giant Brazilian man looming behind her, as he usually is. "You didn't tell me."

Nick catches her elbow, using it to tug her back into his chest. "I didn't know, *querida*."

Because she's incapable of even faking anger towards the love of her life, Amelia directs her frown at Ben and Cass instead. "You didn't tell me either!"

Ben holds up in his hands innocently. "Hey, I was tryna respect their privacy."

We all snort; it's a well-known fact that Ben and privacy are mutually exclusive.

Rolling his eyes, Cass pats his sister on the top of her head. "Sucks to be the last to know something, huh?"

He gets a gut punch for that one, something that half winds him because the tiny redhead is freaky strong and, God, does she know how to throw a punch. Nick stifles his laughter—and his pride—in Amelia's hair, wrapping his arms tighter around her before she tries to launch herself at Cass.

Kate dismisses their antics with an eye roll. "I'm really happy for you, Lu."

Amelia ceases her attempted assault to agree. "Me too."

An ache in my chest urges me forward, has me wrapping my friends in a tight hug, all three of us whispering a synchronous 'I missed you' in each other's ears. Over their shoulders, I catch sight of Pen watching us with a smile. Pulling back, I wave her over, and blue-green eyes narrow at whatever expression she must see on my face.

"Girls," I tug her into my side, interlocking our fingers and squeezing. "This is Pen." When they start to chirp excitedly about finally meeting the infamous Pen, I cut them off, "My sister."

It's kind of funny how we're surrounded by people in the middle of a loud ass party yet I swear I could hear a pin drop. Five forehead creases, five mouths drop, five voices simultaneously screech, "Your *what*?"

God, I shouldn't laugh but I kind of want to. "It's a long story." Pen snorts at that. "One I don't really wanna explain tonight but I will, I promise."

I'll explain everything.

Just not tonight.

I forgot how damn suffocating house parties are. So many drunk, sweaty people and grinding bodies and handsy assholes. Jackson got swept away by the guys for a round of beer pong and I lasted all of twenty minutes without him at my side before sneaking upstairs to his room.

Our room, I guess.

A sigh escapes me as I close the door behind me, a shield against all the noise. I collapse on the bed, unstrapping my heels and wiggling my sore toes, getting comfortable for my wait.

It takes longer than I thought it would for him to find me.

A whole fifteen minutes pass before the door creaks open again. "Party boring you?"

I prop myself up on my elbows, unable to help smiling at the man leaning against the doorway. "You've lost your touch."

His low chuckle hits me right in the stomach, as does the soft click of him shutting and locking the door behind him. I sit up as he advances, legs folded beneath me as I rest back on my heels. My neck cranes back as he stops at the foot of the bed, my hands folded in my lap to stop them from fidgeting in anticipation.

Nothing can stop me from squirming when he brushes his knuckles across my cheek and trails his hand down the curve of my neck, caging my throat to tilt my head back more. The rasp in his voice has an almost embarrassing effect between my thighs. "You are so fucking beautiful."

"You know you don't have to charm your way into my pants, Jackson."

In fact, he doesn't have to say anything at all. He just looks at me and hey, look at that, pants around my ankles.

His own brand of magic.

"I know." His cocky tone has me rolling my eyes, earning myself a tsk-ing sound from those smiling lips. "I like saying it." He dips so his lips ghost my cheek, goosebumps radiating out from the spot he barely touched. "I like how you blush when I say it."

I would roll my eyes again, maybe let out a snort, but I'm way too focused on the hand coaxing me to rise, slipping under my short skirt to palm my ass greedily. A deep grumbling sound vibrates in his chest as his fingers skate upwards and find nothing but smooth skin. "No panties tonight?"

I purse my lips to hide my smile, gripping the arm attached to the fingers wrapped tightly around my neck. "Figured you'd rip them off anyway."

"Smart girl."

A surprised gasp escapes me when both hands cup my ass, squeezing hard enough to bruise as he yanks me forward so our chests are flush against each other. Replacing the grip on my neck with soft kisses, he takes his time, sucking and nipping leisurely, paying no attention to my whimpered moans and pleas for more.

His touch is almost unbearable, feather-light and teasing, roaming all over my body, skimming over the places I want him but never lingering. When his fingers pass the tops of my thighs, just ghosting the aching spot between them, for what feels like the hundredth time, I can't help but groan. "Jackson?"

His breathy murmur feels like fire across my skin. "Yeah, sweetheart?"

"Stop fucking teasing me."

Soft laughter follows the trail his fingers make as he slides the straps of my top off my shoulders. I take that as permission to get busy too, getting his shirt off in record time before clumsily fumbling with his belt. He snickers against my skin. "So fucking eager."

"Yeah, well," his belt hits the floor with a loud clang, soon followed by his jeans, his boxers not far behind, "I was promised things."

Namely the long, hard cock begging for my attention.

A hiss escapes Jackson escapes as my fingers graze the leaking head.

Yeah, two can play at the teasing game.

I keep my touch as light, as slow, as his were as I wrap my hand around his cock, pumping with only half the pressure I know he likes. Leaning forward, I trace my tongue along the length of him, humming, "You're so big."

He jerks, a heavy hand settling on my shoulder, a dark look in his eyes as he gazes down at me. Tightening my grip, I stand, relishing in his sharp inhale. "Please, baby," I kiss the corner of his mouth, "I need you."

I had a hunch those three little words would undo him, and I was right. In the blink of an eye, I'm on my back, my clothes gone, and he's on me before I can take a breath. He kisses me like he's fucking starving, unrelenting and brutal, taking complete control over me. I can't breathe and I don't care; I just wrap my legs around his waist and pull him closer.

Our moans mingle when the hardest part of him grinds against the softest part of me. He rises on his elbows, head dropping to watch his cock sliding through my slick pussy, the head nudging my clit until I'm squirming.

"Fuck, Luna," he groans, a hand sneaking between us to join his cock, fingers pinching my clit and drawing a long moan out of me. "You're dripping all over my cock."

"Please." It's more a moan than a word, dissolving into a whimper when his thumb circles my clit. My heels dig into his ass in an effort to hurry him the fuck up but it's useless.

Instead, he pulls back completely, sitting back on his heels and placing a firm hand on my stomach to stop me from following. When I whine in annoyance, he levels me with a heavy stare. "Just lemme look at you."

And look, he does.

A long, lingering look, like he's committing every inch of me to memory.

I squirm impatiently under his stare, fisting the bedsheets as my hips buck upwards. I swear to God, a tear of relief leaks from my eye when he slips two fingers inside of me, curling and instantly finding the spot that has my head lolling back, a fucking feral noise ripping from my throat.

"Such a pretty fucking pussy," he murmurs, eyes trained between my legs, watching as him move in and out of me, fast enough to set me on fire but too slow to get me over the edge. I yelp when he pulls out abruptly, his hand coming down on my clit in a light slap, the sting quickly soothed by his weight returning on top of me and his cock nudging my pussy again as his teeth nip my bottom lip. "You kept it from me. Eight long fucking months."

All I can do is cry out when he dips inside me, just the tip but enough to make me squirm.

"You gonna make it up to me?"

I nod as frantically as I writhe.

"Good girl." Rolling us over, he settles me on top of him, and I eagerly straddle his waist. "Show me how sorry you are, sweetheart."

He doesn't have to tell me twice.

All my breath leaves my lungs in one sharp cry as I sink down on his cock, half a dozen curses falling from my lips too when he bottoms out inside me. My hands shake as I brace them against his chest, my eyes squeezing shut as I wait for my body to adjust, for the sting of pain to recede. Fucking hell, did he get bigger? He feels bigger. Longer. Thicker. God, I've never felt so full. It feels like he's in my fucking brain.

My eyes flutter open when knuckles graze my cheek. Jackson gazes up at me, the picture of strained concern. "You okay?"

I nod shakily, nails digging into his skin.

He doesn't look convinced. "Am I hurting you?"

My hair falls in my face as I shake my head, clamping down around him and making him groan when he tries to lift me off him. "So good, baby," I manage to croak out, rocking my hips ever so slightly and shivering at the sensation that causes. "Too good. Can't breathe."

Almost involuntarily, as if my compliments spur him on, his hips flex, forcing himself deeper and I almost scream at the painful plea- sure. My stomach clenches, my body crumpling forward slightly when a hand sneaks between my legs, thumb going to my clit and circling languidly. Jackson takes advantage of the position, leaning up to suck a hard nipple into his mouth, sending sparks down my spine as his tongue and teeth get to work.

Tension builds in my stomach as his hands and mouth work in tandem until all I can focus on is them. It builds quick, completely wiping out any semblance of pain and replacing it with an intense want for more. Slowly, I rise up until just the tip of him is inside of me before slamming down again, my mouth dropping open as heat floods my body.

"That's my girl," Jackson croons, ceasing his assault on my chest so he can watch me writhe on top of him.

I go slow, rising and falling and rocking my hips leisurely, partly because I feel like I might split in half if I don't, partly because I'm enjoying the reaction it's drawing out of Jackson. He looks like he's torn between being frustrated at the tortuous, languid speed and entranced by the controlled way I move.

Maybe, just maybe, I put on a bit of a show, caressing up my sides, cupping my tits and maybe squeezing them just a little before tangling my hands in my hair, gathering it up and away from my neck.

The bob of Jackson's throat as he swallows hard is unmistakable, as is the lustful glint in his eyes.

Fuck, I forgot what it feels like to be looked at like that. Like you're the most important, precious thing in the world. I forgot what it feels like to be cherished. Loved. It's a welcome reprieve when his gaze drops to watch himself disappear in and out of me, because that look is almost as overwhelming as the feel of him deep inside of me is.

"You're taking me so well, sweetheart." My pussy clenches at the praise and Jackson's groan vibrates through me, eyes screwed shut and jaw slack as his head falls back against the pillow. "*Fuck*, do that again."

I do, and it sets him off. Hands on my waist shove me down as hips piston upwards, drawing a scream out of me as he somehow hits even deeper, practically rearranging my fucking organs. I lose control of my body when he does it again, falling forward and burying my face in his neck to stifle my cries, vision blurry and ears fucking ringing.

Jackson doesn't relent, even as my nails bite his skin hard enough to draw blood, he just keeps pounding into me ruthlessly. Sacrificing half of his grip on my hips, he yanks my head back my hair, forcing my gaze to his.

Fuck, I'm obsessed with the way he looks. Hooded eyes and dark and wild, flickering between my face, my bouncing tits, where he disappears inside of me. Hair all messy and disheveled, mussed by my hands and our vigorous movements. Muscles twitching wherever my touch lands.

Just as desperate for me as I am for him. Just as affected by me as I am by him.

Just looking at him has a long, low moan ripping from my throat. "I'm so fucking close, Jackson."

His thrusts speed up, balls slapping against my ass loudly as his cock twitches inside of me. "Come with me."

One more thrust of his hips is all it takes to shove me over the edge, the pressure in my lower stomach erupts violently. I feel the moment he comes, and even as he explodes inside of me, he keeps fucking me hard, his spasming movements and the growled sound of my name only prolonging my own orgasm.

After what feels like a lifetime, he finally stills, allowing my spent body to collapse on top of him. Our heavy breathing fills the room as we lie there, bodies still twitching with the aftershocks of a fucking monumental orgasm, relishing in the feel of each other. He's still inside of me, still twitching and throbbing and barely even soft. I'm soaked between my thighs, impossibly wet from a mixture of our release.

Oh, fuck.

My tired body screams as I sit up too quickly, swearing loudly as Jackson pulls out of me and streaks of white gush out with him, dripping down my thighs.

Fuckity, fuck, fuck.

When Jackson follows my line of sight, he swears too. "Fuck. I completely forgot."

I did too. God, the concept of a condom didn't even cross my mind.

"I'm so sorry, Luna." Jackson rakes his hands through his hair, head flopping to face me as I collapse beside him. "I didn't think."

"It's okay. Not your fault." Takes two to tango, and all that. We're both at fault. Well, mostly my greedy little vagina is to blame, really, for being a horny bitch and clouding my judgement. "I still have an IUD. And I'm clean." A flush reddens my cheeks as I clear my throat. "Are you?"

"Yes." Jackson rolls to his side, tucking a strand of hair behind my ear before cupping my cheek. "I haven't been with anyone in a while."

Don't ask. Do not ask.

"How long is a while?"

Damn it.

The corner of his mouth twitches. "September, I think."

"Fuck off," I blurt out before I can stop myself. "Really?"

He hums a laugh. "Really."

Jesus. *September.* That's a while. No wonder I'm fucking coated in him.

As selfishly pleased as his confession makes me, it also incites a pit of guilt to settle deep in my chest. I shift awkwardly, curling into a ball on my side and dropping my gaze to a random spot on his chest.

"I, uh, slept with a few people," I admit quietly. "A few one-night-stands and the guy from my office."

The former, I barely remember. They were done in a drunken haze, nothing memorable about them. And Paul, I haven't touched in months. Not since I started talking to Jackson again. "I'm sorry."

"Don't apologize, sweetheart. We weren't together."

His words do nothing to soothe the guilt heating my skin, spreading nausea all through me.

"Lu," Jackson sighs quietly, gripping my chin and forcing my gaze to his. "It's okay. I'm not angry. You didn't do anything wrong."

"But-"

"No buts," he insists firmly. "Do I like it? No. Am I jealous that someone else got to have you like this? Fuck yeah."

It's sick, really, that the concept of him being jealous sets something churning excitedly in my lower stomach. He knows it too, because his eyes spark for a brief moment, his grip momentarily tightening, before his expression softens.

"You did nothing wrong," he repeats, so sincere and sure of himself that I can't help but believe it. "You sleeping with other people when we weren't even speaking, let alone together, does not change how I feel about you."

My forehead rests against his, our noses brushing as I whisper, half-joking, half, serious, all terrified, "You still love me?"

"Always."

53

JACKSON

I WAKE up to the dulcet tones of my girlfriend screaming.

And not the kind of screaming she was doing last night. This is the banshee-esque, furious kind she does when she's pissed off.

God bless whoever the victim of that scream is.

Sighing, I roll out of bed and amble towards my ajar bedroom door, remembering I'm butt-ass naked at the last second and quickly tugging on some sweats. I yank the door open just in time to catch Luna kicking Cass in the shin, simultaneously socking him in the gut. "You little shit!"

Cass yelps, trying and failing to evade her attack. "I'm sorry!"

"Liar!"

My second sigh in the space of a minute escapes me as I hook an arm around my girlfriend's waist and scoop her up. Perfectly manicured hands slap at my forearm, sharp nails digging into my skin. "Let me go!"

I drop my head, brushing my lips against her cheek because that usually calms her down. Not today, apparently, because her escape attempts don't cease. "Explain why you're beating up Cass first."

"He fucked my sister!"

Well, fuck.

Wasn't expecting that.

For the first time, I notice Pen lurking in the hallway too, lingering just in front of Cass' open bedroom door. One of his jerseys is draped over her body, so big on her it slips off her shoulder slightly and reveals an array of reddish-purple marks scattered across her neck and chest. She's trying not to laugh, a hand slapped over her mouth hiding her smile but there's no doubting the humor sparkling in her eyes.

Really? I mouth at her. *Cass?*

Pen winks and holds up her hands, palms facing each other as she positions them a generous distance apart, wiggling her brows at me. When I cringe at her implication, she erupts into silent cackles.

Yeah, it's a bit too early for that kind of information.

Distracted by Pen and trying to shake off the nausea that hits when my friend's dick is the subject of conversation, I accidentally loosen my grip on Luna. The second she wriggles free, she launches herself at Cass. The poor guy is completely defenseless, trapped between the wall and the very angry fake-brunette pummeling him. "One person, Cass! *One person* you were supposed to keep your nasty dick away from!"

"Hey!" Cass' face tightens in a scowl as he batts Luna's slapping palms away, thumping her back for good measure. "My dick is not nasty!"

"I second that," Pen chimes in, shoulders shaking with the effort of stifling her laughter, and Cass's scowl shifts into a smirk that he directs her way.

In the blink of an eye, Luna steps into his line of sight, rising up on her tiptoes like she's trying to hide Pen from his view. "*No!*" She shoves him backwards with a frustrated groan before screeching again. "Amelia!"

It's comical, how quickly Cass' smirk disappears and morphs into pure panic. "Don't! I'm-"

The door of Nick's recently vacated bedroom creaking open interrupts Cass, and I swear the guy shrinks about a foot in height as a rumpled Amelia creeps out into the hallway, face creased in confusion as she rubs her eyes. Behind her, an equally disheveled, considerably angrier Nick follows. "Why the fuck is everyone yelling?"

An accusing finger jabs Cass in the chest. "Your brother put his dick in my sister!"

A bark of laughter disguised as a cough escapes Nick while Amelia cringes. "Seriously, Cass?"

"It was an accident!"

"Tell me, Cass." I'm not even remotely surprised when Ben appears at the end of the hallway, Kate hovering behind him, the former cracking an amused smile while the latter sighs and shakes her head. "How do you accidentally put your dick in someone?"

Oh, if looks could kill.

"Shut up," Cass snaps at Ben before turning to Amelia. "You can't say shit, Tiny. And *you*," he directs at the Brazilian contingency of our friend group, "stop enjoying this."

Nick's Cheshire cat grin goes nowhere. "I'm sorry, I was just remembering something," he drawls sarcastically, pretending to think. "Sisters are off-limits, was it?"

"I wanna punch you."

I grab Luna before she can deliver on her growled remark, clamping her arms to her sides. "Don't punch him."

"Let her," Nick calls out. "He tried to punch me."

"That's true!" Ben nods in agreement. "It's only fair."

"Okay, enough." Before fists can fly, Pen reigns in her laughter and steps between her latest conquest and her sister. "I appreciate the love, Lu, but I'm a big girl. I can fuck who I want."

Luna wrinkles her nose. "But it's *Cass*."

Cass throws out his arms in bewilderment. "Hey?"

Pen's cheeks twitch, her lips pressing together to hide the smile that's begging to curl her lips. "Jesus Christ, Luna, we're not getting married. It was just sex."

"But we're moving in here," Luna reminds her with a groan and a pout. "It's gonna be weird now."

"No, it's not." Pen cups her sister's face, hitting her with a no-bull-shit deadpan look. "It was a one-night stand, LuLu. Let's not act like you're unfamiliar with the concept of sleeping with someone once and only once."

Luna's defensive stance softens under my fingers. "Low blow."

Pen chuckles as she pecks Luna's cheek. She grabs her hand, tugging her out of my grip and towards the stairs. "Come on. I was promised breakfast."

Luna bristles at the expectant look Pen tosses Cass over her shoulder, even more so when he attempts to follow them downstairs. She darts in between them again, ushering Pen down the stairs and walking backwards after her, mouthing *stay away from her* at Cass with narrowed eyes.

The second Luna disappears from sight, I'm taking her place, flicking Cass on the forehead. "Seriously?" I flick him again for good measure.

Cass howls dramatically, scowling as he lifts a hand to rub his head. "God, you two are fucking violent."

I roll my eyes. "Of all people, Cass. C'mon."

"What? She's hot. I'm hot. Together, we were very, very hot." A smirk curls his lips as he pumps his brows. "All night."

"And on that note," Amelia shivers before practically throwing herself down the stairs, "I'm leaving."

Nick follows, giving Cass a shove and a smug smile on his way past. "I fucked your sister, you fucked Luna's sister. Funny how the world works, huh?"

Cass gags. "Ew, Nick."

"Sorry, my bad." His smile widens. "I *fuck* your sister."

"Nick!" Amelia screeches from somewhere downstairs. "Stop antagonizing him!"

Nick just laughs, unfazed by the anger in his tiny redhead's voice, or the steam practically pouring out of Cass' ears. Mischief written all over his face, he leans forward and pats Cass on the cheek. "But it's so easy."

It feels like old days again, my house destroyed from a party and filled with my hungover friends.

Breakfast was kind of hilarious. It involved a lot of Luna glaring at Cass over her coffee cup and him avoiding her gaze, looking downright terrified. Honestly, I don't think Lu has to worry about them living together being weird; Pen and Cass get along ridiculously well. There's none of that lingering awkwardness that happens sometimes after you've seen someone naked, and when all your friends know you've seen each other naked. And they clearly did more than just see each other naked so it's a miracle, really.

I think, deep down, Luna is fine with them hooking up. She's not the kind of person who polices sex. I think she's just focusing all her attention and energy on this one thing, instead of letting other things cloud her mind. Namely the fact she's going for lunch with the girls with the intention of telling them everything.

She's nervous as shit and she's not even trying to hide it. The girls are doing their best to reassure her but since they have no idea what they're reassuring her about, it's not exactly helping. I tried my hand at calming her down too; in the shower, and then on the bathroom counter, and on my bed a couple of times, too.

And it worked, on some level. By the time the girls cleared out of here, she was too wrecked to be stressed.

I'm changing my sheets when my phone rings, the ringtone specific to Lux filling my bedroom. I dive for my phone, snatching it off my desk before the first ring even finishes. "Everything okay?"

"Everything is fine, *Dad*," Lux groans. I can just picture her rolling her eyes. "I'm just calling to tell you that the ad you put up got a few responses."

My shoulders slump in relief. The ranch hand position. I forgot about that. I swear, every time she calls—or even if she doesn't, honestly—I get this voice in the back of my head convincing me that something's wrong with her, or the baby or the girls or the ranch.

I like to think I'll calm down a little when the baby arrives, but really, I have a hunch that when the new tiny, incredibly fragile addition to our family arrives, the permanent pit of worry in my stomach is only going to expand.

"Okay." I balance my phone between my ear and my shoulder as I toss dirty bedsheets in the laundry basket. "I can come up sometime next weekend to interview some of the applicants."

Like I knew she would, Lux objects. "I can do it."

"I wanna be there."

"But I get the final say."

"Stop being difficult."

"I'm-"

"Enough," I cut her off with a huff. "This isn't up for discussion. If we're inviting a stranger to work on our land, to *live* on our land, to constantly be around my nephew and my sisters, you bet your ass I'm going to be there to vet them."

It's a testament to how tired my sister is, proof she really is in desperate need of some help, that she doesn't argue further. She just sighs and mutters a reluctant agreement before swiftly changing the subject, launching into the latest gossip floating around our hometown.

Unsurprisingly, most of it pertains to her new situation; once that belly started showing, word got around real quick. And God, did those words get twisted.

One version of the story is that she got pregnant on purpose to trap Mark. Another is that she was cheating on him all along with not one but both of the ranch hands and the baby isn't even his. It sounds like the newest one claims that he found out she was pregnant when the rest of the town did, and now she's trying to keep the baby from him.

It's funny how, in every tale, Mark escapes unscathed.

Fucking small towns.

Lux is a better person than I am because she laughs it all off, like she does now. Her cackles drift through the phone as she recites an encounter with the matriarch of the town's gossip hierarchy, a woman I'm pretty sure is older than all my sister's and I combined. "God, I thought Sue Allen's ancient head was gonna pop off when Line threw her out of the store for talking shit about me."

"Wait, what?" Line? As in *Caroline?* The way Lux suddenly shuts up answers that question before I can even ask it. "Since when do you hang out with Caroline?"

"I don't hang out with Caroline," Lux snorts a little too dismissively. "She's our flower supplier. I was just picking up an order."

"You called her *Line.*"

"Did I?" She clears her throat. "Weird. Anyway, it was badass. She basically grabbed the old bat by the scruff of her neck and tossed her on her ass."

Caroline. Badass. Manhandling old women for the sake of my sister's name.

Weird.

"You know, if you're friends with Caroline you can-"

"So, next Saturday works best for me," Lux smoothly changes the subject, cutting off what I was about to say. I roll my eyes but I don't push, mostly because pregnant Lux is even scarier than regular Lux and I really don't want to set her off. "The twins are coming down so everyone will be home."

"Sounds good to me."

"Will anyone be joining you?" God, Lux fucking sucks at subtlety.

"Maybe." I haven't asked Luna yet but I plan to. My gut feeling says she'll say yes; she loves Serenity Ranch, and her and Lux have that weird bond thing going on so she'll probably want to see her, and the bump.

"Have you told her about the ranch yet?" Lux asks the same thing she does every time we talk, as consistently as I ask about her wellbeing.

"She knows I'm moving back when the baby's born."

"That's not what I was asking and you know it. You have to tell her, Oscar."

"I know." And I will. I'm just letting us have a little bit of uncomplicated, undramatic time together first.

Honestly, I'm worried she'll freak out. It's very... permanent. I just think it's a good idea to wait until we're a bit more settled before I drop the 'hey, I bought a massive ranch and will probably be living there for the rest of my life' card on her. Shit, I barely even managed to convince her to kind of move in with me. I can't imagine she'll be willing to move to the ass crack of nowhere halfway across the state, and I don't think we're built for distance.

As if my thoughts summon her, knuckles rap against wood and Luna appears in my bedroom doorway. Perfect timing. Perfect timing. Bidding a hasty goodbye to Lux, I hang up and gesture my girl over.

"Hey, sweetheart." My desk chair creaks as she settles herself on my lap, curling into a ball and clutching my t-shirt. "Everything go okay?"

She sniffles into the crook of my neck. "It went well."

Her weak tone is less than convincing. "Lu."

"I'm okay, I promise. It was just..." She trails off, her sigh heavy. "Overwhelming."

I bet. "I'm proud of you for telling them."

"Don't," she whines, her voice all wobbly. "I'll start crying again."

Wisely, I don't mention the tears already brimming. "Wanna get some food? See a movie or something?"

"Can't. We're doing a girls night. Do me a favor and keep Nick occupied?"

God, that's an almighty fucking favor. Keeping that guy away from Amelia is a borderline impossible task. I find myself promising I will anyway, even though we both know the first chance he gets, Nick will be scampering home to smother his girl with affection. "I'll see you tomorrow, then."

"I have class. And work. And then class and work again." A groan escapes me, coaxing a laugh out of her. "But I'm free the day after tomorrow. I'm gonna need help packing my stuff up. If you haven't changed your mind, that is."

I snort. Un-fucking-likely. "Haven't changed my mind, and I'm not gonna."

"Okay." I hear the smile in her voice as much as I feel it against my neck. "I love you."

Not in a million lifetimes do I think I'll get tired of hearing that. "I love you, sweetheart."

54

LUNA

SOMETHING ABOUT STARTING your morning being bent over the bathroom counter by your hot boyfriend just puts a girl in a good mood.

I don't even mind that I'm spending a beautiful afternoon behind a desk tucked away in a stuffy, minuscule cupboard of an office. When the office assholes make their usual snide comments about my coffee-making abilities, they just roll off my back. When I'm asked to copy something for the thousandth time that day, I do it with a smile. And when, while sorting through a mountain of paperwork, I glance up to find Paul paying me a visit, my smile doesn't fade. "What can I do for you?"

It doesn't take long for his surprise at my pleasantries to fade into a slick smirk. "Someone's in a good mood." His knees knock against mine as he rounds my desk and props himself on the edge. "Happy to see me?"

My smile twitches ever so slightly. The wheels of my chair creak quietly as I roll away from him. "Did you need something?"

"Yeah." He inches closer again. "You."

Ah, shit.

Paul's fingers brush my thigh and I shift out of his reach, crossing my legs and angling them away from him. His forehead creases in a frown. "You've kinda disappeared on me lately."

"Right." I clear my throat. "Yeah, I, uh, got back with my ex." *Ex*

445

doesn't feel like the right word to describe Jackson but it's the only one I can think of right now. "So we can't... you know, anymore."

Paul's smile drops. "Oh." He huffs out a dull laugh, an irritated gleam in his eyes. "Recently, I'm guessing? Or were you fucking both of us at the same time?"

I flinch at his tone. "Don't be a dick, Paul."

"I'd rather be a dick than a slut."

Charming.

With a sigh, I stand. Stalking towards the door, I hold it wide open with one hand, gesturing for him to leave with the other. "Get out, Paul, or I'm reporting you to HR for harassment."

A simple, empty threat but it's enough for him to concede. "Whatever," he stomps towards me. "You're not even worth it. Just a shit, easy fuck."

"What did you just say?"

Both of us freeze. Our gazes snap towards the man lingering just a few feet down the hall. A paper takeout bag from Greenies in one hand, a bouquet of flowers in the other, Jackson grasps the latter so tightly, I'm surprised the stems don't snap. He stands stock still, shoulders squared and body taut, almost like he's ready for a fight, but there's this eerie calm expression on his face. Calculating, almost.

When no one replies, Jackson cocks his head slightly, dark eyes burning into Paul. "I asked you a question."

"Mind your own business." Paul scoffs but it's shaky. He tries to slip away but Jackson is in front of him in a flash, blocking his escape.

"Jackson," I say, an edge of warning to my voice, my eyes darting around the office. It's almost empty at this time, with most people out on their lunch break and anyone still here has their gaze trained on a computer screen but still. I don't want to make a scene in front of the handful of people lingering.

Jackson's gaze flickers to me for a moment, and none of the anger lurking in there is directed at me but it still knocks me back a step. Yeah, he heard exactly what Paul said.

And he is *pissed.*

"Listen," Paul raises two pacifying hands, "I didn't say anything. We were just talking."

"No, *she* was asking you to leave. *You* were being rude."

"I get why you're pissed. I'd be pissed too if my girlfriend was ran through by half the office. But don't take it out on me."

Motherfucker.

"You lying little-"

One kiss of Jackson's teeth thwarts my intention of slapping some manners into Paul.

It shouldn't be hot, the threatening look he pins Paul with. It shouldn't send a shiver up my spine, the single step he takes towards him, just enough so he invades his personal space. And the voice Jackson addresses Paul with, the low, quiet one loaded with something subtly menacing definitely shouldn't send heat pooling between my legs.

"Talk about my girl like that again and we're gonna have a problem."

Whatever effect he has on me, he has the opposite on Paul.

The guy pales, shrinking as his shoulders slump. On the contrary, Jackson seems to grow, getting taller and taller until he's towering over Paul. A firm hand on his shoulder stops any more escape attempts. "Apologize."

"It was just a joke."

"I'm not laughing."

Paul swallows.

A full minute passes before he looks my way, cowardly staring at a miscellaneous spot above my head and mumbling a weak apology.

Jackson's brows shoot up. "What was that?"

Pursing his lips, Paul readjusts his gaze to meet mine. "I'm sorry."

"Good." Jackson nods, clapping Paul on the shoulder before not-so-gently shoving him away. "Now, fuck off."

Without waiting to see if he listens, Jackson ushers me into my office, shutting the door behind him with a little more force than necessary.

"You didn't have to do that," I admonish without meaning it, pecking his cheek and taking the stuff from his hands. A small smile curves my lips as I sniff the pretty flowers, a welcome addition to this dreary hole, before setting them on the desk, dropping the takeout next to them. "You brought me lunch?"

The quiet snick of the door locking is his only reply.

~

Turning around slowly, I find Jackson still lingering by the door, an overwhelmingly tense expression on his face. "That him?"

I don't need to ask for further clarification. "Yes."

A deep noise grumbles in his chest as he leans against the door, no distrust or anger in his tone when he asks, "Why was he in here?"

Just concern.

Okay, yeah, and maybe a little jealousy.

As much as I know the truth will piss him off, I know lying is much worse. "He was hitting on me."

"By calling you a slut? Charming."

Locking my hands together behind my back, my thumb goes to town on my ring. "I told him to leave."

"I heard." Slowly, Jackson advances until he's close enough to touch me, a hand cradling one cheek while lips graze the other. "I can't believe you were fucking that tool."

I huff. "Me neither."

Two hands clamping down on my ass draws a surprised yelp out of me, closely followed by another one when I'm suddenly hoisted up and deposited on the desk. His hands coast up my thighs, dragging the tight, pencil skirt I chose to wear this morning up with him so he can part my legs and stand between them. His fingers splay across my skin, thumbs stroking my inner thighs. "I fucking hate that he got to have you for a little bit."

"I'm-"

"Don't apologize." Feather-light touches morph into a tight, possessive grip. "All mine now."

Rolling my eyes, I shove at his chest gently, grumbling 'caveman' under my breath but I can't keep the grin off my face. *Damn right.*

He smiles back but it's tense. *He's* tense. All rigid and wound up, and I do the only thing I can think of to calm him down; I lock my legs around his waist, fist his t-shirt between my fingers, and drag his mouth to mine.

It's instantaneous, the shift in his demeanor. He's still a solid wall of muscle beneath my palms but the stiffness recedes as he melts against me, pressing every inch of him against every inch of me.

Somehow, it's still not enough. The clothes separating us is too much, but Jackson's making fast work of solving that problem.

Nimble fingers deftly unbutton my blouse, untuck it from my skirt and toss it aside in one smooth move, my bra following close behind. A little voice in the back of my head reminds me that only a locked door separates me from my co-workers, but it promptly shuts the fuck up the moment his mouth clamps around a pert nipple. The other one, he rolls between his thumb and forefinger, rapidly creating an ache only he can soothe as white-hot pleasure shoots down my spine and settles between my thighs.

He grunts against my skin, slipping a hand between my ass and the desk so he can hoist me higher, get more of me in his mouth. I arch my back to achieve the same thing, one hand needily gripping his hair, the other clamped over my mouth in a weak attempt to stifle the noises escaping me.

When my hips start grinding against his, he releases my nipple with a wet plop and I groan in quiet protest. I try to guide him back to where I want him but he resists, his stubborn smirk burning my collarbones. Leaving a trail of wet kisses up my neck, he tugs my bottom lip between his teeth. "How many times did he fuck you, Luna?"

I don't answer at first. I barely even hear him. I'm way too caught up in the hand hovering above the waistband of my skirt, the muscles in my stomach contracting downright painfully in anticipation. Rough fingers tweak my nipple. "Answer me, sweetheart."

"Eight." Eight times. Easy to remember because it was eight times I felt guilty as hell. Eight times that instead of enjoying the post-orgasm haze, I drowned my sorrows in wine and ice cream. Eight times that I showered with the water on boiling hot in the hopes it would erase the icky feeling from my skin.

Teeth nip at my jaw. "Did he make you come?" I know better than to hesitate this time, nodding jerkily. A displeased noise rumbles in his chest. "How many times?"

"Every time."

"That's eight orgasms you owe me," he murmurs huskily, snapping my waistband when I dare to protest. "But I'm gonna round it up to ten. And I'm gonna start collecting today. That okay with you?"

I nod so fast my head spins a little.

Jackson wastes no time yanking my skirt up and slipping a hand between my thighs, a groan escapes him when he finds me soaking wet and throbbing for him. Two fingers slip inside me easily, his thumb rapidly circling my clit. That combined with his head dropping and his teeth tugging on my nipple again is all it takes for me to clamp down around him, muffling my moans in his neck as I come, hard.

I feel his smirk against my skin. "One."

He barely gives me a chance to recover before I'm being gently pushed onto my back, my hips lifted off the desk so he can shed the rest of my clothes. I prop myself up on my elbows so I can watch as he gets down on his knees, throwing my legs over his shoulders.

I promptly fall back again when he disappears between my thighs.

Keeping my whimper in is an impossible task as his tongue slips inside me, fingers digging into my ass and lifting me closer to his mouth. He fucking devours me, unrelenting, a man on a mission and that mission is to drive me out of my fucking mind.

And he's succeeding. I'm incoherent. Nothing but a boneless puddle, limp on the desk. Tears brew in my eyes from the effort of keeping quiet, and I have to squeeze them shut because watching him fucking destroy me is too much. Teeth graze my clit and I'm undone again, drawing blood with how hard I bite down on my lip. I've barely ridden out the second one before the third hits, and I'm convulsing on the desk, soaking the wooden surface, drenching his face.

I'm panting like I've just run a marathon when he finally relents, wiping his sodden lips on my inner thighs. "Two." His lips press just below my belly button, tongue flicking out to momentarily catch the jewelry dangling there. He rises higher, giving my nipple piercings the same treatment before his smug face hovers above mine. "And three." The corners of his mouth twitch as he gazes down at me, eyes tracing every inch of my slack body. "You ruined your desk."

I just about manage to lift a limp arm enough to pinch his bicep. "Shut up."

I barely get the words out before he's kissing me, cupping my cheeks with both hands as he helps me sit up again. I'm spent, or at least I thought I was until he flexes his hips against mine and I get a feel of the throbbing erection straining against his sweats trying to get to me, and suddenly I'm desperate again.

Realizing he's still fully clothed and I'm entirely naked—bar the heels on my feet—I hurriedly rid him of his t-shirt before tugging down his sweats. My actions are foiled halfway there when I'm abruptly lifted and spun around, my wobbly legs barely supporting me as I'm bent over the desk.

A heavy, delicious weight settles over me, Jackson's breath tickling my ear. "Did he fuck you in here?"

I hesitate briefly before nodding. The first time, it happened in here. It was the week after Thanksgiving, the week after what would've been our anniversary. I was sad, and I was so sick of being sad, so when we happened to be the last two people left in the office one night and he was a little flirty, I reciprocated.

The warmth enveloping me disappears as Jackson pulls back, one hand creeping up my back to tangle in my air, the other smoothing over my ass. "I'm gonna fuck you now, sweetheart."

My fingers curl into fists, knuckles white and palms stinging from my nails digging into them. "Please."

Gently, he rocks his hips into my ass. When I push back against him greedily, he chuckles. "It's gonna be hard and fast but you'll take it like a good girl." I whine in response, earning a harsh slap on the ass. "Yes, Luna?"

"*Yes.*"

There's the brief rustling of fabric before I feel his bare flesh against mine, his hard cock sliding between my thighs, the head nudging my clit, teasing me. Greedy hands spread my ass as he eases inside my pussy, a simultaneous low groan escaping us as he sinks into the hilt. He only gives me a second to adjust, just enough for the breath to return to my lungs and the stinging pain of him stretching me wider than what scientifically should be possible to reduce.

And then he does exactly what he said he was going to do.

I grip the edges of the desk for dear life. Every long, hard, deep thrust threatens to knock me off-balance. It's loud, the sound of his skin slapping against mine, too loud, and I should be worried about it but I can't quite bring myself to be.

The hand in my hair jerks my head to the side, a silent demand for me to look at him, and I crane my neck as much as possible so I can.

"Every time you sit at this desk, you're gonna think of me." He punctuates his grunted words with an extra-enthusiastic thrust. "Not him. *Me.* You're gonna think about me fucking this tight little pussy. You're gonna think about how good I felt inside you. You're gonna remember how you moaned my name and how you soaked my fucking cock."

"Jackson," I beg, I'm not sure what for, I just know I need something from him. Hands on my hips rearranging me, lifting me higher, and I cry out as he hits a spot inside me that has my vision going blurry. "Fuck, please don't stop."

He doesn't. He keeps pounding away, keeps hitting that spot. He shifts his weight so he's covering me, sweaty skin flush against sweaty skin as his chest hits my back. "You're gonna spend the rest of the day with my cum running down your thighs and you're gonna fucking like it."

Another thrust and those dirty fucking words are what it takes to send me over the edge, dragging him with me. He catches my lips with his as we both come, his kiss as frantic as his thrusting as he empties inside of me, so much so that I feel his release dripping down my thighs before he's even done.

It takes a while for our breathing to regulate, for our bodies to stop quivering. His forearms brace either side of me so he doesn't crush me under his weight, his lips pressed to my bare, clammy shoulder, his breath hot against my flushed skin.

It's a stark contrast to minutes before, the gentle way his lips caress my shoulders and neck, the delicate way he cups my chin and turns me to face him. "You're mine, Lu," he murmurs softly, nothing but brutal sincerity glowing in those brown eyes I love. "I'm not giving you up again."

55

JACKSON

"WE'RE HERE!"

Mere seconds pass after I shoulder open the front door before a bundle of dark hair throws herself at us, one arm wrapping around my neck while the other hooks around Luna's.

"You're here!" Eliza squeals, the smile on her face is nothing short of ecstatic. "And you're together."

"Eliza," I warn but I'm unable to keep my lips from tipping upwards. I knew she'd be happy to see Luna. I'm glad she's happy to see Luna. Fuck, *I'm* happy to see Luna on the ranch again, and because of some family emergency, and she looks happy to be here. "Where are the others?"

"Lux is coming downstairs now," Eliza tells me, releasing me but showing no signs of letting Luna go. "So she'll be here in, like, thirty minutes."

"I heard that, brat," Lux huffs as she waddles into the kitchen. If I thought Luna looked happy before, it's nothing compared to how her face brightens when she catches sight of Lux, mimicking one of Eliza's excited shrieks as she rushes to her side. Hands reaching out in front of her, she waits until Lux nods her permission before setting them on her rounded stomach. "Look at you," she coos, smoothing her hands over the bump affectionately.

"I know," Lux grunts. "I'm huge."

Luna flicks her gently. "You're glowing."

"You're full of shit," Lux retorts, nudging Lu's hands away and pulling her in for a side hug. Ruffling Eliza's hair before detaching her from me, I move to kiss the eldest of my sisters on her cheek, studying her carefully.

Relief floods my body, relaxing permanently tense muscles. She looks good. Tired and more than a little uncomfortable if the way she keeps rubbing her back and scrunching her face is anything to go by, but good. Healthy. Looks can be deceiving though so I ask anyway, "You doing okay?"

"Yes," she replies a little too quickly. "I'm fine. Everything is fine."

Huh.

Believable.

Grace ambles into the room just in time to catch the end of that sentence, and she comes to an abrupt halt. She narrows her eyes at Lux, and Lux narrows hers right back. Some kind of silent conversation transpires between them, one that ends with Lux huffing in annoyance as Grace turns to me. "Her blood pressure is shit. Doc said she needs to take it easy but she's not listening."

"You are such a tattle-tale," Lux hisses. Glancing at me, she holds up her hands innocently. "I'm fine. I promise, I'm fine."

"A medical professional seems to disagree."

"I'm taking it easy!"

Grace snorts.

"*My blood pressure is fine.*" Lux insists shrilly. "I was just having a bad day."

Unconvinced, I shoot her a look, pulling out one of the chairs tucked under the kitchen table and staring at it pointedly. An almighty huff leaves my sister as she reluctantly plops herself in it, muttering what I'm sure are all kinds of threats against my life.

I rest my hand on her shoulder, leaning down to murmur in her ear. "It's not just yourself you gotta take care of anymore, Lux."

She scowls but it's half-hearted. Two protective hands settle on top of her belly. "I know."

"Then stop being a dumbass and listen to the damn doctor. Okay?"

She grumbles something that I'm pretty sure is an agreement, swatting me away when I kiss her cheek. "Yeah, well, I learned how to be a dumbass from you."

Rolling my eyes at my sister, I plop down on the chair beside her. "So who's this guy we're meeting?"

~

I don't like him.

He's only been in the house for a half hour and I already don't like him.

Maybe it's the fact he's yet to crack his smile. And his version of a greeting was grunting his name with a firm nod. And every question I ask, his answer is annoyingly monosyllabic—I didn't clock his southern accent until at least the ten minute mark.

Or maybe it's that despite said lilting accent and the fucking cowboy boots on his big ass feet, he's still intimidating as hell.

Or it has something to do with him shaking my hand and crushing my fingers with what I'm pretty sure was maybe a quarter of his grip strength.

Or it's the fact that Lux's mouth has been watering since the enormous man interviewing to be our newest ranch hand plodded through the door.

I didn't know that brawny and big enough to wrestle a fucking hippo was her type but Lux has stars in her eyes. And a weird high pitch to her voice as she lays out what his duties would be, this odd nervous energy to her that I don't think I've ever seen in my life.

Whatever the reason, I am positive that I don't like him.

But my sister clearly does, and as she so likes to remind me, she's got final say.

I have a feeling that no matter how much I protest, Hunter Whitlock is about to become a permanent fixture on my ranch.

"I like him," Lux murmurs the moment Hunter's out of earshot. He wanted to check out the barn and the horses, and Lux, obviously, told him to knock himself out. As he jogs towards the paddock where Clyde and the Scooby Gang are hanging out, the earth practically shakes beneath his thunderous strides. "I really like him."

"I don't."

Lux's head whips towards me, a completely bewildered expression on her face, like she can't possibly comprehend what I'm saying. "Why not?"

"He seems like a dick."

"Maybe he's shy," Lux vehemently defends the man she met less than an hour ago. When I scoff, she rolls her eyes. "Come on, Oscar. You said I needed help. He can help. Look at him." She gestures towards the mountain of a man. "He could probably bench press Clyde. One of him is, like, four of anyone else you might hire."

Her eyes drift back over to where Hunter has climbed up the paddock fence and settled astride the thick logs, his gaze trained on the horses eyeing him warily. "Besides, if I'm gonna be a useless human incubator confined to the porch swing for the next few months, I deserve a little eye candy."

"Gross, Lux."

"He's got experience. He can clearly carry his weight around here. Clyde likes him and he's an excellent judge of character. He's perfect, Oscar."

I side-eye Lux, a sigh escaping me as the only acceptable answer becomes clear. It's not like I really had a choice, anyway. She was always going to hire him, whether I agreed or not. But I appreciate her effort at pretending like I'm included in the decision. "Fine."

My twenty-one-year-old sister squeals like an overexcited child.

Looping her arm around mine, she tugs me towards Hunter, leaning on me as I help her down the porch steps.

She was right, he's got Clyde eating out of the palm of his hand. Literally; the guy must've snatched a bunch of apples from the stash in the barn. Shit, Clyde isn't even this comfortable around me or Lux. Luna's the only person he nuzzles the way he's nuzzling one of Hunter's big ass thighs.

Damn it.

"Hunter!" Lux calls out when we get close enough. He swivels to face us, the same impassive expression on his bearded face that he's been wearing since he got here. "When can you start?"

He doesn't move from his positions atop the paddock fence. "Whenever you want, ma'am."

Ma'am.

Jesus Christ.

Lux's smile is colossal. She elbows me, shooting me a brief look as if to say *'see? Look how polite he is.'* "Great. Does Monday work? The cabin you'll be staying in is ready now but I assume you've gotta go get your stuff."

Hunter swings his leg over and hops off the wall, way too gracefully for a man of his bulk. Once on solid ground, he nods his head towards the battered piece of metal he calls a truck and utters the longest sentence I've heard from him yet. "I've got my stuff with me. I can start right now, if you want."

"Oh." I didn't think it was possible but Lu's smile grows. I get another look, this one saying *'see? Fate.'* "Even better. Eliza!" She yells the last bit over her shoulder.

Comically quickly, Eliza's head pops out the kitchen window, where she's been lurking and oh-so-discreetly creeping on the new addition to the ranch. Grace is somewhere in there too, for some reason doing her college work at the kitchen table instead of at the perfectly good desk in her room. Even Lottie stopped being a brat long enough to gawk. I'm grateful Luna was on the phone with Pen when Hunter arrived, because otherwise she'd probably be gaping too and I'd like him even less.

"Can you show Hunter to his cabin?"

God, if my sisters keep smiling like that, their faces are going to split in two.

"Of course I can!" Eliza disappears, reappearing less than a second later as she barrels out the front door, almost breaking her neck in her quest to get to us as quickly as possible.

With a smile like butter wouldn't melt, Eliza grips Hunter by one huge bicep and drags him away, already babbling a mile a minute. I think, for the first time, I see an emotion cross the cowboy's face; surprise. I'm convinced I even see a hint of a smile but it smoothes out too soon for me to confirm my suspicions.

My youngest sister is helping Hunter get his meagre amount of belongings from his truck when a horn honks, dusk kicked up by the wheels of a car rolling down our driveway.

Before she even gets out of her car, Caroline's blush is visible, her wide eyes clearly latched onto Hunter.

I groan. God, this guy's gonna be a fucking hazard.

Smoothing down her sundress, she pastes on that signature Caroline smile before approaching the newest addition to the ranch.

I can't hear what they're saying but I hazard a guess that she's introducing herself when she holds out a hand for him to shake. Even from a distance, I can see Caroline's face drop when Hunter shakes her hand—probably begrudgingly because I think that's his default setting—but does absolutely nothing else, not the least bit interested in participating in the conversation she's trying to start.

She dithers unsurely for the briefest moment before she shakes her head and heads towards Lux and I. "Sheesh," she mutters when she gets within earshot. "I thought cowboys were supposed to be nice."

Lux snickers. "Don't need to be nice when you look like that."

A soft sigh escapes Caroline as she glances over shoulder, dramatically wistful. "I'm so jealous you get to stare at that all day. You think that shirt's gonna come off when the summer heat hits?"

Lux copies her sigh. "A girl can only hope."

"What're we hoping for?" A hand slips into my back pocket as a lithe, warm body presses against my side.

Lux simply nods toward Hunter as if that's explanation enough. And apparently, it is. The guy is fucking miles away yet my girlfriend's eyes go wide, lips pursed as she whistles quietly. "Who's the hot cowboy?"

When I clear my throat pointedly, blue eyes roll. "Baby, I love you," Luna croons, rising on her tiptoes to peck my cheek, "but I have eyes."

"Close 'em," I grumble back, slipping a hand around her waist and yanking her closer.

Luna doesn't immediately melt into me as she usually does. Instead, she leaves a sliver of space between us as she smiles softly, almost apologetically, at Caroline. "Hi, Caroline."

To her credit, Caroline doesn't look the least bit phased. "Hey, Luna." They share a weird moment of intense eye contact before Caroline breaks it, her attention shifting to Lux as she hip bumps her gently. "Ready?"

Lux nods, jerking a thumb towards the house. "Just needa get my bag."

"Where are you going?"

"Line's gotta go to the flower market before it closes and I said I'd help." I open my mouth, but Lux cuts me off before I can even begin to form a protest, narrowing her eyes and giving me a warning look.

"And before you start, yes, my swollen ankles will be able to support my weight for a few hours."

Luna laughs quietly and Caroline's gaze flicks back to her. "You wanna come?"

Lu glances between her and I, seeming to ask both of us, "Do you mind?" When we both shake our heads, Lu breaks out in a smile. "I'd love to."

Caroline and Lux head towards the former's car but Lu lingers beside me, wrapping her arms around my waist and propping her chin on my chest. "You sure you don't mind if I disappear for a while?"

"Nah, go for it." I lean down to brush my lips against hers. "Keep an eye on Lux for me?"

She hums against my mouth. "If you're lucky, I'll bring you back a present."

My hands drop to palm her ass, squeezing gently. "I like roses."

A few hours later, the biggest bouquet of roses I've ever seen lands on my desk, closely followed by the ass of my smirking girlfriend as she perches on the edge. I lean back in my seat, glancing between her and the flowers with a smile. "For me?"

"No, for Hunter. I just wanted to get your opinion first."

Scoffing, I tug her onto my lap, kissing the smirk off her face. She relaxes into me easily, a content noise leaving her when I wind my hands through her hair. "Have a good day?"

Lu hums happily. "It was fun. Line and I made Lux sit down every twenty minutes. She put up a fight but we're very persuasive."

Jesus, again with the *Line*. "I can't believe my sister and Caroline voluntarily spent several hours together without pulling each other's hair out."

"They're friends." Luna shrugs. "I think Line's been helping her a lot lately."

I must not hide my skepticism very well because a bony elbow jabs me in the stomach. "Come on, it must be pretty lonely here, everyone gone all the time. You should be glad she has a friend."

"I am." But I just kind of wish my ex-girlfriend wasn't that friend. "You don't think it's weird? Her being around a lot?"

"You mean am I jealous?" Lu smirks, hands creeping up my chest to curve around my neck, leaning forward to rest her forehead against mine. "No. You love me. I know that." Her head dips to catch my lips for a moment. "Besides, believe it or not, you're not hot enough for Line to risk the wrath of me and Lux by trying something on you."

"If you're trying to sweet talk me, it's working."

That laugh I love tickles my cheek, as does her hair when she shifts a little, turning to glance at my desk at the beginning of a sketch starting to take shape. "What're you working on?"

One hand clamps down on her hip to stop her from leaning forward, the other hastily covering the work-in-progress. "Nothing good."

Nothing I want her to see yet.

I draw her attention back to me by tapping her thigh. "You wanna take Clyde out for a while? He's missed you."

She's up and out of my lap so fast I almost get whiplash. "God, I thought you'd never offer."

56

LUNA

It's wild how much things can change in a year.

A year ago, I didn't know who my dad was. I didn't know I had a sister.

A year ago, I was breaking up with the boy I loved because I couldn't bear to drag him down the shame spiral quickly descending on me.

A year ago, I felt like my life was ending.

A year later and I'm watching the love of my life cross a stage to receive his diploma, screaming myself hoarse and deafening everyone in my general vicinity.

In my defense, I'm not the only offender. Jackson's sisters are giving me a run for my money. They're all here, even Lottie who's trying her best to keep up the sullen teenager act but I swear I see a sheen to her eyes that isn't usually there as she watches her brother. And Lux, who most definitely shouldn't be here considering she's about to pop but God help the person who tries to stop Alexandra Winona Jackson from watching her brother graduate, eight-pound baby in her uterus or not.

Ben might be on the opposite end of the row, but I can still hear him loud and clear. He managed to sneak one of those party noise-maker things in here, and he's been blowing it non-stop, much to the chagrin of... well, everyone. Amelia's sobs are loud enough to burst an eardrum but I don't even blame her. All the emotions I'm feeling,

Mils has got to be feeling tenfold. I've just got my boyfriend up there, she's got Nick and Cass to cheer on. I thought her eyeballs were going to burst with how hard she was crying when Cass did that weird hand signal thing they do to each other before his games, and she returned it with wobbly hands. James, Cass' brother, had to clamp an arm around her shoulders to stop them from shaking with her sobs.

Everyone else—Kate, Sydney, Pen, the parents—is fluctuating between pretending they don't know us and cheering on our friends.

My chest feels like it's about to burst. My heart is so full it hurts. I'm so proud of him that I physically can't fucking take it.

As he returns to his seat, proof that he made it in his hand, brown eyes lock on me. A smile splits his face as one eye winks shut. I pause my incessant whooping to stick my pinkies in my mouth and whistle as loud as possible, and he brightens, his hair falling in his face as he shakes his head in a laugh.

When—a veritable lifetime later—the ceremony finally ends, I hang back as everyone makes a beeline for the graduates, letting the girls congratulate their brother before I elbow my way in. I watch as they all borderline tackle Jackson, him staggering back a step as they attack him with hugs and kisses and excited congratulations.

I hold myself back all of five minutes before launching myself at the love of my fucking life.

Jackson catches me with a laugh, my legs flailing as he swings me around. "Congratulations," I sniffle into his neck, clutching tight at the back of his shirt.

"Thank you, sweetheart."

He tries to put me down but I don't let him go, not yet. "I'm so proud of you."

Fingers tug on my hair gently, pulling my head back so I see his smile just before it descends on me. His lips caress mine softly, and I clutch him tightly, savoring him. I'm going to savor him all summer long because while I know I'll be in Sun Valley next fall, I have no idea where he'll be.

"Can you two detach for, like, two minutes so we can get a picture?"

Lux applauds sarcastically when Jackson reluctantly puts me down, scowling at his sister. Over her shoulder, Nick smirks at us, the camera Amelia's been guarding with her life all day slung around his neck and poised in our direction.

I try to step away, assuming they're angling for a family photo, but Jackson slings an arm around my waist and pulls me in, refusing to let me slink away. Tears that have been threatening to spill all day sting my eyes but I swallow them down. The girls fill in around us, Lux brushing against my other side, her fingers pinching my arm.

"Smile nice and big, okay?" she whispers in my ear, throwing her arm around my shoulders. "This one's going on the window sill."

Despite the fact the sweltering June heat has well and truly set in, I swear the guys' house feels colder than usual. Maybe it's just me being dramatic because this is quite possibly the last time we'll all be in this house together but I'm positive there's a weird chill in the air.

I'm not the only one who's feeling it. Everyone is weirdly sombre, despite the fact we're supposed to be celebrating. Amelia's bottom lip has a constant wobble to it as she peers around the house that pretty much changed her life.

I know how she feels.

Everywhere I look, I'm assaulted by a different memory.

Downstairs is bad but upstairs is worse, and maybe, just maybe, when I slip into my new room, a few tears fall.

It's well and truly my room at this point; there's more of my stuff in here than Jackson's. It makes me sniff a little harder, seeing our stuff together. My mug next to his on the desk cluttered with my text-books and Jackson's sketchbooks. My perfumes on the chest of drawers next to his cologne. My clothes spilling out of our closet, very much encroaching on what's supposed to be his side.

I swipe hastily underneath my eyes when the door creaks open and Amelia creeps into the room. She pauses in the doorway, that damn wobbly bottom lip and tear-stained cheeks pulling at my heart-strings. "Cass' room is so empty."

I collapse on the bed and pat the spot beside me. "C'mere, crybaby."

Red-rimmed, unnaturally green eyes roll, a fist jutting out to catch my shoulder. "Shut up. I'm allowed to be emotional."

"You're gonna cry yourself into severe dehydration."

"Amen to that," Ben chimes in as he shoulders his way into the room, Kate hot on his heels. The latter pats my head affectionately as she perches beside me, linking her hand with mine and tugging it onto her lap, her head falling on my shoulder. Ben eyes Amelia suspiciously as he chucks himself on the bed too. "Are you pregnant or something? You're extra weepy lately."

"No!" Amelia splutters, whacking the back of his calf. "God, please don't joke like that around Nick. We'd never have sex again."

Kate, Ben, and I all snort simultaneously. "Please, the day that man puts a baby in you is gonna be the best day of his life."

"Have you seen him around Lux and the bump?" Kate reaches over to nudge our blushing red-headed friend. "I give him a year before he starts dropping hints."

"A year?" I join in, lips pursed to hide my smile. "Six months, tops."

Ben rolls onto his stomach, propping his chin in his hand and regarding Amelia mischievously. "I say she's knocked up before the summer ends."

"I hate all of you," Amelia mutters, flopping onto her back before digging her nails into my thigh. "And you're one to talk. Jackson's gonna take one look at Baby Jackson and go full-dad mode."

I huff a laugh; Baby Jackson isn't even here yet and Big Jackson has already gone full-dad mode. Well, full-uncle mode.

Dad is a long, long way off. I'm twenty-one, for God's sake, and I haven't even graduated college. I've barely gotten my life back on track after what I've chosen to refer to as The Dark Months. And Jackson and I only just got back together.

When I tell my friends as much, Ben pats my shoulder in an almost pitying gesture. "Lu, sweetie, I hate to break it to you, but I think you're gonna take one look at that man with a baby strapped to his chest and your ovaries are gonna start crying."

I shove him so hard he almost falls off the bed because fuck him for vocalizing a very real fear of mine.

Don't get me wrong, everything I just said rings true but *fucking hell*. He tried on a baby sling the other day and I actually had to leave the room.

My friends' mocking laughter is interrupted by the mission trio filing into the room, crowding the bed too. "What're we laughing at?"

Ben side-eyes me with a smirk. "Nothing."

Jackson eyes me suspiciously as he stretches out behind me, dropping a kiss on my shoulder and winding an arm around my waist. Nick scoops up Amelia easily and settles her on his lap, kissing away the tears lingering on her cheeks, an action that apparently only makes her tears fall faster. Cass perches on the end of the bed, wrapping his hand around his sister's ankle and squeezing.

And we just... sit. Quietly. Squashed together. Limbs tangled. The heavy knowledge that everything is about to change hanging over us.

"I feel like the band is breaking up."

Kate flicks Ben on the forehead. "Don't say that."

"We're still gonna see each other all the time," Cass adds, directing his words at his sister, shaking her a little. "No one's dying."

"Well," Ben starts, and I swear I hear the words before they even leave his mouth, "Nick might be. Old age is really creeping up on him."

A pillow hits him in the face before he even has the chance to dodge it. He screams, literally screams, as Nick pins him underneath one strong leg and proceeds to dig his knuckles into his chest, rubbing hard. "Stop!" Ben wriggles beneath him, pulling on his leg hair. "You have brittle bones! You might break something!"

Wild laughter fills my bedroom as Ben shrieks and squirms, and we only laugh harder when Nick finally relents and our young friend sits up, hair all over the place and an adorably angry scowl pulling at his features. "Jesus, Grandpa. You could've broken a hip."

A flick of Nick's foot is all it takes to send Ben flying off the bed, the yelped sound that escapes him and the heavy thud of him hitting the floor setting us off again.

"Uh, guys!" A yell from downstairs interrupts our antics. Thunderous footsteps sound before Grace appears in the doorway, her eyes wide and downright terrified. It's immediate, how the look on her face causes us all to sober up, Jackson springing to his feet and rushing to his sister. Grace swallows hard.

"I think Lux's water just broke."

57

LUNA

HE IS PERFECT.

The little human staring up at me is completely and utterly perfect. The dark crop of hair on his tiny head, the long lashes framing big brown eyes that, if you didn't already know, tell you exactly who his mother is, those chubby fucking thighs that do weird things to my heart. For such a small thing, he's so fucking warm, like a hot water bottle cradled in my arms.

"He looks like Lux," Jackson murmurs quietly, stroking a finger down one chubby cheek.

That's undeniable. The baby is the spitting image of his mother. But there's something there, something that's undeniably someone else. "He looks like you."

Jackson beams.

He's smitten with his new nephew, completely fucking smitten. Every single thing about the kid fascinates him. Right now, it's the way he's wrapping his tiny fingers around Jackson's thumb, gnawing on it and gurgling happily.

It's been two weeks and the novelty of baby cuteness has yet to wear off. Even when he's screaming his head off and keeping everyone awake and shitting and pissing everywhere. You get mad for a moment and then he does something adorable and you forget he vomited on your favorite shirt. I don't think any of us have ever been so unbothered while so sleep deprived because the kid is too fucking sweet.

Lux has taken to it all like a duck to water. Ironically, the only one who wasn't freaking out after her water broke was her. Grace looked terrified, Eliza looked like she was about to vomit, Lottie was yelling because she had Lux's bodily fluids all over her shoes, and Jackson... God, I don't even want to remember what Jackson was like because honestly, it hurt to watch.

But through it all, Lux was calm. Stoic, almost. She handled it like a fucking badass and an ungodly amount of hours later, she held her little boy for the first time and cried her fucking eyes out.

For a whole fortnight, she's refused to leave his side but today, at the more than a little insistent prompting from her brother, she left us in charge of the kid. She was reluctant—if there's anything she hates more than taking her eyes off her kid, it's accepting help—but the allure of a bath and her bed was too strong.

"Hi, Alex," Jackson coos softly, rubbing his nephew's plump little tummy. "You did so good today."

I snicker quietly. "I still can't believe she actually called him Alexander."

We thought she was joking, at first. We all had a little *ha-ha* moment before we caught Lux's deadpan expression and realized she was serious.

"What?" she'd said. *"Men name their kids after themselves all the time, and they don't do any of the hard shit."*

And, well, shit. How can anyone argue with that?

Alexander Oscar Jackson.

Named after the two best people in the family, Lux joked.

Named after her two favorite people, she added, but I have a feeling one half of that joke is very, very genuine.

"Really?" Jackson chuckles quietly, tearing his eyes off the new love of his life long enough to look at the old one, brown eyes sparkling humorously at me. "I'm surprised she didn't go the full mile and call him Lux."

My chest shakes with a laugh, disturbing the baby nestled against me. He cries out in a little whine and not a second passes before Jackson shushes him gently, carefully transferring Alex from my arms to his.

Sitting back in Lux's ridiculously comfortable new rocking chair, I watch the two of them and, not for the first time, I fear Ben was right.

Something about a man and a baby really does make your reproductive organs weep.

Like I said, the man is smitten. Bottle feeds, diaper changes, baths, he does all of it with a smile. Every waking moment of Alex's day, he's got his uncle doting on him. I never thought I'd be jealous of a baby but, yeah, I'm a little jealous.

Jackson catches me staring and whatever expression I'm sporting earns me an amused look. "What?"

"You look good with a baby." *The understatement of the century.*

His deep, husky laugh fades into a winced groan when Alex tugs on a strand of his hair. Carefully detangling his grabby hands, his head drops to kiss Alex's cheek before he returns his attention to me. "Line's gonna watch him tonight for a few hours."

"Oh?"

Jackson hums, the noise vibrating through Alex's cheeks and making him kick his chubby little legs wildly. "I wanna take you somewhere."

I perk up. "Really?"

"Why do you sound surprised?"

"Just can't believe you can tear yourself away from him."

Cradling the baby in one hand, he cups my cheek with the other, smoothing his thumb over my skin. "Feeling neglected?"

I scoff. "No."

Jackson chuckles quietly. Urging me to stand, he takes my seat before pulling me down on his lap, carefully resituating Alex so he's cuddled between us. "In case I haven't said it, thank you for helping so much the last few weeks."

Shrugging, I catch one of Alex's kicking feet in my hand. "I don't mind."

"I know you don't." Fingers curl beneath my chin and tilt my head towards Jackson. "But thank you anyway."

Unable to help myself, I steal the lightest of kisses. "You're welcome."

"Where are we going?" When my question is met by nothing but annoying silence, I groan. "Come on, not even a hint?"

More silence, only the twitch of his lips letting me know he heard me. With a huff, I slump in my seat and squint at our surroundings.

Trees. That's my only clue. We drive past trees, and trees, and more trees. Vaguely familiar trees but trees all the same.

"Are you taking me to meet the new ranch hand?"

The excitement in my tone earns me some serious side-eye. It's not my fault; I've only been blessed with the man from a distance but Lux's very detailed descriptions would spark anyone's curiosity.

Save a horse, ride a cowboy, is her new favorite motto.

For God's sake, even Caroline blushes at the mere mention of the man.

Squeezing my thigh, Jackson promises, "We'll be there soon."

He sounds weird. He's *being* weird. Acting all nervous. Shifty-eyed and twitchy. Stealing my move and tapping his fingers haphazardly against the steering wheel.

It's freaking me out more than a little, especially because the only thing coming to my mind that explains why the fuck he's acting this way is honestly fucking terrifying.

"Are you proposing?" I blurt out before I can stop myself, and Jackson jolts in his seat. "Jackson, I love you, but I swear to God if you're proposing when I haven't gotten my nails done in almost a month-"

"Relax." I'm not sure if he laughs or chokes. "I'm not proposing."

"Then why are you being all weird?"

"I'm not-" He cuts himself off, shaking his head. "Just wait, okay?"

Wait.

Hm.

I've never been particularly good at that.

What feels like an hour but is realistically no more than a few minutes later, our surroundings become more recognizable.

The lookout point where I told him I loved him for the first time looks as beautiful as it did last year, except there's something remarkably different about it.

What once was an empty clearing is now what looks to be the beginnings of a construction site. There's nothing but a raised foundation and some wooden framing, but I can tell it's the shell of a house.

What. The. Fuck.

"Jackson," I breathe shakily, feet a little unsteady as I clamber out of the car. "What the hell is this?"

"My house." Shaky voice? Check. A touch of determination? Also check. "Well, it will be. When it's built. I only finished the designs last month so it won't be ready for a while."

I blink at the enormous unfinished structure decorating what's arguably my favorite spot on the ranch, and then I blink at its owner. "You designed this?"

He nods, lips tipping up in a boyish grin. "Can't quite build houses but I draw them pretty well."

So you build houses?

God, I remember that like it was yesterday. Seeing him in the art store and being so damn flustered, I blurted out the most dumbass question.

I knew what a goddamn architect was. I knew they didn't *build* houses. But, for the first time of many in Jackson's presence, I panicked and my inner bimbo eagerly rose to the surface.

But then his mouth stretched in a smile, the first proper one I ever got from him, and my embarrassment dissipated. I remember thinking, damn, I'd embarrass myself every day of my life for the rest of my life if I got that smile as a consolation prize.

It's the same smile he wears now as I stare blankly at him, my mind working overtime sifting through a million questions.

"Your grandparents let you build here?" I wouldn't think they'd let him do anything that doesn't directly benefit them and building a house on a prime location for some new touristy shit doesn't seem very beneficial.

"Uh, not exactly." That nervous energy returns full-force, making him shift from one leg to the other, crossing and uncrossing his arms over his chest. "They don't own the ranch anymore. I do."

There's a pause. A long-ass pause in which those two words repeat on a loop in my head until they lose all meaning. "You do."

Jackson barely nods.

"You own the ranch."

He nods again, a little more sure this time.

"You bought this ranch."

"Yeah, sweetheart, I did."

"You bought Serenity Ranch and you didn't tell me."

Jackson winces.

"When?"

"Uh." One big shaky hand comes up to scratch the back of his neck. "The beginning of the year."

"The beginning of *this* year?"

He winces again.

Months.

Months ago he bought this place.

Months in which *we were together*. "And you didn't tell me?"

"I didn't want to freak you out."

He didn't want to freak me out.

That, at least, I can understand.

He didn't want to drop a ranch-sized bomb right when we were getting back to normal.

How nice of him.

"So you're gonna live here? Permanently?" *Hours away from me?*

Jackson's sad smile conveys he's thinking the exact same thing. "That's the plan. I'm sorry I didn't tell you sooner."

"It's okay." And it is. I think, deep down, I suspected he'd move back here. He never really suited the city, not like he suits this place. I'm not, like, mad or anything.

I'm just not quite sure where it leaves me.

Swallowing hard, my gaze drifts back to the bare-bones structure. "Big house for one person."

"That's true." Tentative steps approach me from behind, nervous hands settling on my hips. "Gotta have room for my sisters."

"Obviously."

"And one for Alex."

"I'd be surprised if there wasn't."

"And an apartment above the garage for Ben."

That pulls a laugh out of me. "Of course."

Strong arms lock across my stomach and pull me back against a hard chest, warm breath tickling my cheek. "And room for all your shit."

My breath catches in my throat. "I think you underestimate how much shit I have."

"There's room, sweetheart. Whatever you want, there's room for it."

I turn in his arms, my fingers grasping his collar so tightly I practically have him in a chokehold. "Are you serious?"

"As a heart attack."

The back of my hand meets his chest. "Don't tease." His mischievous smile smoothes out into a serious expression, and I try again. "This isn't us sharing a room. This is sharing a *house*."

A whole ass house. *Our* house. A very fucking permanent house that he designed for his family. For us.

Don't cry.

"Luna," Jackson says softly, both hands moving to tuck my hair behind my ears before cupping my face. "I know this isn't very romantic and you're supposed to be romantic when you're asking someone to live with you." A very ugly noise rips from my throat. "If you say no, I'll understand. I'll still love you."

I wait for it. I wait for the voice in my head to tell me to run, for the 'leave first before they leave you' mentality to kick in and ruin everything.

I almost cry when it doesn't.

It takes several deep breaths and a brief moment of internally bullying myself to suck it up, but I eventually manage to breathe out, "Go on, then. Ask me."

He laughs so hard it vibrates through my entire body. "You wanna make this our house, sweetheart?"

For maybe the first time in my life, I don't hesitate.

"Fuck yeah."

EPILOGUE
LUNA

I DON'T KNOW *why I'm doing this.*

Amelia suggested it. Said it would help cuz I've kind of been struggling since Jackson moved home. We had a great summer on the ranch, hanging out with his sisters and Alex and building the house, but it was bittersweet. I couldn't stop thinking about how I was leaving and he wasn't. He's only a few hours away but it might as well be the other side of the world.

I'm being dramatic, I know. We see each other at least once a month, and we talk practically every minute of the day, but after three straight months of being together nonstop, it feels... wrong? Yeah, being apart feels wrong. I don't know.

Maybe I'm just a clingy bitch.

But yeah, anyway, Amelia says writing shit like this down helps. Her therapist suggested it to her and Dr Resnick is basically God in Amelia's eyes, and Nick's, so I thought I'd give it a go. I did some research and apparently, it's good for people with ADHD too. Helps you process emotions and big events and shit like that.

I don't know. We'll see. I'll give it a try, I guess.

It can't hurt.

∾

I saw him on campus today.

Just for a moment, in passing, when I was on the way to class. It was...

473

weird. How apathetic I felt. Considering all the anger and hurt and betrayal I've felt in the past, it was odd to feel nothing for once. I might as well have been walking past a stranger.

The only speck of emotion occurred when I clocked his ring-free finger, and that was pride because fuck yeah, Jennifer. It took longer than it should've because Professor Jacobs is a dick and he fought her every step of the way but she made good on her promise to divorce his sorry ass.

She doesn't look at me that way anymore. The sad way. The way that kind of makes her look like she's in pain. Now, there's nothing but warmth in her gaze. She calls me Pen's sister and she calls Pen and I 'her girls.'

I'm glad I don't hurt her anymore.

Speaking of Pen, she was with me when we saw the sperm donor. As much as he didn't react to me, he didn't even blink an eye at Pen either. I know Pen tries not to care but I could tell it crushed her a little. She hates the man, she hates what he did, but he's still her dad. I know it's hard for her to connect the man who raised her with the cheating asshole he turned out to be. She's coping though. She's got me and her mom and my mom to help her through it.

Kind of a fucking power team, to be honest.

Alex has gotten huge.

Six months old and still an angel.

We spent Christmas on the ranch, all of us, even Cass. I think that was the longest he's spent in one place since graduating. He's kind of hot shit now, which is weird. We went out for dinner in town one night and got papped which is even fucking weirder. The next day our faces were splashed across the front of some stupid tabloid, the highlight being a picture of Cass cradling Alex and the headline wondering who the MLB's newest star pitcher knocked up.

We checked on the house's progress too. It's almost time to start painting and decorating and doing all the fun shit and I can't fucking wait. Ma's already made a million things, from paintings to vases to mugs to those weird little decorative ceramic bowls that aren't big enough to have an actual use but they're cute and they kind of make a place feel lived in.

I'm excited, I'm really fucking excited, to make that building site into a home.

Our home.

We did a walkthrough of the finished house today. Electrical, plumbing, all that shit is done now. The fun can start. Well, kind of fun, kind of incredibly fucking stressful. I don't know if it looks bigger because it's empty but the place is fucking enormous. Like, excessively so. Like, more rooms than we can fill. It almost feels wrong, the two of us owning something so extravagant but I love it, I really do.

Modern farmhouse, I think Pinterest would call it.

It creeps me out a little, being all blank and empty and echoey inside, but Jackson promised the next time I'm there it'll be a little livelier.

I wish I could stay there all the time. I'm so fucking close to being done with college. I don't know what I'm going to do after but I'm leaning towards taking a year off to figure it out. UCSV has a JD program that I'm looking into. But that's another three years in Sun Valley and I don't think I really wanna do that.

Whatever. I'll figure it out. It's not like I'm in a rush.

I'm a college graduate.

A miracle, really, considering how much of a fucking ride the last couple of years have been. I can't believe I did it.

Shit, I'm kind of proud of myself.

It was a bittersweet day. We had to pack up the house, for real this time. Ben's moving in with some other friends for his senior year, Pen's moving in with her new boyfriend, so it was time to actually say goodbye. We all had a little cry.

But we got to move into our house. God, I love it. I love it so fucking much. Jackson was right about brightening it up; he did all the painting himself and every inch of the house has a little touch of his handiwork. I can tell Line has been here because there are fresh flowers everywhere, and Lux must've popped in to stock the fridge at some point. They're nowhere to be seen now though.

I'm glad because we plan on thoroughly christening every inch of this place.

~

Fuck.

Fuckity fuck fuck.

We have royally fucked up.

Two months.

My IUD was taken out two fucking months ago. It needed to be replaced and I put off getting a new one because the fucker hurt like a bitch going in the first time, and coming out, and I was hyping myself up to go through that again.

I took the pill while I made up my mind.

We used condoms.

And he still managed to knock me up.

Motherfucker.

Now I wish I'd sucked it up because God knows what's coming out of me next is going to hurt a fuck ton more than an IUD.

I don't know what I'm going to do. This wasn't the plan. Jackson's going to freak out. No, that's a lie, he's going to remain calm and levelheaded and pragmatic while I freak the fuck out.

We can't have a baby. We already have a baby; the ranch. And for fuck's sake, we're practically still babies.

I've got options. I'm pretty sure it's still early so I've definitely got options.

I just... I don't know.

I don't fucking know.

~

I saw your heartbeat today.

Strong like your mom, is what your dad said. He cried, like he does at every single appointment, just like he cried when I told him about you. He went white as a sheet and then he cried and then I cried and he held me and he told me whatever I wanted to do, he would be there for me. I'd already decided by then, and I knew that no matter what he would support me, but hearing it made me cry harder anyways.

He's so fucking proud of you already, little guy.

You kicked for the first time last week and he practically threw a party, and then you threw a fist at my kidney and he claimed you were practicing *your pitch. I swear, he's going to be unbearable when you pop out in a few months. Which you need to do gently and on time, by the way, because you're going to be stuck with me for a really long time and starting our life together by pissing me off is not a good idea. Just ask your dad.*

We figured it out, how we're going to make it work. I found a part-time program, two nights in person a week, the rest of it online. You'll be here at the start of summer, I can start classes in the fall. And your dad, Jesus, I don't think I've ever seen someone so happy to be a stay-at-home dad, ever.

We love you so much already.

Even when you use my organs as squeeze-toys.

Okay, I love you, but you need to get the fuck out now.

I'm sick of this. I don't know what the fuck those people who spout on about the beauty of pregnancy and how they never want it to end have been smoking because I am done.

I haven't slept in a month. I pee every two seconds. Jackson won't let me eat sour sweets anymore because they give me heartburn even though every-thing gives me heartburn lately. And he read some article about how some types of herbal teas are bad for pregnant women and now I can't even have a cup without him giving me this stupid fucking pouty face of disapproval. And god, I'm sore. So sore. I can't remember what it feels like to be comfortable.

So please, little guy. Please get out.

I'm a mom.

Weird.

If you'd told me a couple of years ago that I would be the first in our friend group to become a mom, I would've laughed until I vomited. My money was on Amelia. All of ours was, really. Clearly, I didn't take that Jackson family competitive nature into account.

Isaac's inherited that shit, I can already tell. Barely six months old and he's already giving his cousin a run for his money. Alex is obsessed with him, almost as much as Jackson. Lux and I have started calling them the triplets because they're practically identical, the three of them.

I might be biased but my kid's the cutest. He looks just like Alex did when he was a baby. Except those big blue eyes, they're all mine. His hair is a little lighter too, not quite blonde but not quite brown. The perfect mix of the two of us. Thank God because I think I actually would've pitched a fit if he came out looking exactly like his dad.

I think I want another one. It's early, I know, but I love this kid so fucking much, and I see how much Jackson loves him and I want more. I love my boys but a girl would be nice. I'm not picky though.

Anyway. One thing at a time. Should probably do something with the rock on my finger first. I'm pretty powerful but planning a wedding with one kid is hard enough. Two kids might kill me.

One day, though.

I'll bide my time.

THANK YOU FOR READING

If you enjoyed the book, please consider leaving a review on Goodreads and the site you bought it from.

ACKNOWLEDGMENTS

To the three little old women who adopted me in spirit and always share the wisdom they've learned in their very long lives. Hannah, Becka, Ki, in a couple of years when you are too old to care for yourselves, I promise to put you in the very best care homes.

To Alejandra, for putting up with a hundred voice notes at all hours of the night and doing many, *many* vibe checks. I have no idea what this book would look like without your endless help.

To Norhan, because even though your suggestions were almost always useless, at least you tried.

To all my beta readers, from the bottom of my heart, thank you.

And to everyone I met from all over the world while editing this book, thank you for reminding me how fucking cool it is that this is my job.

ACKNOWLEDGMENTS

To the three little old women who adopted me in spirit and always share the wisdom they've learned in their very long lives. Hannah, Becka, Ki, in a couple of years when you are too old to care for yourselves, I promise to put you in the very best care homes.

To Alejandra, for putting up with a hundred voice notes at all hours of the night and doing many, *many* vibe checks. I have no idea what this book would look like without your endless help.

To Norhan, because even though your suggestions were almost always useless, at least you tried.

To all my beta readers, from the bottom of my heart, thank you.

And to everyone I met from all over the world while editing this book, thank you for reminding me how fucking cool it is that this is my job.

ABOUT THE AUTHOR

EJ Blaise is an Irish author of all things romance. When she's not creating unrealistically perfect men, she can be found traveling, reading, and dreaming of running a bookstore café.

Printed in Great Britain
by Amazon

28202082R00280